Lauren Rowe

HERO

THE MORGAN BROTHERS

USA Today and International bestselling author

Lauren Rowe

Hero Copyright © 2018 by Lauren Rowe

Published by SoCoRo Publishing
Layout by www.formatting4U.com
Cover Model: Jason Dickinson.
Photographer: Wander Aguiar Photography www.WanderBookClub.com

Cover design © Sarah Hansen, Okay Creations LLC

To Brad.

Chapter 1
Lydia

Seattle, Three Years Ago

I look at my watch. I'm surprised Darren isn't home yet. He said he'd be home by six.

"What if I do extra chores?" my seven-year-old son, Theo, asks.

I smile to myself. The kid is a fantastic negotiator, just like his father. "Nope," I reply firmly. "You can't have dessert until you've eaten every spear of that broccoli."

"I'm eating my broccoleeee, Mommeeeee," my four-year-old daughter, Isabella, sings, wiggling in her chair. "See, Theo?" She shoves another piece into her mouth. "Yummeeeeee!" She smiles at me like a goof and the green in her mouth pokes out from behind her two front teeth.

"Don't talk with your mouth full, Izzy," Theo snaps at his little sister.

I shoot Theo a warning look. "I'd mind my own business if I were you, mister. It seems to me you've got bigger fish to fry than worrying about your sister talking with her mouth full. There's a big ol' chocolate cake sitting on the kitchen counter, if you haven't noticed, and Izzy and I are going to eat it with Daddy when he gets home. I'd sure hate for you to be left out of our celebration because you didn't eat one itty-bitty pile of broccoli."

Theo scowls again and it takes all my self-restraint not to laugh at his adorably dour expression. Oh, God, how I love this headstrong boy. He's just like his daddy.

"What are we celebrating again?" Izzy asks, popping another piece of broccoli into her mouth.

1

"Daddy gets to be a detective now, not just a police officer," Theo says. "He's gonna help people even more now."

My heart swells with pride. "That's a great explanation of it, Theo. Daddy would love to hear you say it that way." Speaking of which... I look at my watch again. *Where is he?* Darren knows the kids and I are waiting to celebrate his big promotion. I pull out my phone and tap out a quick text: *Hey, hot stuff. What's your ETA?*

"All done!" Izzy says, drawing my attention away from my phone to her empty plate.

"Good job," I say. I high-five my mini-me and shoot a snarky look at Darren's. "See, buddy? That's how you make broccoli disappear."

"Broccoli all gone!" Isabella sings out. She wiggles in her chair again and does a spastic motion with her arms.

I laugh. "Do you need to go potty, honey?"

"No, Momma! I'm *dancing*!" She wiggles again, making me laugh.

There's a knock at the front door and I rise from my chair to answer it. "So what's it gonna be, Theo?" I ask as I head toward the door. "Cake or no cake?"

My son crosses his arms over his skinny little chest and scowls. "I don't even want cake. I'm not gonna eat anything that's bad for me ever again so I can grow up and get big muscles like Daddy."

"Wow," I say as I open the door. "I'm proud of you for making such a healthy..."

My blood runs cold.

There are two police officers standing on my porch, their expressions unmistakably grim. I don't know the white officer on the right, but the black one on the left is Dwayne Piedmont. Darren loves him like a brother. My chest tightens.

"Lydia," Dwayne says softly, his eyes glistening. "May we come in?"

"Daddy!" Izzy shrieks gleefully behind me, and before I can say or do anything to stop her, she's standing at my leg, doing a little shimmy. "Oh, hi, Officer Dwayne. Are you here for Daddy's celebration? He's a detective now so we're having chocolate cake."

"Hi, honey," Dwayne says. "Can you please go into the other room with Officer Navarro here? I need to talk to your mommy for a second."

I feel my knees begin to wobble, but Dwayne grabs my arm to steady me.

"Go with the officer, Izzy," I say, my entire body trembling.

"But I want cake!" Izzy sticks out her little belly and pats it. "I ate all my broccoleeee, so now I get to have cake. Right, Momma? Theo didn't eat his broccoli, so he doesn't get to—"

"*Isabella!*" I bark. "*Go with Officer Navarro!*"

In a flash, Officer Navarro escorts my stricken daughter away from me.

Bug-eyed, I return my attention to Dwayne. I'm vaguely aware Izzy's whimpering about my sharp tone in the other room, but I can't focus on that right now. "What happened?" I whisper.

"He's been shot."

I gasp.

Dwayne tightens his grip on my arm. "I came straight here as they were loading him into an ambulance. I'm here to take you to the hospital. We need to go."

"But is he...?" I trail off, incapable of uttering the word on the tip of my tongue.

"I don't know anything about his condition. All I know is we need to go." He peeks behind us, presumably double-checking that my children are out of earshot. "Officer Navarro will stay with the kids until someone else can come. Do you have someone who can come?"

My brain is freezing up. Panic is rising up inside me, scraping my insides like shards of glass. I motion toward the house next door. "My neighbor."

"I'll call Officer Navarro from the hospital to let him know. Is this your purse?"

I stare blankly. Darren got promoted today. I baked him a chocolate cake. And I've got exciting news to tell him—the best possible news.

"*Lydia. Is this your purse?*"

I nod dumbly and Dwayne puts his arm around me and guides me toward the front door—the door Darren will walk through any minute now because this isn't happening and we're going to eat chocolate cake.

As I walk toward the patrol car in the driveway, I shiver.

"Do you need a jacket?" Dwayne asks.

I look down at my arm. There are goose bumps rising up across my light brown skin—but I can't feel the coolness of the air. I can't feel anything. Because this isn't real. "He was alive when you left him?" I blurt as Dwayne settles me into the passenger seat of his patrol car.

Dwayne presses his lips together. His Adam's apple bobs. "I don't have any information about his condition," he says stiffly. "I'm sorry. I'm just here to take you to him." He shuts the passenger door, cutting off any more questions, and a moment later, we're racing down the street, sirens blaring.

As the car careens through traffic, I don't speak. At this point, I know if I open my mouth, I'll scream like a madwoman or vomit or both. And so, I stare silently ahead, convincing myself this is a nightmare and I'll wake up any minute now next to my husband's warm body in our comfy bed. Yes, any minute now, I'll wake up next to Darren and snuggle close and he'll do what he always does in the middle of the night: pull me closer to him in his sleep, instinctively keeping me safe and warm and protected at all times. And then I'll drift back to sleep in my husband's strong arms, grateful and relieved this was all just a very, very, *very* bad dream.

Chapter 2
Lydia

I'm sitting next to Darren at the hospital. His brown eyes are closed. A mechanical ventilator is attached to his mouth. *Beep, beep, beep.* Over and over again, the heart monitor attached to my husband tells me he's alive. And yet the doctor sitting next to me has just said the words "no longer with us."

I don't react to the doctor's words. It's not that I don't understand them. I've got a doctoral degree in physical therapy, so I fully understand that humans need a living, functioning brain to be considered alive. But the thing is, science doesn't know *everything*. What's true for one patient might not be true for another, especially when that patient is Darren Decker. The reality is that my husband isn't like anybody else. He's the strongest, most determined, and most exceptional human being I know. Trust me, if anyone can bounce back from brain death, it's him. I grasp Darren's strong hand in mine, admiring the tapestry of his light skin intertwined with mine.

"Do you understand, Mrs. Decker?" the doctor says.

I don't know what she's asking me. I stopped listening the minute she said "brain-dead." But it seems she's waiting for a response, so I say, "Just give him some time to recover."

The doctor looks sympathetic. "I'm sorry, Mrs. Decker, but Darren isn't going to recover. That's what I've been explaining to you. Brain death is death. He's legally and clinically dead. We're keeping his body alive to harvest his organs, if that's something you wish to do."

I gaze at Darren's face. His eyelids. I touch his cheekbone, careful not to touch the respirator. His skin is warm to the touch. Other than the bandage wrapped around his head and the respirator protruding from his mouth, he looks as blissfully asleep as he does

5

every morning lying beside me in our bed. "I believe in miracles," I say softly.

There's a beat.

The doctor shifts in her chair. "Mrs. Decker, let me be clear. An essential chunk of Darren's brain is physically *gone*. If I took off those bandages, you'd lose all hope of him recovering. I really don't want you to see that, so please take my word for it."

"Take off the bandages," I say flatly, not taking my eyes off Darren's sleeping face. "I want to see."

The doctor hesitates. She tells me this will surely be highly traumatizing to me. Something I can't un-see.

"I'm a medical professional," I explain. "I can handle it. I want to see."

The doctor reluctantly complies with my request... and the minute the bandages are unwound and I get a solid glimpse of the back of my husband's cratered head, I lean over and barf all over the linoleum floor.

***

I'm calm now. Darren's head is bandaged again and I'm holding his hand. His skin against mine is warm, just like he's sleeping. As before, the heart monitor assures me my husband is alive and well and will be opening his chocolate-brown eyes any second now. But, of course, I've now accepted that the heart monitor is a fucking liar.

I've asked for some time alone with my dead husband before my parents and Darren's arrive and all hell breaks loose. I'm using this time alone with the love of my life to memorize every inch of his face, every pore, so I'll never forget. I touch his soft lips—the lips I've kissed since age seventeen. The only lips I've ever kissed. I trace his eyebrows and Roman nose and steel jaw, as best I can with the respirator sticking out of his mouth. And then I lean forward, press Darren's muscled forearm between my two slender ones, and proceed to tell him The Story of Darren and Lydia.

I begin my story at the beginning, of course—the moment I first laid eyes on Darren in chemistry class at age seventeen. "I felt like I'd been struck by a thunderbolt," I whisper, smiling through my tears. "It was love at first sight."

And it was.

Darren was the mysterious new boy in school with swagger for days—the fresh meat every girl wanted to claim. And yet he went straight for me, a pastor's daughter who'd never been kissed, like I'd ordered him from Lululemon.

"We both just knew, didn't we?" I whisper. "One glance and that was it for both of us."

I talk about how we went off to college together, as far away as we could get from the small minds in our small town, all the way to Seattle, even though our parents said we were too young to move so far away together. Too naive to understand words like "soulmates" and "true love" and "forever." I remind him of the time his piece-of-shit, racist uncle pulled Darren aside at Thanksgiving to tell him he'd best reconsider "getting serious with a black girl, even a light-skinned one like Lydia who's only half black, because, even though she's sweet as can be and I personally like her a whole lot—I really do—a white boy hitching his plow to a black girl will wind up being far more trouble than she's worth, I don't care how good the pussy might be." I grip Darren's hand. "Thank you so much for throwing that punch, my love. No matter what I said at the time about turning the other cheek, that was just my years of Sunday school talking. The truth is, I was elated you broke that bastard's jaw. It was then that I knew you were my knight in shining armor and always would be. It was then that I knew you'd always protect me." I barely choke out my next words. "And you always did." I lay my head on his arm and speak through my sobs. "You've been the best husband and father and protector a man could ever be, Darren Decker."

I can't talk anymore. I'm crying too hard.

With my forehead still pressed against my husband's arm, I let the memories of our life together flood me. Darren the boyfriend. Husband. Father. *Third time father-to-be*. Crying, I stand and place Darren's limp hand on my flat belly. "I wish I'd gotten the chance to tell you about our third baby. I took the test after you left for work this morning and didn't call because I wanted to see your face when I..." I simply can't continue. With a whimper, I throw myself across Darren's muscled chest and lose myself to violent, wracking sobs.

Chapter 3
Lydia

I'm calm again. Staring dumbly at Darren's closed eyelids. The nurse sitting next to me has brought me the consent form for organ donation.

"Darren was a hero in life," she says. "And now, he'll be a hero in death, too."

Oh, how I wish she'd shut up. I'm quite familiar with the concept of organ donation. I work in a hospital and I've personally got a little pink dot on my driver's license. Frankly, I don't want to talk about how much Darren's going to help people as a result of his untimely death. I just want to sign the papers and not think about them cutting open my husband and taking him apart. I don't want Darren to be a hero in death. I just want him to be alive so he can un-heroically watch his kids grow up.

"Where do I sign?" I say flatly. And when the nurse slips the clipboard under my nose, I scribble my name onto the designated lines and fall apart.

***

I escort my children into the room, breathing deeply to keep myself from passing out or vomiting. I don't know if bringing them in here is the right thing to do. In fact, my gut tells me this is a terrible idea. But the child psychologist who recommended it assured me it will help them with their healing in the long run.

When we get inside the room, Izzy rushes to her prostrate father while Theo remains frozen near the door.

I put a hand on Theo's slender shoulder as we watch Izzy throw herself at Darren's chest. "It's okay, buddy," I whisper to Theo. "Daddy knows how you feel."

Across the room, Izzy is sobbing so violently at Darren's bedside, she's literally gagging.

I take two loping steps toward my daughter to comfort her, but the second I leave Theo's side, he breaks down behind me.

I stand frozen between my two kids, my brain melting. I can't process this much grief all at once. Izzy's. Theo's. My own. The grief embedding itself into the tissues of my unborn child.

It's the worst moment of my life.

And I blame that fucking child psychologist.

My entire body shuddering, I stride toward Izzy, grab her tiny arm, and yank her toward the door. But Izzy shakes free of my grasp, lurches to Darren again, and wails like she's vomiting up shards of glass.

Oh, God. I can't do this. I can't be this strong. In this moment, all I want to do is fling myself off a bridge. "Please, Izzy," I choke out, my voice cracking. "Daddy has to go to heaven now. He's got a flight to catch and he can't be late or else he'll miss it." I touch Izzy's shoulder. "Please, honey. We don't want Daddy to miss his flight to heaven, do we?"

My shameful lie works. Izzy releases her grasp on her father's arm and lets me usher her and Theo to Darren's parents on the other side of the door.

Darren's parents.

Oh, God.

They finally got here after being helicoptered off their anniversary cruise in Greece. It was supposed to be the trip of a lifetime for them—a twenty-day Mediterranean cruise they'd saved for five years to take. And now, much to their shock and devastation, they're no longer drinking Greek wine overlooking the Acropolis, they're standing in a drab hospital room in Seattle saying goodbye to their only child. The son they love more than life itself.

After getting my children situated with their grandparents, I head back into the room for my last goodbye. I take Darren's hand in mine, sobbing. "I'll always love you," I whisper. "I'll never love another man, Darren. My heart will always belong to you."

It's the last thing I say to my beloved husband before two men in

9

scrubs come in and take him away to a room down the hall where a surgeon will cut him open and take him apart and scatter him far and wide to people who've been praying for a miracle. To people whose families will get to continue hugging their loved ones tonight.

For a long moment, I stand frozen in the middle of the empty room, incapable of moving.

He's gone.

I'm alone.

The heart monitor is now quiet.

I'm twenty-nine years old.

A mother of two with another on the way.

My husband, the only man I've ever loved—the only man I've ever *kissed*—the great love of my life and the father of my children... is dead.

Chapter 4
Colby

Seattle, Present Day

I rub the top of my boxer Ralph's soft head. He's lying to my right in my warm bed, snoring away in the pre-dawn light without a care in the world. Oh, to be my snoozing dog right now. "I don't have a 'fear of commitment,' Candice," I say groggily to my girlfriend of three months. She's lying to my left in the bed, naked, her long limbs intertwined with mine.

I rub my sleepy eyes and look at my alarm clock. *4:48.* Jesus Christ. Candice wants to talk about this *now*? My alarm went off three minutes ago, my brain feels like it's covered in a sheath of cotton, and I've got morning wood. Oh, and did I mention, we've only been dating for three months? Hardly enough time to even *think* about having this conversation. "I didn't say I'd *never* get married under any circumstances," I say. "All I said was I'm not a guy who's gonna get married simply because my parents did or society says it's what I'm supposed to do. If you met my parents, you'd understand. They've set the bar impossibly high." Ralph shifts his position next to me and I pat him gently, my stomach churning.

"And what about kids?" Candice says. "Is that something you can envision for yourself at some point or is that a 'maybe, maybe not' for you, the same as marriage?"

"Yeah, I want kids. Actually, my whole life, I've pictured myself having five of them, the same as in my family."

"*Five* kids? And yet, you're not completely sure you ever want to get married, huh? Interesting."

I close my eyes and exhale. "Never mind about the five-kids

11

thing. I was just saying that's always been my fantasy—that I'd have a crazy, loud, chaotic family, just like the one I grew up in. But, obviously, given that I'm a thirty-year-old man who's not thinking about getting married any time soon, I'm well aware five kids isn't going to happen for me." I pause waiting for Candice's reply, but she remains mute. So, I continue, "I'm just being honest here, Candice. It's not like I'm some eighty-year-old commitment-phobe who's never been in a serious relationship. I only turned thirty last week."

"Yeah, well, if you want five kids, you don't have as much time as you think, Colby."

I exhale with exasperation. "Forget the five-kids thing. Fuck. I was saying I used to imagine that for myself because I loved my own childhood so much. That's all I meant."

I glance at the alarm clock again. *5:04*. Shit. I didn't set my alarm to go off almost three hours before the start of my twenty-four-hour shift because I wanted to have plenty of time to talk to Candice about marriage and kids. To the contrary, I set my alarm for this early thinking Candice and I would wake up and have some awesome morning sex, the same way we always do whenever she sleeps over, and that, following that bit of awesomeness, Candice would kindly head off to work and leave me to my usual pre-work routine: taking a six-mile jog with Ralph, lifting some weights in my spare bedroom, showering, eating, and then dropping Ralph off at my parents' house on my way into the fire station.

"I think it's perfectly reasonable after six months of dating for me to ask about the trajectory of our relationship, Colby," Candice says, her tone turning snippy. "Maybe your biological clock isn't ticking at thirty, but mine sure is at twenty-nine."

Um... wow. Where to begin? First off, Candice and I haven't been dating for six months. We met and hooked up at a wedding *five* months ago, almost to the day, and then didn't start actually dating until a couple months after that because, as we talked about *explicitly* that first night, we were both fresh off break-ups and wanted to take things slow. And, furthermore, why does me turning thirty a week ago mean I've suddenly got to start thinking seriously about marriage at all, but especially with someone I've dated for mere months?

"I just don't understand why you haven't introduced me to your family yet," Candice says. "If *my* whole family lived in Seattle, then I would have introduced you to them by now."

"I've introduced you to two of my brothers," I say lamely, even though I'm well aware I'm painting the walls while the house is on fire at this point.

Candice sits up in the bed, obviously annoyed. "Having drinks with Ryan in a bar while Dax performed onstage with his band doesn't count. We couldn't even *talk.* What I want is for you to take me home and introduce me as your girlfriend to your family."

I'm speechless. Wow. We're *really* not on the same page.

"You had the perfect opportunity last week to introduce me to everyone at your birthday dinner and you didn't even invite me. I know you said it was just going to be family, and I respected that, but then I overheard you talking to Ryan a couple days ago about how sad your sister looked because her new boyfriend cancelled on coming to dinner at the last minute."

I close my eyes. *Shit.* I thought Candice was in the shower when Ryan and I talked about that. "Candice," I say, exhaling. "If Kat wanted to bring some guy home on my birthday, it means she thinks he's The One. That's the only reason any of us brings someone home for dinner—because we're intending to send out a smoke signal that we've met that special someone. Hence, the reason I've never brought anyone home for a family dinner—because I've never, ever been that sure about a relationship."

Candice looks like she feels sick. "So you're not that sure... about me?"

Crap. How could she possibly think I'm *that* sure about her? *We've been dating for three months!* I take a deep breath and force myself to answer honestly. "I'm not. No."

Tears prick Candice's eyes. "Why not? Have I done something? *Not* done something?"

I consider the question, trying to decide how honest to be. Should I mention that time, a few weeks ago, Candice blasted that poor, frazzled waitress for screwing up the dressing on her salad? Or the time right after that when Candice whispered that nasty comment to her bestie about some poor woman walking by, simply because the woman had the audacity to wear tight leggings without having the body of a supermodel? No. If I cite those examples to Candice, she won't understand my larger point—that I could never settle down with a woman who doesn't make kindness her default mode. "No," I

13

say. "You've done nothing, Candice. It's not you. You're great. One day, you're going to make a fantastic wife for someone. Unfortunately, that someone just won't be me."

Chapter 5
Colby

I open the passenger door to my truck and Ralph hops in without so much as a gesture from me. He knows the drill. As I walk around to the driver's side, my phone buzzes with a text from my brother, Ryan.

Happy Saturday, Cheese. You up?

I push the button to call him as I pull out of my driveway.

"Mornin'," Ryan says, answering my call.

"I'm up," I say. "I'm on my way to Casa Morgan now to drop off Ralph before heading into work."

"Oh, you're working today? Crap. I thought you had the day off."

"I switched shifts with a guy so he could go to his parents' anniversary party," I say. "What's up?"

"I'm fishing with Keane today. Thought you might like to join."

"Oh, no. I'm so sorry to miss that," I say sarcastically.

"You love fishing."

"Not with *Keane*. He's always so damned loud, he scares away all the fish."

"When he was ten, maybe," Ryan says. "Not when he's *twenty-two*. But, regardless, who cares? Fishing isn't about catching fish. It's about hanging out and drinking beer. You know, making memories."

"Well, it's a good thing you feel that way, seeing as how you're about to go fishing with a guy who scares away all the fish. Did you lose a bet or something?"

"Dude, you're the one who asked me to talk to Peen at your birthday dinner," Ryan says. "Were you drunk?"

15

"I didn't mean for you to trap yourself in a rowboat with the guy for God knows how many hours on a Saturday. I just meant for you to pull him aside for fifteen minutes after dinner and ask him if something was bothering him."

"You can't just pull Keane Morgan aside for fifteen minutes and ask him if he's okay. No matter what's actually going on with him, he'll say he's 'handsome and happy all the livelong day.' Getting Peen to take off his mask and get real takes *time*. It's a *process*."

"Now see?" I say. "That's why I always make you talk to him. You just get that fucker like nobody else."

Ryan chuckles. "God help me. So, hey, you talked to Kat yet?"

"I left her a voicemail, but we haven't connected yet. I'll call her tomorrow after I get back from my shift."

"Let me know what she says. If it turns out that new boyfriend of hers didn't come to your birthday because he was being a prick, I'll unleash the Morgan Mafia on his ass before he knows what hit him. What's that bastard's name again?"

"Jeff? Jason? I dunno. Something with a 'J.'"

I can hear Ryan's jaw clenching across the phone line. "Well, whatever that motherfucker's name is, it'll be 'Please, Don't Hurt Me, Captain Morgan!' if it turns out he's being an asshole to our little sister."

I smile to myself. God, I love Ryan. "*Down, boy*," I say. "All I said was she looked bummed out at my birthday dinner and I didn't believe her new boyfriend had to work. Let's not jump to conclusions about him being a prick just yet. So, hey, as long as we're talking about our siblings, how was Dax's show last night?"

"Oh, I didn't wind up going," Ryan says. "Olivia and I got distracted and never made it out of my house." He snickers.

I roll my eyes but remain silent. I was with Ryan when he met his current distraction in a bar about a month ago, and I told him that very night the woman made my psycho-bitch radar go off like gangbusters. But did my younger brother listen to his Master Yoda? *Nope*. On the contrary, he took that smoking hot blonde with crazy-as-fuck eyes back to his place that very night and banged the fuck out of her. So now, as far as I'm concerned, my brother is on his own with that one, come what may.

"I heard that, Cheese," Ryan says.

16

"I didn't say anything."

"You rolled your eyes about Olivia. I could hear it."

I laugh. "Speaking of bat-shit crazy girlfriends, I broke up with mine this morning."

"Are you sad about it?"

"No."

"Then, congratulations. You're single and ready to mingle, yet again."

"No, just single. I've had it with the mingle. I hate that shit, man."

"Yeah, I know. It totally sucks out there, doesn't it? It's painful. So what happened with Candice? Did she turn out to be a mean girl underneath that perfect face?"

"Exactly. How'd you know?"

"Just got a vibe that time I met her."

"Why didn't you tell me?"

"You didn't ask. So what triggered the break-up?"

"It turns out she's got a lead foot."

"Uh oh. Now that's a shitty combination: mean and in a hurry. Biological clock ticking?"

"Yep." I tell Ryan about my conversation with Candice this morning and he gasps and groans at all appropriate intervals.

"What's the damned rush?" Ryan asks.

"I have no idea. No sane person would even *think* about marriage and children that fast, let alone want to have a conversation about it."

"I blame Disney," Ryan says. "They've brainwashed an entire generation of little girls into thinking love at first sight is not only real, but to be expected."

"Frankly, just between you and me, I'm not even sure I believe that shit happened for Mom and Dad."

"Agreed. The more likely scenario is that Mom was so damned hot, Dad was willing to say whatever he had to say to bone her."

I grimace. "*Dude.* Don't use 'bone' and 'Mom' in the same sentence. *Please.*"

"What? You've seen Mom's college photos. She was hot as fuck."

"Stop."

Ryan laughs.

"Okay, fucker," I say, "I'm pulling up to Mom and Dad's now, so... Oh, *hello*. Guess whose motorcycle is sitting in the driveway?"

"Sounds like someone got his ass up early to ask to borrow his oldest brother's truck."

"*Again.*"

"Actually, he must have spent the night there," Ryan says. "There's no way in hell Dax would get his rock star ass up this early on a Saturday, even to sweet-talk you about your truck."

"Shit. The last time Daxy borrowed my truck, he was an hour late to pick me up the next day at the end of my shift."

"Don't even try to pretend you're gonna say no to him, Bee," Ryan says. "Daxy could finger paint with his feces and you'd be like, 'It's a Picasso!'"

I chuckle. He's right. "I'm just impressed with the guy's work ethic. He's working his ass off to make 22 Goats take off, plus he's got a full course load at school. And let's not forget he's the one who made me the best damned carrot cake I've ever had for my birthday last week. What did *you* do for my birthday?"

"Get you drunk on the finest tequila."

"Exactly. And I felt like shit the entire next day, so thanks for nothing." My phone pressed against my ear, I get out of my truck and walk around the back to my passenger door. "Come on, Ralphie."

Ralph lurches out of the cab and bounds toward my parents' front door and I amble behind him as Ryan continues talking in my ear.

"All right, Big Brother," Ryan says. "I've arrived in front of Peenie Weenie's apartment building. Time to storm the castle and drag my quarry out of bed."

I fumble for my parents' house key. "Keane doesn't know he's going fishing with you today?"

"Of course not. Dragging Peen out of bed at seven on a Saturday morning is the best part of fishing with him."

We both laugh.

"Have fun," I say. "Call me tomorrow to tell me about the fishing trip."

"Will do. Be safe out there today, Cheese."

"Always."

Chapter 6
Colby

When I enter the living room of my parents' house—surprise, surprise!—I discover my baby brother asleep on the couch, looking more like the four-year-old I taught to throw a football than the twenty-year-old aspiring rock star he's become.

I flick Dax's forehead. "Rise and shine, sweetheart." But he doesn't stir. I nudge his shoulder. "Hey, Dax." Still nothing. For a split-second, I consider leaving Dax here without waking him. But then I remember I'm not a total dick. If the guy dragged his ass all the way out to my parents' house from his gig in SoDo last night, then he must *really* need to borrow my truck. "Yo, Rock Star," I say, nudging Dax again, this time quite a bit harder than the last time. And, finally, my brother stirs.

"Oh, hey, Bee." He rubs his eyes. "What time is it?"

"Just before seven." I sit on the edge of the couch. "How was your gig last night?"

"We *slayed*. The bar owner already invited us back for two more shows next month."

"Awesome. Congrats."

Dax rises up onto his forearms, clearly energized by whatever he's about to say. "Oh, and get this. You know that guy Kat's been dating?"

"The one who was supposed to come to my birthday?"

"Yeah. Josh Faraday. It turns out he's best friends with *Reed Rivers*! Can you believe it? Kat gave me some money she won in Vegas and told me to record an album with it. And she said when I'm done, she's gonna send it to Reed motherfucking Rivers!"

"I bet knowing who Reed Rivers is would make that story a whole lot more exciting."

19

Dax laughs. "Reed Rivers owns an indie record label called River Records. You know that song 'Shaynee' that's all over the radio right now? It's by Red Card Riot, one of the bands signed to River Records."

"Holy shit. Kat's boyfriend knows that guy?"

"He doesn't just *know* him. Kat said Josh has been best friends with Reed Rivers since they went to UCLA together."

"That's huge, Dax. Wow. Good luck."

"I don't need luck when I've got Kitty Kat Morgan working all the angles for me, son. The girl's pure magic."

"Except when she's playing foosball."

We both chuckle.

"Speaking of Kat," I say. "Have you talked to her since my birthday? She seemed pretty bummed about Josh not making it to the party."

"Um, yeah. I took her to the airport on Thursday, actually. She was flying to LA to spend a long weekend with Josh."

"Really? Did she seem happy?"

"Um. Yeah. As far as I could tell."

Oh, God, my baby brother is the second-worst liar in our family—second only to me. "Okay, Dax, spit it out."

"Spit what out?"

"Whatever secret you're sitting on."

"I don't have a secret."

"Your blazing cheeks tell me otherwise."

Dax sighs. "It's not my secret to tell."

"Okay. Fine. Suit yourself." I slap my palms on my thighs and rise from the couch. "I'm gonna head to work now. *In my truck.*"

"Aw, come on, Bee. That's extortion, man."

"Call it what you want." I turn on my heel to leave. "Have a good gig tonight."

"*Colby.*"

I stop.

Dax exhales again. He looks toward the kitchen and then whispers, "You promise you won't tell anyone?"

I nod.

"*No one*. Not even Ryan."

"You have my word."

Dax looks around again, apparently making sure our parents aren't within earshot. "Kat's preggers."

My heart stops. That's not at all what I expected Dax to say.

"It's a total oops," Dax continues. "The biggest mistake of the poor girl's life. The good news, though? Josh is for sure the father and Kat's head over heels in love with him. Plus, Josh is rich as fuck. Not that Kat's a gold-digger, obviously, but if she's gonna get accidentally knocked up by someone, a gazillionaire she actually loves is a good choice."

I clench my jaw, suddenly realizing why Josh didn't come to my birthday dinner. "Is that asshole denying the baby is his?"

"No, no. *Down, boy*. Kat hasn't told Josh about the baby yet. No need to go all Ryan Morgan on the guy's ass quite yet."

"Why hasn't she told him yet?"

"He's mentioned a couple times he never wants kids and she fucked up by missing a pill or two. She's hoping maybe the situation will go away on its own before she ever has to tell him."

"Why the hell did she tell you and not me? Kat always comes to me with her problems."

"She's not telling anyone. Not even her bestie. She only told me because she had to pull over to barf while I was driving her to the airport."

My heart is aching. "I've got to call her. I'm always her shoulder to cry on."

"No, Bee. Kat would kill me if she found out I told you. She doesn't want anyone to know before she tells Josh. Just wait for her to tell you, okay? I mean, this isn't the kind of secret the girl can keep forever. Sooner rather than later, she'll have to tell you and everyone else."

My shoulders sag with resignation. I nod.

"So, hey," Dax says. "On a lighter note, can you guess why I happen to be here at chicken-thirty on a Saturday morning?"

"I'm too beaten down by this thing with Kat to summon the energy to make you beg," I say. I hold out my car keys. "Take it."

Dax whoops and takes my keys. "Thanks, Bee. Fish's van is on the fritz and we've got to haul our gear to a gig all the way in Lakewood tonight."

"But I swear, Dax, if you're not at the firehouse tomorrow morning at seven twenty-nine with a full tank of gas and Ralphie sitting in my passenger seat, then I'll never let you borrow my truck again."

"Got it."

"Roger?"

"Rabbit."

Dax beams a wide smile at me. "You're a life-saver, Colby."

"Do *not* make me sit at the station after work for an hour like last time, Dax."

"I won't. I promise." He fist bumps me. "You're the best big brother in the world."

I put out my palm. "Your keys?"

Dax rummages into his rumpled jeans on the floor and lays his motorcycle keys in my palm.

"Helmet?"

"Kitchen."

I head off. "Have a great gig tonight, Rock Star. And don't be fucking late tomorrow or I'll kill you."

***

In the kitchen, I find the usual scene: Mom and Dad sitting at the table, drinking coffee while Ralph is perched next to Mom, staring at her adoringly.

After the usual greetings, I stride to the cupboard, grab a to-go mug, and ask, "So what are you two crazy kids up to this fine Saturday?"

"Oh, we're going to have big fun," Mom says. "I need to find an antique dresser for a client, so I'm dragging your father to a bunch of estate sales."

Dad shoots me a pained look that makes me laugh out loud.

I secure a lid onto my mug, grab Dax's helmet off the counter, and head toward the doorway. "Enjoy. Dax will pick up Ralphie tomorrow morning and bring him to the station."

"He's borrowing your truck again?" Dad asks.

"He's working his ass off. It's the least I can do."

"Such a sweet big brother," Mom says.

"What can I say, I've got a soft spot for the kid."

"Be careful out there," Mom says.

"Always. Have fun today, kids. Love you both the most."

Chapter 7
Colby

The heat.

Oh, fuck.

It's almost unbearable.

Thick, billowing smoke is banking down in the room. Visibility is horrible. I do a quick scan with my imager, but there's no sign of the baby. Fuck! Where is she? I make a concerted effort to slow my breathing, trying to make the air in my tank last as long as possible, but it's awfully hard to breathe slowly and calmly with almost a hundred pounds of gear weighing me down and my adrenaline surging.

When the four of us firefighters arrived at this house mere minutes ago, we immediately began unfurling the hoses and getting geared up, per usual protocols. And that's when a hatchback raced up to the scene and its driver, a woman in her late twenties or so, tore out of her car and sprinted like a madwoman toward the blazing structure, shrieking at the top of her lungs that her baby girl was trapped inside with a babysitter.

My heart racing, I intercepted the woman and physically held her back from running into the house until, mere seconds later, a bystander thankfully assumed the job of detaining her. Jesus Christ! But before the guy had a firm grip on the woman, she broke free of his grasp, grabbed ahold of my arm, and hysterically begged me to please, please, *please* save her beloved baby.

Oh, man. I've seen all kinds of people in crisis during my five years on this job. Every single shift, I see people on the worst, most catastrophic day of their life. But that woman's hysteria was the most heart-wrenching display of the emotion I've ever seen in my life. And I must admit, it rattled me.

I'll get her.

That's what I said to the hysterical woman as that bystander pulled her off me—and the minute those words left my mouth, I knew they were wrong. I should have said *I'll do my best*. Obviously. But, shit, there was no stuffing the words I'd said back into my mouth. And so, off I went to finish gearing up, bound and determined to keep my promise and bring that woman's baby back to her.

In record time, I locked my breathing apparatus into place, secured my hat, double-checked my air gauge and straps and axe and radio and gloves, and then, carrying a hose, I followed my fellow firefighter, Jake, into the burning house while my captain and another guy stayed outside to fight the blaze from the outside and await backup.

Right off the bat, Jake and I found an older woman keeled over a kitchen table, her jaw and eyelids already showing signs of rigor mortis. We radioed to the guys outside regarding our gruesome discovery, did a quick, fruitless sweep of the first floor, and then barreled upstairs.

And now, here we are having just arrived on the second floor, and it's clear time is running the fuck out on this search. In just the few minutes since we entered this house, the smoke has thickened exponentially, making visibility almost zero at this point, and the flames are noticeably gaining ground. Twice now, as we've progressed through the house, Jake has shot water to the ceiling and the water has instantly evaporated into steam. That's *no bueno*. It tells us the heat in a particular room we're trying to enter is too hot for us to survive, regardless of our turnout gear. So we've had to flood and wait. Flood and wait. Which means progress has been incredibly slow. Shit. I've got to imagine the guys outside aren't having much luck trying to contain this motherfucker.

I look down at my air gauge. *Fuck*. I'm breathing way too fast. My yellow light's been flashing for a couple minutes now, warning me my air is only half full. In training exercises, I always make it much longer than this before my yellow light starts flashing. But in simulations, there's not a real baby whose life is on the line. And there aren't flames burning out of control all around me, either.

Yet again, I try to slow my breathing, but it's almost impossible to do. I'm in serious danger here, the worst of my life, and I know it.

24

As Jake continues hitting the flames with the hose to stall their progress, I feel my way out of the room with my right hand, exactly as I've been trained to do when leaving my line and moving through a smoke-filled room. Any second now, I'm sure the red light on my gauge will start flashing, signaling I'm down to the last quarter-tank of my air supply, but I'm going to keep my word to that mother and find her baby if it's the last thing I do. Maybe literally.

Okay, I'm in a hallway, I think. Oh my God, the smoke is so thick, I can't see more than an inch in front of my face. I feel my way along the wall and come upon a door I'm almost positive we haven't checked yet. Flames are fingering out from the top of the door and feathering across the ceiling. Every molecule in my body is telling me to get the fuck away from that door. To save myself. But my brain knows if I leave now and find out later that baby girl was trapped inside this particular room, I'll never sleep soundly again. I sidestep some fallen debris engulfed in flames and inch closer toward the door.

My red light begins flashing. My warning alarm goes off inside my mask, telling me to get out.

But I persist. Breathing hard, I feel my way and enter the room.

Flames are licking up the walls. The smoke in this room is a deep black. That's *so* not good. Black smoke is flammable. This place could blow at any time. I radio for Jake's benefit, "Firefighter Morgan. Engine 262. Black smoke. Abort mission. Get out, Jake. Get out!"

But I don't follow my own advice.

Because I promised that mother.

If the baby's not in this room, okay, I'm out. I'll have done all I can do.

But I'm not leaving until I know for sure if that baby is in here or not.

I stop just inside the doorway and scan with my thermal imaging camera... *and there she is*! My imager plainly shows me the body heat of a small figure on the floor about fifteen feet away. I barrel toward the figure as best I can through the opaque black smoke, crashing into something as I go—a dresser? Shit! I'm feeling my way, frantically chasing the red and yellow constellation I see on my imager.

Finally, I reach the baby and get down low under the bank of smoke where visibility isn't quite so poor. She's splayed out on the floor, still conscious and crying her little head off. When she sees me, she reaches her tiny arms up for me, begging me to pick her up. Begging me to save her life. There's terror in her eyes... and *relief*, too. Relief that someone has come to rescue her from this nightmare.

My heart racing, I scoop her up and cradle her protectively in my arm, shielding her from the unbearable heat with my turnout gear as best I can. "Colby's got you, sweetheart," I say, even though I know there's no way in hell she can hear me through my mask, let alone through the roar of the flames around us. But I figure she can see my mouth moving. See the assurance in my eyes.

I get on my radio. "Firefighter Morgan. Engine 262. I've got the baby. *I've got her*. I'm on the second floor, Charlie side. I think I'm close to the Charlie-Bravo corner. My air is low. My red light is flashing. I'm off my line, but I'm going to feel my way toward the hallway and try to locate it. Get ready for us. We're gonna follow the line out."

I feel my way with my left hand, exactly the way I've been trained to do, while shielding the baby with my right arm. But, shit, the smoke is so thick, I'm all turned around. The air around me is undulating from the heat, like I'm underwater. Through my peripheral vision, everything looks like I'm surrounded by stained glass.

The fire is closing in on me.

Oh, God, I'm so fucked.

I decide to make a run for the hallway leading to the stairs... to where I think the hallway is, anyway. But I've no sooner taken two loping steps toward what I think is the right direction than a beam comes crashing down right in front of me, blocking my escape. *Shit*! A wall of flames instantly springs up in front of me. *I'm trapped.*

I activate my personal alert system, signaling to the guys outside I'm still alive but in deep shit.

I get on my radio again. "Mayday, mayday, mayday!" I shout. "Firefighter Morgan! Engine 262. I'm trapped by debris in a room, second floor on Charlie side, and unable to get to the stairs. I've lost my line. Repeat, I've lost my line. I'm on the second floor, Charlie side. Charlie-Bravo corner! Air is low. Almost empty. If there's a window on Charlie side, request ladder immediately. I'm going to search for a window now. *Get that ladder ready!*"

A wall of fire rises up a foot away from me and I barrel blindly away from it, slogging through thick, opaque smoke without a clue if I'm heading toward safety or incineration. Feeling my way with one hand through the smoke while clutching the baby with the other, I say a prayer. *Please, God, let there be a window on the other side of this room.* Because if there's no window, or if, God forbid, it's covered with bars, then I'm toast. Literally.

As I barrel through the thick black smoke, visions of my family members' faces flash before my eyes. If I die today, especially like this, my poor mom will never recover. Same with my dad. And Ryan. Fuck! *Ryan.* In a heartbeat, I have a thousand thoughts, all at once. That I'll never see Kat's baby. Or watch Dax become the rock star I know he'll be. Or laugh at one of Keane's outrageous stories again.

How did I get here? When I woke up this morning next to Candice in my bed and looked out the window at the rising sun, I had no idea I was seeing my last sunrise. I thought I had fifty years' worth of sunrises ahead of me. When I told Candice I was open to maybe getting married *one day,* it didn't occur to me I was already all out of days.

I take a deep breath. *Okay, Colby, you need to stop freaking out. You need to slow your breathing and use your training and calm the fuck down.*

Oh, thank God. I think I see a window. It's barely visible through the bank of dark smoke, but I'm almost sure that's what it is. I radio to the guys and scream with what's left of my air that I see a window on the second floor. "Charlie side near the Bravo corner!" I shout. "Get me a fucking ladder!" I bolt toward the barely visible square of light, clutching the baby like a football in the crook of my arm... when, out of nowhere, I'm taken down.

I'm on the ground. Unable to move. What the fuck just happened?

It takes me a half-second to realize a flaming beam has crashed down from the ceiling and taken me with it. I grit out a string of expletives as pain flashes through my left leg. I try to pull myself to freedom, but my left leg is pinned underneath the beam.

The baby.

My heart stops.

She's not tucked in my arm anymore.

I look around frantically and, thank God, discover her on the floor right above my head. I reach up and grab her just as my gauge vibrates and flashes a sustained red. *I'm completely out of air.*

I grab my radio. "Mayday, mayday, mayday!" I shout. "I'm pinned underneath a beam. My air is gone. Repeat: *no air left*! The smoke is black as fuck, guys! Get me that ladder! I'm pinned but I'm coming!" I get off the radio. "*Fuck!*" I scream. "Fuck!" But then I remember I've got no air and screaming is an exceedingly bad idea.

My personal alert system starts going off like gangbusters, telling the guys outside I've been immobile for twenty seconds.

Still holding the baby, I try to push the beam off my leg, but it's way heavier than I'd realized.

I'm dizzy. Out of air. I feel like I'm about to pass out.

I shake it off. If I pass out, I'll never wake up again. I know it for a fact.

I put the baby down next to me, gather every last drop of strength in my body for one last attempt and, somehow, I'm able to push the beam off me just enough to let me roll my hips and kick with my right leg and wriggle free. In one fluid motion, I scoop up the baby off the floor and crawl like an injured alligator toward that motherfucking window, my twisted left leg dragging uselessly as I move, the baby tucked in my left arm.

When I get to the window, I pull myself up, grab the axe off my belt, and smash the fuck out of the glass... and the minute the glass breaks, dark smoke whooshes out of the room through the gaping hole. I smash away again and again, clearing shards of glass from the frame, and then hang my entire torso out the window, gasping for air. I look down. No ladder. Fuck! It must be at another window. I'm desperate to rip off my mask to breathe, but I don't dare—not with the flames licking at my back.

"Mayday, mayday, mayday!" I shout into my radio. "I'm hanging out a window! Need a ladder! I need a ladder!"

I'm gasping for air. On the cusp of passing out. My lungs hurt. I feel like my turnout gear is about to melt from the heat. It's got to be a thousand degrees in this fucking room! I hold the baby outside the window like she's the Lion King, trying to keep her from the heat and flames.

Thank God, a ladder clacks loudly against the window sill and I quickly shift position, intending to climb out feet-first and slide down by holding the rails, but then I remember I've got the baby and the bailout maneuver I've trained on over and over again isn't going to work. Fuck! There's no drill I've ever run that has taught me how to do a ladder bailout with a useless leg while holding a baby. Should I lower her down with a rope to make sure she...

Boom!

The hanging black smoke explodes behind and around me. Oh, God, I'm so fucked. I know from my training I've got seventeen seconds *at most* before my turnout gear fails and I'm dead. So I do the only thing I can do: I jump. I dive headfirst out the window and down the ladder, clutching the baby with all my might while trying desperately to slow my descent at least slightly with my free arm and good leg. But this is pure chaos right here. I'm bouncing down... and then free-falling. The world turns upside down on me for a split-second. And then there's a weird and terrifying weightlessness before I crash onto my left shoulder and land with a sickening thud to the ground. I flop and roll and wind up on my back, on my tank, gasping for air and screaming in pain. Fuck! I think I just dislocated my left shoulder! Or maybe I broke my collarbone? For sure, I broke some ribs. I don't know. All I know is I'm in excruciating pain pretty much everywhere. And that I can't fucking breathe.

The baby.

I look down and discover I'm miraculously still holding onto her and she appears to be in one piece. She's burned badly, though. Her hair has been completely singed off and her skin is now blackened. She's unconscious and flopping in my arm like a rag doll.

There's a commotion above me. Boots. Someone grabs the baby from me. And then I'm dragged away, away, away from the inferno.

I'm convulsing in pain.

Drawing my dying breath.

I can't breathe.

My lungs are on fire.

The dragging stops. My helmet and mask are ripped off. An oxygen mask is placed over my nose and mouth. I gasp and gag and then... *breathe.* Shaking, I take a long, gulping breath of sweet air. Oh my fucking God, breathing has never felt so... *painful.*

What the fuck is wrong with my lungs? They're in excruciating pain.

Tears streak down my hot face. Tears of pain. Relief. Fear. Joy. I'm quaking with adrenaline. With aftershocks of my terror. My throat and lungs are on fire. I'm in more pain than I knew was possible. But none of it matters in the end because I'm alive.

I'm alive!

They load me into an ambulance.

I'm gasping for air.

Maybe I'm not free and clear yet, after all.

Oh well. At least I brought that baby girl back to her mother, the way I promised to do. That's what they'll tell my parents and siblings. That's what they'll say at my funeral. That I traded my life for the baby's.

Service before self.

It's the last thought I have before my eyes roll back into my head and the world mercifully fades to black.

Chapter 8
Lydia

"So Queen Bea is a happy camper, then?" I ask.

I'm sitting in the break room of the hospital where I've worked for the past year, talking on the phone with my babysitter about my two-and-a-half-year-old, Beatrice. A reporter on the local news is talking about the weather on the TV behind me and a small group of nurses is chatting and laughing at a table to my right.

"Oh, my, yes, little miss is having a grand ol' time," my babysitter, Rosalind, says. "I think that Tylenol you gave her this morning did the trick. She hasn't been fussy about that new molar at all."

"Oh, thank goodness."

"She's in the sandbox now, happily telling all the other two-year-olds at the park how to bake a chocolate cake just like her mommy does it."

"Aw. Give her a kiss for me."

"I sure will. As soon as she's done bossing everyone around."

We both chuckle.

"Oh, hey," I say. "When you pick up the older kids from school, will you remind Theo to call me if that Caleb kid gave him any grief today? I texted him about it, but it wouldn't hurt for you to remind him."

"What'd his teacher say when you met with her this morning?"

"She said she'd handle it. But, still, I want to be sure."

We say our goodbyes and I return to the file of my next patient—an elderly woman who had spinal surgery yesterday.

The newscaster on the TV behind me says, "And in some harrowing news out of the Queen Anne neighborhood, a Seattle

31

firefighter is being hailed as a hero today after being injured in a house fire while rescuing a baby girl."

"Oh, they're talking about him!" one of the nurses at the adjacent table says, and everyone in the room, including me, focuses on the TV.

All day long, I've heard nurses whispering about the "gorgeous" and "brave" firefighter who was rushed into surgery earlier today, but I haven't heard any details about his condition. All I know from my eavesdropping is that he's now out of surgery and in the ICU with his family.

I must admit my interest is piqued. Nurses frequently talk about particularly attractive male patients, especially first responders. But I've never heard so many nurses and other assorted medical personnel whisper *this* much about a patient before. Seriously, this guy must be quite the specimen.

"This is amateur footage of the fire," the newscaster says, and the screen switches to video of a two-story house engulfed in flames.

"Holy crap," I whisper, my skin prickling with goose bumps.

"When firefighters from Station 9 arrived at the house, they were told there were two people trapped inside—sixty-year-old Margaret Corman and fourteen-month-old Lupita Guerra." We see a photo of the adult woman mentioned and then the image of smiling Baby Lupita—an adorable baby girl with big brown eyes who reminds me of my own two daughters at that same age. The newscaster states the firefighters quickly found the older woman deceased during their frantic search and that they then headed upstairs to search for Baby Lupita. "Ultimately, it was Firefighter Morgan who found the little girl," the newscaster says solemnly. "And then became trapped himself."

The screen switches to a smiling stock photo of the trapped firefighter, Colby Morgan, and my heart skips a beat at the sight of him. *Bloody hell.* He's in his late twenties or early thirties, I'd guess, with blonde hair and the most shockingly blue eyes I've ever seen. He's got a chiseled jaw. A spectacularly fit body. A cleft in his steel chin. Basically, if there were a movie about a fireman-by-day turned stripper-by-night who gets turned into a crime-fighting superhero after being exposed to radiation, Colby Morgan would be the star of that movie.

The newscaster concludes her report by saying, "Firefighter Morgan and Baby Lupita are both listed in critical condition. We'll have more on this tragic story as it unfolds."

I spring out of my chair, my thoughts racing. Does the firefighter have a wife and kids? Is there some young woman sitting at his bedside right now who's about to experience exactly what I did with Darren three years ago? I'm trembling at the thought. If some young woman is about to become a widow, then I want to be her lifeline. When Darren died, the outpouring of support I received from the community, and especially from other young widows of first responders, was my saving grace.

In a surge of determination to be of use any way I can, I grab my patient file off the table and bolt out of the break room.

Chapter 9
Lydia

As I approach the firefighter's room, I hear the sound of female weeping wafting through the open door. That, and the beeping of a heart monitor. *Beep, beep, beep.*

I freeze.

Anxiety floods me.

What if the firefighter is brain-dead? Am I truly ready to insert myself into a situation like that? I touch the tip of my left thumb against the base of my left ring finger. Touching my wedding band has been my nervous tic since Darren died... but, for the first time in three years, my ring isn't there.

My heart stops with panic... until I remember I moved my wedding band to my right hand last week.

There was no particular reason to do it. I woke up one morning after an amazing sex dream starring some random guy from a sitcom and realized it was time to overtly signal to the world that I'm single. Did I switch the ring because I'm hoping to fall in love? *Hell no.* I honestly just felt ready to get laid for the first time in three years. By whom and how I'd possibly finagle such a tryst with work and the kids taking up pretty much all my time, I had no idea. But I decided it sure as hell wasn't going to happen if I kept wearing my wedding band on my left hand. So I moved it, went to my gynecologist and got an IUD implanted, and then... promptly forgot I'd done either until now.

Beep, beep, beep. The heart monitor draws me out of my thoughts and back outside the doorframe of the firefighter's room. Please, God, don't let the firefighter be brain-dead.

I peek through the doorway into the room and my heart stops.

He's on a ventilator.

It's protruding from his mouth.

I didn't expect that. Does that mean he's brain-dead?

There are... one, two, three... *six* people crammed in the small room, variously slumped, standing, or leaning. And all of them are unmistakably grief-stricken.

They all look closely related to each other. Definitely a family by blood.

The middle-aged man and woman are clearly the firefighter's parents. The younger four—three broad-shouldered, fit-looking guys and a spectacularly beautiful blonde woman—would appear to be the firefighter's siblings. All four obviously share the middle-aged couple's DNA.

One of the three hunks, a gorgeous dude in ripped jeans and a black T-shirt, is sitting next to the bed, holding the firefighter's limp hand. A second guy with tattoo sleeves on both his sculpted arms is sitting in a corner with his hands over his face and his shoulders shuddering with sobs. A third guy with tousled hair and a ridiculously perfect face is sitting next to the sobbing guy with the forearm-tattoos, patting his shoulder and whispering to him.

My eyes flicker to the young blonde woman. She's standing next to the older couple, her cheek resting on the older woman's shoulder. Okay, there's no way that young blonde is the firefighter's wife. She's the spitting image of the older woman and the young dude in ripped jeans. The three of them are like Russian nesting dolls.

"Excuse me," a male voice says behind me.

It's Dr. Garabedian, the finest orthopedic surgeon at this esteemed hospital.

I murmur my apologies and step aside, suddenly realizing I'm being a brazen lookie-loo.

Crap. Now that I know the firefighter doesn't have a wife in that room, there's no reason for me to be standing here staring at this poor family in grief.

I pry myself away from the doorway and begin walking slowly down the hallway. But five steps into my journey, I stop and lean my back against the wall, feeling like the floor and walls are warping. A half-minute later, as I continue leaning against the wall trying to steady myself, the gorgeous young blonde woman from the firefighter's room glides past me, headed down the hallway toward the double doors that lead to the waiting room.

As if in a trance, I follow her with only one thought in my head: *If that woman is headed to the waiting room to give someone an update on the firefighter's condition, then, by God, I want to hear it.*

Chapter 10
Lydia

The blonde woman walks into the waiting area and straight to a stunningly gorgeous dark-haired man who's obviously not her blood relation like all the people back in the firefighter's room.

"Josh," the young woman says as she flings herself into his muscled arms.

I slip into a chair in a corner and stare at them, incapable of looking away.

As the woman cries in the gorgeous man's arms, he kisses her hair. Rubs her back. Oh, God, his tenderness toward her is breathtaking... and enviable.

I want that.

Not the young woman's grief, of course. Lord knows, I've had my share of grief to last me three lifetimes. But their *intimacy*. That's what I crave. That's what I miss. *That's what I want.*

Three years ago, I wouldn't have thought it possible for me to desire the touch of a man who isn't Darren. But I guess it's only natural I've come to feel this primal ache. To desire fingertips on my flesh again. I'm only thirty-two, after all. And as I've recently come to realize, no woman—not even one as loyal and devoted as I am to Darren—can survive forever on dildos alone.

I continue staring at the couple, my stomach knotted with deep yearning.

The woman pulls away from her lover to pull him down to sitting and says, "I've been holding it together pretty well for my mom, but seeing your face made me lose—" She clamps her hand over her mouth like she's about to hurl, turning the color of Shrek.

"Kat?" the hot dude says, looking perplexed.

37

The blonde takes a few deep breaths and groans like she's about to puke... and, in a flash, I think I recognize the nature of the nausea I'm seeing on this woman's face: *morning sickness*. Maybe I'm crazy. Indeed, I'm probably just projecting. But the blonde's face looks exactly the way I've felt infinite times during all three of my pregnancies. Of course, she might just have food poisoning... some bad chicken, perhaps? But the way it came on so suddenly like that... my gut tells me I'm right.

"Are you okay?" the dark-haired guy asks, looking utterly confused.

Hmm. Interesting. If I'm right about the bun in the oven, then his confusion is throwing me for a loop. Unless, of course, he doesn't know. I glance at their hands. No wedding rings.

"I'm okay," the blonde mumbles. But, clearly, she's not.

"How's Colby?" the man asks.

I sit forward in my chair, my heart pounding.

"The tests came back and it was pretty much all good news, relatively speaking," the woman says, and I exhale with relief. She continues, "Broken leg, ribs, and collarbone."

And his brain?

"Ruptured spleen," the blonde says. "Smoke inhalation—but not too bad, thank God."

My heart leaps. Smoke inhalation! Of course! That must be the reason for the breathing machine—not brain damage!

The blonde continues, "He suffered some burns to his left side where the beam was crushing him, but his turnout gear protected him pretty well. Could have been a whole lot worse."

And what about his brain?

The blonde lets out a huge sigh of relief. "No head trauma at all, thank God."

A little gasp of relief lurches out of me and I cover my mouth, worried I'll be discovered.

"It's gonna be a long road to recovery," the blonde says. "Lots of physical therapy, but he's going to pull through."

My heart skips a beat. *Lots of physical therapy?* Without meaning to do it, I'm instantly concocting my speech to my boss about why the firefighter should be assigned to me.

"But the baby Colby went in to save?" the blonde continues. "She just died in her mother's arms in the pediatric unit."

I clutch my heart, tears welling in my eyes.

The woman says softly, "Her parents came to Colby's room to thank him for what he did to try to save her. He wasn't conscious so they thanked my parents." Tears fall down the blonde's cheeks, mimicking mine. "They said they were grateful to my brother for giving them the chance to hold their little angel one last time and say goodbye."

I wipe my eyes.

She adds, "Oh my God, it ripped everyone's heart out, Josh. All of us were crying, even Ryan, and he never cries." Out of nowhere, the blonde clamps her hand to her mouth again, the same way she did earlier. With an expletive on her lips, she leaps out of her chair and sprints to the bathroom across the hall, her body jerking and heaving as she runs out.

"Kat?" the dark-haired hottie calls after her, his features awash in concern and confusion.

And suddenly, three thoughts simultaneously harden into certainty inside my brain. One, that blonde beauty is pregnant. Probably still in the early days of her pregnancy, judging by her flat belly and queasy stomach. Two, the blonde's hunky boyfriend doesn't have a clue about his girlfriend's bun in the oven. And three, if the firefighter's going to need "lots of physical therapy," as that woman just reported, then I sure as hell want to be the one to give it to him.

Chapter 11
Lydia

It's Monday morning. After a fabulous day off yesterday with the kids—we had a blast using our annual passes to the Seattle Aquarium—I'm back at work, about to head over to the PT desk on the fourth floor. But first things first, I've got to pee.

Just as I sit down in a bathroom stall, someone bursts into the stall next to mine and violently begins barfing. Oh, dear God. Whoever she is, she isn't puking. She's DEFCON-one hurling her large intestines out.

I pull up my pants and bolt to the sink, eager to wash my hands and get the heck out of here before that poor woman comes out of her stall. God knows if it were me in there voiding my body of all its internal organs, I wouldn't want a stranger awkwardly standing next to me at the sink afterwards.

But I'm not fast enough. Before I've finished washing my hands, the stall door behind me flies open and the gorgeous blonde woman from the other day—the young woman I'm pretty sure is the firefighter's sister—emerges and drags her beleaguered body to the sink.

"Hi," she says pitifully, smiling at me apologetically. "Sorry you had to overhear that."

"Oh, no worries," I reply. I motion to my blue scrubs. "Comes with the territory when you work at a hospital. Plus, I'm no stranger to throwing up myself. I had horrible morning sickness with all three of my pregnancies, so I'm quite accustomed to hearing that particular sound, usually made by me."

The woman's exhausted blue eyes flicker to life. "You had morning sickness with *three* pregnancies?" She touches her flat belly. "Wow. I don't know how I'm going to survive doing this through *one*."

40

God, I'm good. "Oh, you're pregnant?" I say. "Congratulations."

The dour expression on the woman's gorgeous face plainly tells me congratulations aren't in order. "Thanks."

"How far along are you?" I ask.

"About eight weeks, I think. I'll know for sure when I go to the doctor next week."

I feel the urge to hug her, but I refrain. "Hang in there. You'll most likely feel a lot better in a couple months."

The woman holds up crossed fingers.

I ask, "You know what helped me get rid of morning sickness?"

She looks at me hopefully.

"Absolutely nothing."

We both chuckle, but her laughter quickly morphs into a pitiful moan.

"Oh, gosh, I'm sorry," I say. "That was my paltry attempt at humor. Forgive me."

"Oh, no worries. I'm used to it. I've got four brothers. In my family, we tease because we care."

"Seriously, though," I say. "There were a few things that helped ease my morning sickness a bit. Nothing helped a lot, to be honest, but every little bit helps, right?" I give her a few tips and she thanks me profusely.

My usual instinct would be to tell a newbie pregnant woman her misery will be worth it in the end—that when she finally holds her precious baby in her arms, all the discomfort she's endured will be quickly forgotten. But I stop myself. This girl's not wearing a wedding ring, and her earlier body language told me this baby isn't happy news.

The blonde finishes drying her hands. "It feels amazing to *finally* get to talk to someone about this, especially an actual mom. Not to mention a mom of *three*."

Interesting. If she yearns for advice from an actual mom, it seems to me she's got a direct line to a mother of *five* down the hall. Does that mean she hasn't told her own mother about her pregnancy yet? "Any time," I say. "I work here, so if you have any future questions and happen to see me walking by, feel free to pull me aside."

"Thanks so much. I'm Kat, by the way."

She holds out her hand and I shake it.

"Lydia. Nice to meet you."

"You, too. Well, my family is probably wondering if I fell into the toilet by now." She flashes me a wan smile—a smile that's so mirthless, it makes my heart pang for her. And then she turns on her heel and heads toward the door. "Have a great day, Lydia."

"You, too, Kat," I reply reflexively... and instantly regret it. Obviously, the girl isn't going to have a great day. She's got an accidental stowaway growing inside her womb and a brother breathing on a mechanical ventilator down the hall. "I meant best of luck, Kat!" I call after her. But the beautiful blonde with the sad smile and heroic brother is long gone.

Chapter 12
Lydia

"Considering what you went through with Darren, I think it will be particularly gratifying for you to work with him," my boss, Janice, says. She's talking about the firefighter, of course. And, instantly, a tidal wave of nerves floods me. As determined as I was when I left that waiting room on Saturday to get assigned to the firefighter, I wound up chickening out and not requesting him, simply because I started second-guessing myself. Would working with the firefighter trigger too many memories of Darren?

"Aw, don't be nervous, Lydia," Janice says, apparently reacting to the look on my face. "I think this journey will wind up being cathartic for you. And if not, then, it's still a win-win. The firefighter will get the best PT on my staff and you'll get to spend the next five to six months helping a courageous first responder get his body back. Not a bad thing, either way, right?"

I nod, despite the clanging of my heart.

We talk about the firefighter's physical therapy program for a bit. He'll get flexibility and range-of-motion therapy for the first six to eight weeks while his broken bones heal. During that time, he'll be relegated to a wheelchair, rather than a walker or crutches, due to his broken clavicle. After that, once his clavicle has healed and he's finally cleared to put partial weight on his shattered leg, he'll use a walker for a few weeks, just because he'll probably have quite a bit of muscle atrophy after so many weeks in a wheelchair. After that, he'll progress to using two crutches. And then one. And, of course, the minute he's out of his wheelchair, he'll start strength training, ever so conservatively at first, probably including quite a bit of aqua therapy.

"You'll see, Lydia," my boss says. "You're going to be this poor

43

man's godsend. And if I were a betting woman, I'd say he's going to be yours, too."

***

Adrenaline coursing through my bloodstream, I enter Room 402 and park myself just inside the doorway. All six of the firefighter's family members are here again. Colby Morgan is asleep in his bed on the far side of the room. And I'm trembling.

"Hi, everyone," I say quietly. "I'm Lydia Decker. Colby's physical therapist."

Everyone greets me.

"Do you need to do something to him right now?" his mother asks. "He had a really bad night last night. Lots of pain. I'd love for him to sleep a bit longer."

"Oh, no need to wake him," I say. "I need to do a PT screening at some point today to get a baseline on him, but it's not urgent. I'll start working with Colby in earnest once he's off the breathing machine and out of the ICU." I gaze at Colby's sleeping form across the room. Is it weird I'm physically aching to hold his limp hand and send him every bit of healing energy I can muster?

I remain rooted to my spot inside the door, chatting quietly with the family. As it turns out, everyone is who I thought they were. The two older people are Colby's parents, Thomas and Louise Morgan. The four younger people are Colby's siblings: Ryan, Kat, Keane, and Dax.

"Where does Colby fall in the birth order?" I ask.

"He's our first-born," Mrs. Morgan says wistfully, looking at her sleeping son. "He's the one who made me a mother."

"Uh oh, Keane," Ryan, the one with the tattoo sleeves, says. "Looks like Colby has knocked you out of Mom's top spot."

"Damn that Colby Morgan!" Keane, the one with tousled hair, says, shaking his fist, and everyone chuckles. But then Keane gazes over at his prostrate brother and his gorgeous face turns somber. "Actually, just this once, I won't fight for Mom's top spot. Colby can have it."

"Wow, that's awfully big of you," Ryan says dryly.

"In fact, I propose a new rule to the game, guys," Keane says magnanimously. "From now on, whichever one of us rushes into a burning building to save a trapped baby and winds up in the ICU with broken bones and internal bleeding and on a breathing machine, he automatically gets Mom's top spot for... I dunno. Should we say a year?"

"A *year*?" the youngest one, Dax, says. "Bah. A week, tops."

"Agreed," Ryan says. "Or else it'd just be *way* too easy for all of us to keep knocking each other off the top spot week after week."

Everyone chuckles. But it's the kind of laughter people share at a funeral.

The playful conversation between Colby's brothers continues, and as it does, my eyes wander to Kat in the corner... only to find her staring at me with laser-sharp focus. Having caught my eye, she makes a face that nonverbally screams at me not to mention the bun in the oven she admitted to me in the bathroom.

I nod, making it clear I've received her message loud and clear.

Mrs. Morgan asks me a question about physical therapy in general, drawing my attention away from Kat, and I answer her. We talk easily for several minutes, until Ryan stands, yawns, and says, "I need a change of scenery for a bit, guys. I'm gonna grab some coffee at that place across the street. Anyone want anything?"

"I'll come with you," Dax says, standing and stretching— thereby showing off his beautiful lean muscles.

Keane stands. "Morgan family field trip."

Colby's parents and sister look at each other, like, "Should we go?"

"If you three want to join them," I say, "I'd be happy to sit here with Colby 'til you get back. If he wakes up, I'll do my PT assessment."

"And you'll sit with him until we get back?" Mrs. Morgan confirms. "I don't want my son to be alone."

"I promise," I say. "I've a couple hours before I need to be at the outpatient clinic next door for my only scheduled patient of the day. You can take all the time you'd like."

Mrs. Morgan looks relieved and, after a bit of prodding from her family, decides to join them.

A moment later, the Morgans are gone and I'm alone with their first-born son. Who's on a ventilator. And attached to a heart monitor that's going *beep, beep, beep.*

Shit.

My heart racing and my mouth dry, I take a deep breath... and cross the room.

Chapter 13
Lydia

I arrive at Colby's bedside and gaze down at him.

Closed eyes.

Ventilator.

Heart machine.

Beep, beep, beep.

I grip the bed railing, trying to steady myself.

Just as I feared I would, I feel like I've just stepped out of a time machine, its dial set to The Worst Moment of Lydia Decker's life.

Reflexively, I look at the back of Colby's skull, my eyes searching for the crater I'm terrified will be there—but this man's head isn't cratered. No, it's whole and perfect and beautiful. *"He's not Darren,"* I whisper, my body trembling. *"He's Colby."*

At the sound of my voice, Colby stirs.

I grip the railing even more tightly and wait, holding my breath.

Colby stirs again, grimaces, and slowly opens his eyes.

And, just like that, I'm yanked back to the present.

Blue eyes.

Not the chocolate-brown ones I was expecting to see.

"Hi," I whisper, peering down at the man's blue gaze. "I'm Lydia, your physical therapist." I lower the bed railing and slide my palm into Colby's. "Your family went across the street for coffee. I'm here to do a PT screening, just to get a baseline, and then—"

Colby grimaces and squeezes my hand, hijacking the rest of my sentence.

"Are you in pain, Colby?"

He nods pitifully and squeezes my hand again, this time several times in a row, telling me the answer to my question about him having pain isn't yes, it's *fuck yes.*

46

I call for the nurse and she rushes in. She asks Colby to rate his pain on a scale from one ten and he weakly shows her eight fingers. She checks her chart and confirms the physician's orders regarding pain management and then quickly adds what seems like a rather large dosage of powerful pain meds to Colby's IV bag.

"There you go, sweetie," the nurse coos. She pats Colby's arm. "In a couple minutes, you'll be feeling like you're floating on a cotton candy cloud."

The nurse leaves the room and I take my seat next to Colby again. To my surprise, he immediately slides his hand into mine again, picking up right where we left off.

I sit silently with him for several minutes, just holding his hand, letting my racing heart calm down. Finally, when I'm feeling steady and the muscles in Colby's handsome face have visibly relaxed, I ask, "Are you feeling better?"

His eyes are glassy now. His brow is slack. He nods weakly.

"Are you floating on that cotton candy cloud the nurse promised you?"

Colby winks at me like a cartoon rabbit and I chuckle at the surprising gesture.

"That good, huh?"

Colby winks again, this time with even more panache.

"Wow," I say. "Even drugged up and breathing through a machine, you're quite the charmer, Mr. Morgan."

His left arm is immobilized in a sling, so he releases my hand in order to brush some imaginary dirt off his left shoulder—a gesture I'm interpreting as his silly way of telling me, "I've got charm for days, babe."

"Oh, I don't doubt it for a minute," I say.

Colby slides his hand in mine again.

"You're a real smooth operator out there in the real world, aren't you, Colby Morgan?"

He nods and winks, yet again.

Oh my God, he looks so freaking stoned right now. Loopy as hell. And so ridiculously beautiful. "Well, it's lucky I'm finding out you're a flirty devil *before* I start working with you three times a week for the next five to six months, huh? Now I know to keep my eye on you, mister."

Colby disengages from holding my hand again and touches the bare ring finger of his immobilized left hand.

"Huh?" I say.

He repeats the gesture.

"Are you telling me you're single?"

He nods. And then flashes me an okay sign.

"Ah. I see. You're saying it's fine for you to be a flirty devil who leaves exploded ovaries in your wake because you're single?"

He points at me as if to say, "Bingo."

I giggle. "Are you single and ready to mingle, Colby?"

This time, Colby wags his index finger at me and furrows his brow. Clearly, I've said something wrong.

"No?" I ask.

Again, he wags his finger at me.

"Single and... *not* ready to mingle?"

He nods.

"You're not interested in dating or you're just not a fan of cheesy pickup lines?"

He makes a vague hand gesture I can't quite interpret. And then he points with great intention at me.

"What?" I ask.

He repeats the gesture.

"Are you asking if I'm single and ready to mingle?"

He nods.

"Well, gosh, that's a bit personal, don't you think?"

Colby shakes his head and slides his hand into mine again. I feel his thumb exploring my ring finger, looking for a ring, and when he doesn't feel one, he releases my hand to point at me and then himself.

"What about us?" I ask.

Again, he gestures to his bare ring finger.

"You're saying we should get together?"

He nods emphatically and then points at me. *Bingo.*

I laugh. "Are you always this forward or just whenever you happen to be on powerful drugs?"

He points to the respirator protruding from his mouth.

"Only when you're on a ventilator?"

He nods and I laugh. How the heck is he managing to be funny under circumstances like this?

"Go for it, Colby," I say. "Milk that ventilator for all it's worth."

He raises his hand like he's a puppeteer with his hand inside Kermit the Frog's head and then he makes his hand puppet laugh enthusiastically.

I giggle. "Is that you laughing?"

He nods and points at me. *Bingo.*

"What are you laughing about?"

He points at me.

"You think I'm funny?"

Another nod.

"Well, you're wrong about that. I'm freaking *hysterical.*"

He raises his hand puppet and makes it laugh and I can't help but giggle.

Again, Colby points to his left ring finger and then at me.

"You're asking me if I'm single again?"

He nods.

"Persistent, mofo."

He nods again.

I shift in my chair. This is a first. I've never in my life been asked this question before, other than when I was filling out a form for the Census Bureau or something. Why would anyone ever have asked me my marital status? From age twenty-one until a week ago, I wore a wedding band that made things awfully clear. And if the band didn't do it, the kids I've been toting around for a decade sure did.

Again, he points at me, asking me if I'm single.

I clear my throat. "Okay, enough chitchat," I say. "Time for your PT screening now, Mr. Morgan."

I perform my screening, surveying his battered and broken, but utterly beautiful, body, and when I'm done, I sit back down... only to feel Colby grab my hand, yet again. And, this time, he intertwines his fingers with mine like he's been doing it forever.

"God, you look stoned as hell, Colby," I say, my hand clasped in his.

He nods.

"Are you feeling any pain at all?"

He shakes his head and does a silly loopy thing with his eyes.

I chuckle. "Are you riding a purple unicorn down a rainbow highway, honey?"

He nods effusively.

Oh, God, his face is stunning. As I sit here, holding his hand, listening to the heart monitor, gazing at his perfect face, it's taking all my strength not to stroke his cheekbone and eyebrows and nose, the same way I stroked Darren's that last horrible day. I lean back and take a deep breath. "You should get some sleep now, Colby," I say. "You need your rest."

He shakes his head, releases my hand, and adamantly indicates his bare ring finger on his immobilized left hand.

"Oh, *that*," I say. "I thought you'd forgotten about that."

He raises his eyebrows as if to say, *I'm waiting*.

Well, damn.

At my prior job before Darren died, I was hit on a few times by patients, despite the wedding band on my finger, but my would-be seducers were always elderly patients who were clearly being playful. Which meant all those times I felt comfortable saying something along the lines of, "Well, gosh, Mr. Rosenbaum, I don't think my husband the six-foot-four police officer would appreciate me dating another man, especially one as handsome as you." But this time... well, this feels different. Colby isn't an elderly patient. Despite his present condition, Colby Morgan is a gorgeous man around my age. Of course, I realize he's high as a kite and out of his head and that this conversation is drug-induced and meaningless. But, still. Saying the words "I'm single" out loud to a handsome man like Colby will be a first for me.

I clear my throat. "Yes, I'm single."

Colby motions to me and him.

"Correct. We're both single," I say.

Colby rolls his eyes and gestures to the two of us again.

My stomach is doing somersaults. "What?"

Again, he gestures to the two of us.

"We should get together?"

He nods.

"Because we're both single?"

He shakes his head.

"No? Not because we're both single?"

Colby looks vaguely frustrated. He motions to me and him again. Then he makes a gesture toward the ceiling like he's spraying a pocketful of stars into the sky. And then he nods and winks.

"So elaborate, Colby Morgan." I chuckle. "You're a performance artist."

He does it all again.

"You're saying we should get together because... what? We're meant to be? We're written in the stars?"

He nods profusely and places my hand over his chest. *Over his heart.*

I retract my hand, suddenly feeling like it's on fire. "Wow, you're a smooth dude," I say, forcing my voice to sound light and bright, despite my racing heart. "Hitting on a woman while intubated? That's some serious swagger, man."

If eyes can smile, then that's what Colby Morgan's blazing blues are doing now.

I clear my throat. "Well, thanks for the flattering offer. And don't get me wrong, this is the best conversation I've had with a man in three years, but I think we should keep things professional between us."

He slides his hand in mine again, his facial expression telling me he disagrees wholeheartedly with my statement. Or, wait, does that expression mean he's in pain again?

"Are you in pain, Colby?"

He nods.

I stand. "You want me to call the nurse?"

He shakes his head, gestures for me to sit again, and then touches his chest, like he's gripping his heart.

I know he's intending to be funny. He's telling me my rejection of him has broken his heart. But a joke like that isn't funny in a hospital. So that's what I tell him.

Immediately, the humor on Colby's face vanishes. His hand on his heart sags. And I know in my heart of hearts, he just realized he wasn't actually joking: he's genuinely in the depths of the worst emotional pain of his young life.

My heart aching along with his, I grab Colby's hand and squeeze, suddenly feeling called to fix this brave and beautiful man. "Colby," I whisper softly, my eyes trained on his. "I don't know exactly what you're going through, but I do know what it feels like to have your life unexpectedly turned upside down on a dime. I want you to know I'm going to do everything in my power to get you back to being *you* as quickly as possible. I'm going to fix you, Colby. *Heal* you. You can lean on me—literally and figuratively."

Colby scrutinizes my face for a long moment. His eyes trained on mine, he makes a groggy writing gesture in the air.

"Sure thing," I say. "I'll be right back. Don't run off on me, okay?" I head to the nurse's station and grab a small white board and erasable marker and quickly return to my helpless hero. "Here you go."

As I hold up the whiteboard for him, Colby writes something on it with great care, his eyelids fluttering with his acute need for sleep the whole time. When he's done writing, I tilt the board to peek at his message... and my heart stops at the sight of it.

Chapter 14
Lydia

Beautiful.

That's the word Colby just wrote on the white board.

And it rendered me speechless.

Yes, Colby flirted shamelessly with me a few minutes ago—as much as a guy on a ventilator can flirt, I suppose. But everything he did before this moment seemed like nothing but painkiller-induced bravado. Loopy fun. But this word he's written... and the way he's looking at me right now... This moment feels real. Completely stripped down and raw. Like we're staring into each other's souls and connecting in a way I've only felt once before in my life.

"Thank you," I manage to say, my heart whacking against my sternum. "You're beautiful, too, Colby. Stunningly beautiful. What you did in that fire..." I swallow hard. I can't say more. I'm too overwhelmed by this unexpected flood of emotion I'm feeling.

Colby motions for the white board again and I move it into place for him.

Soul, he writes. And then he points at the word *Beautiful*. And then at me.

Warmth floods my core. "Thank you," I say, clutching my chest. "You have a beautiful soul, too. You're a man who's willing to risk your own life to help a stranger in need. That makes your soul more than beautiful. You've got a *heroic* soul."

Colby waves away my comment and motions for the board again.

Is baby OK?

Oh, for the love of... Colby doesn't know the baby died two days ago? How is that possible? Has his family actively withheld the tragic news from him to keep him calm while his condition remains precarious? Or was he simply not conscious enough before now to ask the question?

Colby taps the pen against the white board, asking his question again.

Crap. Shouldn't someone in his family be the one to tell him this awful news? How the hell is this up to me?

Again, Colby taps on the board. His eyes are practically rolling back into his head at this point, but he's apparently not going to allow himself to slip into unconsciousness until he gets his damned answer.

Sighing, I cradle Colby's hand in both of mine and say softly, "The baby died on Saturday evening in her parents' arms."

Colby closes his eyes.

"It's my understanding the baby's parents came to your room on Saturday to thank you for giving them the opportunity to hold their baby one last time. I heard Kat say that you were unconscious when her parents came, so they spoke to your parents and expressed their gratitude."

Colby opens his beautiful blue eyes. They're glistening.

I take a deep breath. "I know this is sad news. But take comfort in knowing you gave those parents an amazing gift. Getting to say goodbye to a loved one before..." Without warning, emotion surges inside me and I choke up. I pause for a long moment, swallowing hard, and finally say, "Getting to physically touch someone you love one last time before they're torn away from you forever and ever..." I stop again. Clamp my lips together and swallow hard again until I'm finally able to continue. "Colby, you gave that baby's parents a precious gift. Even if she didn't survive, what you did wasn't in vain."

A lone tear falls out the corner of Colby's eye and trickles toward his temple.

I squeeze his hand. "I don't presume to know what you're feeling," I whisper. "But whatever it is, however hopeless you might feel, or heartbroken, please know you're not going through this alone. I'm going to heal you, Colby. Not just because I'm your physical therapist, but also because..." I swallow hard again. "Because I feel *called* to help you." I clutch his hand in both of mine fiercely. "I'm going to fix you, Colby. I'm going to heal you and make you as good as new."

We sit quietly together for a long moment, our hands clasped. Finally, when it seems the poor man's eyelids can't stay open a moment longer, he motions to the white board again and scrawls a sloppy, illegible message.

"I can't read that," I say, tilting my head to the side. "*Apple*? You're saying you want an apple? Because that's a firm no."

With a roll of his eyes, Colby rewrites the word, this time with great care and attention.

ANGEL.

"*Oh*. Yes, the baby's an angel in heaven now," I say. "I believe that, too."

Colby shakes his head. He points at the word on the white board and then at me. But before I can reply, Colby's eyes flutter and close.

I wait to see if this is it, but, nope. He claws his way back to consciousness and motions for me to tilt the white board toward him again.

"This is the last time," I say. "You need your rest, Colby."

Colby writes with great care again. But when I turn the board to take a peek, his drug-induced handwriting is so jumbled, I can't make it out.

"Hmm. You lost your first kite?"

He points at his latest scribble, clearly exasperated.

"I'm sorry," I say. "I just can't..." I squint at his sloppy writing for a moment. "You lick your friends at night?"

Colby's glazed eyes are practically rolling back into his head. He writes on the board again. *Slowly*. Like a drunkard taking a written field sobriety test. When he's done scribbling, his arm thuds to the mattress, pen still in hand. His eyes close and remain that way. He's out like a light.

I tilt the board around to read his message... and feel my heart lurch and bound and leap out of my chest... and finally explode through my sternum and splatter against a far wall.

Chapter 15
Colby

I wake up to find my six family members camped around my room. Dax is softly strumming his acoustic guitar in the corner while Kat gazes out the window. Keane and Ryan are huddled together, looking at something on Ryan's phone. Mom and Dad are chatting quietly.

And the angel in the blue scrubs is nowhere to be found.

I pat the mattress and quickly locate the white board she brought me. Did she write me a goodbye message after I drifted off? The last thing I remember writing on the board was a question about the baby. Is it still there, or has it been replaced by something she wrote to me?

But, no, the only thing scrawled on the board is a rather detailed cartoon of a hard dick and balls. I roll my eyes. It's Keane's signature doodle. His graffiti tag, so to speak. A nod to his penile nickname since middle school.

Believe it or not, as immature as Keane can be at times, he's not quite as sophomoric as that dick-and-balls doodle would suggest. Keane leaving that little gem in covert places for my mother to discover is a long-running family gag. It started when Keane drew the stupid thing on a school notebook at age thirteen. Mom saw it and read him the riot act for drawing it on something he'd brought to school. But instead of owning up to his stupidity, Keane instead went with the well-worn strategy of *deny, deny, deny* and swore up and down the cartoon was nothing but the innocent depiction of a rocket at lift-off. And what did Mom do in the face of such foolish audacity? True to form, she broke down and laughed. And, thus, a longstanding family joke was born. Call our family's sense of humor immature, but, to this day, we all think it's hilarious when our dick-and-balls

56

Banksy leaves his mark in yet another unexpected place for us to stumble upon. Really, at the end of the day, he's making fun of himself—chiding the thirteen-year-old version of himself who actually believed our mother was idiotic enough to think her naughty son was nothing but a sweet little boy dreaming of outer space.

"He's awake," Kat says softly, drawing my attention away from the white board. She lopes to the edge of my bed and lovingly takes my hand in hers. "Hi, Cheese and Macaroni," she whispers, smiling down at me sweetly. "Did you sleep well?"

I nod.

"Are you in pain, honey?"

Yes, I'm in pain, but not physically. But since there's no way, or reason, to tell her that, I simply shake my head.

Did I imagine that beautiful angel in blue scrubs telling me the baby died? It's possible. I mean, no mortal woman, other than maybe Beyoncé, could possibly be that beautiful without Photoshop. I don't think I imagined those beautiful hazel eyes staring into my soul, but just to be sure, I grab the marker next to the white board and write, *Is baby OK?*

Kat reads my words and, instantly, by the look on her face, I know I didn't imagine the beautiful angel in the blue scrubs.

"Mom? Dad?" Kat says, tilting the board for them to see.

My parents come over and gently tell me the horrible news. As they speak, I close my eyes. But I don't cry this time. I've already heard this news, after all. Besides, I never cry with my family. I'm everyone's shoulder to cry on. It doesn't work the other way around.

"Dax, play him a song," Kat says. "He looks sad."

My entire family gathers around my bed and Dax begins playing "Lean on Me" by Bill Withers... and the minute I hear Dax's soulful voice calling me "brother" and telling me to lean on him, emotion rises and bucks inside me, straining to get out.

I can't believe I'm lying here, broken and breathing on a fucking machine. I can't believe I went through hell for nothing. That I failed that poor mother after promising her I wouldn't. I can't stop thinking about the excruciating pain that little baby must have felt in the fire while I remained safe and protected in my turn-out gear. I can't stop thinking of her face when she raised her arms to me, nonverbally begging me to rescue her.

I close my eyes again, willing the torturous thoughts and images to stop. I pray for serenity to overtake me, but it's no use. I can't escape the visions. Over and over again, all I can see is the look of relief on that little baby's face when I showed up to save the day, immediately followed by her charred, unconscious face when someone ripped her from my grasp.

Visualize something happy, Colby, I tell myself. *Something that makes you feel calm.*

Ralph.

I force myself to think about my sweet dog's face... but, immediately, that image gives way to...

The angel.

Hazel eyes.

Mocha skin.

A smile that touched my soul.

I feel calm again.

At least for now.

I gently grab that woman's beautiful face with my palms and pull her toward me and lay a soft kiss on her full, luscious lips... And then I kiss and kiss and kiss her, fusing my tortured spirit with her healing one, until, finally, blessedly, whatever is dripping into my IV bag does its job and everything fades to black.

Chapter 16
Colby

It's a Thursday morning, five days since the fire. A couple hours ago, I was finally taken off the breathing machine for good following a couple-day weaning process, and now I'm in my new room in a step-down unit.

To celebrate my progress, my entire family is here plus four guys from the fire department, including my battalion chief. They're passing around the blackened, melted helmet I wore during the fire while my chief tells everyone some stats about the fire and the turnout gear that saved my life.

And I'm silently losing my shit.

I know it's a huge honor that my chief came here today. He's a bigwig and he's got shit to do. And I also know he brought that melted hat as a sign of deep respect for me and what I went through. In the world of firefighting, nobody wants to wear a fresh-looking hat. We all want to wear a hat that bears the marks of battle in one form or another. But nobody in their right mind would want a hat that looks like mine. It's horrifying to think that thing was on my head.

"His jacket was exposed to temperatures of close to a thousand degrees," my chief says. "The stitching actually melted, which means..."

I tune out so my heart rate won't spike and send a nurse rushing in.

Jesus Christ. I don't want to hear about the fire. Why would I want to do that when the fire is all I keep thinking about, night and day? When I'm plagued by horrific nightmares? Good lord, every time I close my eyes, I see that poor baby's charred face. Or the way she looked at me when I first showed up to save the day. Or I'm in the house, surrounded by raging flames and unable to breathe. I swing at the window with my axe, but it doesn't break because my axe is made of rubber. Or it's a chicken. And then the baby's flopping in my arms and I'm screaming and crying and gasping for air... and I suddenly realize the axe in my hand is wilted over like a drooping flower. And that's when I know for a fact I'm going to die...

The beeping of my heart monitor speeds up, so I breathe deeply and force myself to think about Ralph. But flames begin lapping at my brain again, so I quickly ditch Ralph and imagine myself kissing the angel in the blue scrubs again.

And that does the trick.

Man, she's better than painkillers.

My rendezvous with the beautiful angel with the light mocha skin and full lips and hazel eyes is interrupted by a female voice at the door. I shift toward the interruption and my heart rate spikes. *It's her.* The angel in the blue scrubs! Although this time, she's the angel in the *aquamarine* scrubs. But, whatever. She's back and she's way, *way* more gorgeous than I remembered her from the other day.

"Lydia!" my mother says brightly, surprising me. I hadn't realized my entire family had met this woman. When did that happen? Mom continues, "Come in, honey. These are Colby's friends from the fire department."

Lydia says hello to everyone and crosses the room to me, a warm smile on her gorgeous face. "Hi, Colby," Lydia says. "I don't know if you remember me coming into your room the other day. You were pretty doped up." She holds out her hand. "I'm your physical therapist, Lydia Decker."

"Of course, I remember you, Lydia," I say softly, taking her hand. "Although I must admit, I had no idea you were my physical therapist."

She chuckles.

"Honestly," I say, "I don't remember more than bits and pieces of our conversation. But I certainly remember *you.* You're unforgettable, Lydia."

Lydia bites her lower lip and says, "I'd be interested to know which 'bits and pieces' of our conversation you remember. You were flying pretty high on pain meds when we first met."

"Oh, God, I hope I didn't embarrass myself."

She smiles. "To the contrary, you were quite the charmer, especially right before you passed out cold. The very last bit of our conversation was particularly entertaining. Do you remember it?"

Fuck. I don't know what she's talking about. Is she referring to when I asked her about the baby? No, the smile on her face tells me she's not talking about that. But that's the last thing I remember. Did I write something inappropriate to her on the white board? Oh, shit. Was it me who drew that dick-and-balls doodle on the white board?

"I'm thrilled to see you off the ventilator," Lydia says.

"I'm thrilled to be off it," I say.

"Does your throat hurt?"

"A lot."

"Yeah. That's from the intubation. It won't last too long."

"Good to know."

"You look like you're feeling a whole lot better than the last time I saw you," she says.

"Yeah, I am. You're looking even more beautiful than the last time I saw you, if that's possible."

Keane mutters, "Go get her, Tiger." And everyone chuckles.

Let 'em laugh. I realize I'm never forward like this—it's just not my style. But now that I've been to hell and back, I'm feeling like my normal shyness is a colossal waste of time. In fact, I'm probably being *too* reserved with Lydia right now. I should just tell her how I'm feeling—that I've never been so attracted to a woman in all my life.

I open my mouth to say something incredibly charming to Lydia, I'm sure, but my plan is thwarted by a nurse coming into the room and checking my vital signs.

"Is he on a healthy dose of pain meds right now?" Lydia asks.

"Yup," the nurse replies, and they both giggle.

"I can tell," Lydia says. "He's got that same look in his eye he had the other day. Like he's sliding down a rainbow on a purple unicorn." Lydia looks at me. "Can't wait to find out what you're like when you're not high on drugs, Colby. If you're half as entertaining as you are *on* drugs, you're going to be a lot of fun."

"He's normally much more subtle than this with women," Ryan says.

Okay, that comment kind of pisses me off. Is he apologizing for

61

me? Well, fuck him. And fuck subtlety. Subtle Colby is the old me, son. The new me has been to fucking hell and back and lived to tell the tale. The new me knows in a whole new, concrete way tomorrow isn't guaranteed. As a paramedic-firefighter, I've seen a whole lot of death from responding to car accidents, fires, overdoses, and various other medical crises. That's why I got my chest tattoo a couple years ago. *Here Today, Gone Tomorrow.* But seeing other people die is something quite a bit different than coming face to face with my own mortality. Now that I've experienced the precarious thread between life and death for myself, I feel even more urgency to live my life to the fullest. Hell yeah. The new me is going to go after whatever and whoever he wants, no holding back... starting with this profoundly beautiful woman with the mocha skin, large breasts, and kind, hazel eyes.

Out of the corner of my eye, I can plainly see that my siblings and firefighter buddies are exchanging loaded smiles and looks, presumably amused at the intense way I'm looking at Lydia and plotting to make her mine the minute my body is able to do my bidding. Well, fuck 'em all. Let them snicker and chuckle like school kids on a playground. I don't care if they all see how badly I want her. I don't care if they all think I'm loopy because of the meds. It's not the meds making me want her, motherfuckers. All you have to do is look at her to know that. She's objectively perfect and sexy as fuck, even in scrubs. And not only that, she's as sweet as can be. The woman is Mother Earth incarnate. Everything about her makes me want to ring her bell the minute my body is capable of doing it.

Oh.

Apparently, while I've been having a lengthy conversation with myself about Lydia inside my drugged-up head, the chief has been telling the object of my desire loads of details about the fire. Just as I've tuned back in to the conversation in the room, he pulls out my melted helmet again, and, predictably, Lydia gasps at the sight of it.

"Oh my God, *Colby*," she breathes. She looks at me, poised to say more—perhaps to ask me a question? But when she sees my face, she stops herself. Without missing a beat, Lydia peels her eyes off mine and says, "Okay, everyone. I'm sorry to shut this party down, but it's closing time at the bar. Colby and I have some physical therapy to do."

Relief floods me. That's exactly what I was wishing she'd do—clear them all out so we can be alone.

Goodbyes are said. Hugs are administered. And, finally, blessedly, it's just Lydia and me.

"Alone at last, Mr. Morgan," she says, taking the seat next to my bed.

I slide my hand in hers. "Alone at last, Miss Decker. There is a God."

She smiles. "You might not say that after I get through with you. Some of what we're going to do together is going to be extremely frustrating for you, I'm sure."

"Bring it, beautiful lady. As long as you're the one administering the torture, I'll enjoy every second of it."

She rolls her eyes. "Okay, Mr. Flirty Pants. Enough with that. Let's get serious for a second. Okay?"

I smile broadly. "What? I can't say you're beautiful? Because you are. You're drop dead gorgeous, actually. I've never seen a more spectacularly gorgeous woman in my life."

She's fighting not to smile too big and it's adorable. "Thank you. Sweet of you to say. Incredibly ridiculous, but sweet. Unfortunately, though, we don't have time to sit here and talk about my earth-shattering beauty all day. You're not my only patient."

"I wish I were."

"So do I."

My heart lurches.

She clears her throat. "I shouldn't have said that. Forget I said that." She blushes. "Momentary insanity brought on by your outrageous charm." She takes a deep breath like she's pressing some internal restart button. "Okay. In all seriousness. This is going to be a long, hard road for you, Colby. But I want you to know you're not walking it alone. Inch by inch, step by step, I'll be right here with you, okay? My job is helping you get back to being *you* as quickly as possible."

Electricity surges through my veins, and not because of her words. Because of the zap I feel through the touch of our palms. Her incredible energy is physically palpable. "Thank you," I whisper, my eyes locked with hers, my fingers zipping and zapping with the influx of her energy into my body. "I wouldn't want to be on this journey with anyone but you, Lydia. I don't want anyone else."

63

"Thank you," she says. She leans forward like she's going to kiss me, like I'm the great love of her life, and whispers, "I'm going to bring you back to life, Colby Morgan."

I'm too overwhelmed with the energy I feel coursing between us to speak, so I simply nod.

"It's my job, of course," she says. "But I must admit, with you, it feels more like my calling."

Again, I nod. But this time, it's because I feel like I'm about to cry. *Again.* And God help me, I don't want to do that. What is it about this woman that makes me feel like she's cracked me wide open and she's peeking at my very soul? I swallow hard and then whisper, "Thank you."

She gives me an overview of my physical therapy regimen, and I must admit, the process sounds overwhelming and fills me with dread. If it weren't for the deep compassion I'm seeing in her eyes right now, I'm sure I'd feel downright hopeless about everything she just told me.

"Do you have any questions for me?" she asks tenderly. "Any concerns about your physical therapy?"

She's hope for the hopeless.

A blazing tiki torch in a dark cave.

I shake my head. "I'm in your capable hands and that's all I need to know."

"Alright," she says. She squeezes my hand, sending electricity coursing through my body again. "Then let's get started, shall we?"

"I'm all yours."

Chapter 17
Lydia

It's Tuesday afternoon and I'm sitting in the break room at work after having just come from Colby Morgan's room... *again*. Since Colby got off the ventilator and out of the ICU five days ago, other than my day off on Sunday, I've been to Colby's room an embarrassing amount of times. Four times a day. It's utterly ridiculous, I know. Indefensible. But I simply can't help myself.

More often than not, I go to Colby's room to work with him in my official capacity, and during our time together, I help him with all the usual stuff for this stage of the game. I've taught him how to sit up in bed. Not an easy thing for someone with Colby's injuries to do. I've shown him how to slowly swing his legs over the side of his bed. To safely transfer into and out of his wheelchair, on and off the toilet, and into and out of his bed.

But, of course, the bulk of my time with Colby has been spent touching his broken body as he's lain in bed like a beautiful racehorse felled on the track. I've massaged his sore muscles and manipulated his stiff and aching joints and done my best to infuse him with every drop of healing energy I can possibly muster. And, through almost all of it, we've talked and talked.

But all that accounts for about half the time I've spent with Colby in his room. Admittedly, the other half of the time, I've been a very bad girl, dropping by Colby's room to say hello to him and whatever family members happen to be there, just because I love spending time in his room. And on those occasions, despite my best intentions, I always wind up staying much, much longer than intended.

Okay, fine. I admit it. I can't stay away from Colby Morgan. I crave the touch of his skin under my fingertips. The sound of his masculine voice. Not to mention the sight of his perfect face. Even broken, Colby Morgan is a breathtakingly beautiful man. His blue eyes are mesmerizing. That little cleft in his chin is to die for. Oh, and his lips! The man is a superhero, even when lying in a bed. I swear to God, every time I look at that bruised and battered man, I think: "If Superman had a blonde brother who'd maybe been in a horrible car accident, he'd be Colby Morgan."

But even better than Colby's stunning eyes and smooth voice and steel jaw and that swoony little cleft in his superhero chin, it's Colby's personality that makes him so damned alluring to me. Talking to him feels like the most natural thing in the world. Now that he's on a much lower dosage of pain meds, his cockiness has measured off into a kind of humble confidence I find utterly irresistible.

"Well, look at you."

I look up from the patient file I've been pretending to read to find my co-worker, Ramona, another physical therapist, standing next to my table in the break room. *Ramona.* She's not my favorite person, to say the least. Indeed, she's a bitch and a half. She sits her hot little body down next to me and places a coffee mug on the table that reads, *I'm not bossy, I'm right!*

Ramona smiles thinly and says, "Someone looks like she's thinking highly pleasant thoughts."

I straighten up in my chair and clear my throat. "Hi, Ramona. How's the personal training going?" Of course, Miss Perfect Body moonlights on evenings and weekends as a personal trainer—and, man, does she make sure everyone knows it.

"Great." She leans back in her chair. "I assume that dreamy smile you had on your face two seconds ago has something to do with the hunky firefighter you've been lucky enough to get to work with?"

I sip my coffee rather than reply.

Ramona continues, "I've noticed you've been visiting the firefighter's room twice as much as necessary the past few days. Two-a-days, Lydia? *Oh my.*"

My cheeks flood with color. Good thing she hasn't noticed I've actually been going to Colby's room *four* times a day.

Ramona smirks. "Hey, no judgment, girl. If I'd been assigned to the firefighter, I'd find any reason I could think of to sneak into his room, too. And I'd no doubt have a swoony smile on my face and drool running down my chin all day long, the same as you."

I fight the urge to wipe my chin.

Ramona takes a long sip of her coffee. "Or maybe you've been visiting the firefighter's room so much as an excuse to see his brothers? Holy hot damn. Those Morgan men are smoking hot. Every last one of them."

"Yeah, they're a ridiculously gorgeous family, all around," I say. "His parents and sister are stunning, too. Have you seen them? His sister could literally be a supermodel and his parents could be one of those elegant older couples they always put on Viagra commercials."

Ramona chuckles.

I continue, "But, trust me, Ramona, no matter how physically gorgeous the Morgans are, it's nothing compared to how beautiful they are as people. They're the most loving, funny, devoted..." I trail off. Why the heck am I doing this? Did I just fall off the turnip truck? Ramona doesn't give a shit about this. Clearly, she sat down here for a reason, and it wasn't to hear about the good-heartedness of the Morgan clan or to foster a genuine friendship with me.

The first day I started working here a year ago, my boss, Janice, a friend of mine from my old job before Darren died, warned me, "Watch yourself with Ramona, hon. She'll pretend to be your best friend, but it's bullshit. She applied for my position at this hospital and was passed over for it, and now she's a bitter little barracuda about it. She's gunning for me and anyone she sees as my friend. So just keep your friends close and Ramona even closer."

Ramona coils a lock of her auburn hair around her finger and flashes a smile that doesn't reach her eyes. "Did you know I asked Janice to assign *me* to the firefighter when he first got here? But she said nope, it had to be you. I reminded her I've got seniority by almost three years over you, not to mention everyone knows I always call dibs on any hunky first responders. But Janice said, 'I think Lydia would be a better fit for this one, Ramona.' She assured me she'd assign me to the next single, hunky first responder, but something tells me no one will ever compare to Colby Morgan. He's the holy grail of hunky first responders, don't you think?" Ramona pauses, apparently waiting for me to agree with her. When I say nothing, she adds, "Any idea why Janice would think you're a 'better fit' to work with the firefighter over me? I've racked my brain about it, especially given my seniority, and just can't seem to come up with a plausible answer." She shoots me another fake smile.

I return Ramona's plastic smile and say, "I have no idea why Janice assigned me to the firefighter. If you're curious about it, ask her." *Screw Ramona.* I have zero desire to tell her about Darren. My life's biggest tragedy is none of her fucking business.

Ramona narrows her eyes and drops a booklet onto the table in front of me. "On a totally unrelated topic... ever seen this before, Lydia?"

I look down and see a booklet I've never seen in my life.

"It's the hospital's employee handbook," Ramona explains, her tone frosty.

My stomach clenches. I say nothing.

"I'm just wondering if you're aware of Section Three, Point Two-A? That's the policy prohibiting all caregivers, *including physical therapists*, from engaging in 'romantic relations' with any patient they're currently treating."

My stomach flips over. My chest feels tight. *Shit.*

With a devilish smirk on her face, Ramona opens the handbook to a specific page and points. I glance down briefly, just to confirm she's not completely full of shit and, yep, it appears to state I'd lose my job and possibly my state licensing, too, if I were to engage in any sort of "romantic relations" with a current patient.

Crap. How have I never heard of this policy before? I guess somewhere in my brain I've always known sexual contact with a patient wasn't allowed. *Of course.* But since I've always been married and never in any kind of situation that would even remotely have led to me having sex with a patient, I've never given the rule much thought. Suddenly, my mind is teeming with a thousand thoughts. What constitutes "engaging in romantic relations"? That sure sounds broader than having sex itself. Oh, crap. Have I violated this policy by brazenly flirting with Colby? Could someone claim I've acted inappropriately toward him?

Ramona closes the handbook with relish. "I hope you know I'm only looking out for you. I'd hate for you to do something stupid, just because he's so gorgeous, and lose your job."

Holy shit. Colby's made it abundantly clear he's attracted to me. Indeed, the other day, he said something brazen about his plan to seduce me the minute he's physically able. He was joking around, sort of, but his message was clear: he's gunning for me. *And I didn't dissuade him.* On the contrary, I encouraged him. Subtly, of course. But it was there. Have I unwittingly made myself a target for Ramona's vindictiveness, just because I've been so sloppy about my attraction to Colby?

Obviously, I'd never engage in any inappropriate touching or sexual contact with Colby while he's still so broken, both emotionally and physically. But, yeah, if I'm being perfectly honest, maybe I was kind of imagining myself jumping his bones one day down the line, when he's healed and strong again. When he's stopped having those horrible nightmares and flashbacks he's been telling me about.

Of course, I'd never engage in romantic relations with Colby or any other man before first telling him about the existence of my three kids. Unless, I suppose, if I was just looking for some meaningless sex... not that I can imagine sex with Colby being anything other than deeply meaningful to me. But, yeah, back to the point: I wouldn't engage in "romantic relations" with Colby unless I'd told him about the existence of my kids—which is something I haven't yet done because it just hasn't seemed like the right timing. Mentioning my three kids to Colby will undoubtedly prompt him to ask me about the status of my relationship with their father. And I have no desire to talk about Darren with Colby. The man has been going through enough emotional trauma of his own without me dumping my baggage on him, too.

". . . and so that's the only reason I said anything," Ramona is saying, drawing me out of my rambling thoughts. She's got the employment handbook open again and she's pointing at something specific in it.

"Ah, yes, I see," I say, pretending to look at whatever she's pointing out. "You're so sweet for looking out for me, Ramona. Thanks." I push the employment handbook back toward her across the table. "But I assure you, there's no need to be concerned. I'm well aware of my ethical and professional obligations and the rationale for the rules. Colby Morgan is my patient and nothing more and he'll stay that way throughout the entire course of his physical therapy with me."

Ramona shoots me a fake smile. "Great, but if you find yourself having a hard time maintaining professionalism with the firefighter, I'd be happy to step in for you."

"No, thanks," I say. "I think I'll keep him."

Oh, those were fighting words, apparently. Ramona leans forward, her eyes blazing. "Watch yourself, Lydia," she spits out, her smiling morphing into a sneer. "Temptation can get the best of anyone. I'd hate to see you lose your license because you couldn't control your hormones."

I lean forward and mimic her exact facial expression—which ain't pretty. "Colby and I are just friends, Ramona, and we're going to stay that way until he's cleared for work again. When he's no longer my patient, will I 'engage in romantic relations' with him? Quite possibly. But until then, I suggest you stay the hell out of my business."

Chapter 18
Colby

It's Wednesday morning in the hospital room that's come to feel like my iron cage, other than when my beautiful Lydia is here with me and I'm able to forget how miserable I am. Thank the lord, though, my doctor has finally cleared me to get the hell out of Dodge later today. In a couple hours, Kat and Ryan will come to whisk me away to my parents' house where I'll recuperate for the next six to eight weeks, for however long I'm stuck in a wheelchair. But before I head out, my gorgeous and sexy and funny and sweet physical therapist, the only good thing about being trapped in this broken and aching body, is here to work her magic on me, yet again.

Today, as usual, as Lydia has been manipulating my muscles and joints, we've been chatting nonstop. And by that I mean *I've* been talking just as much as Lydia, if not more. It's crazy, I know. Anyone who knows me is well aware I talk infrequently in most social situations. Yeah, I mean, I *talk*. Especially with Ryan and my family. But even then, I don't contribute nearly as much to conversations as everyone else. In my family, if you want someone to tell you a rip-roaring story or bust your gut with a joke, then you want Keane or Ryan or Kat. They all inherited Mom's sparkling gift of gab. But, on the flipside, if you want a Morgan who tends to sit back and listen and observe much more than speak, and then pipe in with a zinger only when he thinks he's got something worthwhile to say, then you want Dad, Dax, or me.

And yet, whenever I'm with Lydia, my normal reserve flies out the window. Honestly, I wouldn't be surprised if Lydia has wished a time or two that the doctor would shove that ventilator back down my throat.

Over the past week together, Lydia and I have covered endless

71

topics in our conversations. The usual stuff, of course, like where we went to school, our favorite music, movies, and TV shows. She told me about her schooling to become a physical therapist. I told her about mine to become a paramedic-firefighter. The other day, I babbled to Lydia about Ralph, and that prompted her to tell me about the Australian shepherd mix she grew up with—Ginger. And, man, the way she described that poor, bedraggled, fucked-up puppy she rescued from a dumpster as a kid... That's when I thought to myself, "This woman is going to make a fantastic mother one day."

And now, here we are again, just the two of us, chatting enthusiastically again.

When Lydia got here a half hour ago, I asked her to tell me about her childhood in Kentucky, and that's what she's done. She's told me story after story. Some of them funny. Some poignant. She's touched on what it was like to have a white mother and black father and how she often felt like she didn't fully belong in either racial group. And I've loved every minute of listening to her. Man, just the sound of her voice is a salve for my splintered and broken soul.

"But enough about me," Lydia says as she moves to gently manipulate the muscles of my left arm. "Tell me a story from your childhood. How about a funny story this time."

I purse my lips, considering, and finally say, "'Ryan and the Shitty Towel.'"

She giggles. "Oh boy."

I tell Lydia the whole tale—the story of seven-year-old Colby, five-year-old Ryan, and the shit-streaked towel Ryan re-hung on a towel rack. "It was that very day The Morgan Mafia was born," I say, and Lydia throws her head back and whoops with sexy, throaty laughter, instantly making every cell in my body vibrate with longing to muffle that laugh of hers with a deep kiss.

"Tell me another one," she says. "I'm a kid in a candy shop with these stories."

I tell Lydia a couple more stories, ultimately telling her about the time I helped Dax Superglue our mother's prized crystal vase back together and she didn't discover our crime for five full years.

"Was Momma Morgan pissed when she found out?" Lydia asks.

"As *hell*," I reply. "But Dax was like, 'Look, Mom. If you haven't noticed our shitty-ass Superglue job in five full years, you obviously don't care about that dang vase as much as you say you do.' And she had to begrudgingly concede he was right."

Lydia giggles. "You and Dax seem like you're cut from the same cloth."

"We are. Exactly."

She asks some questions about Dax and I tell her about his indie rock band, 22 Goats, and how he's working his ass off to make his musical dreams a reality.

"Did you ever dream of being a rock star?" Lydia asks.

"Oh, God, no. Just getting up in front of a class in high school to give a speech about alternative power sources practically killed me. I play piano, but only because my mom made me take lessons for years. I don't have actual talent like Dax. My brother is a true artist. I'm more like a highly competent factory worker."

"I noticed the piano keys on your arm." She motions to a tattoo I've got on my right forearm. "I highly doubt factory workers get tattoos of the factory equipment they operate."

"Yeah, okay, I admit it: I love playing piano," I say. "But, honestly, not because I'm any good at it. Just because it gives me time to think and decompress. As far as the tattoo goes, I have Ryan to thank for that. His favorite thing in the world is getting me drunk on tequila and taking me to a tattoo parlor to get another round of fresh ink."

"Did Ryan get a tattoo with you when you got the piano keys?"

"Of course. That dude can't walk into a tattoo parlor without getting something. That particular day, he got a sword in the exact same spot on his forearm as my piano. Yet another entry in Ryan's collection of pirate-themed tattoos."

"I've noticed. Why does Ryan like pirates so much?"

"'Yo ho ho and a bottle of rum,'" I say. "Ryan's initials are R-U-M, so everyone calls him Captain Morgan."

"Ah."

"Not to mention Rum Cake, Bacardi, and Rummy-o. Anything rum-related. Ryan's a commercial real estate broker, but his dream is to open a bar called Captain's one day."

"Oh, that's cool." She begins rotating my right elbow. "So what's your dream? You've told me about Dax's and Ryan's. What's yours?"

"I've already made my dream come true: I'm a paramedic-firefighter in my favorite city in the world. Doesn't get any better than that."

"Wow. Not too many people can say they're living their dream."

"Pretty cool, huh? I used to dress up like a firefighter for Halloween every year growing up. It's all I've ever wanted to be."

"What about goals? Got any of those?"

"Of course. I'd like to do another triathlon with Ryan someday. Beat my last time. We love doing races and fitness challenges together." My stomach flips over as I suddenly remember the body I'm currently trapped in. "I guess I'd better adjust my goals, huh? At this point, I should probably aim for being able to go for a light jog again one day."

Lydia stops what she's doing and levels me with an intense hazel gaze. "You'll get there, Colby. Don't despair. It's going to be slow-go, yes, but you *will* get there."

I nod but don't reply. My brain believes her, but my heart and body aren't so sure.

We're silent for a long beat, both of us lost in our thoughts, apparently. Finally, Lydia says, "So what about Keane? Is he a dreamer like the rest of his brothers?"

"Oh, Keane's a *huge* dreamer. That's all that guy does is dream. Unfortunately, he recently hit a dead-end on his dream, though." I tell her about how Keane has always aspired to become a major-league pitcher, ever since he could throw a baseball. "I know he presents himself like a goofball-slacker, but trust me, Keane Morgan worked his ass off playing baseball his whole life. He was a star in both high school and college, and then he got drafted and tore it up in the Cubs' minor league system."

"Wow."

"And he was absolutely slaying it in the minor leagues. *Slaying it.* He got all the way up to triple A in record time, which is really, really hard to do. His coach told him he was about to get called up to the bigs any day and that's when Keane's elbow crapped out on him and he needed surgery."

Lydia looks stricken. "Oh no."

"Unfortunately, surgery and rehab didn't go as planned. It was one letdown after another for the poor guy. We just found out last night he officially got cut from the team's roster a few weeks ago. He told my entire family about it right here in my hospital room after you left to go home. It was heart wrenching. Keane started crying while telling us about it."

"Poor Keane."

"He's devastated. He doesn't know who he is if he's not a star pitcher. He loves the game and pushing himself to be the best. Not to mention, he liked the adulation and attention that went along with being a star. Honestly, I think Keane's been having somewhat of an identity crisis since baseball ended for him."

"I never would have known he's having a tough time," Lydia says. "Every time I've been around Keane, he's been the one laughing the loudest and telling the funniest jokes."

"Yeah, I know. That's Peenie Weenie for ya. The class clown. I always say he's not our family's *black* sheep—he's our *neon* sheep."

Lydia laughs. "Perfect."

"Trust me, though, Keane's not handling the end of his baseball career well. Underneath those dimples, he's most definitely not smiling."

Lydia looks sympathetic. She puts down my right leg and gently begins working on the other one. "How old is Keane?"

"Twenty-two."

"Still plenty of time for him to chase another dream. Does he have any idea what he'll do next?"

"Funny you should ask that. Right after my parents left the room last night, Keane told my siblings and me about the new 'career' he's started pursuing. We kids already knew he'd been dabbling in it part-time, along with bartending, but now Keane, in his infinite wisdom, has decided to become... a full-time... *male stripper*."

Lydia gasps. And then snickers.

"Honestly, I think he'll be great at it," I say. "It might even wind up being the dude's calling, for all I know. He's an incredible dancer and the biggest flirt you'll ever meet. Oh my God, Lydia, girls have always lost their minds over Keane Morgan. I'm sure he'll clean up on tips."

Lydia levels me with the sexiest look she's ever bestowed upon me and says, "From what I've observed, Colby, I don't think Keane is the only Morgan brother the girls lose their minds over."

Heat spreads throughout my core. Please, God, let that be Lydia's coded way of telling me she's as insanely, intensely, ridiculously attracted to me as I am to her. Please, please, please, don't let that be a generalized observation about all four of us.

There's a rare moment of silent awkwardness between us, simply because I'm too electrified by the possible implications of what she's just said to speak. I *think* she was talking about me, specifically, as opposed to the four of us Morgan boys in general. But if not, if I'm reading too much into Lydia's comment, then I don't know what to say. In truth, yeah, the four of us Morgan boys have always done exceedingly well with the ladies. Some of us in larger volumes than others, simply by choice and personality type, but I can't remember the last time any of us, including myself, didn't get a resounding "yes" from whichever girl we'd decided to pursue.

"So does Keane have a stripper name?" Lydia asks. "Something like Thunder Balls or Jesse Schlong? Or is it just an urban legend that male strippers go by silly names like that?"

I laugh. "I don't know what other guys in the profession do, but my brother is going by *Peen Star*."

Lydia giggles uproariously.

"Believe it or not, it's not just an overt reference to his dick. We've always called Keane 'Peen.' Ever since he was in middle school."

Lydia shakes her head. "The Morgans and their beloved nicknames."

"Oh, you've noticed we like our nicknames, have you?"

"Just a bit."

We both chuckle.

Lydia asks, "So is there a story behind Keane's nickname or did you just like that Peen rhymes with Keane?"

"There's a story. Keane had used some of Kat's expensive makeup for Halloween or something. He was twelve or thirteen. So Kat was furious about it and started chasing him around the house, screaming at the top of her lungs, 'You're such a fucking penis, Keane Morgan!'" I laugh. "So, of course, Ryan and I thought that was beyond hilarious, and for like a week after that, we amused ourselves by constantly screaming at him, 'You're such a fucking penis, Keane Morgan!' We said it on a running loop all the freaking time, more to mock Kat than Keane. So, of course, that catch-phrase quickly led to Keane getting called 'Fucking Penis' by all of us. Which over time got shortened to Fucking Peen. And then Keane's best friend at school, Zander, came over one day and adopted the nickname, so Keane just sort of became 'Peen' in all aspects of his life. And that was that. He's been Peen and Peenie and Peenie Weenie ever since, plus every variation of Peen we can possibly think of. Peen Star. Peeno Noir. Rumpelstilts-Peen. Peen-elope Cruz. Peen-ta-gram. It's never-ending."

Lydia giggles. "God, I love your family. I mean I really, truly love your family."

Goose bumps erupt on my forearms. Hearing Lydia say those words is suddenly making me realize she's the first girl I've been attracted to in a long time, maybe ever, who's met every single member of my family. Granted, I didn't bring Lydia home to Meet the Morgans in the conventional way, but the result is the same: a girl I'm seriously digging has met my entire family and everyone loves her.

Lydia grabs my hand and gently bends my palm back, giving my wrist a much-needed stretch. "Does this feel good?"

"It feels amazing," I say, heat flooding me at her touch. "Thank you. Everything you do always feels amazing, Lydia. When I'm with you, I forget to feel miserable."

"Yeah, well, don't get too used to feeling good around me," Lydia says. "I assure you, when we get started with strength training in six weeks or so, there will be plenty of times when you're cursing my name."

"Lydia, I assure you: your name is and will forever be a sacred prayer to my lips."

She makes an adorable face. "There he goes again. Such a charmer."

I wink.

She gently twists my hand in another direction. "Okay, so tell me the scoop on Kat. Dreams? Nicknames?"

I take a deep breath. Damn, the last thing in the world I want to be doing right now is talking about my sister, no offense to her. I suddenly want nothing more than to strip those scrubs off Lydia's body and kiss every inch of her body. But since that's obviously not going to happen, I nut up and say, "Kat. She works in PR. Dreams of owning her own PR company. She loves to party and have fun. Hence, one of her many nicknames is Party Girl. At the moment, she's been living up to her nickname by dating some über-rich dude from LA who drives a Lamborghini and hangs out with music moguls and rock stars. God help us all, I'm praying he's not a douche because it appears he'll be hanging around for a very long time."

"You haven't met Kat's boyfriend yet?"

I shake my head. "He was supposed to come to my birthday dinner a couple weeks ago, but he had to cancel at the last minute."

"Why do you think he might be a douche? Is Kat attracted to douches?"

"Not any more than the average fun-loving girl. I just figure any guy who drives a Lamborghini, it's fifty-fifty he's a douche."

"I don't think he's a douche. I saw Kat with her boyfriend the day you arrived at the hospital, and he struck me as a real sweetheart. Or at least, if he's a douche, then he's a douche who genuinely cares for your sister. And that's all that matters in the end, right?"

I ask Lydia for details and she tells me about how she watched Josh comfort Kat in the waiting room the night of the fire.

"Why were you in the waiting room watching them?" I ask.

Her cheeks blaze. "I was just taking a little break."

She's lying. I can't fathom why, but she is. But, oh well. It's a question for another day, perhaps. "I'm relieved to hear Josh seems like a good guy," I say, "considering he's going to be part of my family forever, whether we like it or..." I abruptly shut my mouth. *Shit.* What am I doing? I promised Dax I wouldn't say a word to anyone about Kat's bun in the oven. I clear my throat. "I'm not allowed to finish that sentence, actually. It's a secret."

One side of Lydia's mouth curls up. "If you're talking about Kat's secret, I already know. Kat told me herself."

I look at Lydia sideways, not sure if we're talking about the same secret. "You know Kat's secret?"

"Well, I know one of Kat's secrets. The one that would make Josh a part of your family forever, whether you like it or not."

"Holy shit. Kat told you?"

"Correct."

"And told you not to tell anyone?"

"Not in words. But she made this face when I entered your room right after she'd told me." She makes a funny face—exactly duplicating Kat's "shut the fuck up!" look.

"Great impression," I say, chuckling. "So tell me this: Is the secret you know the kind a woman can't keep hidden forever?"

"Yes."

"Holy shit. How did it come about Kat told you? She didn't even tell me. She told Dax and he told me on the sly."

Lydia tells me a story in which Kat told her, a complete stranger at the time, about her pregnancy in a bathroom while the two women happened to be washing their hands side by side at the sink.

"Jesus Christ," I say, blown away. "You want to know the irony of us keeping Kat's secret like this? My sister is the biggest blabbermouth you'll ever meet. In fact, one of my sister's many nicknames is The Blabbermouth."

Lydia laughs and begins massaging my quad muscle. "What are her other nicknames?"

"Oh, God, she's got the most of all of us, even more than Keane. Kat is Kitty, Barf-o-matic, and Kumquat to me. To the rest of my brothers, she's also every slang term for semen you can possibly imagine."

"What? *Why*?"

"Her initials are K-U-M."

Lydia rolls her eyes. "Good lord. Your family is freaking brutal."

"Yes, we are." I laugh. "But, like I said, I don't join in on that one. My *brothers* call Kat all the semen names. Kum Shot and Jizz, mostly. But also Protein Shake, Baby Gravy, Jizzy Pop, Jizz Master Flash, Cream of Sum Young Guy, Baby Batter, Jerk Sauce. It literally never ends. I'm sure Ryan and Keane are cooking up some horrendous new semen-name right now."

Lydia shakes her head.

"Don't worry about Kat. Honestly, I think she'd be bummed if they stopped calling her that stuff."

"So you're telling me Kat has Stockholm syndrome?"

I chuckle. "Yes."

"Why don't you call Kat semen names like your horribly mean brothers do?"

"Because I'm the only one who's old enough to remember the day my parents brought Kitty home from the hospital as a newborn. I looked down at her perfect little angel-face in my arms and felt this overpowering need to protect her. Even at six, I thought to myself, 'I'd do anything for this little person.'" I shrug. "To this day, when I look into Kat's face, I still see that same baby face I fell in love with. And there's no way in hell I'm going to call that face Splooge or Dickspit."

Something unmistakable flashes across Lydia's face. *Desire.* Oh, man, if I had my old body right now, the look on Lydia's face would be my cue to take her into my arms and kiss the hell out of her.

"What are you thinking?" I whisper, my heart thumping.

Lydia shakes her head and whispers back, "I shouldn't answer that question honestly."

"Please do," I whisper.

She looks toward the doorway and then back at me and says softly, "I'm thinking things I shouldn't be thinking. Because you're my patient."

Okay, that's it. I've got to have this woman. The nanosecond my body's capable of doing the deed, whether that's four weeks from now or fourteen, I'm going to make her mine. I look toward the door of my hospital room and whisper, "I assure you, Lydia, whatever inappropriate thing you're thinking, I'm thinking it, too."

She bites her lip and her ample chest heaves underneath her maroon scrubs. And I'll be damned, the dick that's lain dormant between my legs for the past ten days begins to show signs of life underneath my covers.

"So, hey, Lydia," I say, sliding my hand underneath my covers and pushing my dick down. "My family is having dinner at my parents' house to celebrate me coming home and..."

Lydia's phone rings. When she looks at her display screen, she physically jumps. "Excuse me," she says tightly, cutting me off mid-sentence. Without another word, she shoots up from her chair and races toward the hallway with her phone pressed against her ear.

Chapter 19
Colby

Well, that was weird. Lydia hasn't answered a phone call once during the time she's been working on me. I hope there's nothing wrong.

Five minutes pass before Lydia returns from her call, looking frazzled.

"Everything okay?" I ask.

"Everything's fine," she says, forcing a smile. She takes the chair next to my bed. "What were we talking about?"

"You sure you're okay? You look upset."

"I'm fine."

I wait, expecting her to say more, but she doesn't. Shit. What just happened? Her walls are suddenly up. And damn if that's not the paradox of Lydia Decker right there. She's the most open and warm and earthy woman I've ever met... and yet simultaneously the most mysterious and guarded, too. It sounds impossible to mix that set of traits, but Lydia somehow manages to do it. It's sexy as hell, yeah. But perplexing, too.

"Well, if you need anything," I say. "I'm your guy. Unless, of course, what you need would require me to stand, walk, carry anything with both hands, or throw a punch."

Lydia smiles, but she's obviously preoccupied. "I'll keep that in mind."

There's an awkward beat.

"So, Lydia," I say. I take a deep breath. I can't remember the last time I asked a woman out and felt nervous like this. It's awful. I clear my throat and just spit it out. "My family's having dinner tonight to celebrate me getting sprung from this joint. Nothing fancy—just my immediate family, plus Keane's best friend, Zander." Oh, God, I feel like a freshman in high school asking the prom queen on a date. I take another deep breath and force myself to pretend I'm Ryan—the little trick I used to use in high school whenever I felt shy about hitting on a girl. "So, anyway, Lydia, I'm hoping you'll join our dinner party. It wouldn't feel right celebrating without having you there."

Lydia makes a face that tells me she's about to turn me down...

And I panic.

"Before you answer," I blurt awkwardly, no trace of Captain Ryan Ulysses Morgan in my tone whatsoever, "you should know my mother is making her legendary lasagna and it'll change your life." *Jesus Christ, Colby.*

Lydia smiles. "Wow. I *love* lasagna. And I love your family. But, unfortunately, I've got plans tonight—plans I can't change."

My spirit thuds into my toes. "Oh, no worries," I say. "I knew it was a long shot with such short notice. Maybe another time."

"*Oh, absolutely,*" she says brightly...

And my spirit rockets back up into my chest. "Awesome," I say. "It's a rain check, then. But, hey, if we're going to do dinner another time, then why don't we make it a real date and make it just the two of us?"

There. I said it.

Lydia opens and closes her mouth, suddenly looking flustered.

Fuck. I said it.

Thanks for nothing, Ryan.

Lydia lets out a long exhale. She looks stressed. "Actually, Colby, now that you've explicitly asked me out on a date, I think I'd better say something to you. Maybe I should have brought it up sooner, but I didn't want to say anything unless I was sure you were interested in me romantically." She looks at me sideways. "Wait. You're interested in me romantically, right? You just asked me out on a date because you're interested in me as more than a friend?"

I grin. "Yes, I'm interested in you romantically. And, yes, I want to be much more than friends."

Lydia bites back a huge smile. "Okay. That's what I thought. So, in that case, I think I should mention there's this policy against physical therapists engaging in 'romantic relations' with their current patients. It's against the rules for my employment and the licensing standards with the state of Washington."

I feel like laughing with relief. Is that what's been bothering her this whole time—the reason I sometimes feel her walls shoot up around me? A stupid rule against dating a patient? Ha! A *rule* I can deal with. A *lack of attraction* toward me, not so much.

Lydia continues, "There's good reason for the rule. You're vulnerable, physically and emotionally. The most you've ever been, most likely. You need to be able to put your trust in your caregivers, with no misunderstandings or lines even possibly crossed." She fidgets. "If anything is ever going to happen between us, it will have to wait until you're no longer my patient. Okay?"

And... Captain Ryan Morgan re-enters my body. Only, I'll be damned, he's morphed into Colby Cheese Morgan. "Nope," I say smoothly, without a hint of remorse. "Not okay. I'm not going to wait five months to 'engage in romantic relations' with you, Lydia. Sorry not sorry. The minute I'm able to make a move on you, that's what I'm going to do."

She looks positively flabbergasted. "You're joking, right?"

"No. I'm insanely attracted to you in a way I've never experienced before and I'm positive I won't be able to wait that long to hit on you. So I'm not going to lie to you about it now. *I'm coming for you.*"

Lydia's eyebrows shoot up. "But... *Colby.* You can't. I could get fired."

"Put that aside for a minute. Are you interested romantically in me, Lydia?"

She turns bright red.

"Just tell me the truth. If you're not, then this is a moot point. Just tell me if you're interested enough to want to go on a date with me at some point and see where this thing might lead?"

She takes a deep breath. "Yes."

"Good. Thought so. Then I'm not waiting five months. The minute my body is capable of making a move on you, that's what I'm going to do."

"You can't."

"I can."

"Please don't."

"I will."

"Colby, this isn't a joke. I don't want to get fired or lose my license. *Please.*"

I scoff. "You won't get fired, Lydia. No one will ever know besides us. It'll be a victimless crime. I'm not a child or elderly person. I'm not vulnerable in any way."

"It's not that simple, Colby. The rules are the rules." She looks toward the door and lowers her voice. "There's this PT I work with— and she made a point of telling me about the policy. She's got it out for me and she's just waiting for me to screw up. I need to be careful and toe the line. Plus, like I said, there's good reason for the rule. You may not realize it, but you *are* vulnerable. I need to follow the rule for ethical reasons, not just to avoid getting fired."

I roll my eyes. "Lydia, give me a break. I'm a thirty-year-old firefighter with a major hard-on for you."

She laughs, despite herself.

"You wouldn't be taking advantage of me. I'm of sound mind. Sound body? Not yet. But I know exactly what I'm doing and what I want. And as far as that other PT goes, fuck her. She won't be in the room when we finally 'engage in romantic relations,' will she? So I don't see how she'll ever know what the hell we do behind closed doors."

"That's not the point. Ethics is doing the right thing, even when nobody is watching."

I suddenly feel like the Big Bad Wolf outside the first Little Piggy's thatched hut. I'm completely turned on by the idea of blowing Lydia's little house down. "Ethics doesn't apply here," I say. "It's a paper rule when applied to us. *I'm* seducing *you*. Not the other way around. Trust me on that."

She's blushing. "Okay, stop it. I'm telling you we've got to remain professional until you're no longer my patient and that's final. Whenever I touch you, you need to feel confident I'm touching you appropriately."

I have the urge to say "Please don't." But I refrain. She looks serious and I don't want to push her too hard. So I just sort of half nod, even though I have no intention of sitting back for the next five months and being nothing but her friendly patient. "Lydia," I say. "I can promise you this: I'd never do anything to jeopardize your job or career."

Her shoulders relax. "Thank you for understanding, Colby. I'm sorry if it seems like I led you on. I didn't know about the policy until yesterday, to be honest, and then I didn't feel sure there was any need to mention it to you." Lydia rises from her chair. "Good talk. I have to run to an appointment in the outpatient clinic. Congrats on getting out of here today. Who's coming to get you?"

"Ryan and Kat. Everyone else will be at my parents' house when we get there."

"Awesome. Say hi to everyone for me. I'll see you in two days at the outpatient clinic."

"*Two days*? Holy hell! I'm gonna be in the throes of severe Lydia-withdrawals by then."

Lydia's cheeks bloom. "Yeah, I'll definitely be experiencing severe Colby-withdrawals by then, too." She palms her forehead. "Gah. Now see what you did? I'm weak around you. No more flirting, Colby. I'm serious."

I smile broadly.

She twists her mouth adorably at me, trying and failing not to return my smile, and then looks at her watch again. "Crap. I'm late. Do you need anything before I head off?"

"Nope. Run, Lydia, run."

Lydia looks at me sideways. "What aren't you telling me?"

"Nothing. Bye now."

Lydia turns like she's going to dart away from me but then shocks the hell out of me by pivoting and giving me a hug on my good side. "I hate goodbyes," she murmurs into my shoulder.

Electricity jolts through me. She's never hugged me before. I stick my nose into her hair and breathe in her glorious scent. Stroke the back of her head with my good hand. "This isn't goodbye," I coo. "Just two days of torture and we'll see each other again."

"But we'll never be exactly like this again," she whispers. "The clinic will always be crowded with other people." She pulls out of our embrace and I'm shocked to see her eyes glistening. "The time we've spent together alone in this room has been pure magic, Colby."

I touch her face. "You're the silver lining to the worst storm cloud of my life, Lydia. A beautiful angel."

Lydia smiles through her tears. "That's what you wrote on the whiteboard about me the first day we met in the ICU. *Beautiful angel*."

"I did? Is that the 'entertaining' thing I wrote to you?"

She blushes and it's instantly clear she's hiding something from me—something I wrote to her that's far more "entertaining" than "beautiful angel."

I look at her sideways. "What did I write to you, Lydia? Come on. Give it up."

She presses her lips together, looks down at her watch again, and gasps. "Crap! I'm super late. I've gotta go." She sprints toward the door, waving to me as she goes. "See you Friday, my friendly and professional patient!"

And that's it. My beautiful angel is gone and I'm left wondering two things: one, how the fuck I'm going to survive two whole days without seeing those hazel eyes of hers, and, two, what the fuck "entertaining" bullshit crazy-ass thing I wrote to the woman of my dreams on that goddamned white board.

Chapter 20
Lydia

"I blew it, Ros," I bemoan to my next-door neighbor and babysitter, Rosalind. "I had the perfect opportunity to tell Colby about the kids today and I totally blew it."

"The timing just wasn't right today, honey. You'll tell him whenever it is."

We're having this conversation in an ice cream parlor after having watched Isabella perform in a dance recital at her school—the "prior engagement" that forced me to turn down Colby's dinner invitation earlier today. I'm not complaining about that, of course. I wouldn't have missed seeing my feisty middle child tap-dancing (sort of) to "Who Let the Dogs Out" while wearing floppy ears and a tail for anything. I'm just sorry Izzy's recital and Colby's celebratory dinner didn't happen to be on different nights.

I glance over at Izzy and Beatrice. They're standing on the other side of the large ice cream parlor, licking their cones while ogling a slew of decorated ice cream cakes in a large glass-top freezer. Theo, on the other hand, couldn't care less about ice cream cakes. My almost-eleven-year-old is camped at the far end of our long, pink table, earbuds in, his brown eyes glued to some YouTuber on his phone.

I return my gaze to Rosalind. "He asked me if everything was okay after Theo's call and I totally shut down on him. I'm sure he was totally confused, poor guy." I rub my forehead. "I should have told him it was my son on the phone. That he's being bullied at school and was crying on the phone. Colby's not stupid. He could see I was stressed out. He has to be wondering what the heck is going on with me."

"So why do you think you didn't tell him about Theo?"

"I'd just told him we need to keep things friendly and professional between us. How would laying all my baggage on him, all at once, be keeping things professional?"

"Telling him you have kids is laying your baggage on him?"

"No, not the kids *per se*. But once I tell him about the kids, his next question will be 'What's the status of your relationship with their father?' Mark my words, that will be his next question. And I have no desire to have a teary-eyed conversation about Darren with Colby. Colby's got a hero's heart. If I tell him the story of the worst tragedy of my life, he'll want to fix me. And that's not his job. It's my job to fix *him*."

Rosalind nods. "I can see why you didn't feel comfortable going down that road with him just yet. You still get extremely emotional when you talk about Darren. It wouldn't have been a casual conversation with Colby."

"Exactly. And I didn't have a lot of time, either. I had my next patient and had to rush off to the clinic."

"Makes perfect sense, honey."

I glance at Theo. He's still involved with his phone. Another glance at the girls and I see they're now dancing with some other kids to the loud pop music pumping out of the overhead speakers. I look at Ros again. "So you think I'm not completely crazy for not mentioning the kids to him yet?"

Rosalind puts down her plastic pink spoon. "I think everything you've told me makes perfect sense. But I also think you're not being completely honest with yourself about why you haven't told him yet."

My heart lurches into my mouth. "What do you mean?"

Rosalind looks at me sympathetically. "Honey, I think you're just plain scared to tell Colby about the kids and Darren because you don't want to scare Colby off. You want to keep him interested in you romantically. And, on the flipside, I think you're even more afraid that telling him about Darren and the kids will *not* scare him off."

I stare at her dumbly.

"Because," Rosalind continues, "if Colby finds out about your kids and Darren and he's still interested in you romantically, then you'll have to figure out in earnest if you're genuinely ready to have a romantic relationship with a man who isn't Darren. Maybe even fall in love."

Holy fuckburgers. This woman doesn't mess around.

Rosalind takes a bite of her ice cream. "By the look on your face, I'm guessing I've struck a nerve?"

I nod. "I only just put my wedding ring on my right hand a couple weeks ago—and not at all with the intention of falling in *love*, if you catch my drift."

Rosalind chuckles. "Yeah, I catch your drift loud and clear. I'm old, but I'm not *that* old." She glances at Theo to make sure he's still distracted and then she leans forward and whispers, "Have you been intimate with anyone since Darren?"

I shake my head. "I've never been intimate with anyone besides Darren, ever. I've never even kissed anyone else."

Rosalind looks shocked. And then deeply moved. She touches my hand across the pink table. "Oh, Lydia. No wonder your little brain is melting over this situation with Colby. You're thirty-two chronologically, but emotionally you're still a teenager in some crucial ways. You met Darren at seventeen and that's where your experience with boys ends."

Quickly, I glance at Izzy and Bea. They're still dancing with some other kids to a happy song. "I've never even gone on a simple date with anyone besides Darren. Never even *flirted* with anyone else. Honestly, I don't have a clue how to navigate this situation with Colby. I'm trying to remain professional. I really am. But I just feel giddy around him." I shove a huge bite of ice cream into my mouth. "Plus, let's not forget the dang employment policy. I could lose my job or even my license if I give in to temptation here. And it's not even about losing my job at the end of the day. From an ethical standpoint, my only concern should be his full recovery, not figuring out how soon I can screw him."

Rosalind chuckles. "Okay, so that's your answer. No romance until you're no longer his physical therapist. And in the meantime, whenever the timing feels right, tell him about the kids and Darren."

My stomach clenches. I know in my heart that advice doesn't resolve all the anxiety I'm feeling here. I touch the tip of my right thumb against the edge of my wedding band for a long moment, mulling my feelings. "Even when Colby is no longer my patient, I'm going to have to deal with my anxiety over the fact that he's a first responder, just like Darren. As a firefighter, every time Colby walks out the door, his life is at stake. What if I were to fall desperately in love with him and then lose him the way I lost Darren? I wouldn't bounce back from losing a man I love a second time, Ros."

Rosalind reaches across the pink table and grabs my hand again. "I'm not sure you've got a choice here. It sure sounds to me like you're already falling in love with the firefighter, whether you want to do it or not."

I open my mouth to reply to that statement by saying what, I'm not quite sure. But I'm thwarted by the girls standing at the edge of our table, out of nowhere. Holy hell, I didn't see them walk up. How long have they been standing there?

"I have to go to the bathroom, Mommy," Izzy says.

I pop up like a jack-in-the-box that just got cranked and take my daughter's hand. "Let's go."

We work our way toward the bathrooms at the back of the parlor. And as we walk, Izzy asks, "You're in love with one of your patients who's a firefighter?"

My heart stops. "*What*?"

"I heard Ros say it. Are you going to marry the firefighter?"

My heart explodes in my chest. "No, sweetheart. You misunderstood Rosalind. I was just telling her there's a firefighter I've been working with at the hospital who's very nice. But nobody's marrying anyone."

"But she said you're in love with him. You're not in love with him?"

Jesus Christ. "I'm... he's my patient."

"So you're not going to marry him?"

"Honey, I'm not thinking about marrying anyone. Not the firefighter or anyone else."

Izzy's narrow shoulders slump. She looks crestfallen.

"Sweetie, why do you look sad? I told you I'm not thinking about marrying the firefighter."

"That's why I'm sad," Isabella says. "I've always wanted to go to the Daddy-Daughter Dance. I thought if you married the firefighter, I might finally get to go."

Chapter 21
Colby

Dinner is done. The plates from Mom's lasagna have long since been cleared. Kat and Dax are playing Hearts with my parents in the kitchen while I'm lying on the couch with Ralph, surrounded by Ryan, Keane, and Keane's best friend since forever, Zander—a large, black mountain of a man with a mega-watt smile who's an honorary brother to us all. And, as so often happens when the Morgan family gets together, our neon sheep is entertaining everyone in his orbit with his unique brand of Peenie-ness. Tonight, Keane has been dazzling us with his newly formulated theories on... wait for it... *female mind control.*

"And it's just that simple," Keane says, snapping his fingers.

"Sounds like a bunch of bullshit to me," Ryan says, bringing his beer bottle to his lips.

"It's not," Keane insists. "It works every time. Take yesterday at the hospital, for example. While in line in the cafeteria, I said the thing. I told you about to this thirty-ish physical therapist with a banging body, and not two minutes later, at *her* suggestion, I was pounding her from behind in a supply closet."

"What?" I blurt.

"Which one?" Ryan asks.

"The one across from the cafeteria," Keane replies.

Ryan scoffs. "Not which *supply closet*, you dumbfuck! Which *physical therapist*?"

"*Oh.*" Keane chuckles. "Ramona." But when the name doesn't ring a bell with Ryan or me, Keane adds, "The one with the reddish hair and the tight little body who kept lurking outside Colby's room all week long. You know, the chick who kept looking at me, you, and Dax like she wanted us to make her airtight."

Ryan cringes. "Oh for the love of fuck, Peenie! That's the one

91

with the crazy eyes I told you and Dax about. The one I said kept coming at me in the hallway every time I left Colby's room."

Zander laughs. "Sounds like she struck out on her first choice of Morgan brother and settled for door number two, baby doll."

"More like door number stupid," Ryan says, and everyone, including Keane, laughs.

"Well, shit," Keane says, scratching his head. "I didn't realize Ramona was the bunny boiler you told us about. But now it makes perfect sense. That chick definitely has a crazy gleam in her eye like she's figuring out where to hide the body. That's why I fucked her from behind, actually. That crazy look in her eye kind of freaked me out."

We all lose it.

I say, "Hey, Keaney, here's a tip: If a woman looks so fucking crazy you don't want to look her in the eye while banging her, then that's a pretty good sign she's a hard pass."

We all laugh again.

"All I wanted to do those first couple days at the hospital was sob my eyes out," Ryan says. "But every time I left Bee's room to go to the bathroom or grab a coffee, there she was again, asking me how Colby was doing and flashing me 'Come fuck me in a supply closet!' eyes. She's obviously a grade-A bunny boiler, Peenie."

"Oh, *now* you know how to spot a bunny boiler, Rum Cake?" I say.

Ryan rolls his eyes. "Olivia's not a bunny boiler, motherfucker." He lets out a little puff of exasperation. "I mean, yeah, I admit she's a bit of a drama queen, but she's not a *bunny boiler*."

"Just admit defeat already, Captain," Keane says. He puts out his palm. "I'll take my fifty bucks in four tens, a five, four singles, a nickel, and ninety-five pennies, please."

Ryan smacks Keane's open palm. "Not gonna happen, Peenie Baby. And don't change the subject. I want to hear more about that supply closet. Because, gosh, when *I'm* visiting *my* brother in the ICU who's breathing on a ventilator, the only thing I'm thinking about doing is getting laid by some nut job in a supply closet."

Keane scoffs. "First off, this happened *yesterday,* son. Colby was *off* the ventilator and out of the ICU when I fucked her. I'm not an animal. And, second off, okay, yes, I'll be the first to admit it was beneath me. Not *Ramona.* I fucked her from behind, like I said. But the *situation* was beneath me. Lowbrow, even for me. But in my defense, I was super stressed about my wise and beloved Master Yoda being reduced to a pile of rubble, and I thought playing a little Hide the Bishop with a bunny boiler in a supply closet would make me forget my woes for a hot minute."

"And did it work?" Zander asks. "Did you forget your woes for a hot minute, sugar lips?"

"Not so much, sweet meat. As it turns out, even the mighty pussy isn't powerful enough to make a dude forget certain woes. Unfortunately, the whole thing just wound up feeling super skeevy." He shudders. "But, oh well. I'm a twenty-two-year-old dumbshit. If I'm not having fucked-up, skeezalicious, supply-closet sex in a vain effort to ease my crippling worry about The One I Love the Most, then I'm doing something wrong with what the good lord gave me."

"Damn, that was a whole lot of Peenie-ness all at once," I say, chuckling.

Ryan says, "And what exactly did the good lord give you again, Peen Star? Shit for brains? And fuck you, by the way. I thought *I* was The One You Love the Most."

"Not anymore. Try rushing into a fiery inferno to save a little baby and *maybe* you'll retake my top spot."

Boom.

In a flash, I'm right back in that burning building. Trapped. I hear that poor baby screaming. See the relief in her eyes at the sight of me. She reaches for me. I scoop her up and hug her to me.

Colby's got you.

Oh, God. Those goddamned words will torture me until the day I die.

Ryan says something, but I can't process it. His voice sounds like he's talking through a toilet paper roll.

I stroke Ralph with urgency, my heart beating against my sternum.

Colby's got you.

I drag myself to the window. Break the glass. Terror. That's what I feel. The most acute terror of my life. My throat burns. My lungs sizzle.

Colby's got you.

The gates of hell blast open behind me. A wall of flames roars at my back and reaches for me. I've got maybe ten seconds before I'm burned alive.

Ten... nine...

I stroke Ralph even more fervently, trying to calm myself.

Colby's got you.

Seven... six...

The baby's head lolls to the side. Her face is charred. Her hair singed clean off.

Four... three...

Ryan's voice pings around the edges of my consciousness, pulling me back to the present. He's asking me if I'm okay, but I can't reply. I close my eyes and try to remember the thing that therapist told me about yesterday. That little trick she said I should try when I find myself trapped in the fire again. *Visualize a dandelion,* the therapist from yesterday said. *The dandelion is your panic, Colby. It's your fear. Visualize the dandelion and blow on it. Watch its seeds scatter and float noiselessly into the wind. Off they go, Colby. Away, away, away.*

I take a deep breath and let out a long, slow stream of air from my O-shaped mouth.

Away, away, away.

The flames recede. They're not completely gone, but at least I can breathe again.

Away, away, away.

I open my eyes.

Damn, I guess that therapist knew what she was talking about.

Huh.

I didn't intend to meet with her in my hospital room yesterday. She showed up unsolicited and sat down next to my bed. "My good friend, Lydia Decker, asked me to drop by," she said. "I work in the building next door and she thought I might come by and answer any questions you might have about trauma therapy."

Lydia.

The woman is relentlessly kind.

Just thinking about her soothes my tortured soul. In fact, fuck the dandelion. Next time those flames come for me again, I'll imagine myself camped between Lydia's mocha thighs, my tongue lodged firmly into her sweet wetness. Now that's a visual to make a guy a happy camper again.

"Colby?" Ryan says. He's standing next to the couch, looking down at me, his face awash with concern. "Are you okay?"

I nod and shake it off. "Yeah. I'm fine."

"You're shaking like a leaf," Ryan says. He puts his hand on my forehead. "You're clammy."

I inhale deeply. "I'm okay. I'm just a tad bit fucked up in the head these days. Don't worry. I've got an appointment with a therapist tomorrow. She'll reset my noggin for me."

"Did your doctor give you any anxiety meds?" Ryan asks.

"No. I don't need them. I'm fine."

Ryan looks toward the kitchen, apparently making sure my parents are out of earshot. "Keaney, you got some weed?"

"Are there dicks in gay porn?"

"Give Bee something."

"Sure thing. I've got edibles today, fellas." Keane reaches into his pocket and pulls out two wrapped candy bars. "You want chocolate or peanut butter, sweet cheeks?"

I wave him off. "You know I don't do that shit."

"Well, you do today," Ryan says. "It's not like you're going to be operating a fire truck any time soon, man. You're just lying here like a sack of fucking potatoes."

"Good point," I say. I put out my hand. "Chocolate. But you guys gotta join me so I don't feel like a total loser."

"No need to ask me twice," Keane says. He tosses me the chocolate bar. "Careful, though, Eldest Morgan. That's some strong stuff and your tolerance is for shit. One little bite and you'll be feeling fine as wine."

Fuck it. I unwrap the bar and take a huge bite.

"Holy shit," Keane says, laughing. "You're gonna get batfaced on that, Bee."

I look up at Ryan. "Sit down, Captain. You're freaking me out standing over me like that."

"You look like shit," Ryan says. "I'm worried."

"I was just having some sort of flashback but it's gone now. I've been having them since the fire. Totally normal. Slight PTSD, I'm sure. Like I said, I'm gonna get myself some therapy starting tomorrow and I'll be fixed right up."

Ryan collapses onto the couch at my feet. "You scared me, Cheese." He indicates the bar in my hand. "Gimme some of that, fucker. Jesus Christ, I'm totally stressed out now."

I hand Ryan the bar and he takes an even bigger bite than I did.

He points at Keane as he chews. "This is your fault, dumbfuck. You stressed poor Colby out. I told you not to mention the fire around him. He doesn't need to be reminded of that shit."

Keane looks sheepish. "Sorry. I forgot."

"Aw, leave him alone," I say, stroking Ralph's head. "Me being fucked up isn't Keane's fault." I look at Keane. "You don't have to walk on eggshells around me."

"You're pretty fucked up from the fire?" Keane asks softly.

"I've just got a few kinks to work out, that's all. I'll get me some therapy and I'll be good to go." I put out my hand to Ryan. "Gimme that bar, Rummy-o. You took twice as big a bite as me. I gotta catch up."

"Careful with that, Bee," Keane warns. "It's strong stuff."

"How strong?" Ryan says.

"*Really* strong," Keane replies.

"Oh, well, in that case," Ryan says. He takes another gigantic bite and then hands the rest to me. "Eat the rest, Bumble Bee. We'll go down the rabbit hole together."

I eat the remainder of the weed-bar to match Ryan's share, and Keane and Zander look at each other like, *Oh, shit.*

"Atta boy," Ryan says, patting my foot.

"Don't say I didn't warn ya, fellas," Keane says, laughing. He breaks the peanut butter weed-bar down the middle and hands one half to Zander. "Bottoms up, baby doll." They tap their halves together like two dudes enjoying a pint in a pub, and then they cram the entirety of their large chunks into their mouths.

"Hey, you need a ride to the therapist tomorrow?" Ryan asks.

"Yeah, if you don't mind. Mom said she'd take me, but I'd much rather go in your slick new ride."

"You got a new car?" Zander asks.

Ryan tells Zander about his fancy new sports car. "I get a woody every time I get behind the wheel."

"Hey, will my wheelchair fit in the back of that thing?" I ask.

"Oh, shit. I forgot about that," Ryan says. He furrows his brow. "I think so. But if not, I'll just borrow Mom's car to take you."

I laugh. "Then shouldn't I just let Mom take me?"

We both find that comment completely hilarious and start laughing our asses off.

"So tell us the story of how you wound up screwing that

physical therapist in a supply closet," Ryan says to Keane. "We got distracted when you turned poor Colby into a zombie."

Keane looks stricken. "Hey, I'm really sorry about that, Bee. I was just trying to lighten the mood."

"I know you meant no harm, baby doll," I say. "You're a lover, not a fighter."

Keane sighs with relief and flashes me his dimples—and, of course, I melt like I always do when he hits me with those damned things. Or, wait, hold up. Maybe I'm *actually* melting into the couch? I look down at the weed-bar wrapper in my hand and blink hard, trying to clear my head. But I can't. My vision is tunneling.

"Wow, this stuff is strong," I mutter.

"Told you," Keane says.

"So tell the story already, would you?" Ryan says. "Any minute now, I'm gonna start barking like a seal or belting out 'Wind Beneath My Wings' to Colby and I want to hear your goddamned story before that happens."

Keane looks earnest. "Okay, okay. But first can I just say I love you, Bee. I don't tell you that nearly enough. When Mom called and told me what happened to you and that she didn't know if you were going to live or die, it was the worst moment of my life. The mere *thought* of something happening to you..." Keane shakes his head.

Zander puts his hand on Keane's broad shoulder and squeezes.

Keane's Adam's apple bobs for a moment and then he continues, "I don't want to live in a world where you're not around to call me dumbshit, Colby. I love you."

My chest feels tight. "I love you, too, Peenie. All you guys."

"I love you, too, brother," Ryan says. He squeezes my good leg. "More than I could ever say with words."

Zander's dark eyes are glistening. "You've always been my hero, Colby." He forces down a lump in his throat. "I love you, man."

I look down at the weed-bar wrapper in my hand again. "What the *fuck* is in this shit, Peen?"

We all burst out laughing at ourselves and wipe our eyes.

"In all seriousness, though, guys," I say. "When I was trapped in that fire and thought I was done, it was the thought of never seeing you guys again that made me..." I'm too choked up to continue, so I just shake my head.

We're all quiet for a long beat, wiping our eyes and smashing our lips together. Holy hell, there are a whole lot of bobbing Adam's apples in this living room.

Finally, I pull myself back together and say to Keane, "Just tell us the goddamned motherfucking story of how you banged that physical therapist in the supply closet, you dumbshit. I was mentally prepared to cry in therapy tomorrow morning, not tonight with you guys."

Keane leans back in his chair, spreads his muscular thighs, and says, "*Shit.*" He rubs his face and takes a deep breath. And when he comes out from behind his hands, he's got his game face on. "Okay, baby dolls. Here's the story. Fasten your seatbelts, because the smarm train is about to leave the station."

We all laugh, relieved to get this party back on track.

Keane leans forward. "I was in the cafeteria line getting a banana and Ramona beelines over to me to introduce herself. It felt exactly like when girls used to wait outside the locker room after games for me. You know, she gave me that *look.* So she asks me about Colby. We make small talk. Blah, blah, fucking blah. 'Oh, he's so brave!'"

We all chuckle.

"So the whole time, it's obvious to me she just wants to bang and she's looking for her angle. So, finally, she asks if I have any fun plans for the weekend and I say, 'Yeah, I've got a couple gigs.'" He grins, the cat who ate the canary. "So Ramona's like, 'Oh, you're a *musician?*' And that was that. Ka-*bam,* son! I told her what I do and two minutes later, it was Bonin' Time in the supply closet."

Ryan and I look at each other like, *What the fuck?*

"Um, I think you left a little something out of your narrative, son," Ryan says.

"I left out nothing, *son,*" Keane says. "You wouldn't believe how fast women offer themselves to me when they find out I'm a stripper. They're ten times more aggressive with me than they were when I played ball—and, as you know, women weren't exactly shy with me back in my pitching days. I dunno. When they find out I'm a stripper, they forget I'm a human being. They think I'm *literally* nothing but abs, a dick, and balls."

"You're not?" Ryan says.

"Keane," I say. "Just tell us how you got from point A to B."

"Dude, it was like sending a greased pig down a chute. I told her I'm a stripper named 'Peen Star' and she goes, 'Oh, I'd love to get a private lap dance some time.' So I give her my card, just to be a smart-ass, and she goes, 'Actually, I've got thirty minutes right now. How much would you charge me for a private show now? Would twenty bucks get me twenty minutes with you, Peen Star?'"

"Ho-lee shit," Zander says, laughing. "Not beating around the bush, that one."

"No, that one took a weed wacker to the motherfucking bush," Keane says. "You want to know the skeeziest, most demented part? When we were done, she *actually* handed me that twenty bucks and said, 'Nice job, Peen Star.'"

"No fucking way!" Ryan says.

"I know, right?" Keane says. "I thought she was kidding about the twenty bucks. Plus, *twenty* bucks? How insulting. I gave that woman three O's in twenty minutes and she gave me *twenty* measly bucks? On the open market, three O's would normally get me *at least* a C-note!"

"Oh, fuck," I say. "Please tell me you're joking about knowing the market for something like that."

"*Of course*. What do you take me for?"

"Um, a gigolo?" Ryan chimes in.

"A male prostitute?" I add.

"No, no, no," Keane says. "Nobody's payin' for layin' when it comes to Peen Star's peen." He chuckles. "Which isn't to say Peen Star's peen isn't getting any action. Jesus motherfucking Christ, I've never had so much pussy thrown at me in my life. At this bachelorette party I did on Saturday, this one really classy-looking MILF with a diamond ring as big as Zander's head flat-out offered to get her knees dirty for me."

My brother and I erupt in disbelief while Zander nods knowingly and laughs. Apparently, Z's already heard this particular story.

"Did you say yes to the MILF?" Ryan asks.

"No, I didn't say *yes,*" Keane says, feigning offense. His face lights up. "I said, '*Hell* yes!'"

We all laugh.

"The MILF was hot as fuck, brah! Older women always have highly developed skills in the bedroom—the kind of expertise that comes with time and experience. But *this* particular MILF? Holy hot damn. Olympic caliber in the sport of giving head. Ever seen footage of a snake eating a rabbit?"

He mimics what he's talking about and we all lose it for a very, very long time.

"So did the MILF 'tip' you like Ramona did?" Ryan asks when we're semi-composed again.

"Of course not. Well, she tried, actually. But I wouldn't take it. Peen Star's peen ain't for sale, son. Any dabble with a client, it's a dabble on the house. Just for fun."

I shake my head. "I dunno, Peenie Weenie. I'd be careful with that kind of dabble. I think it's the kind that could get you into big trouble."

"Bah. A little dab'll do ya is just one of the perks of the job. It's no different than when groupies used to stand outside the locker room after one of my games, begging me to take them home. I didn't charge the pretty groupies back then and I don't charge the pretty groupies now. It's the same thing, as far as I'm concerned."

"*Dude*. It's completely different," Ryan says. "You're a stripper now, not a pro athlete. Lines are gonna get blurred when you're the guy being paid to take off his clothes versus the guy paid to throw strikes."

"Ryan's right, Keane," I warn. "There could be some big misunderstandings if you're not careful out there."

"It's all good, Master Yodas," Keane says, waving us off. "I've already decided I'm only gonna partake in the dabble when I'm *really* feeling it, and *only* after I've already danced for the whole allotted time *and* gathered all my tips. If I do it like that every time, then what could go wrong?"

"Famous last words," I mutter.

Ryan says, "Yeah, I'm pretty sure the universe is contractually obligated to unleash a shit storm of epic proportions directly on top of any dude's head who's stupid enough to utter those famous last words."

"Well, thanks for watching out for me and The Talented Mr. Ripley, fellas," Keane says breezily. "But we'll take our chances." He flashes his dimples. "So, hey, Bee, speaking of hot women, I've been meaning to ask you: what's the deal with your hot physical therapist? *Damn, boy*. What's her name again?"

"Lydia. And don't even think about giving her a private lap

dance in a supply closet, Peen Star, or I swear to God I'll find a way to beat you senseless, even in my present condition."

"Don't worry," Ryan says. "I'll beat him senseless for you if he so much as looks at Lydia."

"Thank you. That's why I love you the most, Captain."

"*Hey*," Keane says. "I thought you loved *me* the most."

"I've never said or done anything to give you that impression, Keane."

"You're such a dumbfuck, Peen," Ryan says. "Why even joke about hitting on Lydia when Bee so obviously looks at her like he owns her?"

Keane rolls his eyes. "I was *kidding*. We all know Lydia is Colby's girl. He staked his claim on her the day she walked into his hospital room. Actually, he staked his claim on her in high school when he was all obsessed with Beyoncé."

"Oh, yeah," Ryan says, chuckling. "I forgot about that."

Keane says, "I was just playing around—trying to get a rise out of him. Colby's looking catatonic over there. I wanted to make sure his brain still works."

"I'm just lost in thought," I mumble, but my tongue feels thick and weird as I say it.

"Yee-gads, you're stoned out of your mind, Bee," Zander says, laughing. "You're literally drooling." He looks at Ryan. "And so are you, Rum Cake. You both look like fucking jelly fish."

Ryan and I look at each other and laugh our asses off.

"Well, looks like I'm crashing here tonight," Ryan says. "What time's your therapy appointment tomorrow, BeeBee Baby?"

I rub my face. "I have no idea, man."

We laugh again.

"So you're totally into Lydia, huh?" Keane asks.

"Dude, I'm obsessed," I say. "I can't stop thinking about her, day and night. I think I'm falling in love with her."

"Not surprised," Keane says. "It's written all over your face every time she walks into the room."

Keane keeps talking about my obvious attraction to Lydia, and how gorgeous she is, and how much she's my "type," whatever that means, but I tune him out. I lied to the guys just now. I don't *think* I'm falling in love with Lydia—I *know* I am. When I'm not having a

101

nightmare, it's because I'm dreaming I'm having sex with Lydia. Or that we're running on the beach together or otherwise doing something where my body is back to normal. And when I'm awake, I'm consumed with thoughts of her. Take right now, for instance, I'm wondering what Lydia's doing tonight. What kept her from being here to celebrate with us tonight? And who called her today when she was working on me? Man, it's driving me crazy to think whoever was on the other end of the line today said something that upset her.

And not knowing what that phone call today was about isn't the only thing driving me crazy when it comes to Lydia. What 'entertaining' thing did I write to Lydia on that whiteboard that she won't tell me about? Did I write something dirty? Because the woman inspires dirty thoughts in me, that's for sure. I can't imagine I wrote anything too salacious. Painkillers or not, that would have been so outside character for me as to be mind-blowing. Plus, I was on a breathing machine and broken and in pain, so I can't imagine I was even remotely thinking about sex in that moment. *But what if I was*? What if I was so out of my head, my most primal instincts took over the minute I laid eyes on her? I guess it's *possible*, considering how sexually attracted I am to her.

"Hey, Keaney," I say, cutting him off mid-sentence. "Did you draw that dick and balls on that whiteboard in the ICU?"

"Of course. And bee tee dubs? Mom-a-tron totally thought it was a rocket at liftoff."

We all laugh.

"Do you remember what was written on the white board before you doodled your self-portrait?" I ask.

"*Nada.* It was already wiped clean when I drew on it. Why?"

My shoulders slump. "Lydia said I wrote something 'entertaining' on the white board when I was flying high on painkillers, but I don't remember writing a damned thing except a question about the baby. I'm just hoping whatever I wrote to her wasn't something too horrifically offensive. I don't want her knowing this early on what a total perv I am, down deep. Not 'til I can actually *do* something about my pervy thoughts, anyway. I can't begin to tell you how frustrating it is to be trapped inside this useless body around a woman I'm so damned attracted to. She had to help me get onto and off the toilet last week. God, it was so fucking embarrassing."

Keane cringes. "So much for a 'meet cute.'"

I chuckle. "I just wish I knew what I wrote to her. It must have been something pretty outrageous because she refuses to tell me."

"I wouldn't worry about it, Cheese Head," Keane says. "Whether you're on painkillers or not, drunk or stoned or sleep deprived, you're always the same classy dude. Like Superman. You're like 'Truth, Justice, and the American way!'" He holds up his fist. "I'm sure you just told Lydia she's beautiful or something."

"I dunno. I'm so insanely attracted to Lydia, God only knows what depravity might have slipped out of my subconscious in a moment of drugged-up weakness."

"Description of this goddess, please," Zander demands, snapping his fingers like he's summoning a butler.

"Hot. As. Fuck," Ryan replies.

"Hot. As. *Fuckity* Fuck," Keane adds.

"Details, please," Z says, snapping again.

"May I do the honors, Eldest Morgan Sibling?" Keane asks me politely, like we're at a tea party and he's asking to pour my tea.

"Please do," I say. "Just don't make me sic Ryan on you."

"Gotcha." Keane looks at Zander. "Remember Mrs. Dunne from ninth grade English?"

"*No fucking way.*"

"Way."

"Lydia is *that* hot?"

"*Hotter.* Lydia is Mrs. Dunne, only slightly younger and with fuller lips and lighter eyes and way, *way* bigger tits."

"*Keane,*" I say sharply.

"Sorry." He looks at Z. "Way, way more bountiful *breasts.*"

Zander says, "So Lydia's black?"

"Biracial," I say. "White mom. Black dad."

"That counts as a sister in my book," Zander says.

"Call her whatever you want," Keane says. "All I know is the woman is smoking hot."

Ryan says to me, "So have you told Lydia she's in your crosshairs yet? Or are you waiting 'til you can actually pull the trigger to let her know you want her?"

"Oh, I've told her," I say. "I didn't break my *head,* motherfucker."

"Atta boy," Ryan says, chuckling.

"But it's a non-starter for a while. Nothing can happen between us 'til I'm not her patient anymore. Some rule in her employee handbook says a current patient is off-limits to her."

"Bah. Fuck her employee handbook," Keane says. "Get to good will hunting, Matt Damon. Pull out your crossbow to-*day*."

I sigh. "It's a moot point right now. If you haven't noticed, I'm not in any shape to sweep a girl off her feet. I want it to be good when I do it. Plus, not gonna lie, I don't want her to re-break my bones in the throes of passion."

Keane waves dismissively. "Bah. You've got fingers and lips, doncha? Well, then, you're good to go right fucking now."

"It's more than the handbook and my physical condition that's holding me back," I admit. "To be honest, the girl's a bit of a Jenga tower to me. I feel like if I make the wrong move, she's gonna come crumbling down on me and I don't know why. She's got a skittish-kitten vibe." I tell the guys about how I invited Lydia to dinner tonight and she said she had plans without further elaboration. And how her body language was really weird after she took that phone call today, and then didn't give me the slightest hint about who was on the other end of the call. And all the other small times over the past week when I got the feeling there was something she wasn't telling me, despite her being warm and open and earthy most of the time. "I'm thinking maybe there's an ex-boyfriend at play here," I say. "That's the vibe I'm getting. Like her heart's not completely available."

"I dunno, man," Ryan says. "From what I've seen, Lydia is totally into you."

"I second that emotion," Keane says.

I shrug. "Well, something's holding her back. I'm not sure if it's the stupid employment policy, or that I'm a broken pile of bones, or if some other guy has dibs on her heart. All I know is she lights me on fire, I can't stop thinking about her, I miss her when I'm not with her, and I want to kiss her and fuck her like nobody I've ever met before. And yet something is holding her back, big-time, and I'm not buying that it's just the physical-therapist-patient thing." I run my hand through my hair. "Oh, man, I've gotta lock this woman down, guys. I'm going fucking crazy."

"You know what you should do?" Zander says. "If you don't mind me jumping in here."

"Please do, Z. You, unlike your wife over there, only speak when you've got something of value to say."

Keane flips me off.

"Give her space," Zander says. "You've made it clear you want her, right? And she's replied by saying it can't happen while she's your physical therapist. So give her what she *thinks* she wants, by the book, and I guarantee she'll be the one coming after *you*. Reverse psychology, brother."

Ryan nods. "Z's right. It's your best play. Be on your best behavior for a solid month. And then, at the one-month mark, make your move out of nowhere and she'll be so relieved she won't be able to resist you."

"But what if what she *said* she wants is, indeed, what she wants?" I say. "What if she literally wants me to wait five or six *months* to make a move?"

"What are the odds of that?" Keane chimes in. "I mean, come on. You're *you*. Break your bones, put you through a wood chipper, I don't care. You're still gonna be Mr. Dreamy McDreamy-pants to women. But, okay, for the sake of argument. Let's say she's a super straight arrow and she actually cares more about some stupid rule in her employee handbook than what her lady-boner is begging her to do." He rolls his eyes at the thought. "Then it's a no-lose. You'll get points for being respectful of her wishes and the minute you're not her patient anymore you can jump each other's bones. I doubt it'll play out like that, but if it does, it'll be worth the wait." He smiles and his dimples pop. "But I should add, in my experience, women only bring up rules when they want you to break them."

I laugh. "Thanks, guys. Okay, I'll be the perfect patient for a month and then make my move."

"Keep us posted," Zander says.

Before I can reply, my mother's voice sings out from across the room.

"Good night, boys," she says, entering the living room with Dad, Dax, and Kat.

Brief conversation ensues. We find out Mom and Dad kicked the Wonder Twins' asses in Hearts. Ryan confirms he'll get me safely off to bed and help me with whatever embarrassing things I might need assistance with—getting into my pajamas, getting on and off the toilet, etcetera.

My parents hug and kiss me and tell me they love me and thank God I'm alive.

And then, Mom and Dad Morgan finally head off to bed, leaving their stoned-as-fuck children to party on.

Chapter 22
Colby

Kat kicks Ryan off the edge of the couch and takes his place next to me. Dax takes a chair next to Z. And Ryan sprawls out on his back on the floor and immediately begins making floor-angels and laughing like a fool.

"Dude," Dax says. "Is he stoned?"

"I'm stoned out of my mind!" Ryan confirms, still making floor-angels.

Dax peers into my eyes. "Holy fuck! You're *all* stoned?"

The four of us potheads burst out laughing.

"Oh my God," Dax says, holding out his hand to Keane. "Gimme some."

"How do you know it was me?" Keane says.

We all laugh.

"I don't have any left," Keane says.

"Yes, you do," Dax says. "Dig deep."

Keane fishes into his pocket. "Oh, hey, you're right. I've got gummy bears, brah." He places the packet in Dax's palm. "Go forth and prosper, little brother."

Dax rips open the package and pops a couple chewy candies into his mouth.

"Hey, Daxy," I say. "Don't be greedy. Share the wealth with Kumquat."

Okay, yeah, I'm being a sneaky bastard. But I'm dying for my sister to finally come clean about her bun in the oven. It's been two weeks, for crying out loud! The girl's never kept a secret that long in her life.

"No, thanks," Kat says. She glares at Dax, nonverbally telling him to keep her secret, and Dax returns her glare, nonverbally telling her to give up the ghost.

107

I wait.

But Kat remains mute.

Fuck.

I clear my throat. "Everything going well with Josh?" I ask, looking at my sister.

"Things couldn't be better," Kat replies brightly. "He just moved to a fancy new house in Seattle today. He's launching a chain of rock climbing gyms with his twin brother, Jonas, and they've decided to headquarter the business in their hometown. Did I mention he's originally from Seattle?"

"No. You've told me next to nothing about him, actually."

"Oh. Well, yeah. Josh grew up here with his twin brother, Jonas."

"Where'd he go to high school?"

"St. Francis Academy."

"He's Catholic?"

"Raised Catholic. Not practicing anymore."

"And he moved to Seattle *today*?"

She nods. "Sold his house in the Hollywood Hills and bought himself a new place here. Looks like he's going to live in Seattle for good."

I look at Dax and we both nonverbally agree that's damned good news.

"Hey, if you want to ditch my ass and go see Josh now, I won't be offended," I say. "I'm just lying here, broken and stoned. Nothing to see here, folks."

"No, I'm good, honey." She pats my arm. "I've got a big surprise planned for Joshua William Faraday tomorrow night. I don't want to go to him tonight and steal my own thunder."

"You two are getting pretty serious, huh?"

Her cheeks flush. "I love him with all my heart and soul."

Aw, man. She looks so damned vulnerable right now, I just want to hug her. "And he loves you back?" I ask, my stomach clenching with anticipation.

"I truly believe so."

"But you two haven't exchanged the magic words?"

Kat shakes her head. "I'm hoping it happens tomorrow night. I've got a diabolical little plan in place to make Josh say the three little words first."

I slide my hand in Kat's. "Don't worry, Kumquat. Josh will be putty in your hands tomorrow night. How could any man possibly resist you?"

She shrugs. "It's been known to happen before."

"You mean that guy in college?"

She nods.

"Oh, sweetheart, that guy was a fucking idiot. He wasn't worth your tears. This time, all your dreams will come true."

Kat half-smiles at me and, just like that, all I can see is the angelic little baby face I first laid eyes on twenty-four years ago.

"So, hey, Jizzy Pop!" Ryan shouts from the floor. "Are we ever gonna meet this Josh Faraday bastard or what? And if the answer is yes, then for the love of fuck, *please* tell him to bring his Lamborghini when he comes so I can tell him I'm taking his car for a test drive around the block and then gun it all the way to Mexicoooooooooo!"

Everyone laughs.

"Oh, you'll all meet Josh, for sure," Kat says. "And when you do, I'll most definitely tell him to bring his fancy Italian car. But there's no rush on that, guys." She squeezes my hand and smiles at me. "Our family has had enough to worry about lately. No need for me to pile on. Right now, let's just focus on Colby."

Chapter 23
Lydia

It's a Wednesday afternoon, exactly three weeks since Colby got out of the hospital. And for the ninth time in three weeks, I'm standing at a therapy table in the outpatient clinic, gently manipulating Colby's muscles and joints. But unlike when Colby was an in-patient at the hospital, we're not alone here. Physical therapists with their patients are scattered around the large space, including one particularly bitchy PT who just so happens to be working at the station next to mine. *Ramona.* Indeed, in *nine* sessions with Colby, Ramona has just so happened to be working at the adjacent therapy table every freaking time. Not once has she been in the acute care building working with a new patient just out of surgery. Never has she been working with a patient in the swimming pool attached to the clinic. And she's never once been out grabbing lunch, even when I thought I was being clever and scheduled Colby for noon. *Not once!* Clearly, the woman has been checking the schedule religiously for my appointments with Colby and reserving the station next to mine to terrorize me.

I glance at Ramona as I work the rotation of Colby's left hip and discover she's staring right at me as she guides a young woman through exercises with a resistance band.

I try to keep my face neutral in the face of her hard stare and return to Colby. "So how are the nightmares? Less?" I ask quietly.

"So much less," Colby says. "I went to another session with that therapist you recommended yesterday, and last night I slept like a rock for the first time since the fire."

"Oh, Colby. I'm so glad."

"I've still got some things to work through, for sure, but I'm definitely making progress."

"I'm so glad to hear it."

Oh, man, I'm dying inside. These past three weeks, Colby hasn't flirted with me at all the way he used to do in the hospital, though he's been charming and sweet. Honestly, I've started wondering if maybe the brazen way he came on to me in the hospital was more a function of the pain meds than his sincere attraction to me.

When I made him promise not to hit on me again until the end of his physical therapy, I meant it. But now that he's actually complying with my request, I feel a huge loss. And it certainly doesn't help we haven't been alone in three whole weeks. Every time I see him these days, I feel like I'm going to combust.

"So guess what?" Colby says as I maneuver his left ankle. "Kat is *finally* bringing Josh home to Meet the Morgans."

"Hallelujah! When?"

"This Sunday for dinner. My mom is making her famous spaghetti and meatballs. God, I hope my parents don't choke on a meatball when Kat drops her baby bomb."

"You think she'll finally do it then?"

"She's got no choice. She can't keep this secret forever. It's been a full month."

"Is she showing yet?"

"No. Hmm. Good point." He chuckles. "Knowing Kat, she'll probably chicken out and wait until she literally has no choice."

"Well, either way, you've got to promise to tell me everything when you come to your appointment on Monday. Take notes if you have to—I want full details."

"There's no way in hell I'm gonna give you a report after the fact. You've got to come to dinner. I won't take no for an answer this time. Sunday at seven. Give me your phone number and I'll text you the address."

I'm simultaneously elated and crestfallen. Elated he's asking me to dinner again, thereby confirming his continued interest in me, and crestfallen because, yet again, I've got plans. "I'm going out of town this weekend," I say, my shoulders sagging. "Leaving tomorrow. I won't be back until late Sunday night."

Colby looks hugely disappointed.

"I'm sorry, Colby. I truly would have *loved* to come to dinner. I'm so disappointed."

He tries to smile. "No worries. Such is life. Where are you going? Somewhere fun, I hope?"

Oh, shit. My heart rate is suddenly pounding. "The Happiest Place on Earth," I manage to say breezily, though my head is teeming with thoughts. Should I finally tell Colby about the kids now?

"Oh, that's always fun," Colby says. "Have you been there before?"

"Several times," I say. "You?"

"A couple times. I haven't been in a long time, though. Last time we went as a family, I think Dax was, like, ten."

The same age as Theo. Although Theo is turning eleven on Saturday. Hence, the trip.

I suddenly realize the silence between us has become awkward. Colby's obviously waiting for me to elaborate on why the hell a single woman who presumably has no children is going to Disneyland. But I don't feel like now is the time to tell him about my three kids and dead husband. Not here in the clinic with all these people around us. Not with freaking *Ramona* staring at us like a hawk. And, frankly, not when my silence on the topic at this point has become strange and weird and deceitful and I don't know how to dig myself out of this hole.

The truth is the kids and I are flying to California to spend a long weekend at Disneyland with both sets of the kids' grandparents—my parents and Darren's. Is that really what I want to explain to Colby as an opening salvo when I first tell him about my kids? I quickly decide, *Um, no, thank you.* Because I'm a freaking coward.

I clear my throat. "What's your favorite ride?" I ask feebly.

"Space Mountain," he says.

"That's my favorite, too," I say. "You know, if you're in a wheelchair, they let you go to the front of every line. Too bad you're not coming with me. I would have milked you for all you're worth." Oh my God. What am I saying? Colby couldn't possibly come with me to Disneyland with my kids *and Darren's freaking parents*!

"Hey, milk me any time. Please," Colby says, and then he immediately cringes. "Sorry. That came out wrong."

We both laugh. God, he's so cute.

Oh, jeez. I'm in a pickle. I'm having the irrational urge to invite Colby to Disneyland. To tell him about my kids and Darren and tell my parents and Darren's parents about Colby and...

Oh. Wait.

Darren's mother.

Images of her grief-stricken face shooting daggers at Colby and me all weekend long flash across my mind.

Yeah, no thanks.

Never mind.

This isn't the way I want to tell Colby about my kids, anyway. Not like this. I've waited too long to tell him now. I've made it a *thing.* Now, whenever I tell him, which I'll obviously need to do at some point, it's going to be a huge bombshell. Which means I need to do it when we're alone, when we can talk in detail and I can cry and he can say whatever he needs to say about how weird it is that I waited so long to tell him. How hurt he is that I didn't share such a massively important part of my life with him. And *certainly,* whenever it happens, it's got to be when Ramona's not watching me like a prison guard on yard duty.

The clock strikes the hour, signaling the end of my session with Colby.

"Time's up," I whisper.

He sits up and smiles thinly. Clearly, his mind is racing every bit as much as mine is.

"Well, my friendly *physical therapist,*" he says. "Have fun in Disneyland. I'll expect a full report on Monday."

My heart lurches into my throat. "And I'll expect a full report about your family dinner with Josh."

Colby looks at me for a long moment, his eyes scanning mine like an MRI searching for cancer cells. "Have a great long weekend in Disneyland, Lydia."

"Thank you."

"I guess I'll see you on Monday, then."

"See you then."

I'll miss you, I think. But, of course, I don't say it.

I glance at Ramona. She's busy with her patient, so I lean into Colby's ear. "The PT at the next station is the one who has it out for me," I whisper. "The one who told me about that employment policy. She's been watching me like a hawk with you for the past three weeks."

Colby glances at Ramona and then returns to me. His features noticeably soften.

I whisper, "We're not supposed to give our personal numbers to patients, but take mine. I don't want to wait for Monday to get an update about the dinner. Call or text me on Sunday night and tell me everything."

The hardness in Colby's eyes from a moment ago is gone. In fact, he looks elated. "Awesome."

He pulls out his phone and I discreetly mouth my personal cell number.

"I'll text you Sunday night," Colby whispers.

I bite my lip. "Please don't forget. I'll be waiting by my phone."

"Lydia, I think about you twenty-four-seven. I won't forget."

My heart explodes in my chest. *Oh my God! He still feels the same way he did in the hospital!*

Colby glances at Ramona behind my back. "She's staring at us like a sniper right now," he whispers. "Better throw her off the scent." He raises his voice and plasters a fake smile on his face. "Bye, Lydia," he booms cheerfully. "Thanks for being such an amazing and professional physical therapist!"

I laugh. "My pleasure, Mr. Morgan!"

"See you Monday, Physical Therapist Lydia!"

"Okay! See you then, Mr. Morgan!"

I help him into his wheelchair and push him toward the lobby... and we both break down into ridiculous giggles.

Chapter 24
Colby

"Lydia is such a mystery to me sometimes," I say, exhaling with frustration. I'm sitting in my sister's car as she drives me home from my physical therapy appointment, feeling like my head is going to explode. "She's so warm and open and fun ninety percent of the time, but then there's this other ten percent when she turns guarded and skittish on me. I can visibly see her walls going up, right before my eyes, and I have no idea why. It's those times that I feel like there's something big she's *dying* to say, but she's literally biting her tongue to stop herself."

"She's probably just worried about that employment policy you were telling me about. Maybe she's constantly on the cusp of hurling herself at you and ripping your clothes off, and she has to fight hard to keep herself in line so she doesn't get fired."

"I don't think that's it. I think that stupid employment policy is a red herring—something for her to hide behind so she doesn't have to face the *real* thing she's worried about, whatever it is."

"Maybe she's been hurt by some dickhead in the past, so she subconsciously pulls away every time she feels herself going weak in the knees for you."

I purse my lips, considering that idea. "Maybe. Whatever it is, she becomes a scared little kitten stuck in a tree." I indicate my arm in a sling. "And, unfortunately, getting kittens down from trees isn't something this firefighter is capable of doing at the moment."

"How much longer before your arm is out of that sling?"

"Two more weeks. I thought that'd be my cue to make my move with her, but now I'm not so sure. I'm just getting too many mixed signals from her lately."

"What kind of move are you thinking of making?"

I look at her like she's a moron. "How many kinds of moves are there to make, Kat?"

"I mean, like, are you thinking of starting something purely physical with her—like a fling? Or are you wanting to start a serious relationship with her?"

Now I look at Kat like she's got three heads. "Why on earth would I want a fling with someone as amazing as Lydia? That woman is solid-gold *wife* material."

"I know, I just... I'm impressed you're not the teeniest bit daunted by the kid-thing, that's all. I didn't mean to imply—"

"Wait, what?"

Kat looks perplexed. "Huh?"

"*What* 'kid-thing'?" Blood whooshes into my ears as my brain processes the meaning of Kat's words. "*Lydia has a kid?*"

"Well... yeah." Now Kat's looking at *me* like I've got three heads. "Lydia has *three* kids."

"*What?*" I blurt loudly.

"*This is news to you?*"

I'm speechless. I nod.

Kat says, "But haven't you and Lydia been talking each other's ears off for the past month?"

I close my gaping jaw. "Are you sure about this?"

"She said so herself."

"*Lydia said she has three kids?*"

"Yes."

I stare at my sister for a long beat, trying to understand what I'm hearing and finally say, "When did Lydia tell you about this?"

Kat tells a story in which, in her version of events, for no apparent reason other than making small talk, Lydia blurted to my sister, a complete stranger at the time, that she has three kids while the two of them washed their hands in a bathroom in the hospital. And, instantly, I know it's the same conversation Lydia told me about—the one in which Kat blurted to Lydia, a complete stranger at the time, that she's pregnant. But, of course, since my sister *still* hasn't shared her baby news with me, it makes perfect sense she edited her version of the story. Holy fuck! *Is every woman in my life keeping the news of secret babies from me?*

I look out the window of the car, my mind racing through all the conversations I've had with Lydia over the past month in which I would have expected the topic of Lydia having *three* freaking children to come up. "I don't know which is mind-fucking me more," I finally say softly. "That Lydia has three kids or that she hasn't told me about them. It's a tie at the moment."

Kat says, "Aw, Colby. Don't feel too bad about it. Lots of single moms don't want their kids to meet a guy they're dating until they know for sure things are getting serious with him."

"Do lots of single moms fail to even *mention* they have three kids to a guy they're dating, serious or not?"

"Probably not," Kat admits. "But you and Lydia aren't even dating yet, right? You're still her patient. It could be that."

I feel like the air just left my lungs. "True," I say, barely above a whisper, though saying the word physically pains me. "Lydia and I aren't dating. That fact is now abundantly clear to me." I look out the passenger window of Kat's car, feeling utterly deflated. I thought Lydia and I had an unspoken understanding. I thought we both knew the feelings are there, we just can't act on them yet. I thought we were both feeling the same way... and now I'm not so sure. I run my hand through my hair, trying to get ahold of my emotions. "This sucks, Kat. This is making me think I've been feeling a whole bunch of intense feelings on my own. Maybe she honestly views herself as my friendly physical therapist and nothing more. Maybe she never talks about her kids with her patients and I'm just like everyone else to her."

"No way, Colby. Lydia's got strong feelings for you. We could all see it in the hospital, plain as day."

"I would have sworn that to be the case back then, but now I just don't know. Things have been weird between us since I got out of the hospital, to be honest. Way less intimate. Maybe she felt something for me in the hospital but it's gone now. Maybe her feelings have morphed into genuine friendship and nothing more. Maybe she doesn't know how to let me down easy."

Kat looks sympathetic. "I can't imagine Lydia's put you in the friend zone, honey. What sane woman would ever do that with you? You're literally the perfect man."

I stare out the window, my stomach churning. "I don't know,

Kat. If I had three kids and I was interested in a woman romantically, I'd tell her about my three kids. I'd want her to know what she was potentially getting herself into if she got involved with me."

Kat sighs. "Just ask her about it, honey. You're both adults. *Talk.*"

I sigh. "Yeah, you're right. I'll ask her about it at my appointment on Monday. I want to do it face to face. It's too important not to be able to see her face when she explains it to me."

We drive in silence for a long moment, during which I'm feeling physically ill.

"You're hurt?" Kat finally asks.

"Yeah, I'm hurt," I say. "I'm hurt and a thousand other things, too. Confused. Rejected. Kind of angry, to be honest. I mean, I can't help wondering: Does Lydia makes *every* patient feel like...?" I stop, too embarrassed to continue.

Raindrops begin peppering Kat's windshield and she turns on the wipers. "Like what, sweetie?"

My mind is reeling. Have I been imagining my soul connection with Lydia? Do I want her to feel the way I do so badly, I've been seeing signals and green lights that simply haven't been there?

"Does Lydia make every patient feel like what, honey?" Kat prompts again.

I don't reply.

"*Colby Morgan.* Does Lydia make every motherfucking patient feel like *what*?"

I sigh and look at my sister. "Like she's falling in love with him." I swallow hard, stuffing down my emotion. "Every bit as much as he's falling in love with her."

Chapter 25
Lydia

After two full days of making Mickey Mouse our bitch, everyone is now relaxing at our hotel pool for a couple hours before heading back to the park this evening for the Electric Light Parade. At the moment, Darren's father, John, is trying to teach Theo the butterfly stroke with no visible signs of success. My parents are enthusiastically re-enacting scenes from *The Little Mermaid* with Izzy and Bea in the shallow end. And I'm reclined on a lounger with Darren's mother, Michelle, watching the kids, drinking wine, and feeling distinctly like there's a boa constrictor wrapped around my chest.

Has my mother-in-law sharply regressed with respect to her grief about Darren? Or have I progressed so much in my healing in recent months I've left her in the dust? Either way, she seems as raw and tormented and *stuck* in her grief as ever, and I'm finding that extremely hard to be around. Should I be feeling as tormented as she is? Am I betraying Darren by feeling so happy lately? And, most of all, am I betraying Darren by constantly wishing Colby were here with us this weekend? Because that's what I've been doing. Wishing Colby were here.

Darren's mother takes a long sip of her wine. "Watching John with Theo in that pool is bringing back so many memories of John with Darren. Those two used to spend hours and hours in our backyard pool together, just like those two. I'd sit and watch them and smile from ear-to-ear."

I twirl the wedding ring I put back on my left hand Thursday night, right before meeting Darren's parents in our hotel lobby, and say, "Well, that certainly explains why Darren was such a fantastic swimmer."

119

"Darren wasn't just a fantastic swimmer. He was fantastic at *everything* he ever tried."

I nod, even though the statement is patently ridiculous. Darren was fantastic at a whole lot, don't get me wrong—but there were at least a couple things he royally sucked at. But, clearly, that's not something I'd ever say to his mother. Not back when he was alive, and certainly not now when he's become elevated in her mind to saint status.

Michelle continues, "Darren would have loved being here with us all so much. Don't you keep wishing he were here?"

I nod again.

And I'm telling the truth. I've honestly wished Darren were here at least twenty times since we arrived late Thursday night... but I've also wished Colby were here, as well, just as many times, if not more. And realizing that is suddenly making me feel like I'm going to vomit. How can I possibly wish *both* Darren and Colby were here?

"Darren would have adored seeing Izzy's and Bea's faces when they met Jasmine today," Michelle says. "Wasn't that a wonderful moment?"

"It was amazing," I manage to say, despite the boa constrictor increasing the pressure around my chest.

"And he would have loved seeing Izzy on Space Mountain. Oh my gosh! Her little shrieks were so adorable."

My palms feel clammy. My skin is hot. When Izzy screamed with glee on Space Mountain today, I didn't think, "Oh, how I wish Darren were here!" Actually, in that moment, I distinctly remember thinking "Oh, how I wish Colby were here!" But that was only because Colby had expressly told me Space Mountain is his favorite ride and I happen to know for a fact that Darren's was always Pirates of the Caribbean... Oh, God. I seriously feel like I'm going to barf from the pangs of guilt I'm suddenly feeling.

"I miss him so much," Darren's mother says, her voice breaking. "Every single day, it's a struggle to get out of bed."

I grab her hand. "I miss him, too," I say. "So much." But I don't add, "It's a daily struggle for me to get out of bed, too." Because, in truth, it's not. For almost two years, yeah, it was. But this past year, I've honestly found it quite easy to get out of bed every day. I've been excited about my life. Indeed, for the past month, ever since I met Colby, I can honestly say I've *leaped* out of bed every day, feeling almost drugged with excitement and joy. Is it wrong of me to feel happy? Should I still be feeling depressed?

"You still miss him?" Michelle asks, shocking me. In three effing years, she's never once asked me that question. What the hell? She *doubts* I still miss Darren?

"Of course I do," I say, finding it hard to breathe. "Darren was the love of my life, Michelle."

My mother-in-law nods. And then promptly breaks down in tears.

I move to Michelle's lounger and hug her. But, honestly, my stomach is churning. Should I be on the verge of tears at all times like Darren's mom? Should I still be dreaming of Darren every single night? Because, truthfully, I've been dreaming about Colby quite a bit lately. And, sometimes, my dreams are awfully steamy. Other times, Colby's simply standing there in my dream and I say to him, "You're out of your wheelchair, Colby!" And then we both scream happily and dance around. And then there are the dreams where Colby is sitting at the dinner table with me and my kids, or pushing Bea on a swing, or taking my evening jog around my neighborhood with me— and I feel overcome with serenity and joy. But, yeah, mostly, Colby's naked in my dreams and fucking me hard, or licking between my legs and making me moan in ecstasy...

"I have to admit," Michelle says, having regained her composure. "Spending so much time with Theo these past two days has been hard. A joy, obviously, but difficult, too. Theo makes all of Darren's exact facial expressions. Have you noticed that? God, he reminds me so much of Darren."

I look at Theo in the pool. I've always thought of Theo as Darren's mini-me, even though, of course, he's got my skin, hair, and lips. "Yeah, he definitely inherited Darren's facial expressions and mannerisms."

"I love the way Theo's nose crinkles when he laughs," Michelle says. "Just like Darren."

Memories of Darren's laughter flood me in a torrent and my eyes fill with tears.

Michelle grabs my hand and smiles. Clearly, she's heartened to see me crying.

"It's all right, love," she says, patting my hand. "I'm here for you, sweetie. We'll just get through this together, as we always have."

Tears spill out of my eyes. "I almost broke down when we were in line for the teacups today," I admit. "John smiled and winked at me, and he reminded me so much of Darren in that moment, I almost totally lost it."

My mother-in-law's smile widens. "I know, sweetie. Why do you think I'm having such a tough time? I have to live with John every day and he's Darren's spitting image. Every single day, I see the man Darren should have become thirty years from now. Every day I think, 'That's what Darren would have looked like if he'd lived long enough to walk Izzy and Bea down the aisle.'"

Okay, that does it. I cover my face and bawl.

Michelle hugs me, cooing at me the whole time. She kisses the side of my head. "It's all right, love. I know, honey. It's just so hard."

Finally, I pull myself together and wipe my eyes. I haven't cried like this in a full year. I don't feel like myself right now. I feel sick. Weak. Shriveled. Goddammit, I've been doing so well lately! And now I feel like I'm falling apart again. Why is she dragging me back to this dark place?

"I noticed you're still wearing your wedding ring, sweetheart," Darren's mother says.

I reflexively look down. I'm not sure why I moved it back to my left hand on Thursday night, other than I instinctively didn't want Darren's parents doubting my eternal love for their son.

"I'm so glad to see it," Michelle continues. She pats my hand again. "It means the world to me to know you're still so devoted to him, Lydia. I know Darren's looking down on you and thanking you for keeping his memory alive."

I feel physically ill. Confused. Riddled with self-doubt. *Guilty.*

Michelle sips her wine. "So I take it you haven't dated anyone since Darren passed?"

I swallow hard. Does feeling like you're falling in love with a stunningly gorgeous man count as "dating" him? I shake my head, too overwhelmed to speak.

"Not even a date?" Michelle says. "Not even a kiss?"

I shake my head again, my stomach churning. "Nothing."

"Oh, Lydia." My mother-in-law puts her hand on her heart. "I always used to say this about you to Darren behind your back, but I'll say it to your face now: You're the most devoted and faithful wife Darren could have chosen. Thank the lord you care as much as I do about keeping Darren's memory alive. *Thank the lord.*"

Chapter 26
Colby

The Morgan family's Sunday night dinner with Josh Faraday is over and done. As it turns out, Josh is an awesome guy, his Lamborghini and thousand-dollar shoes notwithstanding. As far as I could tell, Josh is sincere, funny, and intelligent. Far humbler than I expected him to be, probably due to his tragic childhood. And, man, did he make it abundantly clear he's deeply in love with my little sister. And the icing on the cake? Right before dinner, after Dax had let all of us hear rough cuts of the first three songs on the album he's been recording, Josh offered to send the tracks to that music-mogul buddy of his, Reed Rivers. As far as I was concerned, it was that precise moment when Josh earned "honorary Morgan brother" status in my book. I mean, obviously, I already knew the guy had impregnated my little sister, thereby reserving him a seat at our Thanksgiving table until the end of time. But, at least for me, a guy sticking his dick inside my sister without wearing a condom doesn't a brother make. On the other hand, a guy wearing his heart on his sleeve about his love for my sister *and* offering to help my baby brother make his lifelong dreams come true? Well, now. That's a guy who just went from being a sperm donor to *family*.

And now the evening is over and the house is quiet and empty, except for Dax and me. Josh and Kat left ten minutes ago, looking happy and relieved about how well both Josh and The Big Baby news were received tonight. Ryan left a couple minutes after Josh and Kat, saying he was headed to Olivia's. Mom and Dad left right after Ryan to take Ralphie for a walk, probably wanting to talk in private about their only daughter's shocking news.

And I'm just hanging, as usual. Specifically, I'm lying on my parents' couch with my leg up and my arm in a sling, thinking about Lydia. Only tonight, rather than thinking about how much I want to fuck Lydia, or how beautiful she is when she laughs, all I can think about is why she's never mentioned she's got three kids. I've thought about it a lot and decided it's not the existence of the kids themselves that bothers me. I like kids. If Lydia had done me the courtesy of telling me about her kids, I would have been down to meet them. A little bit scared? Yes. I admit that. But I certainly wouldn't have run away, screaming. No, the thing that's got me so freaked out about the whole thing is that I truly thought Lydia and I had been building something off-the-charts amazing this past month, that we were making a once-in-a-lifetime soul connection. But now I can't help thinking maybe what I've been feeling is a projection brought on by painkillers and post-traumatic stress and the fact that every time I look at her, I imagine myself with my tongue lodged firmly between her legs.

"Ho-lee shit!" Keane exclaims loudly on Dax's phone, drawing me out of my thoughts.

Due to some high-paying bachelorette party tonight, Keane didn't make the big dinner. So now he's getting the post-dinner scoop from Dax, who's sitting next to me talking to Keane via video chat. From what I can tell from Keane's image on Dax's phone, our neon sheep appears to be sitting in his car, dressed in a black cowboy hat, vest, and a large sheriff's badge.

"Yup," Dax says. "Mom had a photo of you dancing in your G-string."

"Oh, Jesus," Keane says. "How'd she find out?"

Dax tells Keane what Mom told all of us at dinner tonight: that thanks to the adult daughter of one of her friends attending a recent bachelorette party, Mom now knows exactly how her second-to-youngest child makes his living—and it ain't bartending, like he told her.

"Well, when the hell is she gonna tell me she knows?" Keane asks.

"She's probably planning a surprise attack," Dax says.

"Hey, Keane. Just so you know..." I pipe in, and Dax quickly adjusts his phone to capture my face on their video chat. "The three older kids voted not to tell you Mom found out. We thought it'd be funny to let Mom blindside you."

"*Bastards*. Dax is the only one who had my back?"

"Yup."

"Well, that's not nice," Keane says. "If any of you older kids were strippers and Mom found out about you, I'd totally tell you, brah."

"Dude, at age thirteen, you told Mom your dick-and-balls doodle was a rocket at lift-off. You can handle Mom just fine without any kind of heads-up from any of us."

Keane scowls at me again. "This is a tad bit bigger deal than selling a dirty doodle to a damsel, dude." He sighs. "Well, thanks for the heads-up, *Daxy*. That's why I love you the most. Colby?"

"Yeah?"

He smashes his nose right into the camera on his phone and says, "Fuck you."

I laugh.

Keane pulls back again. "So anything else exciting happen at dinner tonight?"

Dax and I look at each other and smile.

"Not really," Dax says. "Oh, wait. Yeah. There was one thing. Kat's preggers."

"What?"

"Yup."

Keane goes uncharacteristically quiet. Finally, he says softly, "Is she gonna keep it?"

"Yeah." Dax tells Keane the whole story and Keane listens intently, occasionally saying, "Whoa!" and "Oh my God."

"I guess I'd better meet this Josh Faraday dude at some point, huh?" Keane says.

"Sure sounds like it," Dax says.

"How far along is she?" Keane asks.

"Twelve weeks."

"Hooooo-leeee shit," Keane says, shaking his head. "Well, fair warning, dudes: the minute that kid is born, I'm gonna be gunning for top-uncle honors."

"Is that so?" Dax says. "Uncle Peen is gonna be babysitting in between shaking his ass for dollah billz and smoking bowls?"

"I never said I'd *babysit*. I'm just gonna, you know, hang with the kid whenever Mom's around to change its diapers and shit." He glances at the dash of his car and his eyes go wide. "Oh, shit. I gotta fly, fuckers. Thanks for the intel, Little Brahito. It's time for me to shake my ass for a room full of horny cowgirls."

"Another bachelorette party?" Dax asks.

"Nope. Just finished one of those across town. Peen Star's doing double duty tonight, pardner. Round Two of the rodeo? A Just-Got-Divorced Celebration with a bunch of MILFs. I got triple my usual fee. *Yeehaw!*"

"Watch yourself, Peenie Weenie," Dax says. "Divorcees are notorious cougars."

"I can only hope and pray you're right about that, son." He snickers. "Over and out, fellas. I'll see you brothers from the same mother on the flipside. Peen Star *out.*" The call disconnects.

Dax plops his phone onto the coffee table in front of us. "I think Peen Star's about to get laid by a divorcee."

"Maybe even an entire pack of them," I say.

Dax grimaces. "My brother is Deuce Bigalow."

"He says his cock isn't for sale. That it's just for fun after he's been paid for his actual services."

"Oh, yeah, that sounds like an ironclad plan."

"Ryan and I told him."

Dax shakes his head. "Fucking Peen."

"Fucking Peen."

Dax pats my good leg. "So it's just you and me tonight, dude. Keane's off getting laid. Kum Shot's off getting laid. Rum Cake's off getting laid. And we're sitting here watching Jimmy Kimmel."

I motion to my bum leg and arm in a sling. "I know what my excuse is. What's yours, Rock Star?"

Dax sighs. "Epic burn-out on the pointlessness of it all."

"Pointlessness? Daxy, for God's sake, you're twenty. You can get laid literally any night of the week. And it's already *pointless*?"

"Dude, I can get laid *too* easily these days. It's actually kind of mind-fucking to have girls be *that* aggressive with me. And this is just the beginning. What's gonna happen if 22 Goats takes off worldwide? We've just been playing local clubs and festivals and the pussy practically rains from the sky. I can't imagine what it's like for bands who play arenas and world tours. It's got to be kind of soul-sucking in a weird way. We're genetically built to have to work for it, at least a little bit."

"You're complaining about girls throwing themselves at you?"

"I'm not *complaining*. I'm just saying it's a head trip, that's all. I've got to consciously work at staying humble, you know? It's hard not to get a little bit jaded when you say hello to a pretty girl and thirty seconds later she's offering to suck your dick."

"Okay, so you're not into groupies. I don't think there's anything wrong with that, Dax. You've always been a deep thinker. I mean, there's nothing wrong with casual sex, but, yeah, it tends to get old for the thinking man."

Dax bites his cheek. "I'm not saying I'll *never* partake in the groupie dabble. I'm not a saint. But I'm feeling like my life is a room with a buffet featuring nothing but donuts these days, and no matter what I do, or which room I try to walk into, I keep getting escorted into that same room with all the damned donuts."

"Any man would get sick of donuts if that's all there was. Like I said, sounds normal to me."

"Right? It's not weird at all to occasionally say, 'Gosh, thanks for all the donuts, universe, but, um, can I maybe get a big ol' steak, once in a while? Maybe a loaded baked potato and some broccoli?"

"Not weird at all. I've been there myself. I'm no rock star, but, trust me, donuts definitely have a thing for firefighters. I'm surprised you're already sick of donuts at twenty."

"Dude. *Again*. Let me repeat. I'm not going cold turkey on donuts. I'm just saying they're starting to bore me, and that's making me question everything."

"Great. Question everything. And then write a song about it."

"I'm one step ahead of you, Master Yoda. Wrote the song last night."

"Play it for me."

"Yeah?"

"Of course."

Dax leaps up, grabs his guitar across the room, and then plays me a song about a guy searching for love that takes my breath away.

"Amazing, Dax," I say. "That right there is why I'm genuinely in awe of you."

Dax beams at me. "Thanks, Bee."

"One day, Baby Brother, the entire world's gonna know how brilliant you are. Mark my words. You're gonna be a star."

Dax's face flushes. "Thanks." He puts his guitar down. "So what about you, Old Man? Have you met any steak and broccoli lately? I noticed you looking at your physical therapist in the hospital like she was a bone-in ribeye."

"Bite your tongue, son. Lydia Decker is the finest filet mignon."

"So you're into her? Not my imagination?"

"I'm totally obsessed with her."

"I'm not surprised. She's hot as hell, man. And exactly your type."

"Daxy, you're a day late and a dollar short with this conversation. I already had the exact same one with Ryan, Peen, and Z the other night when you were in the kitchen playing cards with Kat and Mom and Dad."

"That's what you boys were talking about when you got stoned out of your minds? Ha! I knew it was something good. So what was the take-away? You're going after her, I assume? Or is she already taken?"

I sigh. "Funny you should ask that. Honestly, I don't know what the fuck is going on with Lydia at the moment. I just got some news about her that put me in a bit of a tailspin, actually."

Dax leans back onto the couch. "Lay it on me, Big Brother."

"It's a long story."

"I've got all night. As far as I'm concerned, the donut buffet is closed."

I take a deep breath and launch into telling my baby brother The Story of Lydia, from beginning to end. "I've been *really* clear with her I'm gunning for her," I say in wrap-up. "And she's never once shut me down, other than to say we have to wait because of that policy thing. And then, *boom*. Kat drops the bomb on me the other day that Lydia's got three kids she's never told me about and now I don't know what to think."

Dax purses his lips for a long moment. "Okay, you want my best guess, Cheese?"

"Lay it on me, Rock Star."

"It's a shot in the dark. Just a hunch. But if I were a betting man, I'd say Lydia's still legally married to the kids' father."

I feel like I've been punched in the gut. Just the thought sends my pulse racing. "No way," I blurt. "She told me she's single. She wouldn't lie to me about that. She wouldn't lie to me about anything."

Dax smirks. "Not mentioning she's got three kids after a month of listening to you talk about how much you love your dog isn't kind of lying to you?"

My stomach churns. *Shit.*

"Think back, Cheese. Did you ask Lydia if she's *married* or if she's *single*?"

"The terms are mutually exclusive. You ask one, you get the answer to the other."

"One would think. But maybe in this instance Lydia's interpreting 'single' as 'currently available because I'm separated from my husband.' Maybe she thinks if she tells you about her kids, your next question will be 'So what's the deal with their father?' And she doesn't want to mention that part to you yet because she's technically not single yet."

My stomach flips over. Lydia once mentioned she'd been to therapy in the past and that it had helped her during a "tough time." Was she referring to marriage counseling? Oh, Jesus. My head is spinning. I just don't know what to think. Did she have all three kids with the same guy? And if so, what's her relationship status with him? Has she been married? Is she friendly with the guy or is there some kind of drama there?

"Hey," Dax says, having an epiphany. "Maybe her husband wants to get back together with her. Or maybe he's a dickhead and they're having a huge custody dispute and she wants to finalize the divorce with him before she dives into anything with anyone else. Maybe that's why she's been insisting on waiting for physical therapy to be over before you two dive in—she's actually waiting for her divorce to get finalized."

I bite the inside of my cheek and remain mute. Everything Dax said doesn't sound like Lydia to me... but, then again, she's got three kids and I had no idea... and those kids weren't the product of immaculate conception.

"How long does it take to get a divorce?" Dax asks.

"I dunno. Google it. My laptop is over there."

My baby brother grabs my laptop and immediately begins tapping something out on my keyboard. "Okay," Dax says. "It typically takes anywhere from six weeks to twelve months for a divorce to finalize, depending on a bunch of factors." He looks up from my screen. "One would think it'd take longer to finalize a divorce when you've got three kids, right? Whoa, maybe her husband was abusive."

"Stop jumping to conclusions," I say.

Dax shrugs. "Why else wouldn't Lydia have told you about *three* kids? It's got to be something like she's got a restraining order on her ex."

"Now you see why I'm so tortured right now. It's definitely got to be *something* that's kept her from telling me. But *what*?"

Dax taps on my keyboard again. "I'm gonna research the shit out of her for you, baby doll. What's her last name?"

"Decker."

"Lydia... Decker." Dax taps on my keyboard again and quickly surmises Lydia's not on Instagram, Facebook or any other social media platform. "Interesting," he observes. Again, he taps on my keyboard and says, "Okay, I'm going old-school. Google. I'm searching 'Lydia Decker, physical therapist, Seattle, children, divorce.'" When the search results pop up, Dax positions himself so we can both see my screen. "Anything look particularly interesting to you?" he asks.

I survey the preview panes for the various links and quickly surmise the first page of blurbs is about *physical therapist Lydia Decker* recently helping to organize a fundraiser for a *children's* hospital last year in *Seattle*. "Go to the next page of results," I command.

Dax clicks and scrolls... and then gasps. "Holy shit."

I follow Dax's pointed finger and my heart stops. He's indicating a preview pane that reads:

Seattle *police officer, Darren Decker, age 29, was shot and killed today while answering a domestic violence call in South* **Seattle**. *Officer Decker is survived by his wife,* **Lydia Decker**, *and their two* **children**, *Theodore, age 7, and Isabella, age 4.*

I feel instantly dizzy. Sick to my stomach. And sick to my heart. "Lydia," I breathe. Every cell in my body has instantly awakened with a ferocious urge to comfort and protect her. To *love* her.

Dax clicks on the link and tilts the screen and we both review the article in stunned silence. When I'm done reading the horrific words on my computer, I close my eyes, too overwhelmed with emotion to keep them open.

"*Dax*," I whisper. "Oh my God. Poor Lydia."

"Yeah, I know," Dax says. "This is... *horrible*."

I shake my head. "That beautiful woman's been through fucking hell—the worst hell imaginable—and all this time, I had absolutely no idea."

Chapter 27
Colby

"Hmm," Dax says, his eyes trained on my laptop. "Every mention of Officer Decker's death says he was survived by his wife and *two* kids. Didn't Kat say Lydia's got *three* kids?"

"Yeah, Kat definitely said Lydia has three kids," I say.

"You think maybe Kat heard wrong?"

"No. She was sure."

Dax considers that. "Do you think maybe Lydia had a kid with some other guy after her husband died? It's physically possible. Her husband died exactly three years ago."

I rub my face. I can't process this. Lydia brightens every room she walks into. Her smile lights my soul on fire. She laughs easily and often. She's joy and serenity incarnate. *And she's been through a tragedy like this?*

Dax begins clacking on my keyboard again. "I'm gonna figure this mystery out. If Lydia's got a third kid, I'm gonna find him or her."

I close my eyes again. I can't believe Lydia hasn't once said something like, "Oh, *you're* having nightmares, Colby? Well, let me tell you what kinds of nightmares *I've* had.'"

"Wow, Colby," Dax says, his eyes still trained on my laptop. "It seems like this Darren Decker was a great guy. You totally would have been friends with him. He looks like one of your buddies from the firehouse." He continues scanning my screen. "Oh, here's a headshot. Wow, he was a *really* good-looking dude, huh?" He tilts my screen and I'm met with the smiling face of a guy who for some reason reminds me of Ryan.

"He's Ryan with darker hair and brown eyes," I say.

133

"Totally," Dax agrees. He clacks on my keyboard again. "Oh, *shit*. I found Lydia's third kid, bro." He tilts the computer screen toward me and I'm met with an article dated five months after Officer Decker's death entitled, "Slain Officer's Wife Accepts Posthumous Award for Bravery on His Behalf." Dax says, "Check out the photo."

Dax scrolls down... and there she is. *Lydia*. She's standing with a somber little boy and a heartbreaking little girl on either side of her, holding their hands. She looks devastated. Exhausted. Sick as a dog. *And unmistakably pregnant.*

"Lydia," I whisper. The image before my eyes is too much for my heart to bear. Those three devastated faces. The tragic beauty of Lydia's bulging belly. The Medal of Honor dangling from her little son's neck.

Every fiber of my body wants to leap through my computer screen and comfort those three poor faces. To somehow take away their pain.

"They look just like her," Dax says, referring to Lydia's kids.

I can't reply. I'm too wrecked by the sight of Lydia's swollen belly to speak. Too plagued by images of Lydia crying herself to sleep at night while trying to comfort those two poor kids. Or giving birth without her husband by her side. I keep seeing Lydia dropping her phone and crumpling to the ground after receiving that horrible, devastating phone call.

"Colby? Are you okay? You look pale."

I open my mouth to reply, just as the front door opens and Ralph bounds in, followed by my laughing parents.

"Oh my gosh, Ralph was in rare form tonight," my mother says gaily, putting Ralph's leash on a side table. "We went down to the dog park and Ralphie saw his little poodle friend and—" Mom's eyes lock onto my face and her expression instantly morphs into one of deep concern. "*Colby*? What's wrong?" She rushes to me. "Are you in pain?"

"Colby just found out something tragic about Lydia," Dax explains.

Mom's brow furrows. "Physical Therapist Lydia?"

I bow my head and rest my face in my hand. I can't have this conversation with my parents right now. If ever I wondered about the intensity of my feelings for Lydia before this moment, those doubts

134

have been erased now. Seeing the photo of her standing there with those kids... seeing her pregnant belly... Oh, God, it's now more clear to me than ever before: Lydia Decker owns me, heart and soul.

"This is horrible," Mom says after reading the article about the death of Lydia's husband. "Thomas!" she calls toward the kitchen. "Thomas, come see this!"

Dad ambles in from the kitchen holding a glass of water, a question on his face, and Mom tearfully explains the whole thing to him before turning to me and saying, "Lydia hasn't told you about *any* of this?"

"Apparently, it's not something she talks about with her *patients*."

Mom's face softens. She sits on the end of the couch and grabs my hand. "Sweetheart, you have no idea what's been going through poor Lydia's head—why she hasn't opened up to you about this. There's no right or wrong way to grieve. I'm sure she's doing her best."

"Can I ask you something, son?" my dad asks, and we all give him our undivided attention. Thomas Morgan rarely speaks, so when he does, we sure as hell listen. Dad says, "Do you feel like you're at a place in your life where you're ready to become the only living father figure to three kids?"

I open and close my mouth. *Whoa.* The dude doesn't fuck around.

Dad continues, "If you pursue this woman, there's no room to do it casually, son. You need to do it with a lifelong commitment in mind, at least as a real possibility. Or don't even start with her at all."

"Check out Pops!" Dax says. "Stealing a page from *Jerry Maguire!*"

Everyone looks at Dax quizzically.

"Remember? Cuba Gooding, Jr. told Tom Cruise not to steal the goods from a single mom? Only he didn't say 'the goods.'"

Mom pokes my good thigh. "You hear that, Colby Edwin? Don't steal the goods from single-mother Lydia."

"Okay, Mom," I say. "Got it."

Mom pats my arm. "Good boy. That's why you're my favorite son."

"*Hey,*" Dax says. "You're not supposed to say stuff like that, Mom. You're supposed to make each one of us think we're secretly your favorite."

"Well, of course, *you're* my favorite, Daxy," Mom says. "I'm just feeling sorry for Colby right now, that's all." She puts her hand to the side of her lips and stage-whispers to me, "You're honestly my favorite."

I laugh.

Mom giggles, gets up, and motions to Dad. "Come on, Old Man. Beddy-bye time for the old farts." She looks at Dax. "Will you help Colby tonight with whatever he might need?"

"Yup," Dax says. "I'll get little Colby Edwin into his dinosaur jammies, make sure he brushes and flosses his teethies, and goes peepee. It'll be good practice for when I babysit Kat's baby one day."

Mom rolls her eyes. "Oh my God. I still can't believe our baby is having a baby."

"She'll be fine," I say. "Josh loves her and he's not going anywhere. He's made that clear."

"But he doesn't plan to marry her," Dad pipes in, his tone not at all pleased.

"They don't need the paper, Dad," Dax says. "Josh will always take care of Kat and the baby. She'll be fine."

"Well, either way, there's nothing we can do about it now but love and support Kitty through this," Mom says. "Which we shall do." She grabs Dad's arm and puts her cheek on his shoulder. "Good night, honey pies. Sleep tight."

"Hey, Mom and Dad?" I say, halting their movement. "Can I ask you something?"

They look at me expectantly.

I take a long, deep breath. "Do you think being a father figure for three fatherless kids is something I would do well? I mean, if I were to pursue Lydia after my physical therapy is over, which is what I've been planning to do, do you think I'm up for a job that big?"

Mom smiles. "I can't think of a better man for a job that big, sweetheart."

Dad nods his agreement. "You want my advice, son? Take things slow with Lydia, especially while you're still healing. If you start feeling like the job is too big for you, leave yourself room to bail out before those kids get too attached. Better for everyone to know up front if you're not ready. The worst thing you could do would be to start making implicit promises to those three kids you can't or don't intend to keep. They've already been through enough abandonment. Don't let them get too attached unless you're sure you're in it for the long haul."

I nod. *Holy motherfucking shit. This is intense.*

Dad continues, "I've seen the way you interact with Lydia, son. The chemistry is undeniable. But there's more at stake here than your mutual attraction. There are five hearts on the line here: yours, Lydia's, and those three kids'. If anyone's heart is going to get broken, then be the Morgan man we've raised you to be and make sure the only heart that gets broken is yours."

Chapter 28
Lydia

I pad out of the girls' bedroom after tucking them in for the night and make my way next door to Theo's room. He's in bed in his darkened room, wearing his brand-new Mickey Mouse pajamas and reading the book about animation I bought him at one of Disneyland's souvenir shops with a flashlight.

"Time for bed, buddy," I say softly.

"One more chapter."

I take the book out of his hands and turn off his flashlight. "Sweetie, it's way past your bedtime. Your book will be here tomorrow." I sit on the edge of his bed. "Wasn't that a magical trip?"

"Best birthday *ever*."

"What was your favorite part?"

I'm expecting Theo to name a particular ride or attraction, but he surprises me by saying, "Getting to spend time with everyone."

"I know your grandparents sure loved getting to spend time with you and the girls."

"You think we cheered Grandma up a little bit? I'm not sure we did."

My stomach tightens. "Sure, we did. Spending time with all of us was the best medicine for her."

He looks unconvinced. "Grandma just looks so sad all the time." He chews the inside of his cheek. "Can I tell you something and you promise not to get mad?"

"I'll do my best."

He sighs. "I don't want to be mean, but it's hard to be around Grandma sometimes. I feel like she's mad at me if I'm having fun."

Out of the mouths of babes. "Let's just try to have compassion for Grandma, okay? Everyone handles grief differently."

"Yeah, but I heard her talking to Grandpa about you when we were in line for Thunder Mountain and she said she's not sure how come you're able to laugh and be so happy all the time. She *said* it was a good thing and that she was glad you're doing so well, but the *way* she said it seemed like she thought it was a bad thing you're happy."

My stomach turns over. "And what did Grandpa say in reply to that?"

"I couldn't hear."

I press my lips together. I feel physically ill. "Like I said, we just need to have compassion for Grandma." *Fuck.* "So how's school going, buddy? You haven't mentioned Caleb in a while. I take that as a good sign."

Theo shrugs. "It's okay."

"Is Caleb still teasing you?"

Again, Theo shrugs.

"Theo, tell me what's going on. Is Caleb still teasing you?"

"He doesn't tease me, Mom. He tortures me. But there's nothing anyone can do about it so I don't want to talk about it anymore."

"Dang it," I whisper. "Okay. Here's what we're going to do, honey. I'm going into that school tomorrow and I'm going to talk to Mrs. Dupont and demand—"

"No, Mom," Theo says sharply. "*Please.* Just let me handle it, okay? We've tried all that and it didn't work. No offense, but whenever you've done something to 'help' me, things have just gotten worse."

"But Theo. I can't let you—"

"*Mom, listen to me.* Caleb has way more friends than me. Every time Mrs. Dupont talks to him and tells him to stop being a jerk to me, someone else starts doing everything for him. He's like a freaking cult leader."

"Theo, I can't let that boy torture you anymore. He needs to be expelled from school."

"Just, please, Mom. I just need to turn invisible and get him to ignore me. That's all I have to do. If I need your help again, I'll ask you."

I rub my forehead. It's times like this that I wish Darren were here. He'd know what to do to help our sweet little boy. "Are you planning to physically harm him in any way, Theo?"

Theo scoffs. "Of course not. I'm just planning to be invisible and make him lose interest. It's not that much longer before the school year is over. Once we're in middle school, I'm betting he'll totally forget I exist."

I sigh. I truly don't know what to do.

"Mom, please. I've made up my mind. Just let me try it my way now."

I look into his dark brown eyes and I see Darren telling me to let him try to fight his own battles. "Okay, Theo, I'll let you handle this your way for a little while, just to try it out. But only if you promise me two things. One, you'll come to me right away the second you think maybe you can't handle things on your own."

Theo nods.

"Promise me."

"I promise."

"And, two, you'll always answer me honestly whenever I ask you how school is going. No lies or sugarcoating, ever."

"Promise."

I take Theo's hand and kiss it. "I'm so sorry you're going through this, honey. I'm sick about it."

"It's okay. I'm used to it."

Oh, my heart. I stand and open my mouth to ask if he's wearing his nighttime wetness alarm. It's the same thing I've asked him every single night before heading out of his room for quite some time. But, tonight, for the first time ever, I stop myself. Clearly, my boy doesn't want to be coddled any more. If Theo's not wearing his wetness alarm tonight, then that's his business. Come what may. He knows where we keep the extra sheets if he needs them. "Good night, my love," I say softly, bending down and kissing Theo's forehead. "I love you so much."

"I love you, too, Mom. Thanks again for taking us to Disneyland. It was even better than I thought it'd be."

"You're welcome. It was pure joy to see you having so much fun." *No matter what Grandma thinks.*

I stand over my beautiful son for a long moment, watching him fall asleep, my heart aching with love for him. But after a few minutes of me standing over him, staring at his perfect little face in repose, Theo opens his eyes and whispers, "Um, Mom? No offense, but could you go now? It's kind of creepy having you standing there watching me."

I chuckle, wipe my eyes, kiss his soft forehead one more time, and tiptoe out of the room.

Chapter 29
Lydia

After three nights of sharing a hotel room with my three kids and three days of getting sucked dry by the emotional vampire that is my mother-in-law, it's finally "me" time, baby.

I unlock the top drawer of my nightstand with greedy hands, rummage through my vast selection of vibrators and dildos and G-spot stimulators, and settle upon an extra-long, extra-thick silicone dildo with all the bells and whistles that, when I'm particularly excitable, gives me intense G-spot orgasms that make my eyes roll back into my head. It's not a sure thing with this particular piece of equipment, I must admit. My G-spot is an unreliable little bitch. But tonight my body is telling me to swing for the fences.

I slip into my bed with my chosen toy, my nipples hardening with anticipation, and slide Colby's dick inside me.

"Fuck me, Colby," I whisper softly, licking my lips.

And he does.

Oh, yes, he does.

I swipe into the pictures on my phone and find the one of Colby's smiling face I swiped off the Seattle Fire Department's website. It's the same shot of Colby I saw on TV the day of the fire. The one that made me get up from that table in the break room and head straight for Colby's room in the ICU.

"Fuck me, Colby," I breathe, looking at his gorgeous face and working the dildo roughly inside me.

Oh, yeah, I'm getting close now.

I imagine Colby on top of me. Not the broken and on-the-mend Colby I know, but fully healed version of him. A powerful version. Strong. Animalistic. In charge. My fingernails dig into Colby's muscled back as he thrusts and moves passionately on top of me. "Harder," I whisper softly, working the dildo to maximum effect.

Oh, yeah, I'm on the bitter cusp of cracking wide open now.

I swipe into the next photo on my phone—the photo I took of the message Colby wrote to me on the white board. The words he scrawled just before passing out cold.

After I snapped my photo of Colby's message, I quickly erased it, of course. I didn't want him to wake up and see it and feel compelled to apologize for it or take it back. Intellectually, I knew Colby's note to me wasn't real. That it was nothing but a drug-fueled hallucination. But I didn't care. My body wanted to pretend the words were real. My heart, body, soul... the tingling between my legs... all of those things wanted to believe in fairytales. I've already lived one fairytale, after all. Why not again? And so, I snapped my photo and erased the board, and I've been looking at it nightly ever since.

"Say it to me, Colby," I grit out, staring at the photo of Colby's scrawled message on my phone.

Strong, powerful, sexy Colby whispers the words he wrote on the white board into my ear as he gyrates on top of me and, just like that, my core releases with a powerful orgasm that makes my insides shudder and warp.

When the waves of undulating pleasure stop seizing my womb, I stare at the ceiling, tears welling in my eyes. *I'll never love another man.* That's the promise I made to my husband as I held his hand for the last time. And it didn't even occur to me at the time I might be over-promising. Indeed, when I said those words to Darren's lifeless body, they seemed as safe and true and unyielding as "the sky is blue."

And then I laid eyes on Colby Morgan. And everything I thought I knew about the color of the sky was no more.

My phone buzzes next to me on the bed. I pick it up and gasp. Speak of the devil. It's a text from Colby.

Hey, Lydia. I hope you had fun in D-Land. Can't wait to hear about it tomorrow. Our family dinner with Josh went amazingly well. Kat's baby news is now officially out! I'll tell you everything when I see you. Just wanted you to know I've been thinking about you and realized I owe you a big apology. I was dismissive about that employment policy and that wasn't cool. You're genuinely worried your job might be on the line if you get involved with me or if I flirt with you too much and I brushed off your concerns. I'm sorry. From here on out, I promise to be your friendly patient with a massive but well-hidden crush on you. When you're no longer my PT, I'm going to ask you out on a real date and hope to God you say yes. But until then, I'll keep my feelings well hidden, per your request. You're a beautiful person, inside and out, Lydia. Truly, the most beautiful woman I've ever met. I'd never do anything that even potentially puts your career at risk or causes you a nanosecond of anxiety. See you tomorrow, Beautiful. Much love, Colby

I stare at my screen for a long time, my mind and heart racing in equal measure. After reading and re-reading the message probably ten times, I finally tap out a reply that doesn't reflect how I feel in my heart in the slightest:

Hi Colby. I was just now lying here thinking about you. Thank you for understanding. Honestly, I can't wait for the day when you ask me out on a real date but now is not the time. Thank you for understanding. XOXO Lydia

I stare at the response I just sent, my heart aching, and finally tap out a quick add-on.

P.S. Just so you know, when I'm no longer your PT and you ask me out on a real date, I'm going to say yes.

Chapter 30
Colby

I look myself up and down in the mirror of the changing room, trying to see my nearly naked body through Lydia's eyes. Not too shabby, actually. I twist my torso to get a good look at the burn scars running down my left side, straight into the waistband of my swim trunks. That's a sizeable swath of scarring, but I kind of like it. There's no question I'm battle tested.

I let my eyes slowly drift over my body again—my tattooed pecs, abs, biceps, lats, and legs. I've definitely suffered some muscle atrophy over these past two months. But thanks to years of dedicated working out, I still look like a semblance of me.

And, hey, at least I'm out of that fucking wheelchair. Getting out of that thing has meant I'm living at my condo again. Driving my truck. My brothers and sister have been regularly stopping by my place to help me and walk Ralph, but, otherwise, I'm now able to take care of myself again. Oh, and *hello*! My sex drive is back with a motherfucking vengeance. As Keaney would say, "Yee-boy!" Holy shit, I'm a horny bastard again. Hornier than ever, actually, and I'm including that one crazy month right before college when I dated Megan Friar, the freakiest girl at my high school who, by the way, two years after I dated her became a mega porn star. So, yeah, I'm hornier than the time I dated an aspiring porn star for a month.

But just to be clear: my horniness is directed at one woman and one woman only. Oh, fuck, all I want to do is get inside Lydia Decker. I'm obsessed with the idea. I fuck Lydia in my dreams. And in my waking fantasies. The woman has invaded my cells. Written her name in Sharpie on my dick. And I'm pretty sure she stole off into the night with my sanity in a tote bag, too.

Lydia.

Every night without fail, I wack off, thinking about her. And most mornings, too.

Lydia.

Last week, on two separate occasions, highly attractive women brazenly hit on me. Once in a doctor's waiting room and another time while waiting in line at the grocery store. And I wasn't even remotely tempted either time. Why? *Because my heart belongs to Lydia.*

Lydia, Lydia, Lydia.

She owns me.

Every cell of my body pulses only for her.

Every molecule vibrates in her name.

My heart beats for her.

And yet...

Ever since I sent her that text four weeks ago promising to behave like her friendly patient until the end of my physical therapy, I've kept my word and been a good boy. Of course, I only sent her that damned text as a means to an end—to give Lydia the space and safety I thought she needed to open up and tell me about her kids and dead husband. But in four weeks she still hasn't taken the bait. Talk about a plan backfiring. Thanks for nothing, Ryan. Nice suggestion, fucker.

I take a deep breath and look myself up and down in the mirror one last time.

A promise is a promise, Colby, I tell myself. *No boners today.* At least not until I get into the pool. Yep, that's the plan. Keep myself from popping a boner when I see Lydia in her bathing suit until I'm waist-deep in the swimming pool and can hide it. *Roger that.*

I exhale, grab my walker, and slooooowly make my way through the curtain of the changing room... and instantly see my beautiful, sexy Lydia standing alongside the swimming pool in a bright red, two-piece suit. And, instantly, I know I'd better get my ass into the water *pronto.*

Chapter 31
Colby

No boners, no boners, no boners.

Lydia looks curvy and strong and healthy and smooth standing on the pool ledge in her swim suit. She's mentioned she does yoga in her bedroom every morning and crunches and push-ups every night, and I can plainly see the results of her efforts. She's tight where I like a woman to be tight and soft where I like 'em soft. Hot damn. The woman is much hotter than I fantasized she'd be—and that's saying a lot. In short, she's a goddess.

"Hey," I say, trying to sound casual as I make my way toward her with my walker. I take a deep breath and focus all my energy on not popping a boner underneath my swim trunks.

Lydia's caramel eyes overtly scan the full length of my body and linger noticeably on my tattooed chest. When she jerks her gaze back to my face, she's blushing. "You look great," she chirps, but her eyes tell me her sunny tone doesn't match her inner dialogue. She motions to the stairs of the pool. "Make sure you grab firmly onto the railing as you descend the steps."

With Lydia's help, I transition from my walker to the railing, telling myself over and over again not to pitch a tent until I'm waist-deep in the water.

"Don't put full weight on your left leg as you descend," Lydia warns as I go. "Lean on the railing, Colby."

When I'm about halfway down the steps, Lydia enters the pool and turns around to wait for me. She's waist-deep in the water beckoning me like a siren, her glorious breasts and abs and hips on full display as I slowly walk toward her.

"Good," Lydia says. "Take your time."

Before I've even hit the last step, I feel my dick hardening. Quickly, I shift my gaze to a physical therapist-patient duo behind Lydia in the pool—a male PT and a white-haired old lady—and, thankfully, my dick quiets down just long enough for me to get into the water.

Lydia grabs my hands and guides me into the pool. She says something, but I don't catch it because I'm too distracted by my thickening dick.

"I'm sorry," I say. "What?"

"I was saying that with strength training, we're going to do whatever you can tolerate from a pain standpoint. If you feel pain, we stop whatever we're doing. The key is gradually incorporating more challenging activities each week. It's got to be a slow, gradual process or you might hurt your muscles."

Okay, I can't process any of that. All I know is I'm mere inches away from her and that we're in our bathing suits and our hands are joined. All I know is I want this woman more than I've ever wanted anyone in my life. That I want to fuck her. Kiss her. Lick her. Suck her. I want to touch every inch of her glorious body. To feel myself inside her and hear the sounds of her pleasure. "Great," I reply, but only because it seems like she's waiting for a reply and that one seems like a safe bet.

"How do you feel?" she asks, leading me to walk slowly around the pool like a toddler learning to swim.

"Amazing, actually. The lack of full gravity on my limbs makes me feel almost like my old self."

Lydia peels her eyes off my chest. "I'm sorry. What?"

I smirk. Plainly, I'm not the only one feeling a wee bit distracted right now. "I said I feel almost like my old self in the water."

"Yeah, the gravitational pull on your muscles and joints is much less when you're submerged in water. That's why I'm such a huge fan of aqua-therapy. Okay, let's head over to the ledge now. We'll do some leg lifts." She guides me slowly toward the ledge by my hands.

As we move together, my hard-on is bulging between us. I can't imagine she's missed it. It's mere inches from her crotch and straining toward her like a sunflower leaning toward the sun.

I look down at her breasts. Her nipples are rock hard behind the spandex of her suit. Her skin is truly stunning. Smooth and sexy and a beautiful hue.

We arrive at the pool ledge and she backs me gently against it. She's so close now, I feel her body heat wafting over my wet skin across the surface of the water.

Her hands still clasped with mine, she whispers, "What's the story behind that tattoo on your chest?" She juts her chin at the phrase inked across my pecs: *Here Today, Gone Tomorrow.* "Did you get that after the fire?"

There's a splashing noise in the water behind Lydia's back. The PT-patient duo in the pool is walking behind us through the water, heading for the steps.

I wait, praying they're leaving.

Neither of us speaks.

Please, God, make them leave.

The male physical therapist helps his white-haired patient ascend the steps. He brings her a towel and walker. They chat and slowly walk toward the exit of the pool area. They walk through the door, still talking. And then they're gone.

It's quiet.

We're alone.

In the water.

About eight inches apart.

In our swim suits.

Holding hands.

Lydia's hazel eyes are locked onto my baby blues.

"Your tattoo?" she prompts.

Her chest is heaving. Her breasts look full and inviting at the water line. Her light brown skin is glistening with a sheen of water. She's smooth, curvy perfection.

"I got it two years ago," I say softly. "I've seen a lot of death in my job."

As if in a trance, she nods, unclasps her right hand from mine, and then slowly, ever so slowly, as water drips off her slender hand, she brushes her fingertips across the letters of my tattoo.

And that's it. At the touch of her fingers against my bare flesh, a white-hot rocket of desire shoots straight into my dick and shatters my resolve to keep the promise I made in my text four weeks ago. In a flash of uncontrollable desire, I grab Lydia's face, pull her to me, and crush my mouth greedily against hers.

At the first contact of my lips on Lydia's, she throws her arms around my neck and presses herself against my hard-on, and, just like that, every cell in my body explodes with the most intense desire I've ever experienced—a primal need to claim her, fuck her, lick her. *Own her*.

I open her lips with mine and slide my tongue into her mouth, eliciting a sexy, throaty moan from her that almost makes me come in my swim trunks. I slide my hand down her back, cup her ass cheek in my palm, and pull her flush against my hard-on.

She moans into my mouth and grinds herself wantonly into my dick, pushing my back into the pool ledge.

"Lydia," I breathe. "I've wanted you from—"

"Well, well, well," a female voice says, cutting me off, and we break apart like teenagers caught by a cop with a flashlight.

"Ramona!" Lydia gasps, leaping away from me and wiping her mouth. "This was the first time. This has never happened before."

The woman bends over the pool ledge toward us, a steely smile on her lips, and practically hisses her words. "Save me the bullshit, Lydia. *You're going down*."

"*Whoa*," I say, utterly shocked at this woman's bile. "Let's talk about this rationally for a second. It was just a kiss."

But the bitch doesn't acknowledge me. She's only got eyes for Lydia. Piercing, death-stare eyes. "It was so clever of you to reserve a station in the *clinic* and then sneak him into the pool at the last minute. I guess you figured no one would catch you breaking the rules in here, huh?"

Holy shit. I suddenly recognize this woman. She's that physical therapist who's always at the next station when Lydia works on me. Lydia told me she has it out for her, and that she's the one who showed her the policy in the handbook. What the fuck? I thought Lydia was just being paranoid when she worried about this woman gunning for her...

Lydia looks stricken. "Ramona, listen to me. This was literally the first time we've ever had any kind of sexual contact, ever, and it won't happen again."

Ramona. Wait. Why does that name sound familiar?

"I know what I saw. You were attacking him, Lydia."

"She's telling the truth," I say, my mind searching its memory banks to figure out where I've heard the name Ramona before. "*I kissed Lydia. She didn't kiss me.*"

Ramona shoots me an incredibly fake smile. "Unfortunately, what I saw was Lydia mauling you, Mr. Morgan. And there are clear rules against Lydia doing that—for important reasons, by the way." She straightens up on the pool ledge, a vicious smile on her face. "I'm sorry to say, after what I just saw, there's no doubt in my mind Lydia will lose her job at this hospital, and might not even be able to work anywhere in the state of Washington ever again. Sexual misconduct is a big no-no in our profession."

Lydia lets out a squeal of anxiety.

I grab Lydia's arm to calm her. "Ramona, there's no need for you to go scorched earth about this. I'm a thirty-year-old man. This isn't some form of sexual abuse of a vulnerable patient. I kissed Lydia and knew exactly what I was doing. I'm not some ninety-year-old guy with dementia. I knew *exactly* what I was doing and *I* kissed *her.*"

"There's no such thing as fault in these situations. There's two people kissing and one of them is a physical therapist and the other her patient. It's as simple as that. Even if I wanted to look the other way, I couldn't."

"Ramona, please!" Lydia blurts, her voice steeped in panic. "I don't know why you've had it out for me since I started working here, but I'm begging you to please—"

"I don't have it out for you, Lydia," Ramona says, a wicked smile curling on her lips. "I'm simply protecting your patient."

"What's your problem, Ramona?" I roar. "Are you fucking insane?"

Ramona's smile vanishes. "Keep your temper in check, Mr. Morgan." She looks at Lydia, her eyes burning. "Thanks to her outrageously inappropriate behavior, Lydia has now subjected this hospital to potential liability."

"*What?*" Lydia shrieks. She looks absolutely panic-stricken.

"The rules are black and white," Ramona says coldly. "No sex on the job."

Boom. I just remembered where I've heard the name *Ramona* before. A diabolical smile spreads across my face. "Hey, *Ramona,*" I say calmly. "About that no-sex-on-the-job thing, does that also apply to a physical therapist paying for sex in a supply closet?"

Ramona's eyes widen. She staggers like she's been shot.

I slide my hand into Lydia's, warmth spreading throughout my body. "Guess what Ramona here did back when I was an in-patient at the hospital, Lydia? She paid my little brother twenty bucks to fuck her in a supply closet. The supply closet across from the cafeteria."

Lydia's jaw is hanging open.

And so is Ramona's.

I continue, smiling like an assassin at Ramona. "I can't help wondering what this hospital and the state of Washington would think about a physical therapist paying a male prostitute for sex while on the job."

"I didn't..." Ramona chokes out. "You're lying. It's a fabrication. Never happened."

"Oh, really?" I say. "Because Keane was pretty damned detailed about what happened in that supply closet. He said he felt totally insulted by the twenty measly bucks you paid him to screw you—which he did upon your solicitation, by the way. He felt, based on usual market rates for his services, giving you three O's should have earned him *at least* a Benjamin."

Ramona sputters. Gasps. Looks like her brain is physically melting.

"I gotta figure screwing a prostitute while on duty would be enough to get your ass fired. Add a solicitation of prostitution charge and I'm guessing you'd lose your PT licensing, too. Actually, Keane wanted to rat you out that very day, he was so pissed about what a cheapskate you are. But I told him, 'No, no, little brother. Live and let live. I'm sure that's how Ramona lives *her* life—*live and let live.*'" I smirk. "But I guess I was wrong about you."

Lydia squeezes my hand and I squeeze back. For the first time since the fire, I feel completely like my old self again. And it feels amazing.

"I..." Ramona begins. She looks like she's on the verge of tears. "Your brother's lying. It's his word against mine. Nobody would believe a male prostitute's word over mine."

"Actually, Keane doesn't lie. But it doesn't matter because he's a total perv who took a video of you while he was pounding you from behind. He showed it to me and you can clearly see the side of your face."

Ramona turns sheet-white. "We were both consenting adults. I paid him as a *joke*."

"Oh, yeah? Well, if that's how you want to explain screwing a guy named Peen Star in a supply closet to your boss here at the hospital—oh, and to the cops, too—then be my guest. But that's not what Peen Star will say. He'll say it was a business transaction."

Ramona looks like she's going to throw up. "You're lying about the video."

"I'm not. But, please, test me." I hold her gaze firmly.

She looks like she's on the cusp of hyperventilating. "I want to see it."

"No. You're not in any position to negotiate here, Ramona. All you need to know is it exists and all four Morgan boys have seen it and we'll all support Keane's version of the story."

"Oh my God. Colby, please. Tell your brother to delete that video. I'll do anything."

"Damn straight, you will. You're gonna do exactly as I say. You're gonna turn around and march out of here and forget you ever saw Lydia and me today. You're not gonna say a word about it to anyone and you're gonna stay the fuck away from me and my girl 'til the end of time. Do you understand?"

"Send me that video."

"You're in no position to demand anything. That video is my insurance policy to make sure you keep your mouth shut."

She exhales. "How do I know your brother will keep his mouth shut?"

"You have my word. Keane will keep your dirty little secret if I tell him to because Keane, unlike you, is a good-hearted person who doesn't get pleasure from causing other people pain or misery. But I promise you this as a Morgan: if you ever fuck with my girl again, The Morgan Mafia will come down on your ass so hard, you'll wish you never walked through that door today. Count on it."

Chapter 32
Colby

Just as Ramona careens out the swinging glass door leading out of the swimming pool area, a new physical therapist-patient duo enters. The PT greets us warmly. Makes small talk with us for a bit. And then the pair heads into the pool to begin their workout.

Lydia turns to me, her face on fire, and whispers, "Oh my God, you're my hero. Is there really a video?"

"No. I was totally bluffing. And Keane's not a prostitute either, by the way. Just an idiot. But Ramona doesn't need to know any of that." I glance over my shoulder at the physical therapist and her patient on the other end of the pool and whisper, "God, Lydia, I feel high right now. That kiss felt supernatural. Ripping Ramona a new asshole felt incredible. Your nipples look amazing. Your skin. Oh my God, Lydia, I need to kiss you again as soon as humanly possible."

Anxiety flickers across her face. She glances toward the other people in the pool. "Yeah, about that... Would you be willing to ditch your session and grab a coffee with me? There's something important I need to talk to you about. Something I need to tell you."

My heart leaps. *This is it. Fucking finally.* "Everything okay?"

"It's fine. There's just something I need to tell you and it can't wait and I need to tell you in private."

"Let's do it. But here's an idea: my parents live ten minutes away in Bellevue. They have a small lap pool in their backyard they keep heated this time of year. Why don't we go there and finish today's session in private and talk as we do it? We'll kill two birds with one stone."

"Your parents won't be there?"

"Nope. They're in Portland for my cousin Julie's wedding this

153

weekend. And there's no risk of any of my siblings stopping by, either. Ryan and Keane went to my cousin's wedding. Dax is out of town for a gig. And Kat just got home from her trip to South America with Josh and she's obsessed with getting the baby's nursery ready."

Lydia twists her mouth considering.

"Come on, baby," I whisper. "*Here today, gone tomorrow.*"

Lydia makes a facial expression I can't decode.

Jesus Christ, this woman is a tough nut to crack. I flash her my most reassuring smile. "You still owe me a makeup session from that Friday you took off to go to Disneyland, remember? And now you're gonna blow off today's session, too?"

Lydia glances nervously at the other PT-patient duo in the pool.

"We're just going to talk," I coo. But, of course, I'm lying. I'm not only gonna kiss this gorgeous woman in my parents' pool, I'm gonna fuck her there, too. Because when I'm in the water, I'm feeling damned close to myself. But in this moment, I'll say anything to get her to my parents' house. "Lydia," I whisper. "Just say yes."

She bites her luscious lower lip, but she can't contain her sexy smile. "Text me your parents' address."

Chapter 33
Lydia

"You have reached the destination," the robotic female voice on my phone tells me.

I put my car in park and take in the façade of the Morgans' home. It's precisely what I imagined it'd be—a two-story, Cape Cod-style home on a quiet, suburban street. The exact house I'd scout as a filming location if I were making a movie entitled, "The Morgans."

I slam my driver's door shut and walk toward the house, clutching my purse in one hand and my damp bathing suit in the other. Oh, man, I'm nervous Colby's going to freak out when I tell him everything. And nervous Colby *won't* freak out when I tell him everything. And, oh, God, I'm horny. And relieved to finally get Ramona off my back! Oh, and did I mention I'm *horny*?

These past two months, I knew Colby had to be rocking a breathtakingly beautiful body underneath his hospital gowns and tight T-shirts. But nothing—and I mean *nothing*—could have prepared me for the beautifully scarred golden god in swim trunks I spied today in the therapy pool. Not to mention the hard-on jutting from behind his bathing suit. Even after everything he's been through—and everything he's still going through—Colby Morgan is smoking hot.

Oh, God, the way he tore into Ramona. I've never been so turned on in my life. In that moment, I probably would have dunked underwater to give him a blowjob if we'd been anywhere else.

And that kiss! Whatever self-restraint I've managed to tap into these past two months with Colby flew straight out the window the minute Colby pressed his lips against mine. Kissing Colby, feeling him wrap his arms around me and press his steely hard-on against me, was absolutely electrifying. But if I'm being perfectly honest, it was

155

also confusing and mind-fucking, too. My kiss with Colby today was my first kiss with anyone other than Darren. And it was every bit as enthralling and amazing and sexy and earth-quaking as my first kiss with Darren, if not more so. *If not more so.* And, frankly, that realization is royally screwing with my head right now.

I reach the front door of the Morgan residence. There's a yellow sticky note attached to it.

Lydia. Come in. I'm in the backyard.

When I enter the house, I find myself standing in a living room that's elegant yet warm. Neat and tidy yet lived-in. In other words, the room is the physical manifestation of Mrs. Morgan to a tee.

A bunch of framed photos sitting atop a black piano call to me from across the room so I stride over to them. Not surprisingly, every one of the pictures looks like the kind of stock photography that comes inside frames at purchase. My eyes graze over Morgans blowing out birthday candles. Caps and gowns. The whole clan standing at the railing of what looks like a cruise ship. Keane in a baseball uniform. Dax with a guitar. Ryan in leather pants, smoldering at the camera. Colby in a group photo at what must be the fire academy.

My eyes drift to what looks like a recent photo of Colby and Ryan. They're running shirtless in a pack of other runners in some kind of organized race. Holy hot damn. Both men are ripped as hell, glistening with sweat, and inked with tattoos—though Ryan has three times as many tattoos as his older brother. Oh, man, Colby is sexy as hell in this shot. Absolutely mesmerizing.

I take out my phone and capture a snapshot of the sexy photo—and then immediately crop Ryan out. No offense to Captain Morgan, of course. He's obscenely hot, too. But there's only one man I want to gaze at when I'm alone with my vibrator on a lonely night.

After editing my photo of Colby, I take in the rest of the photos on the piano and lock in on a photo of the five Morgan siblings as kids. Colby looks to be about Theo's age. He's standing before the camera, smiling and cradling the youngest Morgan in his arms who's clad in a diaper and sucking on a blue pacifier. Ryan is standing next to Colby's right shoulder and he's holding Kat—who seems to be about five. He's cradling her in his arms like she's a little baby, the same way Colby is cradling Dax. Indeed, now I get it. Ryan is using Kat as a prop to mimic Colby's exact pose with Dax. And Kat is clearly in on the gag. For her part, she's wearing a white towel between her legs and sucking on a pacifier, the same way Baby Dax is doing. Ah, I see. The towel is meant to be Kat's diaper. Oh, man, Ryan and Kat think they're so clever in this photo. They're laughing their heads off about the way they're copying Colby with Dax. I can practically hear their squealing laughter wafting off the photo. And what is the neon sheep doing in this photo? Well, a handstand, of course, as one does—especially when one is an epic goofball. And, of course, Keane is flashing his show-stopping smile and dimples, albeit upside down and with blood rushing into his adorable head.

Again, I pick up my phone and take a snapshot, simply because I know I'll want to look at this goofy picture of the Morgan Five at some point again, if only to lift my spirits whenever I'm feeling blue. The photo is pure joy incarnate. Silliness. Family. *Love.* Not to mention sweet Colby is the star of the photo in every way. The centerpiece. While everyone else is goofing off around him, he's the quiet port in the storm. The fierce protector. The lighthouse. Just looking at the photo makes my heart squeeze for the grown man the boy in the photo has become.

I stuff my phone back into my purse. What the heck am I still doing in here? Colby is out there in the backyard waiting for me. It's time for me to get out there and tell him the truth. That I'm a widow and mother of three. That I'm damaged—emotionally screwed up, far more than I ever let on. And that, most of all, I'm totally unsure how to do this thing with him, whether there's an employment policy or not.

I take a deep breath, gather my bag and bathing suit, and head toward the backyard. I don't know how Colby's going to react when I tell him I've been keeping the biggest part of my life hidden from him all this time. But there's no turning back now. However he's going to react, I'm about to find out.

Chapter 34
Lydia

I close the sliding glass door behind me and take two steps around a corner and there's Colby, slowly swimming the length of a small lap pool, looking much more like an injured fish on a line than Michael Phelps.

I make my way to the edge of the pool and watch him, gathering my courage. After about a half-minute, Colby spots me and abruptly stops swimming. He stands in the middle area of the small pool, staring at me, his chest heaving. Water is dripping off his muscular chest. His hair is slicked back, making him look like a European commercial for cologne.

"Hi," he says simply, his eyes blazing.

I wave.

Colby tilts his head. "What's wrong, sweetheart?"

I can't speak.

Colby drifts toward me until he's standing directly under me in the pool. "Tell me what's wrong, Lydia."

"I'm scared," I whisper, my voice almost inaudible.

"Of what?"

"I've got something to tell you. Something big I've been keeping from you. And I'm terrified you'll lose interest in me after I tell you."

Colby's beautiful face morphs into a warm smile. "Nothing could make me lose interest in you." He touches my ankle. "Join me in the pool. Tell me all about this big, scary secret down here."

I hold up the damp bathing suit in my hand, indicating I'm not pool-ready at the moment.

"You don't need a bathing suit to get into the pool with me," Colby says, and arousal whooshes between my legs. Colby smiles.

"Get naked with me, Lydia. Figuratively and literally. Let's bare our souls and bodies to each other."

"Colby," I whisper. I didn't expect him to cut to the chase like that. My clit is suddenly throbbing.

"I want you, Lydia. I want you more than I've ever wanted any woman in my life. There's no secret you might have that will change that. Have faith in me. Get into the pool."

I want nothing more than to follow his command, but I can't move. I've never been naked with anyone but Darren. Never been touched. If I do this thing, I'll never again be able to say that about myself—that I was a virgin when I met my future husband and have only ever belonged to one man. Am I truly ready to change that essential part of my life's narrative right here and now? Because, if I do this, there's no going back. I'll never again belong to just Darren the minute I strip off my clothes. Will I be okay with that after the pleasure is over and I'm lying alone in my bed later tonight?

Colby's eyes are smoldering. "How about I show you how it's done?"

I surprise myself by nodding slowly.

A huge smile spreads across Colby's face. He reaches beneath the water's surface, pulls down his swim trunks, revealing his hard dick, and plops them at my feet with a soft *splat* on the concrete.

My eyes train on Colby's hard-on under the water. It can't possibly be that big. Water has a magnifying effect, right? I look at Colby's face again to find him gazing up at me, his blue eyes smoldering.

"Lay yourself bare to me," he says softly, his cock straining. "Whatever you're about to tell me won't scare me off."

I take a deep breath. And then another one. And then I just nut up and blurt it out. "I have three kids." I brace myself for the look of shock that's sure to grace Colby's face—or maybe the look of hurt or anger that I've kept such a huge part of myself hidden from him all this time—but he looks unfazed. And so, I continue. "Theo is eleven. He's shy and introverted and funny. He wants to be a cartoon animator when he grows up. Or a rock star. He's currently taking guitar lessons. He's being bullied at school and I don't know what the heck to do about it. Isabella—Izzy—she's seven. She loves to sing and dance and read. She never sits still. She has no filter, God bless her. And she's a giant beating heart. My baby, Beatrice—Queen Bea—she's two and a half. She popped out kicking ass and taking names and making you work for it. She loves painting toenails— anybody's toenails—and making cakes in the sandbox at the park— but only *her* way." Oh, God. My heart is racing. I clutch my chest. "I love my kids more than life itself, Colby. They're my heart beating outside my body." I choke up. "I'm sure you're wondering about their father. You're probably assuming I'm divorced. But I'm not. Darren, their father, died three years ago. He was a police officer killed in the line of duty. Shot in the head while trying to save a woman from her abusive husband and..." I'm breaking down. Finding it hard to breathe. Staggering in place. "I've wanted to tell you about all of this so many times, Colby. *So many times.* To let you in the way you've let *me* in. I've wanted to be vulnerable and raw with you the way you've been, but I just couldn't do it. At first, it was because I didn't want to dump my stuff on you when you were lying in a hospital bed with broken bones and a broken spirit. And then, as time passed, and I felt so close to you, I admit I didn't tell you because... I was a coward. I didn't want to risk popping the magic bubble we'd created. And then it started feeling like I'd waited way too long to tell you and that I was being dishonest and then I freaked out and started worrying you'd be pissed or hurt I hadn't told you. That maybe you'd question the depth or sincerity of my feelings for you. Or maybe even my character. And I didn't know how to fix that, so I just buried my head in the sand and pretended... I don't know. Colby. I'm sorry. I have three kids and a husband I loved and I don't know how to 'date' and 'flirt' like a normal thirty-two-year-old woman." I wipe my eyes. My face is hot. I'm breathless. "I'm sorry to drop all this on you."

There's a beat. Colby looks nothing but sympathetic. Compassionate. And absolutely smitten.

"Finished?" he says softly.

I nod and wipe my eyes again.

"Well, I'm glad you finally got all that off your chest. But, sweetheart, I already knew about all of it."

I make a face like, "Whachu talkin' 'bout, Willis?"

Colby smiles. "I Googled you a month ago, Lydia. I've just been waiting for you to feel comfortable enough to finally tell me all that."

I'm utterly flabbergasted.

"I'm sorry about your husband," he says. "It pains me to think about what you've been through. It physically *pains* me."

My eyes drift from Colby's blazing blue eyes to his hard dick under the water again, ever so briefly. I can't help myself. He's truly delectable. "The idea of getting involved with me—a widow with three kids—doesn't scare you?" I ask, my eyes settling back onto his face.

"Oh, it scares me shitless," Colby says, making me chuckle. "But how about you let *me* decide what fears I can and can't overcome? Despite my current physical condition, I assure you I'm still me—and I'm not a guy who runs away from what scares me. I run toward it."

I nod. My skin is buzzing. And so is my clit.

"No more secrets," Colby says evenly, his eyes locked with mine.

I nod again, trembling too much to speak.

"I want you, Lydia."

I'm twitching with arousal and nerves. "I've never been with anyone but my husband," I confess. "I'd never even kissed anyone but him until I kissed you in the pool earlier."

Colby's eyes ignite. There's no doubt about it—this revelation has turned him on. "There's nothing to be nervous about. I'm gonna take excellent care of you."

My eyes drift to his hard-on again.

"I want you, Lydia," Colby coos. "Do you want me?"

I peel my eyes off his erection and gaze into his eyes. They're smoldering. Breathtaking. Forget the employment policy. *Here today, gone tomorrow.* "Yes."

A smile spreads across Colby's handsome face. "Then get your clothes off and get into this pool."

Chapter 35
Lydia

My clothes are off and lying at my feet. I look down at Colby in the pool, my clit throbbing and my naked skin erupting in goose bumps. Somehow, I resist the urge to cross my arms over my chest.

"You're a goddess," he says, his hard-on straining. "Get in, sweetheart. I'm gonna make you feel so fucking good."

Twitching with yearning and nerves, I lower my butt onto the pool ledge and then slip into the warm water right in front of Colby. And the minute I'm in the pool, he takes two steps toward me, places both his large palms on my cheeks, nudges his erection into my belly, and kisses me.

I throw my arms around his neck and press myself into his hard-on and then instantly pull back, worried I've been too rough with him. "Your leg," I whisper. "Does it hurt?"

"It's fine. Don't think about me. This is all about you."

"But are you okay?"

"I'm the best I've ever been."

He pins me against the ledge of the pool and kisses me passionately, and when he's got me quaking with desire against him, he slides his fingers inside me and begins swiping at my G-spot with firm, confident strokes. After a while, his mouth leaves mine and travels to one of my hard nipples as his fingers continue working me.

I begin quaking. Oh, God, he's good.

Colby gives one of my peaked nipples a good, strong suck, and my body reacts like he's just sucked on my clit.

"Oh my God," I blurt. My knees buckle, but he holds me up.

I reach down and stroke Colby's erection, eager to give him reciprocal pleasure, but, soon, I'm too enraptured by the movement of his fingers inside me and his lips on my breast to do anything but throw my head back and groan.

Colby kisses my extended neck as I throw my head back. "That's it," he growls. "Let go, Lydia."

I make a sound I've never made before. A kind of guttural groan mixed with a heave.

"That's it, baby," Colby says, nipping at my neck. "Let it out. You've waited a long time for this. Let go and surrender to it."

I feel like my eyes are about to roll back into my head. But I won't let them. Something is holding me back. "I want you inside me," I choke out. "I'm not gonna come. Just get inside me."

"Like hell you're not. Clear your mind, sweetheart. It's like riding a bike. Listen to my voice."

He begins whispering to me. Coaxing me. Seducing me with his voice. His fingers inside me feel insanely good. His wet skin against mine is delicious. And his words are perfect—variously dirty, sensual, adoring. I'm so turned on, I feel like I'm about to lose all control...

And yet...

I just can't get there.

I can't do it.

Something is holding me back.

Out of nowhere, Colby mutters an expletive, picks me up, and places my ass on the ledge of the pool. As water drips from my naked flesh onto the cool concrete, he unceremoniously spreads my legs wide, slides several fingers inside me again—this time deep, deep inside me to a different place than my G-spot—and he begins passionately eating my clit while fingering me.

And that's it.

I come undone into his mouth.

Whether I feel fully ready to do it or not, my body has its own idea.

As my insides twist and warp around Colby's fingers and onto his tongue, I press my palms flush against the hard cement behind me and scream with pleasure. Holy hell. It's so unlike me to scream in the throes of passion. I'm more of a quiet moaner than a screamer. Sometimes, a *whisperer*. Or, at least, I was a whisperer, back in the day. After three years of doing this with me, myself, and I and nobody else, I honestly can't remember what I'm normally like when I have an orgasm with a partner. But I'm pretty sure it's not like this.

In a frenzy, Colby pulls my twitching body off the ledge and into the water. I'm expecting him burrow himself inside me and screw the hell out of me now, but he surprises me by kissing me passionately and sliding his fingers deep inside me again. Deep, deep, deep his fingers go—until he's fingering that same unexpected spot way in the back of my core. A spot I didn't realize was an erotic button until now. But, I'll be damned, in short order, much faster than I knew was possible after an initial orgasm, I begin warping again, even more intensely than last time. Yet again, I shriek with pleasure, and this time the pleasure is so all-consuming, it brings tears to my eyes. Holy fuck, is this an orgasm or an exorcism?

"Are you on the pill?" he grits out.

"IUD. Oh, God, get inside me."

Colby pushes my back against the ledge of the pool, feels between my legs to find his target, and slides his rather impressive cock inside me.

"Lydia," he growls as he thrusts into me. "I've wanted to do this for so long."

I moan into his ear, tears streaming down my face. "This feels so good," I choke out.

"You own me, baby," Colby says. "You have no idea how much you own me."

I close my eyes and grip his broad shoulders, barreling toward another release. I've wanted Colby inside me so badly for so long, dreamed about it. Fantasized. But the reality of him far exceeds any fantasy. He's way better than I thought he'd be. Far better than anything I've ever—

My eyes shoot open.

In the midst of my pleasure, a lightning bolt of guilt shoots through me and settles in my stomach just as Colby stiffens, impales me with his hard cock, and comes like a rocket inside me.

When he's finished, Colby puts his forehead against mine and says, "Now that's what I call physical therapy."

He chuckles but I can't join him. I'm reeling. Bug-eyed. Mind-fucked.

Guilty.

164

How is it possible sex with Colby was *that* good? I knew it would be good, but how could it be better than I remember sex with Darren? I mean, that's crazy, right? I must be so starved for sex after three years, so desperate, I'm simply ultra-sensitive.

Colby kisses my neck, oblivious to the thoughts racing inside my head. "You're like a drug," he says, breathing deeply. "You're better than my fantasies."

I suddenly feel like a deer in headlights.

At my stiff body language, Colby leans back and searches my face. "What's wrong?"

I swallow hard, my heart racing. "I don't think I can explain it."

"Try." He strokes my arm. "Lydia, talk to me."

I wipe at my cheeks. "It just felt so good."

He chuckles, but when I don't join him, his brow knits. He studies my face intently for a long beat like he doesn't understand what he's seeing, and then says, "Come on, sweetheart. Let's get you out of this pool and dried off. Looks like we need to talk."

Chapter 36
Lydia

Colby and I are both wrapped in big, fluffy towels while sitting on a couch in his parents' living room. For the past twenty minutes, Colby has patiently listened as I've stuttered and stammered my way through explaining the cocktail of emotions I felt during sex with him. The pleasure. Euphoria. Relief. Elation. And *guilt*. And he's looked alternately thrilled, crestfallen, and sympathetic throughout my explanation.

Soon, our discussion winds its way to me somehow telling him about my conversation with my mother-in-law at Disneyland. The pressure I feel not to hurt anyone's feelings, to uphold Darren's memory. To be a good wife and mother and fulfill everyone's expectations of what a "good widow" is supposed to do. He asks me if I'm worried my children would react poorly to the idea of me dating someone, and I tell him honestly I think the girls will welcome Colby with open arms but that Theo might take a bit of time to warm up.

"Was that who called that day in the hospital when you were with me?" Colby asks. "Theo?"

"Yeah. Theo's being bullied by this little shit at school. That day, he was having a particularly rough day."

"What's he being bullied about?"

"It's a long story."

"I've got time."

I sigh. "Theo's a bed wetter. He's always had issues with his nighttime bladder control but his problems got much worse after Darren's death. I've tried everything I can think of to help him, both with the bedwetting itself and the bullying about it, but I'm failing him."

166

"How does that kid at school even know about Theo's bed wetting?"

"Sixth-grade camp."

"Ah."

"He was making real progress the month before camp. He hadn't had an accident in a while. So when he insisted he didn't want to bring his nighttime wetness alarm because he thought the other kids would see it and make fun of him, I relented and let him have his way. I packed the thing in a little black bag, just in case, where nobody would see it and know what it was. And then I packed him some extra sheets and pajamas and crossed my fingers and toes and sent my baby off. Turns out, I was sending him off to his slaughter."

"Poor guy."

"And now this boy Caleb calls him 'Pee-o' at school and douses his crotch with water every time poor Theo walks by."

"Jesus. Sounds like this Caleb kid is a serial killer in the making."

Tears well up in my eyes. "I've done everything I can think of to help my baby. The only thing left for me to do is switch him to another school but he absolutely refuses. He's trying so hard to be strong and ride this out until middle school, but I can see my baby's soul withering before my eyes."

"Keane had a problem with bedwetting into adolescence, too. All the way into middle school, I think. I don't remember how he got over it, but I'll ask him."

Relief floods me. For so long, I've wished Darren were here to help me with Theo. For so long, I've felt helpless and inadequate and anxious. I melt into Colby's hard chest. "Thank you so much. I'll take any help I can get."

Colby kisses the side of my head. And then my cheek. I turn my head to greet his lips with mine and, in short order, we're kissing desperately. In a flash, Colby pulls the white towel off my naked body and, as he continues kissing me, he begins massaging my clit.

I sharply inhale. "Oh, God," I choke out, just before a wave of ecstasy slams into me.

"Turn around," he whispers. "I can only lie on this side."

I rearrange myself so that Colby is lying behind me on his good side, spooning me, and two seconds later, he's inside me, thrusting in and out with slow, deep thrusts while reaching around me to swirl my hard, throbbing clit around and around. He moans and whispers into my ear, "I jack off every night thinking about doing this to you."

I moan with pleasure, moving my body with his. He pinches my nipple and bites at my neck and I'm gripped with indescribable pleasure—an orgasm so intense, it causes tears to spurt out of my eyes and roll down my cheeks.

Colby comes on my heels, a groan of ecstasy blurting from his lips.

When his body quiets down, he sighs happily behind me. "God, I love physical therapy."

I covertly wipe my cheeks and remain mute. That felt beyond amazing... *so why am I feeling sick to my stomach right now?*

"Lydia?"

I turn to face him and the minute he sees my face, it's clear he knows I'm feeling the same way I did in the swimming pool.

"I'm sorry," I say. "I thought I'd worked through all my grief, Colby. I really did. But having sex with you—having amazing sex with you—it's bringing up feelings of guilt and grief I didn't know existed. It's like the more intense the pleasure with you, the more intense the guilt."

"Lydia," Colby says, his tone breaking my heart. He covers his face with his hands for a long, nerve-racking moment, his chest heaving.

I wait, my heart thudding in my ears and my skin pricking with goose bumps.

When Colby finally lifts his head, his jaw is clenched. His vulnerability is gone. He looks resolved. Steely. "I've pushed you too hard," he says flatly. "You're not ready yet. I should have listened to you when you tried to tell me, but I listened to my dick instead."

"No, it was both of us. I wanted it, too. I still want it. I don't know what the hell is wrong with me."

"You've got to get therapy. You've got to figure this out. I don't know how to help you. I would if I could. But I don't know what to do."

I nod. He's right. I know he is. "I saw a therapist for a long time. I haven't seen her in a year. I'll go back."

He looks relieved. "You've got to figure this out, Lydia, or else this is gonna shatter me." Color floods his face and he looks down. When he's gathered himself again, he says softly, "I don't want to be your guilty pleasure, Lydia."

I'm too overcome with emotion to speak.

There's a very long moment of silence between us.

The look on Colby's face is pure anguish.

Finally, Colby exhales and says, "No more sex until I'm no longer your patient. I should have let you play by the rules in the first place. And while we're not having sex for the next two months, you're gonna get your noggin fixed up and I'm gonna meet your kids and find out everything there is to know about you."

I nod. "I want you to meet my kids, but I don't want to make it a *thing*. I don't want them to think I'm introducing them to someone I'm dating."

"Josh and his brother are having a grand opening party for their chain of rock climbing gyms on Sunday. Why don't you bring the kids? It's gonna be a big party with hundreds of people. Rock climbing. Live music. A face-painter. Half my family will be there, not just me. The kids will think they're at a fun party and that one of your patients and his family just happens to be there."

Elation floods me. How is this man so damned perfect? I grab Colby's cheeks and lay a passionate kiss on his lips. "*Yes*," I whisper, my heart soaring.

"Yeah?"

"Yes. *Thank you.*"

"For what?"

"For wanting to meet my kids."

"No need to thank me, Lydia. If you haven't figured it out yet, I'm a wee bit smitten with you."

169

Chapter 37
Colby

I'm standing with Mom, Dad, and Ryan at the Climb & Conquer grand opening party, half-listening to Josh Faraday and his twin brother, Jonas, welcome the large crowd and explain their new company's inspiring mission. Okay, that's a lie. I'm not listening to the Faraday brothers' speeches. I'm too distracted scanning the crowd for Lydia and her kids. *Where are they?*

"So, without further ado," Jonas says, "let's let the band play while you guys climb and conquer our rock walls and have a great time."

Josh grabs the microphone from his brother and shouts, "Thanks for coming, everyone. Happy Birthday, Climb & Conquer!"

Everyone in the place claps. Well, everyone except me. Clapping isn't practical for a dude on crutches. Not to mention a dude whose mind is currently preoccupied. Oh, fuck. This feels way more stressful than the handful of times I've met a girlfriend's parents. Kids don't sugarcoat their opinions, unlike adults. If Lydia's kids meet me and decide they don't like me for some reason, they'll surely let her know. I don't think that will happen, of course—kids and animals have always liked me—but I guess there's a first time for everything. What if today is the first time in the history of my life a kid meets me and instantly despises me? What will be my chances for a future with Lydia then?

For a while, I get vaguely distracted watching people get fitted with harnesses and ropes and start climbing the towering rock walls around us. I watch the band for a bit, talk to Ryan and my parents, grab some little sandwiches off a waiter that walks by. And, finally, I watch my sister on the dance floor across the large gym, gleefully shaking her adorable baby bump alongside her best friend, Sarah.

"Colby?" Mom says, drawing my attention to her. "Are you

okay? You look tired. Ryan, honey, go find Colby a chair. He's been standing on his crutches for a long time."

"I'm fine, Mom. Ryan, no. I'm fine."

"You sure?" Ryan asks.

"I'm good."

Ryan is about to say something in reply when Josh Faraday strides up to our group, a huge smile on his face. He greets everyone and makes pleasant small talk, ultimately offering all of us lifetime gym memberships. "Standing offer for you, Colby," he says, indicating my leg. "Whenever you're up to it."

"Thanks," I say. "Gimme three more months and I'll definitely take you up on that."

Josh glances furtively across the room at Kat and says, "Hey, Louise, can I talk to you for a second?"

Mom lights up. "You bet, honey." She takes Josh's offered arm and throws a goodbye air-kiss to the rest of us. "Excuse us, fellas."

"What's up with that?" I ask Ryan. I motion to Josh and Mom chatting furtively about thirty yards away.

"Josh is gonna pop the question to Jizz," Ryan says. "Mom said she went ring-shopping with Josh on the down-low last week, right after Josh and Kat got back from Argentina."

"No shit? Wow. When's he going to ask her?"

"Next couple of weeks, apparently."

"Wow. What the hell happened to 'Josh and I have decided, after discussing it like reasonable adults, we never want to get married, so please respect our decision and don't ask about marriage again!'?"

Ryan laughs. "Yeah, it appears Josh has a different idea."

"I thought he didn't believe in marriage."

"That was the initial scouting report on him."

"You think maybe watching his twin brother get married to Kat's best friend last month inspired him to follow suit?"

"I have no idea. But whatever caused Josh's change of heart, Mom said he couldn't be more excited about the idea now. Apparently, he bought Kitty a massive rock and he's putting together some epic, fairytale proposal for her."

"Awesome," I say. "Kat has always loved fairytales. She deserves to be the princess in her own."

"Speaking of Kat," Ryan says. "I've got to find her and talk to her about something important. Excuse me, brother. I'll catch you on the flipside."

And off Ryan goes toward the dance floor on the far side of the gym, leaving me standing alone with Dad and once again scouring the place nervously for Lydia.

When there's still no sign of Lydia, my gaze wanders to Mom and Josh again, just in time to see a dark-haired beauty tap Josh on the shoulder, talk to him briefly, and shoo him away. Wow, whoever that curvy brunette is, she's *exactly* Ryan's physical type. As I recall, my brother used to have a whopper of a crush on Kat's best friend, Sarah, and this woman reminds me of Sarah to a tee. I reflexively look toward the dance floor, thinking maybe I'll head over there and point out Sarah's doppelgänger to Ryan. From what Keane told me last week, it seems Ryan and Olivia are officially kaput. But, damn, I don't see my brother or sister anywhere. Shit. I want Ryan to see that brunette beauty, whoever she is. Hopefully, seeing someone like her out in the world will encourage him to keep Olivia firmly in his rearview mirror.

Movement in my peripheral vision catches my attention and I turn to find Mom dancing toward Dad and me with gusto. As she bops along, Mom is exuberantly singing along with the Spanish-language song the band is performing, even though, to my knowledge, Louise Morgan doesn't speak a single word of Spanish.

"How the heck do you know this song, Mom?" I ask when she arrives.

"It's 'Bailando' by Enrique Iglesias," Mom replies, as if this fact answers my question.

"But how do *you* know it, woman? It's in Spanish."

"They play it all the time in Zumba. I hear *all* the best songs in Zumba." She hits me with what I'm sure is meant to be some sort of Zumba maneuver and I laugh.

"Who was that brunette you were talking to over there? I should introduce her to Ryan."

"She's Josh's personal assistant. Daddy and I met her at Jonas and Sarah's wedding last month. And when I met her, I swear I had the exact same..."

Lydia.

Sorry, Mom. I'm not listening to you anymore.

My woman and her three kids are finally here.

Chapter 38
Colby

As Lydia walks through the crowd toward me, I stand stock still on my crutches, mesmerized. Her youngest kid, Beatrice, is perched on Lydia's right hip, sucking her little thumb, while Lydia's middle child, Isabella, holds her mother's hand and bops along happily to "Bailando" as she walks. Lydia's oldest kid, Theo, is shuffling stoically behind his mother and sisters looking like he'd rather eat a bag of shattered glass than be here. And Lydia? The sight of that woman always lights my fuse, but today, seeing her dressed in street clothes instead of scrubs—finally getting to see her as the natural mother she is—she looks sexier to me than ever.

Lydia and her kids reach my parents and me, and, while I try my damnedest not to look like I'm about to keel over with excitement and nerves, Lydia greets everyone and introduces her kids.

True to form, Mom jumps right in and begins interacting warmly with Lydia's kids, giving me a much-appreciated opportunity to hang back and observe the situation.

Okay, first observation? Isabella Decker is already Team Colby. She's all but winking at me on the sly. Theo, on the other hand, not so much. I'm not getting active *hate* from the little dude, but he's certainly not here to make new friends. And Beatrice? The jury's out on that little beauty, but only because she won't peek out from the crook of her mother's neck long enough to let me get a read on her.

The band switches songs from "Bailando" to the iconic opening guitar riff of "Play That Funky Music White Boy" and Mom squeals with excitement. She grabs Dad's hand, shouting, "Come on, old man! Momma Lou wants to dance!" and that's that. Off they go to the dance floor, leaving me standing alone with Lydia and her three kids.

173

"What happened to your leg?" Izzy asks, pointing.

I reflexively look down. "I broke it."

"How?"

"I'm a firefighter. I went into a burning house and a beam crashed down on top of it and smashed it."

"You're a *firefighter*?" Izzy looks at her mother, her face aglow. "Are you my mommy's *patient*?"

"Yes."

Izzy looks at her mother as if to say, "Gotcha!" and Lydia gives her daughter a warning look. Huh. *Interesting*. I'm not sure what that nonverbal exchange was about, but by the look on Izzy's face, she's just discovered the secrets of the universe.

"I might want to be a firefighter one day," Theo pipes in, and I peel my eyes off Izzy.

"Oh yeah? I'd be happy to give you a VIP tour of the firehouse sometime."

I'm expecting him to light up at the suggestion, but he doesn't.

"Or I might want to be a detective like my father. Or an animator. Or maybe a rock star or golfer."

Am I imagining the emphasis he just put on the word father? I clear my throat. "Wow, Theo," I say. "Sounds like you're gonna be a busy guy when you grow up."

Oh, shit. Based on Theo's dour facial expression, it's clear I've just royally fucked up.

"I know I can't be *all* those things when I grow up," Theo explains to me calmly—because, apparently, I'm a dumbshit. "I just meant those are all the options I'm currently considering." He leans forward. "*Because I'm eleven*."

"*Theo*," Lydia chastises. She looks at me and grimaces.

But I can't help smiling. Okay, cool. The kid's a smart-ass? Great. That's a personality type I happen to know a lot about. "It's okay," I say to Lydia. "Theo's right. My comment was patronizing. I'm sorry about that, Theo. Won't happen again."

Theo looks surprised. Maybe even impressed. "It's okay," he says, all his bravado from a moment ago gone. "I'm sorry. I didn't mean to..."

"It's all good," I say. "It's been a while since I've had a conversation with an eleven-year-old and I'm obviously pretty rusty at it."

174

The annoyed look on Theo's face from a moment ago is now gone, replaced by vague tolerance. "Hey, I've never talked to a firefighter before, so we're even."

Izzy pipes in out of nowhere, "I don't want a broken leg, but I wish I had crutches!"

I smile at her. "I know it seems like it'd be fun to have crutches, but, trust me, the novelty wears off fast." But then I remember I'm talking to a seven-year-old and hastily add, "Novelty just means it would stop being fun super fast."

"Oh, I know what *novelty* is," Izzy says brightly. "We had it on our vocab list at school."

"You did? Holy moly. What grade are you in?"

"Second."

"Wow. And you already had 'novelty' on your vocabulary list?"

Izzy nods. "I'm in the advanced vocab group. The Blue Angels. We get the biggest words so we can 'fly through the pages.' But I also know that word because my mommy always says, 'Okay enough, guys! The novelty has worn off!'"

I chuckle and shoot a little wink at Lydia—and immediately draw a death-stare from Theo. *Shit.* "Well, Izzy," I say. "I'm impressed. At your age, I didn't know what novelty was. And neither did any of my four younger siblings at that age, either. You're one smart cookie."

Izzy nods. "I'm a *very* smart cookie. They put computer chips inside my brain instead of chocolate chips!"

Lydia and I laugh and Izzy shoots me a gap-toothed smile.

"Man, you're really smart, aren't you?"

She flashes me an adorable look that makes me giggle like a fool.

Still laughing, I look at Theo to see if he's laughing along with me, but nope. That wink I shot at Lydia a minute ago was a deal-breaker for him, apparently. I'm done.

"Does it hurt?" Izzy asks, pointing at my leg again.

I peel my eyes off Theo's pissed off face. "Not too bad. It hurt a lot when I first broke it. But not too much anymore. It only hurts when I overdo it at the gym or when it rains."

"You've been overdoing it at the gym?" Lydia says. "*Colby,* you have to be careful to avoid injury. Slow and steady wins the race."

I shrug. *Of course*, I've been overdoing it at the gym. If I don't get back to my old strength and get back to work as soon as humanly possible, I'm going to combust.

"Your leg hurts when it *rains*?" Izzy says.

"Yup."

"Why?"

"I don't know for sure. I think it has something to do with how the barometric pressure of the atmosphere drops before a storm."

Izzy looks at me blankly.

Fuck. I just said "barometric pressure of the atmosphere" to a seven-year-old. Good God, I'm way worse at this than I thought I'd be.

"Well, if your leg hurts when it rains," Izzy says, "then it must hurt an awful lot living *here*."

"I know, right?" I say. "Welcome to Seattle."

Izzy rolls her eyes comically like rain is the most annoying thing *ever*—like it's a real pain in the ass during her morning commute to her job as an accountant—and I laugh my ass off at her sheer adorableness.

"You don't like the rain, Isabella?" I ask.

"Oh, no. I *love* the rain," she replies. "I love wearing my boots and splashing in puddles."

"Then why'd you make that face about the rain?" Theo interjects, his tone unmistakably annoyed.

"*Because he said the rain hurts his leg!*" she bellows, indicating my leg, her anger flashing from zero to sixty in a heartbeat... and I'm instantly brought back to the thousand and one times Ryan and Kat—whose age difference is the same as Theo and Izzy's—interacted in exactly this same way.

And that's it. *Boom.* I suddenly realize my nerves and awkwardness are totally misplaced here. *I can do this.* I've been training to love these three kids since I was two and a half years old when Ryan Ulysses Morgan came home from the hospital, followed by Kat, then Keane, and then Baby David Jackson. I sneak another smile at Beatrice, determined this time to win her over, but she nuzzles shyly into Lydia's collarbone again.

"Hey, Beatrice," I say softly.

She doesn't look at me.

"Beatrice," Lydia says. "Mr. Morgan is talking to you."

"Colby," I say.

"*Mr.* Colby," Lydia corrects.

I flash Lydia a look that says, *Seriously?* And she shrugs like, *Well, shit, I don't know what the hell I'm doing here.*

"Beatrice," I coo again. "You wanna know a secret? I think you're going to like it."

Beatrice *sloooowly* turns her head to look at me with a side-eye.

"Did you know we've got the exact same name, you and me?"

She knits her little brow.

"It's true. My name isn't Beatrice. It's Colby. But guess what everyone in my family calls me? *Bee*. Because Col-*by*. *Bee*."

Her face lights up with understanding. She points to herself. "Bea!"

I laugh. It's the first word she's spoken to me and her voice is the most heart-melting sound I've ever heard in my life.

"I know!" I reply. "You're Bea and I'm Bee. You're Bea because that's the *first* part of your name and I'm Bee because it's the *second* half of mine. So, if we put our names together we're *Bea-Bee*."

Oh, man, Beatrice loves it. She throws her head back and squeals with delight and every cell in my body surges.

"Bea-Bee!" she squeals, giggling.

Score.

"Hi, Lydia," Ryan says, coming up behind me. He gives Lydia a hug. "Great to see you again. Who are all these people who look strikingly like you only in much smaller formats?"

Lydia laughs and introduces everyone to Ryan, and much to my surprise and dismay, Theo throws nothing but sunshine his way, right out of the gate. *What the serious fuck?*

"Anyone wanna climb a rock wall with me?" Ryan asks.

Theo is instantly all over the idea, but Izzy declines the offer.

"I wanna dance!" Izzy says, doing a little wiggle in place. She motions to the dance floor across the gym.

"Okay, okay," Lydia says, laughing. "Come on, Queen Bea. Let's dance with your big sister."

"No, Mommy," Izzy says sharply. She gestures to me. "I want to dance with *Mr. Colby*."

177

My heart skips a beat. *"Colby,* please." I look at Lydia. "If it's okay with your mom."

"That's fine," Lydia says. "But Colby can't dance, honey. He's on crutches."

"Of course, I can dance," I say. "I'm not going to win any dance contests today, but where there's a will, there's a way. All I have to do is wiggle a little bit, right, Izzy?"

She squeals with delight and wiggles in place. "Let's go!"

Lydia leans into Beatrice's concealed face. "Would you like to dance with Colby, too, Bumble Bea?"

Beatrice shakes her head and burrows into her mother's chest. *Damn.*

"No?" Lydia asks incredulously. "But you *love* to dance, Bea."

Beatrice shakes her head again.

Lydia looks at me apologetically. "I don't know what's gotten into her. She's never shy like this."

Beatrice clutches her mother even tighter.

"No worries," I say. "This party is loud and exciting and I'm some random dude on crutches. If I were her, I'd burrow into your chest, too."

Lydia flashes me warning eyes and I suddenly realize what I've just said. I glance at Theo to find he's not the least bit amused by my unintentionally smarmy comment and that, in fact, he's currently plotting my murder. *Shit.*

I throw Ryan a look that says, "Help me," and my brother grabs Theo and escorts him away to climb.

"Let's go, Colby!" Izzy says, touching my hand and wiggling in place.

Lydia nuzzles Beatrice's face and says, "You wanna dance with Colby and Izzy or help me take some photos of Theo climbing the wall?"

Beatrice covertly peeks at me for a split second. "No," she says, and then she quickly hides in Lydia's chest again.

My heart skips a beat. Damn, she's an adorable kid. "Hey, Bea," I say. "Did you notice there's a face-painter in the far corner?"

Well, that gets Beatrice's attention. She pops her head out of her mother's chest and peers across the gym like a prairie dog on the African plains.

"Over there," I say, pointing. "See?"

"Mommy!" Beatrice gasps, jerking her little body in her mother's arms. "I go face paint! Mommy! Face paint!"

"Okay, Bumble Bea," Lydia says, laughing. She looks at me. "You found her Achilles' heel."

It's quickly decided Izzy and I will dance, just the two of us, and then meet Bea and Lydia at the face painter after they're done taking some photos of Ryan and Theo.

"But we're going to dance for a really long time, right?" Izzy says.

My heart squeezes. "Of course."

"Honey, Colby needs to take it easy. You can dance with him for one song and that's it. You need to be gentle with him. He's still healing."

Izzy's face lights up. Apparently, being gentle is right up this cutie's alley. "Okay, Mommy." She turns to me and pets my forearm with acute tenderness, like I'm a baby bird with a broken wing that just fell out of the sky and landed at her feet. "Come on, Colby," she purrs. "Follow me. I'll be very, very gentle with you while I show you how to do a shuffle ball-change."

Chapter 39
Colby

The Climb & Conquer party is done. The band just now finished playing its final song. Izzy's face is painted with kitten whiskers. Bea's cheeks are decorated with glittery stars. Theo and Ryan are now soulmates for life, having climbed four towering rock walls together over the past hour and a half. And my matchmaker of a mother, God bless her, has just insisted Lydia and her "kiddos" should come for a Morgan family dinner "as soon as we can wrangle everyone's busy schedules."

"Oh, we'd *love* to come for dinner," Lydia says brightly, her face aglow. "Colby has raved about your cooking, Mrs. Morgan."

"Please, call me Louise or Lou," Mom says. "Or call me Momma Lou, if you like. That's what everyone calls me these days."

I look at Ryan like, *What the fuck?* and he chuckles. No one in the history of the world has ever called our mother Momma Lou, as far as I know. And in our family, we don't nickname ourselves. It's just not done.

More conversation ensues and, soon, everyone is pulling out their phones to compare photos from the party. Ryan shows everyone the shots he snapped of Theo at the top of the highest wall. Lydia and Mom follow suit. And, suddenly, I find myself tasked with gathering all the party photos via air drop and putting them onto a Google drive for everyone to access.

"Sorry, I have no idea how to air drop photos to you," Lydia says sheepishly.

"Oh, it's easy," Ryan pipes in. "I'll show you."

Lydia pulls out her phone and hands it to Ryan, just as Izzy tugs on Lydia's shirt and urgently tells her mother she needs to use the bathroom. In a flurry of commotion, Ryan says he'll perform the air drop for Lydia. Lydia hands Beatrice to my mother. Mom and Dad, with Beatrice in tow, take Theo for one last climb while Lydia and Izzy hit the bathroom... and, just like that, I'm standing here alone with Ryan.

After my brother quickly transfers the designated photos from Lydia's phone to mine and his, we begin swiping through the shots together. Ryan stops on a particularly adorable picture of Izzy and me on the dance floor and we both gush about Izzy's unbelievable cuteness.

"She's a cutie patootie, you might even say," Ryan says, doing his best Keane impression, and we both laugh. Ryan adds, "Do you think Izzy was under the false impression it was the crutches that made you such a sucky-ass dancer today?"

"Hey, I'll have you know Isabella said I'm a *phenomenal* dancer," I say. "She told me so *three* times during one song."

"Dude, Izzy didn't compliment you because you've got actual dancing skills. She did it because she's a little girl who's dying to have a daddy."

My heart pangs. Truer words were never spoken. The kid wears it on her sleeve.

Suddenly, the enormity of what I'm embarking on here with Lydia hits me like a ton of bricks. Dad warned me there'd be three hearts on the line along with Lydia's and mine, and I'd approached today's meet-up with that mentality. But no warning from my father or good intentions by me could possibly have prepared me for the look of pure adoration on Izzy's face when we danced together. Or the way my heart ached when Beatrice shouted "Bea-Bee!" at me when Izzy and I approached her at the face painter. Or the envy I felt when Theo looked at Ryan like he was the second coming of Christ.

"Wow, these are great," Ryan says, drawing my attention to Lydia's photos of the party. "Huh. What's this one doing here?"

My eyebrows shoot up in surprise. Sitting on Lydia's phone is a snapshot of me taken when I ran a half-marathon with Ryan last year... except that Ryan is cropped out of the picture.

"I have no idea why Lydia has that shot," I say. "I didn't give it to her."

"You didn't send this to her and crop me out?"

"I have no idea how she has that photo."

Ryan smiles broadly. "Lydia must have pilfered it. Is it up on your Instagram?"

"No. I never post anything there. I just lurk."

Ryan purses his lips. "Isn't this one of the photos sitting on the piano at Mom and Dad's?"

I blush. *Holy shit.* Lydia must have seen this shot at my parents' house, took a photo of it, and cropped Ryan out. Why the hell does that turn me on so much?

Ryan smiles, apparently amused by whatever he's seeing on my face. "You brought Lydia to Mom and Dad's, did ya?"

I can't help shooting my brother a wolfish smile.

Ryan laughs. "Oh my God. You finally got to desecrate your virginal teenage bed, didn't you?"

"No, unfortunately, that fantasy is still unfulfilled." But I can't stop grinning like a douchebag. "We did, however, have sex in the pool and on the couch."

Ryan whoops. "That's the Cheese Head I know! Even one-legged, my Master Yoda still gets the job done."

"Yeah, well, don't get too excited. It turned into a bit of a shit show. As my physical therapist, Lydia's technically not supposed to dabble with me while I'm still her patient. She could lose her job if she gets caught. So, as great as it was, she felt weird about it afterwards and we both agreed not to do it again until I'm no longer her patient."

"But won't that be in, like, two or three more *months*?"

"Yeah. Don't remind me."

"*Dude.* That's a helluva long time to wait for Bonin' Time to come around again when you've already tasted the fruit and know for a fact it's delicious. Why the hell wouldn't you just get yourself assigned to another physical therapist? Problem solved. Bonin' Time restored."

"Yeah, I know that sounds perfectly logical, but it's out of the question. I wouldn't want to be on this journey with anyone but Lydia. And for her, being my physical therapist is some kind of spiritual journey. She's told me so herself. And now that I know about her husband, it doesn't take a rocket scientist to figure out why she wants to be the one to fix me."

Ryan knows all about Darren Decker. I told my brother about

Lydia's dead husband and three kids a full month ago, the day I found out about them.

"Yeah, that makes sense," Ryan says. "I'm sure helping you feels like some kind of therapy to Lydia. Like, she's getting to do the thing she wishes she could have done for her husband and never had the chance. In fact, I bet working with you is bringing up all kinds of memories and grief about her husband."

Jesus.

How the hell did he...?

And how did I *not*...?

Of course.

I suddenly get it in a whole new way. For Lydia, restoring me to my old self again... *healing* me... that's the way Lydia's healing herself. No wonder she wants to fix me so badly. I'm the last phase of her grief counseling.

"Bee? Are you okay?" Ryan asks.

"Hmm?"

"You look like you could tip over. You okay?"

My heart is racing. I clear my throat. "Yeah, I'm fine."

"Hey, let's see if there are any other photos Lydia pilfered from Mom and Dad's besides that one of you running." He clicks into the photos on Lydia's phone and starts swiping.

"Ryan, wait. Don't look through Lydia's photos. She didn't give us permission to—"

"She's got that one of the five of us as kids," Ryan says. "The one where Keane's doing a handstand."

I peek over his arm, instantly forgetting my objections to Ryan invading Lydia's privacy. "Why would Lydia want that one?" I ask.

Ryan grins. "Well, duh. Because she's head over heels in love with you, man."

Every hair on my body stands up at once. "How do you figure that from Lydia stealing a photo?"

"Because Lydia didn't steal *a* photo—she stole *this* photo in particular. This shot more than any other sitting on top of Mom and Dad's piano is a window into your soul, Colby. It perfectly foreshadows the man you became. But never mind. I didn't need to see this photo on Lydia's phone to know she's in love with you. It's clear enough from the way she looks at you."

I can't reply for a moment. I'm too overcome with excitement.

Ryan continues scrolling through Lydia's photos, looking for more of me, while I peek over his shoulder and feel ashamed of myself for not stopping him. "I don't see any others of you," Ryan declares, swiping through photo after photo of Lydia's adorable kids.

"We should stop looking now," I say half-heartedly. "We're invading Lydia's privacy and—"

"Is this Lydia's husband?" Ryan asks, stopping on a smiling photo of Darren Decker. He's in swim trunks, standing on the shore of a lake—and he looks ripped as hell.

"That's him," I say. "Darren Decker."

"What a stud." Ryan swipes again. This time, Darren is canoodling Lydia. Another swipe and Darren is wearing a sharp suit and tie. Another shot, and he's an action hero in his uniform. And now he's laughing on a bed with Theo and Izzy.

I should tell Ryan to stop swiping, but I don't. I should look away, but I can't. An emotion I rarely feel is beginning to bubble and gurgle inside my belly... an emotion I'm intellectually ashamed to feel, but feel nonetheless: *jealousy.*

Ryan continues swiping in rapid-fire succession—so fast, I can barely make out the scrolling images. There's Darren in swim trunks again with abs of steel. Darren holding a newborn, looking overcome with joy. Kissing Lydia's cheek, looking like he thinks he's the luckiest guy in the world. A scrawl of handwriting on a white board and then Darren wearing a pink, floppy hat while having a tea party with a tiny Isabella.

"Go back," I blurt.

"Huh?"

"Go back a couple photos. To the handwriting one." I glance toward the restroom to make sure Lydia's not coming back. "Hurry up."

Ryan swipes. "This one?"

My heart stops.

Love at first sight.

That's what the writing says... on a white board. And it's in my handwriting.

Love at first sight.

Holy fuck, it's the message I wrote to Lydia before passing out in the ICU the first time I met her.

"So that's the 'entertaining' thing you wrote to Lydia on the whiteboard, huh?" Ryan says. "Holy shit, Bee. You don't mess around."

I don't reply. I don't remember writing that message to Lydia, but now that I'm seeing it, I know it's the God's truth. I fell in love with Lydia the moment I laid eyes on her.

"Wow, and to think you were worried you wrote something pervy to Lydia that day," Ryan says.

But I can't speak. Now that I've seen those shots of Darren and my message to Lydia scrambled together, the reality of my horrible situation is slamming into me. I'm head over heels in love with a woman whose heart still belongs to another man. No wonder she cried when I fucked her. No wonder she feels guilty about how good she felt with me. *She's still his.*

"Colby?" Ryan says. "What are you thinking? You look like a madman."

Before I can reply, Lydia's voice rings out over Ryan's shoulder.

"Look who we found!" she says, approaching with Kat and Josh in tow.

My sister says something light-hearted, but I don't reply. If I try to speak, God only knows what madness will come out of my mouth.

Jealousy.

That's what I'm feeling.

Jealousy.

It's a dark bile rising up inside me.

Jealousy.

A dark acid washing over my flesh.

I want her to want me the way she so clearly still wants him.

Ryan hands Lydia her phone and she squeals with delight as she looks at the photos he sent to her—the photos Ryan took of Theo atop the highest rock wall.

"Oh my gosh!" Lydia says. "Look at Theo's face in this one. That's the biggest smile I've seen on that boy's face in three years."

I feel sick. Will Lydia ever be able to give me her whole heart... the way I'm ready, willing, and able to give her mine?

"Can I see that?" Josh says to Lydia, and she shows him a smiling photo of Theo on her phone.

"Would you mind me using this shot in some marketing for

Climb & Conquer?" Josh asks. "I couldn't have gotten a better shot with a paid model and photographer. Of course, we'll pay you for the shot."

"Oh, you don't need to pay me for it," Lydia says. "Of course you can use it."

"Let me pay you something," Josh says. "We're going to want to use that shot far and wide."

Lydia laughs. "Feel free. Theo will be thrilled to find out he's going to be your mascot."

As Josh thanks Lydia and they continue chatting about the photo, I catch Kat's eye and motion for her to come close. When she does, I lean over my right crutch into my diabolical sister's ear. "I need somewhere to talk to Lydia in private. Help a brother out, Kumquat."

Kat doesn't hesitate. "Josh's office in the back. The door locks. Josh and I will keep the kids occupied."

I nod and tune back into the group's conversation to find Izzy begging Lydia to let her climb the tallest rock wall before they have to leave.

"No, honey," Lydia says. "We need to head home for dinner and bath time."

I quickly flash my brother a hand gesture—a double-tap to my right eyebrow that tells him I need a wingman right fucking now—and Captain Morgan springs into action.

"Actually, Lydia. If it's okay with you, I was hoping to climb with Izzy before you guys head out. I got that great shot of Theo—I'd like to get one of Izzy, too. Wouldn't you and Colby like the chance to talk privately for a bit, anyway?"

Lydia looks at me. My jaw is clenched. I nod.

"Please, Mommy!" Izzy shouts.

"Sounds wonderful," Lydia says brightly, her eyes locked with mine, and Izzy squeals with joy.

Kat, Josh, and Ryan escort Izzy away to find Theo and my parents and Bea. And, just like that, I'm standing alone with Lydia... and the ghost of Darren Decker.

"Alone, at last," Lydia says, her hazel eyes darkening with heat.

"Follow me," I say. "We need to talk."

Chapter 40
Colby

During the slow walk on my crutches with Lydia to Josh's office in the back of the gym, I formulate the right words to confess all my sins to Lydia. I plan to tell her I peeked at her photos and saw picture after picture of Darren on her phone. That I saw the shots she pilfered from my parents' house. That I've finally seen the scrawled message I wrote to her on the white board... *and that seeing it made me realize the undeniable truth of my written words.*

But even as I craft my little speech in my head, I know I won't say a word of it to her. Not today, anyway. Not when I've seen the immortal Darren Decker on her phone and I now understand why she can't fuck me without crying.

Of course, I understand intellectually that Lydia will always love her dead husband. That's not a difficult concept for me to get. But in this one-of-a-kind fucked up moment, after spending the day with Lydia and her kids and realizing I truly could love them all if given the chance, after finally getting to see what I wrote to Lydia on that white board intermingled with evidence of Lydia's powerful love for another man, I'm not thinking with my *intellect*. I'm thinking with my big swinging dick. My need. My heart. My *jealousy.*

I want her.

I need her.

I've got to have her.

And I don't want to share.

I've got no right to feel this way and I know it. To feel this way is to be an asshole and a caveman and an idiot. But it's honestly how I feel in this moment. Whether I want it to or not, in this moment, jealousy is consuming me like a pyre.

187

Lydia and I reach Josh's office.

"After you," I say, and she steps into the small room ahead of me. I close and lock the door behind us, turn around, and then throw my crutches to the ground like a madman, pull her to me, and kiss the living hell out of her.

A flurry of greed and want and desperate need overtakes me. I've got her shirt and bra off. She's got my T-shirt up and my jeans unbuttoned. I bend down to suck on her nipple and almost lose my balance, thanks to my precarious one-legged stance, and she expresses concern.

"Get on the desk," I command in a voice that isn't my own. A voice that belongs to an asshole.

Lydia complies, no questions asked. She's breathing with a hiss—the air passing through her clenched teeth laced with ardent desire.

I limp and hop my way the short distance to a nearby rolling chair, glide up to where she's sitting on the edge of the desk, yank her pants and undies off, pull her naked hips into my hungry mouth, and begin eating her out like a starving man. I slide two fingers straight to her G-spot while devouring her clit with my tongue and lips and, within a minute, she's ferociously arching her back and shoving herself into me.

"Say you want me," I bark out.

"*I want you*," she grits out. "Oh, God. *Colby.*"

The sound of my name coming out of Lydia's mouth with such desperation makes my balls tighten and wetness drip from my tip. Still working her G-spot, I get up from my chair, bend over her, and suck her peaked nipple *hard*—brutally enough to make her whimper.

"I want to hear you say my name as you come," I say. "Come for me, Lydia. Say my name and come."

She whimpers again. Groans, growls, and throws her head back. Finally, she arches her back sharply, stiffens, and comes hard, my name on her lips... and then, fuck my life, she immediately bursts into tears.

I stand over Lydia for a half-minute, watching her writhe and twitch in simultaneous ecstasy and torment—and much to my shock, my instinct in this moment isn't to comfort her. It's to pound *him* out of her heart. But I can't take her the way I want to do it. Not with my

188

traitorous left leg, I can't. So I push my unbuttoned jeans down, collapse onto the rolling chair with my dick sticking straight up, and command her to sit on my cock. "I want you to look into my eyes as you fuck me," I seethe, my tone as hard as my dick. "I want you to know it's me who's making you feel so fucking good."

Lydia doesn't hesitate. She clambers off the desktop and straddles me in the chair. With a loud moan, she slams her hot, swollen pussy down onto me with such ease, it feels like she's been greased, and we both groan with relief and pleasure as my body burrows deep inside hers.

"Look at me," I command, holding her chin, and her glistening hazel eyes lock onto mine as she gyrates on top of me.

I grab her hips and guide her gyrations on top of me and she throws her head back and growls.

"No," I choke out, grabbing her chin again. "*Look at me, Lydia.* Look into my eyes, say my name, and come."

"I can't," she chokes out. She clamps her eyes shut and tears squirt down her smooth cheeks.

"Open your eyes and look at me," I grit out as I fuck her.

She opens her gorgeous eyes and I grab the back of her head and firmly hold her gaze in place.

"Look me in the eyes, say my name, *and come for me now.*"

Lydia shudders and moans.

I've never felt desperate like this before. I want to devour her. Ingest her. Take her into my bloodstream and keep her there. Lock her away in a tower and chain her to a cot. I'm a fucking beast, not the prince. I'm not the hero of this story. *I'm the villain.* "Lydia," I say, choking back my rising panic. "I'm all-in, baby. Don't you understand?" I suddenly feel desperate. Terrified I'm going to lose the only woman I've ever genuinely wanted. The only woman in the world who's ever set my soul on fire. *I can't lose her. I have to make her mine.* All of a sudden, a lightning bolt of greed hits me. Fuck him. *She's mine.* Lydia's husband might own her heart, her past, her children, her dreams. Maybe her very soul. *But I own her body like that fucker never did.*

"*Let go, Lydia,*" I growl. "Say my name and come for me right fucking now."

"Colby," she chokes out, her glistening eyes fixed on mine.

I grip the back of her head with one hand and guide her movement with the other. *"You're going to come for me now, Lydia."*

She whimpers. And then whimpers again, even more loudly. "Oh, God, Colby," she chokes out, her voice ragged. "I've never felt... Oh, God. *Colby.*"

Time stops ever so briefly... and then Lydia's muscles begin clenching and unclenching around my cock so forcefully, I can't hang on through it. With a loud moan, I explode into her with the most intense orgasm of my life.

Finally, when my body quiets down, I open my eyes and gaze at Lydia's beautiful face. She looks drunk. Like a woman who's just experienced intense sexual satisfaction. But her wet cheeks tell me she's a woman who feels guilty as hell about her pleasure.

Fuck!

I pass my thumb over her tear-streaked cheek, my heart throbbing even more than my bum leg. *"Lydia."*

She leans forward and puts her forehead on my shoulder. "I'm only crying because it felt so good."

I pull away, suddenly pissed. "No. Fuck that shit, Lydia. Do me a favor and respect me enough not to lie to me anymore, okay? You've lied to me enough. From here on out, you tell me the truth and nothing else, even if the truth hurts. No lies. No half-truths. And absolutely no more secrets."

The shocked look on her face makes me ashamed of the harsh tone I've used with her.

Sighing, I wrap her in my arms. My heart physically hurts. "I'm sorry," I whisper. "I'm losing my mind. Please forgive me."

"No, it's me who's sorry," she whispers.

I hold her for a long moment and finally say, "My instincts were right the other day at my parents' house. We should have stuck with the game plan. I convinced myself I could fix you with my magic dick, but, obviously, I can't. You're trapped, Lydia. You're trapped in a burning building and I don't know how to get you out."

Lydia pulls back from our embrace, her face awash in apology. "I want you, Colby. I honestly do."

"You think you do. But you're clearly not ready for this."

"I *do* want you," she insists. "Every bit as much as you want me."

I exhale a long, dejected breath. "I'm not sure when you say that you understand quite how much I want you."

Lydia opens and closes her mouth. And then hangs her head.

I bite my lip, trying to keep myself from losing it. Oh, God, the torment of this situation is almost too much for me to bear. "This was a mistake," I finally whisper, though it pains me to say it. "We need to go back to the original game plan and stick to it. You need to get some therapy from someone who knows what they're doing and I need to get my old body back so I stop feeling like an insecure little bitch about stuff I have no business feeling insecure about. And then we'll try this again."

Her head still bowed, she nods.

"And in the meantime, you've got to show me everything I've been missing out on, Lydia. The *real* you, including your kids. When we finally reach the finish line of my physical therapy and I'm no longer off-limits to you, I want both of us to be ready to hit the ground running. At the very least, I want you to be able to fuck me without bursting into tears."

She raises her head and puts her forehead against mine. "I'm sorry," she says softly. "I truly thought I was ready for this."

I'm trembling. I feel like my heart is physically breaking inside my chest. "I'm sorry, too," I whisper. "I feel like an insensitive dick for saying this, but the truth is I'm not the kind of man who can be any woman's consolation prize. I respect the life and love you shared with your husband. I really do. But if it turns out you're not capable of giving your heart to me as totally and completely as you gave it to him—if you're *never* going to be able to do that—then..." I trail off. There's no honest way for me to end that sentence. I don't even know why I started it. In truth, there's no circumstance under which I wouldn't continue pursuing Lydia—no pain that would stop me from fighting tooth and nail to make her mine.

"Then what?" Lydia prompts when it's clear I'm not feeling the urge to finish my sentence.

But I'm feeling too emotional to speak.

"Colby, then *what*?" she whispers. "Please, tell me."

I swallow hard and put my palm on her cheek. "Then nothing." I let out a shaky breath, my eyes locked onto hers. "Then you're just going to break my fucking heart."

Chapter 41
Colby

I'm sitting in the passenger seat of Ryan's sports car after the Climb & Conquer party, staring out the window at passing cars while listening to Ryan's playlist. So far, we've been graced by "Bailando," by Enrique Iglesias—what the fuck?—and then, thankfully, "Sex on Fire" by Kings of Leon and "Fix You" by Coldplay, the latter two songs making me think of Lydia. And then the current song came on—"Unsteady" by X Ambassadors—and hit me like a ton of bricks, even though I've heard the song probably twenty times in the past two months while being driven to and from medical appointments in Ryan's car.

When I've listened to the lyrics of "Unsteady" before today, I've always felt like the singer was my surrogate. That he was telling *my* story. Because, obviously, ever since the fire, I've been more than a little unsteady. Physically. Mentally. Emotionally. Spiritually, too, if I'm being honest. But today, after witnessing Lydia's tears, it's suddenly clear to me this song is far more about Lydia than it ever was about me. All this time, the woman I thought was so strong and put together has been broken and held together with Superglue and chicken wire and I didn't even know it. Here I thought I was the one needing fixing, but it was Lydia all along.

"You're awfully quiet," Ryan says, turning down the volume on the song.

"Why the fuck is 'Bailando' on your playlist?" I say. "You never listen to pop music."

"I do now."

I roll my eyes. "Who is she?"

Ryan laughs. "The most incredible girl I've ever met in my life.

192

I've still got to hunt her down, unfortunately, but I will. Mark my words, son. I will."

I shake my head. "You're so predictable. So Olivia's completely kaput, then, I hope and pray?"

"Kaput. I told Keane to tell you last week. He didn't?"

"Oh, he told me. I just thought maybe you were planning to do an on-again, off-again thing with Olivia, so I wasn't holding my breath."

"It's over for good. She's a fucking lunatic."

"Gosh, if only someone had warned you."

Ryan continues looking straight ahead as he drives, but he's smiling.

"So who's this new girl who's making you listen to 'Bailando'?"

"Samantha. She's a flight attendant from LA. I met her in a bar last week. I'm actually kind of in the middle of a big *thing* with her. I'll give you an update when I've got something to tell you. I can't talk too much about her right now or I'm gonna turn into Captain Ahab on your ass and it won't be pretty."

"I have no idea what that means."

Ryan chuckles. "Don't worry your pretty little head about it, Cheese. I'll give you an update when I have one. Now tell me about you and Lydia. How'd it go in Josh's office?"

"Good."

Ryan pauses. "That's it? *Good*?"

"Good."

"Well, at least tell me if you banged the hell out of her in there."

"It wouldn't be polite to tell you that. But yes, I did, as best I can do with my stupid fucking leg. I rang the bell like Paul Revere when the Red Coats were coming... and then she cried. The End."

"She cried? *Nice*. I love it when I ring a woman's bell that hard. So hot."

"No, no, it wasn't like that. She didn't cry tears of *euphoria*. I've gotten those before—and, yeah, they're hot as hell. Unfortunately, these ones were tears of *guilt*."

"*Guilt*?"

"About her dead husband. I'm the only guy she's been with besides him."

"Ever?"

"Ever."

"But didn't you say he died three years ago?"

"Yup."

"Holy shit. Lydia hasn't gotten with *anyone* since her husband died?"

"No one. He was her first at age seventeen—her first for *everything*. I'm the only guy to kiss her besides him, to see her naked, to have sex with her."

"Holy shit, Colby. That's so fucking hot. Lydia's a virgin with three kids."

"Yeah, well, it'd be a whole lot hotter if she didn't burst into tears every time I rang her bell better than her husband ever did." I sigh, my heart aching. "Clearly, her husband still owns her. For some reason, seeing those photos of him on her phone made that clear to me in a way it wasn't before."

"Colby, come on. She's a widow. Of course, Lydia's got photos of her dead husband on her phone. But you know what other photos she's got on there? Your note to her on the white board. That photo of you running that race. The shot of you as a kid holding Dax and looking like a saint."

For a long time, I don't reply. Finally, I say, "I want her, Ry. I *really* want her. And I'm scared to death I'm not gonna get her."

Ryan chuckles. "Colby motherfucking Morgan, don't be a dumbshit. You'll get the girl. You *always* get the girl."

"Maybe not this time. I truly think it's fifty-fifty I don't."

"Pfft. You'll get her. She's just gonna take a little more time and patience than you're used to expending. But it's okay. You already know she's well worth the wait."

A lump rises in my throat. I swallow it down and say, "What if, at the end of the day, Lydia tells me she's realized, thanks to me, she's simply not capable of giving her heart to anyone but him? What if she tells me she can't love me the way I'm so ready to love her? That would crush me."

Ryan looks away from the road briefly to smile sympathetically at me. "Just give her time. You're her first since her husband. Just having another guy's tongue in her mouth must be a huge head trip for her, let alone having another guy's dick inside her."

I swallow down the lump in my throat again. "But I can't

compete with the guy I saw on her phone, Ryan. In life, he was a stud, obviously. But in death, he's frozen in perfection. Larger than life. And to add insult to injury, these days I feel like half the man I usually do. I can't even climb a rock wall with her kid. I need my little brother to do it for me. Oh, and thanks for that, by the way. I really appreciated that. But it sucks, you know? I hate feeling like I can't be me. If I were in my old body, it would have been *me* at the top of that wall with Theo, winning that kid's heart today, not you."

"Colby," Ryan says softly. "I know you don't feel like yourself these days. But hang in there. You'll be back to your old self soon, brother, and then you'll lock your woman down."

I rub my eyes, trying my damnedest to keep my emotions at bay. "I love her," I say softly. "Seeing what I wrote on the white board made me realize that with full clarity. I've loved her since I saw her. And now that I've met her kids, I know I could love them, too. I know it in my bones we could have it all, if she'd give me a real shot. Although, come to think of it, Theo hates me so maybe we're dead in the water, regardless."

Ryan chuckles. "Theo doesn't hate you."

"Oh, yes, he does. The kid caught me winking at his momma. After that, he looked at me like he wanted to cut off my balls."

"Aw, come on. If you were in Theo's shoes, you'd be throwing major shade at the scumbag who wanted to bone your momma, too. Think about it: if Dad died and some dude came sniffing around Momma Lou, you don't think you'd be throwing daggers at the guy?"

"When did *Momma Lou* become a thing? We don't christen ourselves in our family, man. She's crossed a line."

Ryan laughs. "She didn't christen herself. It was Josh. Dad told me our darling momma got shitfaced drunk at Jonas and Sarah's wedding last month and started babbling to Josh about how much she wants the baby to call her Gramma Lou. So, of course, Josh saw the opportunity to kiss her ass and started calling her Momma Lou on the spot and she went batshit for it."

I roll my eyes. "Dude. I like Josh. You know I do. But he's kissing Momma Morgan's ass pretty damned hard these days. Actually, he's kissing all our asses. Lifetime gym memberships for all of us? *Really?*"

"Aw, come on. Kat said he's never had a family before and he's genuinely thrilled to be part of ours. He just wants his girl's family to love him. Is that so wrong? You don't think you'd do the exact same thing in his shoes? In fact, fuck you, you hypocrite. You just did the exact same thing in his shoes at the party. You don't think dancing with Izzy was kissing her tiny ass? I happen to know for a fact you don't dance, *ever*."

The man is right as rain, as usual. "Yeah, well, a lot of good all my ass-kissing did me today," I say. "Yeah, *Izzy* loves me. And Bea vaguely tolerates me, *maybe*. But Theo can't stand me."

Ryan laughs. "He'll come around. He's just going through a tough time."

"Oh, he told you about the bullying?"

"What bullying? No, I just meant he's going through a tough time seeing his mother showing interest in a guy for the first time since his dad died."

"Oh."

"Theo is being bullied?"

"Apparently." I describe the situation as Lydia described it to me and Ryan expresses deep sympathy for the little guy. "I want to help him so much," I say. "I just don't know how to do it, especially now that he hates me."

"Keane had that same problem with bed wetting, remember?" Ryan says. "You should talk to him."

"Yeah, I was planning to do that. Call him now. We're coming up on his exit soon. If he's home, we can swing by and talk to him tonight."

"Great idea. I'll call Zander, though. Peenie never answers his damned phone."

"True, true."

Ryan taps on his phone and the next thing I know, Zander's low baritone fills Ryan's sports car.

"Good evening, Captain Morgan," Zander says calmly. "To what do I owe this distinct pleasure, sir?"

Ryan and I both laugh.

"Hey, Z," Ryan replies. "Are you and the missus home right now? Cheese and I are a couple exits away from yours. We want to swing by and chat about something important."

"Yeah, sure. Come on over. Peenie just now walked through the door with glitter in his hair. We were just gonna chill out and watch a movie."

"Cool," Ryan says. "Put Peenie on for a sec, would you?"

A moment later, Keane's distinctive voice fills the car. "Yo, Master Yodas. What's up?"

"Hey, Peenie," I say, jumping in. "It's Bee. There's something important I want to talk to you about when we get there so put your thinking cap on." I explain Theo's situation briefly.

"Poor little dude," Keane says. "Well, you've definitely come to the right place, for sure. I pissed myself until I was almost fourteen."

"*Fourteen?*" I say. "Wow. I didn't realize it went on that long."

"Not something I broadcast to the world, Big Brother. Hey, should I text Daxy and tell him to get his rock-star ass over here, too? 22 Goats played a festival today. He should be done by now."

"Yeah, great," I say. "You know I'm always down to hang with Daxy."

"What's your ETA?" Keane asks. "I gotta hop in the shower before you lads get here. I've got baby oil and glitter and *eau de bridesmaid* all over me."

"Five minutes," Ryan says. "We're taking your exit now."

"Cool. Hey, do me a favor and swing through that Taco Bell on the way to my place, would ya? Just get me two of everything on the dollar menu."

"*Dude,*" Ryan says, grimacing. "*No.* That shit will kill you."

"*Dude,*" Keane replies. "*Yes.* I'm hungry and poor. And Mom has been so busy worrying about Colby lately, she's barely sent me any home cookin'."

Ryan and I exchange an eye roll.

"We'll get you some real food," Ryan declares. "And don't worry, it's on me."

"Well, gosh, thanks, Rummy-o. That's awfully cool of you. And when I say cool, please know I'm spelling that k-e-w-l. Top honors, brah, because you're the kingpin of kewl."

Ryan and I share a smile. There's nobody like Keane Morgan.

"Oh, hey, Z says he's hungry, too. He says he'll pay you back in cash and lifelong devotion if you pretty-please feed him, too."

"Tell Z we've got him covered and his money's no good to me,"

Ryan says. "Although I'll certainly take Zander's lifelong devotion if he's offering it."

"You sure you've got it? Z and I are growing boys. You're gonna need to get enough for six just to feed us two."

"Yeah, I know. This ain't my first time at the Feeding Peen and Z Rodeo, son. And, yeah, no worries about the money. I just closed a pretty big deal at work, so I'm flush."

"Another big deal? Dude, you're on fire, Captain! You're gonna have enough cash to open that bar of yours in no time."

"God willing."

"Oh, hey, Dax just hit me back. He says he's with Fish and Colin in Fish's van and they're just leaving the festival now. He said they're starving."

"Tell Daxy we'll get food enough to feed twenty. Just tell him to head straight to your place and that all three of them should put their thinking caps on." Ryan looks at me. "Are you cool with Fish and Colin joining the brainstorm, Cheese?"

I nod. "The more brainpower, the better. Sounds like Theo's bully is a particularly virulent strain of asshole. Honestly, I have no idea what I can possibly say or do to an eleven-year-old."

"Yeah, if Theo's bully were an adult, we could just threaten to break his legs," Ryan says. "What the hell do you say to a little punk-asshole kid who's terrorizing our boy?"

My chest warms at Ryan's use of the term "our boy" to reference Theo. Now, see? That's why I love that guy the most.

"Okay, dudes," Keane says, "I gotta jump in the shower and wash the Peen Star off my hot bod before you get here with my grub-a-dub-dub."

"Get to it, Peenie Weenie," I say. "And thanks so much for being willing to help me figure out this thing with Theo. It means a lot to me."

"Are you kidding me? This is the first time you've asked me to help you with anything in my entire life. I feel like I've been knighted or something." He chuckles. "See you soon, big brothers. Peace out."

Chapter 42
Lydia

"It sure sounds like you've kept him at an emotional distance, Lydia," my therapist, Dr. Aabrams, says.

I nod.

"No doubt because of this acute fear of loss we've been discussing. Plus, I'd venture an educated guess you're probably keeping the fantasy alive for yourself to some degree by keeping him in the dark."

I look at her quizzically. "The 'fantasy'?"

"That Colby is Darren," she says matter-of-factly.

My mouth hangs open.

"It's never occurred to you that Colby might, to some degree, be an emotional stand-in for Darren?"

My cheeks feel hot. I shake my head.

"I think it's quite possible your feelings for Colby might, in part, be a transference of your feelings for Darren. In other words, you've been projecting your love for Darren onto Colby and assuming a shared intimacy that just isn't there."

I feel physically ill. I clutch my stomach. "I don't think so."

My therapist presses her lips together. It's what she always does when she thinks I'm full of shit.

"What?" I ask.

"You've expressed how important it is to you to continue being Colby's physical therapist."

"It is."

"And how much you want to be the one to heal him—that it feels like a spiritual mandate for you to be on this journey with him." She raises her eyebrows like she's waiting for me to say "Aha!" And when I don't, she adds, "Lydia, I don't doubt you have strong feelings for Colby. But right now, while he's still your patient and you're caught up in this journey of healing him, not to mention having sex with him—which, as we've discussed, theoretically puts your job and licensing at risk—I think things are way too confusing for you to process all your conflicting emotions. In my opinion, Colby's instincts were right on the money: you should abstain from a sexual relationship with Colby until such time as he's no longer your patient to give you time to sort things out, one thing at a time."

"We've already agreed to abstain. It's only a couple months. It shouldn't be that hard. Before Colby, I went three years without sex."

"That's a start. But fair warning: abstaining alone isn't going to be enough. If you don't use this period of abstinence to achieve genuine emotional intimacy with Colby, then in two months you'll simply be sexless and in the exact same emotional spot as you are right now. You need to let him in during this period of celibacy, Lydia. You need to let down your guard."

"That's what Colby said. He said he wants to get to know the kids."

"Well, that's one aspect, certainly—although I'd caution you not to make implicit promises to the kids about Colby yet. Proceed slowly there."

I nod.

"I'd suggest you cast Colby as your friend until you're confident he's going to become more than that for the long haul."

I nod.

"But besides the kids, what I'm talking about has more to do with you letting Colby get to know the real *you* over the next two months. Talk to him. Tell him everything. Start at the beginning and don't stop telling him."

"Oh, jeez, Doc. That's not going to be a short conversation."

"Good. It shouldn't be. It should be a two-month-long conversation, maybe more. Do it an hour or two at time, if need be. Take it slow. Open up to him. Be vulnerable. Cry if you have to. And by the time you've reached the end of Colby's physical therapy, you'll have forged a genuine, beautiful friendship. And that's when you'll know if you're truly ready to take things to the next level or leave things in the friend zone, after all."

I take a shaky breath. "You think if I do that, I'll be ready to have sex with Colby without feeling all that horrible guilt?"

"I do. I truly do."

I sigh with relief.

"Either that, or you'll realize your feelings for Colby were a transference, after all. Either way, I think you'll have full clarity. Sex—especially good sex—has a way of clouding people's judgment. And it sure as heck sounds like the two of you had some damned good sex."

We both laugh.

"So, yeah, speaking of that..." I say. "Are you suggesting *literally* no sexual contact at all with Colby for two months? Not even kissing?"

She looks at me like I'm a naughty puppy. "*Lydia.*"

I laugh. "Sorry."

"Yes, I'm suggesting you follow the rules of your employment and the state of Washington's licensing for physical therapists and that you toe the line completely, without room for interpretation."

"Damn."

She smiles sympathetically at me. "I think the stress of breaking the rules is one source of your guilt, don't you?"

"Yes, I do. Most definitely."

"You've always been a rule-follower."

I sigh. "Yeah, I know."

"But that doesn't mean you can't touch him. You have to touch him for your job, after all. So here's what I recommend you do: follow the Jane Austen standard of conduct. If Lizzie Bennett and Mr. Darcy would be able to do it in civilized society, it's on the table. Otherwise, don't do it with Colby while he's your patient."

I twist my mouth. "Okay. So touching his hand is okay, then? Because Mr. Darcy touched Lizzie's hand and kissed the top of it."

The doctor laughs. "Already looking for a loophole, are you?"

I blush. "He's really, really hot, Doc."

Dr. Aabrams rolls her eyes. "Sure, go for it. Touch hands. Actually, you know what? Hand-holding can be incredibly intimate and erotic when you're not allowed to do anything else. In fact, bonus points: if you hold Colby's hand while opening up to him emotionally, I think you'll be surprised at how arousing and intimate that simple touch will become for you, especially as you get closer and closer to him emotionally. I actually tell lots of my patients to start with the simplest, least threatening forms of touching when they're dealing with a sexual dysfunction or trauma."

"Oh, I don't have a sexual *dysfunction*, Doctor. To the contrary, I was a bat out of hell with Colby. I'm sure the neighbors thought someone was being gutted in that pool."

She looks at me sympathetically again. "Lydia, sobbing and feeling extreme guilt or shame upon reaching intense orgasm is definitely not *functional*."

I grimace. "Good point."

"But don't worry. I truly think this game plan is going to work wonders for you. Make it a game if you have to. The Celibacy Game. For the next two months, you're only allowed to touch hands while you open your heart to him. Strive for emotional intimacy with him first and, hopefully, physical intimacy will follow naturally and beautifully two months from now."

Blood is whooshing into my ears. Not to mention my crotch. "Okay. Thank you. I'm super excited to give it a try."

My doctor smiles and says, "Lydia, I predict by the time you reach the finish line of Colby's physical therapy, you'll know exactly what you want and won't feel guilt or shame about going after it."

Chapter 43
Lydia

On an evening when Izzy and Bea are getting mani pedis with my next door neighbor and babysitter, Rosalind, and then returning to her place afterwards to watch *Enchanted* (again), Colby, Ryan, and Keane Morgan have "just so happened" to drop by to have chicken pot pies with Theo and me after a brotherly day of fishing. Or, at least, that's our story and we're sticking to it. And so far, so good. Theo doesn't seem to suspect this little dinner party was engineered solely for his benefit.

For his part, Colby has been sitting across the table from Theo throughout dinner, mostly observing the conversation without saying much. It's the same behavior I've seen from Colby many times in group settings: he sits back and lets everyone else take center stage, not speaking unless and until he's got something he deems worthwhile to say. It's not the way Darren always used to behave in groups. Darren was much more like Ryan. A dyed-in-the-wool extrovert. But, I must admit, I find Colby's quiet charisma and calming energy incredibly alluring. Indeed, although he's the least flashy Morgan brother, I consistently find myself staring at him the most and wondering what the hell he's thinking. I've always found strong, silent types incredibly swoony. I've just never been involved with one before.

After listening to Ryan and Theo chat for a bit about their climbs at the party last week, Keane pipes in: "Hearing you two talk, I'm bummed I didn't make it to the party. I was supposed to go, but I was up late the night before and totally flaked." Keane smiles at Theo and two adorable dimples pop out of his handsome face. "Hey, Theo-Leo, do you think maybe you'd be willing to go with *me* to the rock climbing gym some time? I'd love to give it a try with someone who already knows how to slay."

Theo swats at the air adorably. "Ryan's the one who slays, not me. He had to tell me where to put my feet and hands the whole time I was climbing. I'm small for my age, so I could barely reach the hand holds."

"Nah, it was all you, buddy," Ryan says. "I just made a suggestion or two."

"I couldn't have done it without you, Ryan."

"Okay, that settles it, then," Keane says. "All three of us will go together. Just as long as you're there, Theo. I need a little brahito-burrito like you to give me some much needed confidence."

"Much needed confidence?" Theo asks, laughing. "*You*? You seem awfully confident to me, Keane."

"Fake it 'til you make it, brah. The truth is I'm totally afraid of heights. I think if I see you climbing the highest wall, I'll feel like a total chump if I don't do it, too."

Theo laughs. "You can totally do it, Keane." He motions to Keane's ridiculously fit body. "If *I* can do it, *you* can do it."

Keane takes a sip of his beer. "I don't know. I just freeze up when I get really high up. You're seriously not scared of heights *at all*?"

Theo shakes his head proudly. "Not at all."

"Amazing. You've got the heart of a lion, man. When I was your age, I was deathly afraid of heights, plus a whole lot of other things, too."

Theo looks intrigued. "Like what kinds of other stuff?"

"What *wasn't* I afraid of?" Keane says. "The dark. Sharks. Elephantiasis. Flesh-eating bacteria. The list goes on and on. You're not scared of any of that stuff?"

"Just flesh-eating bacteria," Theo admits, and we all laugh.

"Oh! What about botulism?" Keane asks.

"Oh my God," Theo says. "*Yes*! Botulism scares the crap out of me."

Now we're all chuckling heartily and Ryan, Colby, and I are exchanging excited glances.

Theo adds, "We learned about botulism in science class and now I freak out every time my mom drops a can of soup."

"Same here!" Keane bellows. "I always worry I'm gonna wake up one morning with my jaw frozen shut!"

"Me, too!" Theo says gaily, and again, Ryan, Colby, and I exchange furtive glances.

Oh, God, I'm in awe of Keane Morgan right now. The way he's creeping up on his bull's-eye without Theo having the slightest suspicion that's what he's doing is truly masterful to watch.

"When I was your age," Keane says breezily, putting down his beer bottle, "I just couldn't stop worrying about stuff, night and day. I even had night terrors. You ever get those? They're like nightmares on steroids."

Again, Ryan, Colby, and I share a secret look. *Damn, he's good.*

Theo says, "*I get those all the time!*"

"You *do*? Ha! I knew you were my brother from another mother. Put it there, little dude." He fist-bumps Theo. "But I bet I've got you beat on one thing." He looks around like he's about to tell a huge secret. "I don't normally tell people this, but since you're obviously my spirit animal, I'm just gonna go ahead and tell you my deep, dark secret: I was a bed wetter until I was almost fourteen."

Theo freezes, a forkful of food in front of his lips.

Keane continues, "I know, I know. I don't look like a dude who'd pee my sheets into my teens. These days I look like I could leap over tall buildings, right?" He lays his muscled forearms on the table and his biceps flex and bulge with the effort. "But it's true. And I don't mean I peed a little squirt here and there. I mean I had full-on *thar she blows* accidents like a mofo. Thankfully, by my fourteenth birthday, I was as dry as a Mormon wedding and I've stayed that way ever since. Well, okay, in the interest of full disclosure, I peed myself once last year, but that was only because I'd had *waaaay* too much tequila with Ryan."

Ryan laughs, but Colby and I simultaneously bark out, "*Keane!*"

Keane chuckles happily. "My point, little brahito," he says, "is that this too shall pass, whatever 'this' happens to be. All I had to do was get my mind right and my body followed, you know? Sometimes, these things just take time. But it's never hopeless."

Theo's face is bright red. He looks at me for encouragement and I nod.

"Actually, Keane, I've got..." He swallows hard. "The exact same... deep, dark secret as you."

Keane shoves some food in his mouth like what Theo just said is the most normal thing in the world. "Oh, you're a bed wetter, too? Cool."

Theo nods.

Keane puts down his fork abruptly. "Wait. Are you just saying that to make me feel better?"

Theo laughs. *He laughs*! "No. I swear to God, Keane. *I do it all the time*. Just like you used to do. *Thar she blows* and everything."

Keane and Theo both laugh... *They laugh*! And I swear to God, I'm a hair's breadth from bursting into big soggy tears of joy at the sight of it.

"So how did you finally make it stop?" Theo asks.

Keane launches into explaining various tactics he found helpful. It's mostly the same stuff our doctor has told Theo to do a thousand times. The same things I've suggested *ad nauseam* after reading articles and blog posts by other distraught parents online. But, somehow, now that The Mighty Keane is suggesting these strategies, Theo looks open and receptive and determined to follow his advice to a tee.

As Keane and Theo talk, I glance at Colby again to find he's already looking at me, his blue eyes sparkling. I smile at him, thanking him for arranging this magical night for my sweet little boy, and he returns my smile and winks. And, just like that, I'm flooded with a tidal wave of love for Colby. Not projected emotions. This isn't transference. No, in this moment, I'm positive this love I'm feeling for Colby has absolutely nothing to do with Darren. I love Colby Morgan for the man he is. I'm sure of it.

When I tune back into the conversation between Keane and Theo, Keane is suggesting Theo get himself a hobby he can truly master. "Having something you love to do that you do well relieves stress," Keane explains. "And that's the name of the game. For me, that thing was baseball. What could it be for you?"

Theo tells Keane about the animation software I got him for his birthday and then he talks about how he's been taking guitar lessons.

"Hey, you know who you should talk to about guitar?" Keane says. "Our little brother, Dax. Ever heard of River Records?"

Theo shakes his head.

"It's a record label, son. Google it."

Theo reaches for his phone.

"Not right now, brahito. That was a figure of speech. River Records is a record label that has all the hottest bands right now, and the guy who owns it told my baby brother he likes his band so much, he's gonna come to Seattle one day soon to see them play live. And if that guy likes my brother's band, he's gonna sign 'em to a record deal and make 'em huge stars."

"Awesome," Theo says. "When could I meet him?"

Finally, Colby Morgan speaks. "You and your sisters and mom could come to my family's house for one of our Sunday night dinners. Dax never misses those."

Theo's face lights up. "Sounds great." He looks at me. "Can we go, Mom? *Please?*"

"Of course. Sounds great." I smile at Colby. "Great idea."

Oh, how the smile on Colby's face is lighting my soul.

"So what about friends?" Keane says. "Having a best friend helped my confidence. Zander made me feel like being weird was my superpower, not my shame. Do you have a friend who could be your wingman like that? Someone who just totally gets you?"

"No, not really." Theo looks down at his plate. "I'm kind of being bullied at school, actually."

My breath catches. *Jackpot.*

"Oh, yeah? What's going on?" Keane asks nonchalantly, just before shoveling some food into his mouth.

Theo exhales and looks up. "I had an accident at sixth-grade camp three months ago and this kid named Caleb has been torturing me ever since. He calls me Pee-o and throws water on my pants when I walk by in the halls and now nobody wants to hang out with me because they're scared Caleb will start picking on them, too. I'm like the bubonic plague."

I clutch my chest. My heart feels like it's physically palpitating.

"What a little douche!" Keane says. He looks at me. "Sorry, Lydi-Bug, but it had to be said."

"I agree. Unfortunately, I don't know what to do about the little douche. I haven't been able to help Theo with this problem at all, try as I might."

"Caleb just gets madder and sneakier whenever our teacher or the principal talks to him about me," Theo confirms.

Keane scratches his head. "Honestly, I don't know what to do to help you with a kid like that. That's just pure evil. Ryan? You're our family's fixer. What do you think our little brother here should do?"

"Hmm," Ryan says, scratching his steel chin. "I'm honestly not sure. Colby? Got any bright ideas?"

We all look at Colby.

Beautiful, quiet, handsome, kind Colby.

He looks contemplative for a long moment, and then he nods decisively. "Yeah, I've got one idea. No guarantees, of course, but it's worth a shot."

"I'll try anything at this point."

Colby leans forward, steepling his fingers. "Does your school ever have assemblies, Theo? You know, like, they invite people from the community to come in? Like, oh, I dunno, maybe firefighters?"

"Yeah. All the time. We had a police officer come with his German shepherd last year and tell us to say no to drugs. And a puppeteer came once and did this stupid show to teach us that bullying is bad." He rolls his eyes. "Yeah, *that* worked like a charm."

"But no firefighters?" Colby asks.

"Nope."

Colby smiles broadly. "Perfect. Okay, Theo-Leo. Leave it to me. It may take a few weeks for me to get it cleared through the department and your school, but I'll make it happen. Some of my firefighter buddies and I are going to come down to your school in our pretty red fire truck and talk to Caleb. Oh, I mean to the sixth-graders."

Theo giggles.

"And afterwards, hopefully, if I do it right, Caleb will leave you the hell alone."

"But what are you gonna say to him? He's not normal, Colby."

"Just leave it to me."

Theo looks like the weight of the world has just been lifted off his shoulders. "Thanks, Colby."

"Just a heads up, though?" Colby says. "When I choose a lucky kid to sit in the driver's seat of the fire truck and work the siren, don't be mad when it's Caleb and not you."

Chapter 44
Lydia

Ryan, Keane, Colby, Theo, and I are still sitting around my dining room table chatting when the front door bursts open and Izzy bounds in, trailed by Rosalind holding a sleeping Beatrice.

The minute Izzy sees Colby, she beelines to him and throws her arms around his neck, squealing with joy to see him.

"I'll get Queen Bea into her jammies and tuck her into bed," Rosalind says after a quick round of introductions. "Nice to meet you all."

"Great to meet you, too," the Morgan boys reply in unison.

And off Rosalind goes with my baby girl, God bless her.

"Time for you two to get ready for bed," I say to Izzy and Theo.

"Can I practice my guitar before lights out, Momma?" Theo asks.

I look at my watch. "Twenty minutes, buddy. Set the timer and make your minutes count."

Theo says his goodbyes with particularly enthusiastic hugs for the Morgan brothers and then sprints off to his room.

"Isabella," I say. She's currently whispering sweet nothings into Colby's ear and he's giggling adorably with her. "Yo, *Izzy*," I say. "Bedtime, baby cakes."

"Just a sec, Mommy," she says, holding up her index finger. "I'm telling Colby about *Enchanted.*"

"*Izzy*. Right before you came in, these nice gentlemen were just saying it was time for them to head out."

"But Colby can't leave," my daughter says, her hazel eyes wide. "I want him to read me a bedtime story."

A quick look at Colby and it's obvious he's elated about the idea. "If Colby's willing," I say, though it's a foregone conclusion.

"I'd *love* to," Colby says. He quickly tells his brothers to go on without him. "I'll take an Uber home, fellas. Izzy Stardust wants a bedtime story!" With that, he grabs his crutches and follows Izzy to the room she shares with Beatrice, just as Rosalind comes out and says her goodbyes.

I hug Ryan and Keane at the front door, thanking them profusely for their special brand of magic, and then tiptoe down the hall toward my daughters' bedroom. Holding my breath, I peek through the cracked door. Beatrice is splayed out on her tiny toddler bed in the corner, passed out cold. Colby is sitting on Izzy's twin bed, and Izzy is squatting like a baseball catcher in front of her bookcase, apparently mulling her options while talking a mile a minute.

"Oh, really?" Colby says as Izzy talks and talks. "Is that so? Oh, wow."

"Izzy," I say softly through the cracked door. "Just one book, sweetie. Don't ask for two."

"Okay, Mommy." She blows me a kiss and waves. "Nighty-night. Bye."

Well, damn. *Don't let the door hit ya on the way out, Mommy.*

I pivot to leave, but then, on a sudden impulse, stay put and listen at the door.

"Oh, good choice," I hear Colby say. "I've always loved 'Choose Your Own Adventure' books. I used to read them at your age, too."

"You *did?*"

"Yep. We're two peas in a pod. Oh, this is a good one. I love pirates, though not as much as my brother, Ryan. They're kind of his *thing.*" Colby clears his throat and begins reading Izzy's chosen book in a soft, calm voice that sends goose bumps of desire erupting over my skin. God, that man is so effortlessly masculine. I take a step forward, straining to hear above the clanging of my heart. "Should we go into the cave or run away?" Colby asks, his deep voice utterly captivating to me.

"Go into the cave," Izzy's little voice says firmly.

"Good choice. That's what I wanted to do, too."

"Because you're a firefighter."

"Hmm?"

"You wanted to go into the cave because you're a firefighter and firefighters never run away from danger."

"That's true, actually. We run *in* whenever everyone else runs *out.*"

"Because you're *brave.*"

I smile to myself. I can perfectly imagine Izzy's adoring face when she said that just now.

"Thank you," Colby's deep voice replies. "I try to be."

"Do you ever get scared?"

"All the time. But that's what bravery is: doing something even when you're scared, especially something to help someone else in need. Now where were we...?"

"Is that how you hurt your leg? Because you ran in when everyone else ran out?"

"Yep. That's exactly how."

"Were you scared?"

"To run into the fire? No. I wasn't scared to run in. I was excited. I was born to be a firefighter. Every chance I get to use my training, I get super excited. The part that made me scared was when I got trapped and I thought I'd never see my family again. That part scared me a whole lot."

"Oh my gosh. Did you cry when you thought you'd never see your family again? I know I'd cry."

"I sure did. Not at the time, but later, after I got out, I cried a lot. When I was trapped in the house, I didn't cry because I knew I had to keep my wits about me so I could do my best to get out and see my family again."

My heart pangs. I clutch my chest.

There's a long pause. And then a muffled sound followed by Colby saying, "Thank you, Isabella. That was sweet. What was that for?"

Surely, Isabella just hugged him. Or maybe she kissed his cheek.

"Because I'm just so glad you didn't die," Izzy replies.

"Thank you. Me, too."

"Will you come back tomorrow night and read to me again, Colby?"

Tears well in my eyes. *Oh, Izzy.*

"Wow, thank you. That's so sweet of you to invite me. I don't know if tomorrow night will work out, just because your mommy is really busy with work and taking care of you three kids and she might not want me coming around every single night, but hopefully she'll invite me to your house again one day soon. Now, where were we...?"

"I think we should just tell her *I* invited you tomorrow night," Izzy declares.

Colby chuckles. "Oh, God. Please don't get me into trouble,

Izzy. Your mommy is going think I put you up to that. Now, please, let's read so I don't get in trouble—"

"Do you want to marry my mommy?" Izzy blurts.

My heart stops.

"Wow," Colby says. He chuckles. "Um." He pauses. "Do you *want* me to marry your mommy?"

Izzy doesn't hesitate. "Yes."

Holy shit.

"Really? Wow. That's awfully sweet of you to say."

I clutch my neck. I feel hot. Dizzy.

"I think we should read, don't you?" Colby says. "Now, where were we...?"

Izzy says, "If you marry my mommy, you can come live with us and read to me every single night."

"Holy cow. Ever heard the word *persistent*?"

"Never gives up."

"Oh yeah. I forgot you're in the advanced vocab group."

"The Blue Angels. Because we—"

"*Fly through the pages*. Yeah, I know."

They both giggle.

"So will you marry my mommy and come live with us?"

"Sweetheart, let's please not talk about me marrying your mommy anymore, okay? I don't want to get in trouble with your mommy for keeping you up so late. I want your mommy to like me, not be mad at me."

"She already likes you. I heard her say so to Ros."

My skin pricks. *Izzy!*

"Is that so? What did she say about me to Ros?"

"We were getting ice cream after my dance recital and she said she likes you but she's not supposed to like a patient. Or maybe she said she loves you? I can't remember."

I literally stagger in place in the hallway. *Jesus Christ, Izzy!*

"*Really?*" Colby says. "*Interesting.* Can you remember anything else she said about me?"

"She said she wanted to go out on a date with you. And she said you're good looking. Or maybe she said you're hot?"

Colby laughs and I palm my forehead.

"Well, well, well. Thanks for the intel."

"My daddy used to read to me."

There's a long pause. And then, "Do you remember your daddy well?"

"No, not really. But my mommy told me he used to like reading to me and having tea parties with me. I've seen lots of pictures."

My heart pangs.

Colby asks, "How old were you when your daddy died?"

"Four."

"I'm sorry. I'm sure that was really sad for you."

"It was. I was in this room and my daddy was lying on this bed and he had this thing sticking out of his mouth and I hugged him and then my mommy told me he had to go on an airplane to heaven."

A little whimper escapes me and I cover my mouth with my palm to keep myself from being found out.

Colby says, "What else do you remember about your father? Anything happy?"

Isabella pauses. "He used to do this thing on my neck. You know when you go like this?" There's a little raspberry sound. "Only on your neck, not your arm. He used to do that to me a lot."

Colby chuckles. "Did you do it back to him?"

"I don't think so. I'm not sure."

"Well, it sounds like your daddy loved you a whole lot."

"He still does."

"Oh, *of course*. One hundred percent."

There's a long pause. And then Izzy says, "Will you do that thing to my neck like my daddy used to do, Colby?"

Oh, for the love of fuck. My heart just exploded and splattered against the door of Izzy's bedroom.

Colby says, "I don't think I should do that."

"Why not?"

"Because it was a special thing you did with your daddy. I think he'd like keeping it as your special thing with just him."

I wipe my eyes. Oh my God.

Izzy says, "Well, could you maybe do it on my arm, then? My daddy always used to do it on my neck. So maybe my neck could be my daddy's special thing, and my arm could be yours."

There's a brief pause. And then a little raspberry sound followed by Izzy's giggling.

And I'm suddenly overcome with emotion. If I don't leave this hallway now, they're surely going to hear me sniffling out here.

I pivot to leave but freeze when I hear Izzy's next words.

"Please marry my mommy, Colby."

I wait, my heart pounding noisily in my ears.

"Thank you so much, Izzy," Colby finally says. "You're such a sweetheart. But, please, let's read now, okay? I don't want to get in trouble with your mommy for keeping you up too late."

Colby begins reading again.

Izzy makes a little cooing sound that tells me she's snuggled into the crook of his arm or against his chest, and I force myself to tiptoe back down the hall.

Chapter 45
Lydia

Colby enters the living room on his crutches. "Hi," he says from the entryway.

"Hi."

He leans his crutches against the wall and settles next to me on the couch. "Your daughter is amazing," he says. "We read one of those 'Choose Your Own Adventure' books."

"Oh, yeah? Fun."

"It was. We wound up stowing away on a pirate ship on the high seas, kicking some pirate ass, and ultimately finding some buried treasure in a cave."

"I'm sure Izzy loved every minute of it."

"She asked me to do it again soon."

"Well, then, I guess you'd better come back soon. How's tomorrow night sound?"

Colby's face lights up. "Awesome. I'll bring dinner for everyone."

"Thank you. Six thirty?"

"Perfect."

I press my lips together, feeling like every cell in my body is vibrating. "So, hey, um." I clear my throat. "I saw my therapist yesterday. Dr. Aabrams."

"Oh, yeah?"

"Yeah. She had an interesting bit of advice for us. A game plan." I tell him the gist of what Dr. Aabrams advised yesterday and he listens intently.

"So she's an expert in sex therapy?" Colby asks, rubbing the cleft in his chin.

I nod. "Apparently, trauma and sexual dysfunction often go hand in hand."

Colby looks thoughtful for a moment. "Okay. Let's do it. The Celibacy Game for two months. But in exchange for my solemn vow to act like a character in a Jane Austen novel, you've got to promise to tell me anything and everything I want to know."

"That's the most important part of this exercise, apparently. It's what leads to 'emotional intimacy.'"

"Great. There's no time like the present." He grabs my hands... and, immediately, a swarm of butterflies releases into my stomach. "Tell me The Story of Darren and Lydia. Start at the beginning and don't stop talking until you get to this very moment."

"This story is going to take a lot longer than a couple hours to tell."

Colby brings the top of my hand to his soft, warm lips, and the moment his mouth makes contact with my flesh, my clit zings with desire. "I've got all the time in the world, sweetheart. I'm not going anywhere. Just start at the beginning and keep talking for the next two months."

Chapter 46
Colby

"So, does anybody here think they might like to be a firefighter one day?" I ask the assembled crowd of about one hundred sixth-graders at Theo's school. I'm flanked by three firefighters—two guys and a badass woman. A red fire truck is parked behind us, its gleaming doors swung open and its large hoses unfurled across the blacktop.

Keane, Ryan, and Zander are standing off to the side, ready and waiting for their cue, should I give it to them.

Lydia is standing at the back of the crowd with the sixth-grade teachers and about a dozen other mothers, all of whom, oddly enough, decided to take time out of their busy schedules to attend this particular school assembly today.

And for the past fifteen minutes, my fellow firefighters and I have been giving the kids an overview of what it means to be a firefighter.

In response to my question—whether any of the kids is interested in becoming a firefighter one day—a whole bunch of kids raise their hands... including the one Lydia pointed out to me earlier as Theo's tormenter, Caleb.

"Awesome," I say. "Any of you think you might like to become a paramedic, too, like me and my friends Emma and Dave here?"

Again, a bunch of hands go up. *Including Caleb's.*

"That's great," I say. "I love it when I see kids thinking about doing something that helps other people. Let me ask this: even if you don't want to be a firefighter or paramedic when you grow up, does everybody here agree we should all try to help other people now and again?"

Every hand in the place goes up.

"I agree," I say. "You want to know why I'm leaning on these crutches? Because I got hurt trying to help someone who was trapped in a fire."

A hushed murmur rustles through the crowd.

"Because that's what firefighters do. We do whatever we can to help people. That's our motto: *service before self.* Does anyone know what that means?"

A bunch of hands go up. I call on a little girl with ringlet curls.

"If someone needs you, you help them, even if you might get hurt."

"That's right," I say. "Can I get a show of hands if you think it's the right thing to do to help other people who are in need in some way? Even if it's just, you know, being nice to someone who might be sad one day? Someone who maybe needs a friend because other people are being mean to him or her?"

Every hand goes up.

"Man, I'm happy to see that, guys. When someone else is sad or hurt and you make them feel better, then it makes *you* feel better. Like, for instance, let's say someone is being teased or bullied and you stick up for them. Maybe you tell the bully to stop. To the kid who was being bullied, you'd be that kid's hero, wouldn't you? Raise your hand if you've ever been bullied."

A bunch of hands go up, including Theo's. *And Caleb's.*

I turn to my firefighter friends. "Any of you ever been bullied?"

Emma to my right tells the kids a story from her childhood about a time she was bullied because of her nose. And then my buddy Dave tells a story about being teased because of his height.

"See? Everyone goes through something," I say. "My brother, Keane, over there used to get teased a lot, too." I motion to my brother. "Say hi, Keane."

He waves. "Hi."

"Keane just came to watch today with his friend Zander, just for fun. They're not firefighters. Keane was a professional baseball player and Zander is a fitness trainer. But, hey, as long as they're both here, let's find out if they were teased. Zander?"

Zander waves at the crowd and tells everyone a brief story involving him always having the "wrong" clothes.

"Keane?" I ask. "What about you?"

Keane waves at the crowd. "Hey, everyone. Yeah, I was teased at lot in sixth grade for being a bed wetter."

The crowd collectively gasps. Several of them, Caleb included, look at Theo. But, God bless Theo the Lionhearted Boy, he's doing exactly what I told him to do: he's keeping his eyes locked on Keane's.

Keane continues, "I felt super embarrassed about it, but then I met this guy." He indicates Zander standing next to him. "And he threatened to beat anybody up who made fun of me."

Everyone laughs.

I say, "Oh, well, we're not going to do that, though, right, guys? Nobody's beating anybody up. But we're certainly going to stick up for each other and tell bullies to stop, right? Because we've all got something we're embarrassed about. Will you guys make me a promise from now on you'll stick up for someone who's being bullied or teased? We're all in this together."

Unanimous promises abound.

"Thank you so much, guys. You don't have to rush into a burning building to be a hero. You just have to stick up for what's right. So come up here and get a sticker firefighter badge if you're willing to make that pledge to stick up for what's right and be a hero and then anyone with a badge can try on our turnout gear and hold the hoses. And while you're all doing that, I'm gonna select a few of you to sit in the fire truck and work the sirens."

I steal a quick look at Theo. He's looking right at me. And the message he's sending me is unmistakable: *Thank you.*

***

"Press this button here, Caleb," I say, and the little shit presses the button to make the siren wail.

Everyone in the crowd screams and cheers and Caleb hoots.

"Pretty cool, huh?" I say, turning off the blaring sound.

"Awesome," the little fucker agrees.

"So, hey, Caleb," I say. "Have you ever bullied anyone?"

His face flushes. He shakes his head.

"No?"

219

Caleb shakes his head again, looking like he's about to hurl.

"Huh. That's not what I heard. Just between you and me, I'm in love with Theo Decker's mom and she told me there's a kid named Caleb who keeps calling her son 'Pee-o' and throwing water on his crotch when he walks by in the halls. Was she talking about a different Caleb?"

Caleb has gone completely pale. He doesn't reply.

If this little turd were an adult, now would be the time I'd lean in and tell him I was going to break his legs and punch every tooth out of his asshole mouth if I hear even a whisper about him so much as *scowling* at my boy ever again. But, unfortunately, since I can't say shit like that to an eleven-year-old, especially not in my official capacity as a firefighter, I choose a different tack. "Ever heard the expression, 'The oppressed becomes the oppressor,' Caleb?"

He shakes his head.

"It means people who hurt others usually have been hurt themselves." I pause. "Is that what's going on here, Caleb? Has someone been hurting you? Are you having a hard time at home for some reason?"

Caleb's eyes prick with tears. "My parents are getting divorced."

"I'm sorry to hear that."

"My dad screams at my mom a lot. And when I tell him to stop it, he screams at me."

Suddenly, I don't want to rip this kid's head off anymore. I just want to help him. "Do you have someone you can talk to about that? Someone who can help you?"

Caleb shrugs. "My uncle. But he's being deployed next week."

I touch his shoulder. "I tell you what. I'll leave my number with your teacher and tell her to give it to you. If you ever need something, feel free to call me and I'll do what I can to help you."

He nods. "Thank you."

"But I'm not gonna put myself out there to help you if you're gonna keep picking on Theo or anyone else. Is that clear, Caleb?"

He nods.

"Say it out loud for me, Caleb. Promise me you're gonna stop picking on my boy."

"I'll stop picking on Theo."

"And anyone else."

"And anyone else. I promise."

"Awesome. As much as I'd like to believe you, let me give you a little incentive." I squeeze his shoulder. "Make it to the end of this school year without me hearing you've teased or bullied or looked cross-eyed at Theo again, even once, and I'll give you and a friend a VIP tour of the firehouse. I'm talking about a ride-along in the truck. Getting to spray a big hose in the back. The whole nine yards."

"Oh my God."

"But I swear to God, Caleb, if Theo tells me you've so much as looked at him funny the rest of this school year, my offer of friendship *and* the VIP tour are both off the table. And not only that, I'll come to your class and tell everyone what you did and how disappointed I am in you."

"I won't do another thing to Theo. I swear."

"I know you won't." I remove my hand from his shoulder. "Now go over to my boy and tell him you're sorry for everything you've done to him and that you swear to God it won't happen again."

I help him down out of the cab and off he goes, straight to Theo.

As Caleb approaches Theo, I search the crowd for Lydia's face to find her eyes trained on her son, looking like she's holding her breath. Now my eyes drift to Ryan. He's also watching Caleb approach Theo. I find Keane and Zander. They're holding a large fire hose with a line of kids, shouting animatedly about some imaginary fire they're all putting out together. I smile to myself. Why doesn't that surprise me?

Now I return to Theo. Caleb is just now reaching him.

They talk. Caleb gesticulates. Theo looks wide-eyed and incredulous. Caleb puts out his hand and Theo warily shakes it. Caleb pats Theo on the shoulder and walks away. And little, skinny, heartbreaking Theo lets out the hugest exhale of his life.

I look at Lydia to find her already staring at me. She mouths, "Thank you." And I wink.

"Oh my God, Colby!" It's Theo. He's standing in front of me, looking flushed. "Caleb just apologized to me! He said he'd never do it again!"

"Awesome." I high-five him.

"What did you say to him?" Theo asks. "Did you threaten to beat him up or something? I can't believe that just happened."

"I didn't threaten to beat him up. I'd never threaten a kid. I just talked to him. Got to know him a bit."

Theo's obviously not buying it. "But what *exactly* did you say to him, Colby? He said he wants to be *friends*."

"I just talked to him and told him to leave you alone. So, if Caleb comes at you again, make sure you tell me, okay?"

Theo's smile is beaming. "I will. Thank you so much, Colby."

"You're welcome."

"I can't believe you did this for me. *I can't believe it*."

"I'd do anything for you, Theo. Literally, anything."

To my shock, Theo throws his arms around my waist, almost making me lose balance on my crutches. He lays his cheek flush against my abdomen and whispers, "Thank you, Colby. I'm so glad my mom picked you to be her boyfriend."

Chapter 47
Colby

My phone beeps on my nightstand with a text and I check it. *Lydia.*

"Kids are asleep," she writes. "Wanna come over and talk and hold my hand again, Mr. Darcy?"

"See you in 20, Lizzie," I reply. "Need anything?"

"Milk, if you wouldn't mind."

"Don't mind at all," I write. "What about beer? Any left from last time or should I grab more?"

"More. Oh, and ice cream, too, please."

"You got it, baby," I write. "Flavor?"

"Surprise me."

"Ooooooh. Sexy girl. Just popped a boner. How much longer again?"

"Tooooooooo looooong," she writes."

"I got home from our PT sesh today and wacked off thinking about your titties."

"LOL. What a coincidence! I masturbated in the shower this morning with a big, fat waterproof dildo, thinking about your beautiful ass."

"BONER!"

"LADY-BONER!"

"Walking to my car now," I write. "Gotta stop texting. See you in 15."

"Call me as you drive. I want you to talk dirty to me."

I start the engine of my truck and place the call.

"Hey, gorgeous," Lydia says.

"Hey, beautiful," I reply.

"Exactly how much longer 'til Bonin' Time?" she asks.

"Eighteen days," I say, sighing. "Nine days 'til I leave for Maui. A week while I'm gone. I'll arrive back home on a Sunday. We'll have our final PT session the next day at eleven and then it's Bonin' Time!"

"Bonin' Time!" she shouts. "Woohoo!"

We both laugh.

"Please change your mind about coming to Maui with me," I say in my most charming voice. "*Please*."

"We've talked about this, sugar. I'm not going to change my mind."

"But I'm gonna die after a week without you. I will seriously, literally, physically *die*."

She giggles. "Just think of the fireworks when you get back."

"Tell that to my balls."

"Hey, Colby's balls: 'Just think of the fireworks when you get back.' Does it make it better or worse if I tell you I had an incredible sex dream about you last night?"

"It makes it worse, but tell me more."

She describes her dream in explicit detail, and I swear to God I almost come in my jeans as she talks.

"And then," she concludes, "I woke up having a little orgasm. It was unbelievably delicious. That's why I brought my dildo into the shower this morning. I woke up coming. Not a bad way to wake up."

"You're killing me. You're fucking killing me, Decker. I'm physically *dying*."

She makes an incredibly sexy sound... a sexual sound that tells me she's masturbating on the other end of the line. "Hey, baby," she purrs. "Do you think Jane Austen would approve if we were to get naked and masturbate together tonight, instead of our usual talking and holding hands?"

"Oh, Jesus. Yes."

"I'll give you a little show with my dildo," she purrs.

"Oh, fuck." My cock twitches. I can barely breathe. "Hey, baby," I manage to say. "How much do we really need milk and ice cream and beer?"

Lydia laughs. "We don't. On second thought, just get your beautiful ass over here as soon as humanly possible."

Chapter 48
Colby

I park my truck in front of Lydia's house, shift my boner in my jeans, grab my single crutch (yeah, thank God, I'm down to one crutch now), and make my way up Lydia's walkway. Holy fuck, I'm so horny, I can barely breathe. And so in love with Lydia, it's a miracle my heart hasn't physically burst by now.

Lydia, Lydia, Lydia.

It was six weeks ago that Lydia first sat me down and told me about her therapist's brutal advice. Six weeks of me going to physical therapy sessions at the clinic by day and sneaking over here at night to talk and hold hands. And crazy enough, as torturous as the idea of celibacy for two months sounded to me at the time, it's turned out to be the best advice imaginable. It's pure insanity, I know, considering Lydia and I haven't so much as kissed this whole time, but these past six weeks have been the best of my life. Obviously, knowing there's a definitive finish line to the pain has made it doable and, actually, kind of fun. Painful, yes. A slow death. But totally, thoroughly awesome. It's felt a lot like training for a marathon or triathlon, actually. Grueling. Painful. Horrible. Torturous. But you just stick with the training program and trust euphoria will come on race day as you cross the finish line. Oh, and the craziest part of this Celibacy Game we've been playing? How erotic the slightest touches have turned out to be for both of us. Especially after last week, when our little game took a decidedly kinky turn.

For the first two weeks or so when I raced over to Lydia's house after her kids went to bed, we held hands and she doled out yet another heartbreaking or heartwarming chapter of The Story of Darren and Lydia. Sometimes, she cried. Sometimes she laughed. But through it all, her walls came crashing down.

225

And then, about three weeks in, our conversations evolved from Darren and the kids and the story of her past to the story of who she is today. And it was then that our hand-holding evolved into something indescribably sensual. We caressed fingers. And then wrists and palms. And then we fudged a little and started laying soft, passionate kisses on each other's palms and fingers and wrists. And then we stretched the rules again and progressed to laying wet, greedy kisses on each other's hands and fingers and wrists and forearms. And then little nips and sucks. And, I'll be damned, the sensation of her stroking and kissing my forearm and fingers and palms started feeling almost as hot as if she'd been stroking or sucking my dick. It was the damnedest thing ever.

And then, just over a week ago, our late-night conversations and confessionals took an intriguing turn. We started playing a sort of Truth or Dare game... which led to us asking each other pointed questions about all manner of sexual topics and answering them with brutal honesty... which led to me asking Lydia about her masturbation practices a few days ago.

And that cracked the whole thing wide open.

From that moment forward, we ditched Lydia's couch and started having our "conversations" in her bedroom. In our underwear. Physically showing each other what we meant when we said, "I like it like *this.*" It was FaceTime phone sex without the phone. Fucking without the fucking part. And, oh my God, it was hot.

Four nights ago, I think it was, after Lydia had finished whispering to me about how much she was dying to suck my cock and telling me exactly how she'd do it, she surprised me by grabbing my hand and sliding my finger into her mouth and sucking it off exactly the way she'd just described she wanted to do... and I broke down. Without asking if it was permissible under the rules of our fucked-up game, I pulled out my dick, pumped my shaft no more than ten times, and came all over her tits. And that's when Lydia did something that told me she was no longer the sobbing mess I'd fucked almost two months ago. She scooped up my cum and licked every drop of it off her fingertips with a wide, curling tongue.

Oh, Jesus fucking Christ. I'll never forget that moment as long as I live. I knew right then the therapist had given Lydia the best advice possible. And I also knew that, if I could just hang on a little while longer, I'd be handsomely rewarded at our impending finish line. Indeed, I'd get to experience the best sex of my life. And so, although every fiber of my being wanted to rip Lydia's panties off and plunge myself deep inside her right then and there, I kept my eye on the prize and recommitted myself to the game, albeit this new, revised one in which we both sent Jane Austen turning over in her grave.

And now, it's time for me to raise the stakes, yet again. Lydia's offered to fuck herself with a dildo for my viewing pleasure tonight. *And I can't wait.*

I reach Lydia's front door and knock. Seconds later, when her door opens, my balls tighten at the sight of her. She's wearing a white tank top and underwear that complement her mocha skin beautifully. Without a bra, her ample tits look incredible. Her thighs look strong and smooth. Her cheeks are blooming.

"Hi, baby," Lydia says simply, leaning her shoulder against the doorjamb.

"Hi, sweetheart." Her dark nipples are taunting me through the thin fabric of her tank top. "Are you trying to torture me, wearing that?"

"Yes."

"God, your nipples look amazing. I'd commit murder to get to suck those things tonight."

"Patience."

"Torture."

She smiles. "Sorry I texted so late tonight. Bea's molar is still coming in so it took forever for her to fall asleep."

"The Tylenol didn't help this time?"

"She was too wound up. I just rocked her and sang to her for a bit and she finally calmed down." She visibly puts her game face on. Shifts her weight. Juts out her incredible breasts. "So, hey, sexy man, you want to head to my bedroom for a little show or what?"

I shift my hard dick in my pants, enter her house, and close the door behind me. "*Fuck yes.* Lead the way."

Chapter 49
Lydia

The vast assortment of dildos and vibrators I've acquired over the past three years is lying next to me on the bed. "Which one?" I ask softly, goose bumps covering my naked flesh.

I never once masturbated in front of Darren. There was never a need. Once we got started having sex six months into dating as teenagers, we had sex virtually every day and were basically never apart.

"Don't use your dildo to start," Colby says. "I want your fingers first. Your fingers are my tongue. My voice is my cock."

"Ooooh. Delicious."

Colby strips off his clothes and takes his usual chair at the foot of my bed and I'm struck by how strong and powerful his body looks nowadays. Other than those burn scars marking the left side of his torso and, of course, the slight limp he still bears—which should be completely gone within the next three weeks or so—there's nothing about Colby's appearance that even hints at the horror he went through mere months ago.

Settling into his chair, Colby spreads his thighs to give me an unimpeded view of his hard cock and balls. Even from here, I can see the glistening wetness already seeping from the tip of his erect penis.

"You're already wet for me," I whisper. "God, I wish I could lick that up."

He swirls the wetness pooled at his tip with his fingertip. "Tell me how you'd do it."

Rather than tell him, I show him by lapping my tongue against the tip of my thumb, and Colby reacts by groaning and gripping his cock. "And then I'd take you into my mouth, all the way, and suck you until you were shooting your load straight down my throat," I add. It's the dirtiest thing I've ever said out loud in my life. And, man, it felt delicious to say it. Indeed, if I'm being honest, all this dirty-talk I've been doing with Colby this past week hasn't just made me feel naughty or sexy. It's made me feel *free.*

Colby increases the speed of his hand job. "Touch yourself now, sweetheart. Open your folds wide and show me every inch of you. I wanna see your hard clit. Oh, yeah. That's it. Now, suck on your finger. That's it, baby. Make your fingertip extra wet and then swirl your clit around with it and pretend it's my tongue."

I do as I'm told and softly moan with pleasure.

"Now move your clit back and forth. Side to side. *Slowly, baby.* One... two. What's your rush? Slow it down. One... two. Thaaaat's it. Nice and slow for me. Oh, yeah, you're a sexy little thing." Colby shifts in his seat and emits a tortured sound that sends a shockwave of excitement zinging into my epicenter as I fondle myself. "Good girl. I wish your finger could be my tongue so fucking bad." He licks his lips. "I remember how good you taste. I'm counting the seconds until I get to taste your sweet pussy again."

My toes are tingling. My core is tightening into a dull, delicious ache. "Colby. Oh, God. I need to go faster."

"No, baby. You do as I say. Nice and slow. One. Two. One. Two. Just like that." He pumps his shaft slowly in synchronicity with the way I'm touching myself.

I rarely have orgasms by touching myself. I'm a dildo kind of girl. And I've certainly never gotten off by touching myself this slowly before... But, I'll be damned, a couple more purposeful touches at the rhythm commanded by Colby and, suddenly, I'm hit with a slow-rolling orgasm that rips a long, low moan from my throat. "*Oh.* I'm coming in a deep rumbling wave."

Colby's eyes darken with heat. "You look so sexy when you get off, Lydia."

I bite my lip. "*I want you.*"

"I know you do. That's the idea. Now let's get you there again before I fuck you with that dildo."

"I want you inside me. I don't want the dildo. I want *you.*"

"I know you do. And, believe me, I want you, too. I'm imagining myself balls deep inside you right now, fucking you so hard your eyes roll back into your head. But we've come this far. We're gonna go all the way. I made a promise and I'm gonna keep it."

I groan. "Let's do it, Colby. Forget our promises. I don't feel guilty. I feel free. I feel sexy. I want you. *Please*. I'm ready."

A wicked smile spreads across Colby's glorious face. He licks his lips while continuing to pump his shaft. "I love hearing you beg. You have no idea how much it gets me off. But we're gonna stick to the program. No regrets that way. I'm still your patient, remember? And torture is part of our fun. Now grab your dildo, baby. The pink one. And slip the tip inside you. Just the tip."

Shaking with arousal, I do as I'm told.

"Spread your thighs wider. I want to see every inch of your pussy as it widens to let it in. Oh, God. That's nice. Now slide it all the way in slowly."

I begin sliding the dildo inside me.

"Even slower than that, baby. Yeah, just like that. Oh, for the love of fuck. So good." He quickens the movement of his hand on his cock. "Now fuck yourself with it."

I'm trembling. Quaking. This feels so... erotic. Why the hell is this turning me on so damned much?

"Beg me again. I love hearing you beg."

I beg him again. And then again and again and again. Until, finally, a whimper of agony escapes my mouth and an orgasm slams into me.

"So sexy," he says when I come down. He sucks in air through his gritted teeth while stroking his dick. "Now turn the dildo on the lowest setting. Just the thruster. No vibration on your clit just yet."

I comply. . . and instantly, at the sensation of the dildo knocking against my G-spot, I'm clinging to the edge yet again.

His blue eyes darkening with desire, Colby leaves his chair, crawls to me like a panther, straddles my hips, places his hand over mine on the dildo, and assumes control of the movement of my toy. He leans over me and whispers into my ear, letting his warm breath tickle my cheek. "I'm fucking you, Lydia. So hard, my balls are slapping against you. My face is buried in your tits. I'm sucking your nipple. My finger is up your ass."

I cry out with excitement.

I feel the warmth of his lips hovering just over my ear. "Now turn on the rabbit. Lowest setting."

I follow his instructions and the minute the silicon rabbit vibrates against its target, I jerk violently, immediately on the cusp of a savage orgasm. Without meaning to do it, I brush my knuckles lightly against Colby's balls, just barely, and he jerks and groans like I've sucked his tip.

At his reaction, I lose all self-restraint. I brazenly stroke the underside of his balls. "Fuck me," I grit out. "Forget the game. I won't feel guilty. I'll feel nothing but good."

He's shuddering at my touch. "Quiet now, baby. Keep your hands to yourself." He lets out a ragged breath. "*Lydia.*"

I arch my back and run my fingernails lightly across his balls, determined to break him. But I've miscalculated. At my touch, Colby gasps, stiffens on top of me, and shoots his warm load all over my breasts.

"Oh, fuck," I grit out, my arousal boiling over and releasing into an orgasm. I moan and writhe, reveling in the naughty pleasure I'm feeling.

And my eyes stay dry.

And it's no wonder: I feel nothing but pleasure. No guilt. No shame. No conflict. This is the man I want—the man I love—and anyone who doesn't like it can go fuck themselves. Including my mother-in-law.

When my climax subsides, I feel ravenous for Colby. I swipe my fingers into the puddle on my chest and suck it off my fingers, my eyes trained on Colby's, and he exhales like he's in acute pain.

"You're trying to break me," he whispers, his chest heaving.

"Yes."

"Why?"

"Because I'm ready."

He winks. "Good things come to those who wait." He moves off me, turns me on my side and spanks my ass, making me yelp. And then he laughs, slides off the bed, and walks slowly to the bathroom.

"You're still supposed to be using a crutch, Mr. Morgan!" I call after him.

"Thanks, Physical Therapist Lydia! How's my cum taste?"

I giggle. "Great! Did you do those stretching exercises I gave you as homework?"

231

"I sure did! Plus I wacked off thinking about you twice!"

I sink into my bed, smiling from ear to ear. "I don't think I'm going to survive eighteen more days."

"We've come this far. We're going to see it through. If I fuck you now and you shed a single tear, I'll never forgive myself." I hear the shower turn on. "Get in here with me, babe. You're gonna wash yourself for my pleasure."

I get up from the bed. "I can't wait eighteen days, Colby. I'm serious. I'm gonna crack. I apologize in advance, but I'm gonna freakin' crack."

"I'll stay strong for both of us," Colby says. "You forget I've run marathons and triathlons. I know what it means to stick to a training program and never deviate, no matter the pain involved. That's all we're doing here, baby. Training for race day."

I stand in the doorway of the bathroom, my arms crossed over my bare chest, looking at my superhero through the clear Plexiglas of my shower door. "You look amazing, Colby. You're a new man."

He flashes an adorable smile. "Thanks to you."

I watch him showering for a moment, mesmerized by the movement of his soapy hands across his beautiful, muscular body.

"Hey, do me a favor," he says as he slides a bar of soap across his tattooed chest. "The day of our last appointment the Monday after I get back from Maui, clear your entire calendar that day, besides me. We're going to have our first official date right after my appointment."

"Ooh la la. Sounds fun."

Colby smiles. "Hey, pervert," he says. "Quit staring at my balls and get your gorgeous ass in here. I want to wash you from head to toe."

"I wasn't aware Jane Austen took hot showers with her gentlemen callers."

"I'm not gonna touch you. The *washcloth* will. Same thing as me fucking you with a dildo."

I giggle and glide happily toward the shower. "We're never going to make it another eighteen days, Colby. You realize that, right? We're hanging on by the barest of threads."

"Speak for yourself. I'm totally gonna make it. And in the meantime, I'm gonna make sure we have as much fun torturing ourselves as humanly possible."

Chapter 50
Colby

Mind officially blown. It's Sunday night at my parents' house and I'm surrounded at the dinner table by the usual suspects: my entire immediate family, plus Josh and Zander. But, for the first time ever in my life, a woman I've invited home for dinner is sitting at the table next to me... oh, and her three kids, too.

Of course, I realize Lydia's already met my entire family, so this isn't quite as dramatic an episode of Meet the Morgans as it otherwise might have been. But, still, I'm *officially* bringing a girl home for dinner with my family for the first time in my adult life. Add the woman's three adorable kids to the mix and there's no missing the smoke signal I'm sending out to my family tonight: *these four humans are officially mine.* Sitting here now, feeling like Lydia and her kids belong to me, it's crazy to think about how I reacted when Candice got all butt-hurt I hadn't invited her home yet. I feel like a different man than I was back then. Since that day, I've traveled to hell and back and somehow wound up in heaven.

I look down at Isabella sitting to my left, twirling spaghetti on her fork, and my heart skips a beat. When my sweet girl notices me looking at her, she smiles at me, displaying the front-tooth gap she acquired two nights ago when she bravely let me tie a strand of dental floss around her dangling tooth and *yank.* I snake my arm around Isabella's shoulders and she leans her cheek against my shoulder, making it abundantly clear she's my girl.

Reflexively, I glance down the long table at Beatrice, hoping she's catching sight of my lovefest with Izzy—perhaps noticing what she's missing out on. But *nope.* My nemesis is currently perched on Zander's lap, draped over his hard chest like a kimono, looking like

233

he's the man of her dreams. I force myself not to let out a long, *jealous* sigh. Fuck me. If I'd known all I had to do to win Bea's heart once and for all was let her paint my toenails the way she painted Zander's earlier tonight, I would have suggested she paint mine a long time ago.

Of course, Zander didn't mean to steal Beatrice away from me earlier today—not that I ever had her in the first place. He was just standing there in the living room, laughing with Peen, being his gregarious and mountainous self, when Beatrice walked into my parents' house for the first time, spied him, and visibly lost her ever-loving mind. Without missing a beat, Beatrice beelined straight for Zander, batted her long eyelashes at him, and asked him in that adorable little voice of hers if she could "pwease" paint his toenails with a certain sparkly pink nail polish that was, at that moment, tucked inside the Princess Jasmine purse slung over her tiny shoulder. Of course, Z replied that, yes, he'd be honored to receive a pedicure from such a lovely pedicurist, and that was that. From that moment on, Zander Shaw owned Beatrice Decker's heart. And I was chopped liver.

I peel my envious eyes away from Bea and Zander at the other end of the dinner table and steal a quick peek at Theo. He's seated between Dax and Keane, looking happy as a clam at high tide. Man, Theo's a whole new person these days compared to the sullen and skeptical creature I met at the Climb & Conquer party two months ago. Thankfully, ever since the school assembly, Theo's no longer being terrorized at school. To the contrary, he's now got a couple friends who frequently come over to the house after school. Last I heard, Theo and his buddies were thinking about starting a band.

"Oh, that sounds amazing!" Mom gushes, and I tune back into the conversation at the table. Apparently, Kat and Josh have just told the group about the exciting list of activities they've lined up for their "weeklong wedding shindig" in Maui next week.

Of course, I tried to convince Lydia and the kids to be my "plus four" on the trip, but Lydia turned me down.

"If it were just me, I'd say hell yes," Lydia said when I asked her to join me in Maui. "But I've got to consider what's best for the kids."

"What's best for the kids is getting to go to Maui for a week, all expenses paid," I replied.

But Lydia wasn't convinced. "Everything I've read on the topic of integrating kids with a boyfriend says I should proceed prudently and cautiously," she explained. "A week with my boyfriend and his entire family before we've even come out as an official couple to the world? It would just be too much, too soon."

One side of my mouth hitched up. "I'm your *boyfriend*?" It was the first time Lydia had called me that word and it electrified me, as goofy as that sounds.

Lydia flashed me a sexy look that shot tingles straight into my dick. "Slip of the tongue. You're my *patient*. No more or less."

I leaned in and whispered into her ear then, even though we were alone. "Do you regularly lick your patients' cum off your tits?"

She grazed the tip of her nose against my jaw, sending shivers across my skin. "Only when I *really, really* like the patient."

"Come on, baby," I pleaded. "Come to Maui."

But she wouldn't budge. "It's a moot point, anyway," she said. "I don't have enough vacation time to take a full week off for Maui and then again when I visit my parents over the holidays."

And that was that.

I was officially going stag to Maui.

"Oh my gosh!" Mom gushes, once again drawing my attention to the table conversation. "A chartered plane for all fifty of us? Josh, that's too much!"

Kat strokes Josh's cheek adoringly, and the basketball-sized sparkler on her left hand glints in the light of the overhead chandelier. "Josh is pulling out all the stops for this trip."

Josh grabs Kat's hand and kisses it. "Actually, *T-Rod* is pulling out all the stops. I'm just pulling out my wallet."

"Please don't think you need to be so fancy with us," Mom says to Josh. "We're all perfectly happy to fly coach on a commercial flight."

"It's all good, Momma Lou," Josh replies. "T-Rod says with such short notice, chartering a flight for fifty people is what makes the most logistical sense."

"But isn't it crazy-expensive?" Mom asks.

Josh waves at the air. "I'm only getting married once. And like I said, T-Rod said it's the best way to get everyone there on short notice."

"Who's *T-Rod*?" Zander asks, and I can't help noticing Beatrice snuggling closer into Zander's chest as his deep baritone voice rumbles against her cheek.

"Theresa Rodriguez," Josh says. "My personal assistant for the past six years."

"T-Rod's the absolute best," Kat says. She rests her hand on her ever-growing baby bump. "Without her, we never would have been able to throw together a destination wedding for two hundred people on such short notice."

"Did you christen her T-Rod or was that Josh?" Lydia asks Kat.

"That was all Josh," Kat replies.

Lydia laughs. "I just assumed it had to be you because of the Morgan family's love of nicknames." She looks at Josh. "Now I see why you fit in so well with this family."

I glance at Keane, assuming he's going to chime in on this particular topic. We all love nicknames in this family, but Keane and Ryan are by far the most talented at giving them. But Keane looks lost in thought. Exhausted. Kind of miserable, as a matter of fact.

My eyes shift to Ryan. Whenever Keane looks like a lost puppy, I like to call Ryan's attention to the situation so he can pull Keane aside and find out what's up. But, much to my surprise, Ryan looks as lost in his thoughts and miserable as Keane.

"I know, right?" Josh says to Lydia, laughing. "These Morgans take the sport of nicknaming to Olympic levels. I'm a rank amateur compared to them."

Lydia giggles. "Me, too. When I first met the Morgans in the hospital, I needed a spreadsheet to keep track of everyone."

"Same here," Josh says. "I needed a spread sheet to keep track of *myself*." He launches into listing the various nicknames he's been christened with since meeting the Morgans and everyone laughs and throws a few more at him, just for good measure. "What about you?" Josh asks Lydia. "What have they done to you?"

Lydia laughs. "So far, they haven't been too brutal with me. I'm Lydi-Bug and Flip Yer Lyd."

"Nice," Josh says, laughing.

"I'm Theo-Leo," Theo pipes in. "Ryan called me that when I made it to the top of the highest rock wall at Climb & Conquer because I'm lionhearted."

"And also because you were 'King of the world!'" Ryan adds.

Theo looks at Ryan blankly.

"You know, Leonardo DiCaprio in *Titanic*?"

Theo shakes his head.

A flurry of commentary occurs about the awesomeness and horrendousness of that movie, depending on who's talking, and, ultimately, my mother winds up offering to have the three Decker kids over for a slumber party one night soon so that she can watch *Titanic* with Theo after the girls have gone to bed. "We'd have a grand ol' time," Mom says to Theo and the girls. "Popcorn. Hot cocoa. Maybe a little Monopoly. Plus, I think your mommy and Colby would appreciate having a date night." Mom glances at me, her eyes sparkling, and I can't help shooting her a grateful smile. *Best. Mom. Ever.*

I squeeze Lydia's hand under the table. Hot damn, I love my matchmaking mother. And, motherfucking hell, I know *exactly* which night to put on the calendar: the night of my last physical therapy session with Lydia, the day after I get back from Maui.

"Thanks so much, Momma Lou," Lydia says, returning my hand-squeeze under the table. "Doesn't a slumber party here sound fun, guys?"

Izzy expresses extreme excitement. Theo is polite but sweet about it. But Beatrice's isn't having it.

Lydia looks at me. "Will Ralph be here for the slumber party, too, Colby?"

"He sure will. And I'm sure he'll want to sleep with Beatrice, if she'll let him."

Okay, that does it. Beatrice is now absolutely ecstatic about the sleepover.

More conversation ensues—random topics that zigzag all over the place, as is pretty typical around here. And, finally, Josh says, "So, hey, Dax, did you ever hear from Reed about that demo of yours? I sent it to him and he said he loved it, but I haven't heard anything since."

Dax forces a fake smile and explains that, yeah, Reed Rivers contacted him to say he loved the band's sound but that he wanted to see 22 Goats perform live before discussing the possibility of the label signing them. "It's okay," Dax says. "I know Reed is a busy guy."

"It'll be good for you to meet Reed in Maui," Josh says. "Maybe that'll remind him to carve out some time to come to Seattle to see you play."

"Or Dax's band could play a show for Reed in Maui," Lydia says softly, almost to herself.

"Oh my gosh," Kat says, her entire face lighting up. "Why didn't I think of that?" She pat's Josh's arm. "Honey, text T-Rod about this idea. She'll need to make arrangements."

Josh pulls out his phone and taps out a text. "Consider it done, Dax. We'll make it happen, one way or another."

"Holy crap. Thanks so much, guys," Dax says. He shoots Lydia a grateful look that melts me. "Thanks for the idea, Lydia."

"No problem. I was just thinking out loud."

I squeeze Lydia's hand under the table again, lean into her ear, and say, "If I didn't already love you, Lydia Decker, I swear to God I would have fallen head over heels in love with you just now."

Chapter 51
Colby

While everyone else is in the family room, eating cake and listening to Dax and Theo play their guitars, I pull Ryan into the kitchen.

"What's up with Keane?" I ask. "And what's up with you, for that matter? You both look like you've been rode hard and hung up wet."

"I'm in hell," Ryan says. "The girl of my dreams isn't working out. Don't ask. And Keane is just coming off a massive shit storm. It seems Peen Star got himself into a bit of hot water last week with some crazy-ass client. But he's all good now. I roped in Josh and Josh roped in this friend of his named Henn who's a miracle-worker and it's smooth sailing for Peenie now."

"Oh, thank God," I say. "What happened? Did sex with a client come back to bite Peenie Weenie in the ass?"

"*Bingo.* But he's gonna be okay. He killed off Peen Star. May he rest in peace. He's gonna start over with a brand-new stripper name and a new, reputable booking agency. He said he's gonna recharge his batteries in Maui and come back fresh and squeaky clean and start slaying again—this time without the laying."

"What's his new stripper name?"

Ryan laughs. "Ball Peen Hammer."

"Oh, for the love of fuck."

"Don't be too hard on the kid," Ryan says. "He's young and women were throwing themselves at him in ways he just couldn't resist. Trust me, he's learned his lesson."

"You sure about that?"

"Positive. He's gonna take the job seriously from now on and make a real go of it. He knows he dodged a major bullet."

239

I rub my forehead. "Thanks for dealing with that. Jesus, that kid gives me a heart attack."

"Fucking Peen."

"Fucking Peen."

"So, hey, enough about Magic Mike," Ryan says. "Today's a big day for you, Superman: Colby Morgan bringing a girl home for the first time. You do realize Momma Lou thinks you've brought home her three future grandkids, right?"

"As far as I'm concerned, those kids are already mine in my heart. But I'm not thinking about actual marriage any time soon. I only just now told Lydia I love her for the first time a few minutes ago."

"A few minutes ago?"

"Just now. Sitting at the dinner table."

"With everyone there?"

I grimace. "Yeah. Bad, huh?"

"*Colby.*"

"Shit. It just slipped out."

Ryan chuckles. "Uncharacteristically dumbshit move."

"I know."

"Well, did she say it back?"

"No. But it's okay. I didn't say the actual magic words. I said it so off the cuff, there was no chance for her to reply."

"What did you say?"

I tell Ryan word for word what I said and then palm my forehead as I realize how stupid I am. "Crap. That was the world's worst first 'I love you' in the history of time, wasn't it?"

Ryan laughs. "Pretty bad."

"Shit," I say. "I've got to go out there and pull Lydia aside and fix this. I've got to tell her for real." But before I've made a move to leave, Lydia's voice calls to me from the entryway of the kitchen.

"Colby?" she says.

I turn around to find Lydia looking... highly aroused. Her cheeks are flushed. Her eyes are blazing. *I know that look.*

"Can I talk to you for a minute?" she says.

My dick is tingling. There's no way I'm imagining the sexual look on Lydia's face right now. "Sure thing," I say smoothly. "See ya later, Captain." With that, I grab Lydia's hand and lead her slowly out of the kitchen toward my mother's office down the hall—the closest room with a lock on the door. I just became crutch- and cane-free yesterday, actually, so I'm pulling Lydia along pretty slowly. But, oh my fucking God, I'm walking as fast as my legs will carry me.

Chapter 52
Colby

I shut and lock the door of my mother's office behind me and the second I turn around, I'm pinned against the door and met with the crush of Lydia's lips on mine. My dick hardening, I wrap my arms around her and return her kiss with everything I've got. Everything I am. After almost two months of kissing nothing but Lydia's fingers and wrists and palms, this kiss feels like the first time. No, better than the first time, actually. I've never felt quite this kind of connection with anyone before, the rush of my soul fusing with its mate. After two months of getting to know each other inside and out, this kiss isn't a kiss—it's a communion.

"I can't say it back yet," she whispers against my lips. "I'll say it back when it's not tainted by me breaking the rules."

"Fine. Whatever, baby. The way I said it was stupid, anyway. It's fine."

"But I want you to know I *feel* it, Colby," she says, furiously unbuttoning my jeans. "I want you to know hearing you say those words set me on fire." She rips open the front of my unbuttoned jeans and pushes down the waistband of my briefs and my hard cock pops out. It occurs to me this is definitely not Jane-Austen-approved behavior, but before I can muster the willpower to say or do a damned thing about that, Lydia drops to her knees before me and licks me from ball to tip.

My knees buckle. Oh, God.

For a split-second, I contemplate telling her we should wait. But that impulse passes when Lydia wraps her lips around my cock and *sucks*, jolting my entire body with so much arousal, all at once, I damn near explode into her mouth.

242

"*Lydia*," I breathe. I tilt my head back against the door and concentrate hard on not losing it too fast. "Oh, Jesus," I whisper. "It's been so fucking long."

Within seconds, I'm quaking, desperately trying to hang on. It's been so long since my poor cock has been touched by anything other than my own palm, I feel like a virgin in her mouth. I breathe deeply, focusing all my energy on not coming, but when she massages my taint while continuing to devour me, I lose myself with a loud groan into the back of her throat.

When I'm done climaxing, I pull her up to me and hold her face in my palms and whisper, "Come to Maui with me. *Please*. I can't be away from you, Lydia. I'm physically addicted to you."

She skims her lips against mine and smiles. "I told you: I don't have enough vacation time to come. That was the truth. And it's for the best, anyway."

That last comment pisses me off. "Why is it for the best? I just told you I love you, Lydia. I'm obviously not going anywhere. I've walked through fire for you. What's holding you back now? *What?*"

Lydia jerks her head back, clearly shocked at my sudden show of anger. But, seriously, what the fuck? I'm not a fucking saint! How many dragons do I have to slay before this woman will finally surrender to me completely?

"*What?*" I ask when she doesn't say anything.

"I just meant..." She opens and closes her mouth. "I don't know."

"No. Don't chicken out now. You meant *something*. Have the balls to say it. No holding back. No sugarcoating. What's got you skittish now, Lydia? Lay it on me."

Lydia steps back. "Why are you so angry? I don't understand."

"You don't understand? *I don't understand.* I've been patient. I've been compassionate. I've put my heart on the line. Just tell me what's left for me to do and I'll do it."

"There's nothing for you to *do*, Colby. I just think..." She sighs. "Our relationship hasn't been road-tested yet by you walking out the door to go to work and put your life on the line every day. It's easy for me to be sane and calm and collected when you're not working—when every day I know you're safe and coming back to me. We haven't seen how I'll react after you go back to work and every day is a crapshoot whether you'll live or die. I just want you to be ready for the fact that I might turn into someone you can't love anymore when you're finally back to doing what you were born to do. I'm scared I'll push you away but won't be able to stop myself."

I gape like a fish on a line for a moment, flabbergasted. Jesus Christ. I had no idea I had this final dragon to slay before Lydia could be mine. That my last hurdle would be convincing her to take a chance on me regarding the very thing that makes me *me*. The one thing I'm most proud of about myself. I rub my face for a long moment, anger and hurt and panic bubbling up inside me like lava gurgling inside a volcano. Will I ever be good enough to win this woman? Or has Darren fucking Decker fucked this up for me 'til the end of time? Is she telling me in code she *still* might not be able to love me at the end of all this?

I grab Lydia's face and grit my teeth, near-desperation flooding me. I have to have this woman. I literally can't live without her. "Here today, gone tomorrow, Lydia," I grit out, my face an inch from hers, my eyes on fire. "*I love you, Lydia.* At some point, you're going to have to figure out how to take a leap of faith. Because love doesn't come tied up in a nice little box with a ribbon around it. Love is messy and scary and full of risk. Love *is* risk. It's walking on a tightrope between skyscrapers. It's being shot out of a cannon and jumping out an airplane at thirty thousand feet and you trusting your parachute will open. And, sometimes, love is watching the one you love walk out the door and knowing he might never come home again because it's who he is—but you're willing to love him anyway."

Lydia is trembling in my hands. She nods. And then throws her arms around my neck. "I'm sorry." She nuzzles into my neck. "Don't give up on me. I promise when you get back from Maui, I'll be ready. I promise, Colby. I'll get there. Please don't give up on me. Never, ever give up on me."

Chapter 53
Colby

It's been an incredible six days in paradise.

Tomorrow is finally the big day. The wedding of the century. And then it's back to Seattle the day after that, followed by my last physical therapy session with Lydia on Monday, followed by fucking her brains out at my condo. And then... the rest of my life.

Of course, I'm dying for the sex part of that itinerary. Oh, dear God, I'm aching for it. But it's so much more than the idea of fucking Lydia again that's been turning me inside out this past week away from her. It's the idea that she promised to be ready to give herself to me completely when I get back from this trip. Not just her body. *All of her.* And I'm scared to death, after everything we've been through, she'll realize she can't deliver on that promise, after all.

Being here this week with my entire extended family has made me realize just how much Lydia and the kids belong here, too. Indeed, as much fun as I've had, I never want to attend another family wedding or trip without Lydia by my side, ever again. She's the air I breathe. My port in the storm. She's the beat of my heart. And those amazing kids only serve to amplify the love I feel for Lydia threefold. What if Lydia ultimately decides she can't stomach being with me because I'm a first responder? God help me, I won't survive it.

"You're walking really well, Bee," Zander says, drawing me out of my thoughts.

Ryan, Zander, and I are walking along a winding pathway from the private beach to the hotel after having spent the last couple hours kayaking together. The sun is setting behind us over the spectacular aquamarine ocean. The smell of plumeria fills the air.

"Yeah, I'm almost as good as new," I reply to Zander. But what

I'm thinking is, *I've got to get back to my room for some FaceTime-sex with Lydia.*

"Lambo!" Ryan calls out next to me, and my eyes lock onto our brother-in-law-to-be about thirty yards ahead of us on a perpendicular pathway, walking with his closest crew—his twin brother, Jonas, that hacker guy, Henn, a couple of Josh's fraternity brothers I haven't interacted with too much this week, and, Mr. Big-Dick himself, Reed Rivers.

There are greetings. Shit-talk ensues about the corn hole tournament we all played earlier today, during which Ryan and I eked out a win over the mighty Faraday twins. And then Josh invites Ryan, Zander, and me to his bungalow for an impromptu bachelor party. "We're just gonna smoke cigars and play a little poker," Josh says. "Come with us. I need as much help as I can get to kick Reed's ass. The last time we played cards, Mr. Rivers wiped the floor with me."

Ryan and Zander accept the invitation, but I decline. It's nothing against Josh. I've come to love the guy like a brother, especially after this awesome week. And the few times I've interacted with his core group of friends, I've liked all of them, too. Well, other than Reed Rivers. He seems like a douche, though, of course, I'm thrilled the guy signed my brother's band to a record deal earlier this week. It's just that no bachelor party poker game could ever compete with Lydia's tits on FaceTime.

And so, I offer my regrets, wish everyone good fortune, and head toward my room on the far side of the resort.

On my way to my room, I notice my cousin Julie lounging poolside with her husband while her stepdaughter, Coco, splashes happily in the water. *Perfect.* I've been meaning to pull my cousin aside all week to ask her a few questions.

I head into the pool area and sprawl myself out on a lounger next to Julie and her sleeping husband. After ordering myself a mai tai from the roving cocktail waitress and making small talk with my cousin about today's fun, I finally ask my cousin some questions about what it's like to be a stepparent.

"My biggest worry," I admit, "is that I'll do or say something to make them think I'm trying to take their father's place or somehow dishonor his memory."

"They would never think that because you'd never be disrespectful."

"But what the hell would they even call me?"

Julie laughs. "They'd call you Colby."

I run my hand through my hair. "I'm overthinking this, aren't I?"

"A little bit."

"I just don't want to screw up. Those poor kids have been through enough."

"Colby!" Coco yells from the pool. "Will you come play dolphins with me again?"

"You bet, Flipper!" I shout back. "Just give me another couple minutes, okay?" I return to Julie. "So do you have any final advice for me, Jules?"

My cousin shrugs. "Not really. Just lead with love and you'll be fine."

"Colby!" Coco calls from the swimming pool. "Flipper needs her trainer!" She lets out a hilarious dolphin mating call and Julie and I laugh.

"Sounds like someone has fallen deeply and totally in love with you," Julie says. "The same way those three kids surely have, as well. The same way *everyone* does when they spend any kind of time with you." She touches my arm. "Because to know you is to love you, Colby."

I'm genuinely surprised by my cousin's kind words. It's not that I have an inferiority complex or anything. I know I'm a great guy. It's just that I've always been fairly quiet around Jules and our boisterous side of the family. For her to say something like that about me, she would have had to notice my quiet charms in the midst of abundant chaos, not to mention she would have had to notice me in the midst of my four gregarious siblings. "Thanks a lot," I say. "I think the same of you, Jules."

"Thank you."

I take a deep breath. "Man, I'm excited to get home and start my life."

The song blaring overhead changes from a Coldplay song to the one that's been following me around more than any other these past few months: "Unsteady" by X Ambassadors. As I listen to the familiar song for a moment, I suddenly realize that, for the first time since the fire, it's not telling my story anymore. And it's not telling Lydia's, either. I don't care what fears Lydia admits she has about me being in a high-risk profession, the two of us are rock solid and steady as she goes now. I know it in my bones. Individually. Together. We've made it through the fire, literally and figuratively, and now we're in it for the long haul.

"Colby! Pleeeeease!" Coco calls from the pool. She's flopping around like a dolphin.

I laugh. "Coming, Flipper!" I get up from my lounger. "Thanks, Jules. You have no idea how excited you've made me to get back home and start my new life with my little family."

With that, as that X Ambassadors song continues blaring, I take four bounding steps, launch myself into the air, and cannonball into the pool.

Chapter 54
Lydia

"Say *aloha* to Colby," I say to the kids. I flip my iPhone around so the kids can see Colby's handsome, smiling face, and they all wave and say *aloha* and good night.

"Good night?" Colby says, surprised.

"We're three hours ahead of you, remember?"

"Oh, yeah."

Without warning, Izzy grabs my phone from me and kisses the screen, and I hear Colby laughing wildly and kissing her back.

"Guess what, Izzy Pop?" Colby says.

"What?"

"I got you and your sister the cutest hula-girl outfits you ever did see today. You and Bea Bop a Lula will have to give me a little hula show when I get home, okay?"

Izzy squeals.

"I also got you the prettiest shell necklace you've ever seen, too, honey. I can't wait to see it on your pretty neck."

Izzy gasps. "Can I see it?"

"Nope. It's too pretty to show you on the phone. I want to see your eyes light up in person."

Izzy wiggles with excitement. "I can't wait!"

Colby laughs. "God, I miss you, sweetheart. So, so much."

"I miss you, too," Izzy says. She sighs like a Disney princess looking into a wishing well. "I love you so much, Colby."

My heart stops. Holy shit. Izzy's never said those words to Colby before. Indeed, none of us has ever said those magic, sacred words to Colby before. Not even me. But, of course, leave it to Isabella Rose to lead the charge on kicking down any remaining walls.

249

"I love you, too, my beautiful, smart, silly, sweet Isabella," Colby says, a huge smile on his gorgeous face. "I'm counting the days until I get to see you all again."

Izzy coos like a pigeon and kisses the phone again and Colby leans in and says, "Mwaaaah!"

Without warning, a lump rises in my throat and I swallow it down.

"Put Theo on now, sweetie," Colby says, his smile dazzling. "I have to go to a rehearsal dinner in a bit for my sister's wedding tomorrow and I want to make sure I talk to each of you before I have to go."

"One more kiss," Izzy commands.

They kiss through the phone one last time and then Izzy holds out the phone toward her brother. "Your turn, Theo!"

Theo grabs the phone from his sister and starts excitedly telling Colby about a physical fitness test he took and passed at school today, during which he was required to climb a rope hanging from the school gym's high ceiling.

"Awesome," Colby says. "That's because of all the rock walls you've been climbing, dude."

"When can you start coming to C&C with Ryan and Keane and me?" Theo asks. "You won't believe how good I've gotten."

"I should be able to climb with you in a couple weeks," Colby says. "Believe me, going to C&C with you and my brothers is at the top of my To Do List."

"Can we maybe go just you and me for your first time?" Theo says. "I love going with Ryan and Keane, but maybe we could make your first time something special for just you and me."

Again, I feel choked up.

"Awesome," Colby says, smiling broadly yet again. "So, hey, Theo-Leo, you wanna see what I bought for you today in Hana?"

"For *me*?" Theo says, sounding genuinely flabbergasted.

"Heck yeah, for *you.* I've been missing you and your sisters all week." Without further ado, he pans his camera to a gleaming ukulele sitting on his hotel bed and Theo loses his freaking mind.

"That's for *me*?" Theo shouts.

Colby's face returns to the screen. "Yup. It's a nice one, too. Not a tourist piece of junk. Dax helped me pick it out. He got the same

250

one for himself. He's been playing his all week and loving it. He said when he gets back he'll give you a lesson on it, if you want. He said the ukulele is a lot easier for little hands to play than a guitar."

Theo thanks Colby and they high-five through FaceTime.

"Put on my nemesis now, please," Colby says.

"Okay. I love you, Bee."

Oh my God. Tears prick in my eyes. I didn't mean for my kids to fall in love with Colby just yet. My intention was to take things slow. Keep them and their hearts guarded in case things between Colby and me didn't work out... In case I found I simply couldn't stomach watching him walk out the door every third day to risk his life.

But it's clear to me now, watching them with Colby, that trying to take things slow, whether for myself or my children, is futile. We all love this beautiful man. Lock, stock, and barrel. And there's simply no turning back. No saving ourselves from potential loss or pain. We're all-in.

Theo hands Beatrice the phone.

"Hello, *Newman*," Colby says, and I burst out laughing through my emotion. Beatrice would never get Colby's *Seinfeld* reference, of course, but I sure do.

Colby tells Bea about the presents he got her—a hula-girl outfit, a coloring book, and "a beautiful headdress so you can look just like Moana." And Beatrice loses her mind.

"I love Moana!" she shrieks.

"Yes, I know."

"Say thank you to Colby, honey," I say, wiping my eyes.

"Thank you, Bee!"

"You're welcome, Bea."

"Bea-Bee!"

"That's right. I miss you, sweet pea. Sweet dreams. I love you."

"Okay," she says.

Colby laughs and mutters, "Glad I got those feelings off my chest, Newman. Put your mother on now, Bumble Bea."

I take the phone from Bea's outstretched hand and look at Colby's stunning face. He looks positively euphoric.

"Hi there," I say. "Well, that was adorable."

Colby bites his delectable lower lip, instantly sending goose bumps of desire across my flesh. "Did you get the presents I sent you?" he asks. "I sent them yesterday via overnight shipping. Should have arrived this afternoon."

"Oh. I saw some boxes arrived, but I haven't opened them yet."

"Don't open them with the kids around. They'll be scarred for life."

"*Oh.*"

"Yeah, your presents aren't from Maui. They're just a few things I saw online. Things I thought you might particularly enjoy while I'm still here."

"Sounds intriguing."

"Get the kids to bed, open your presents in your bedroom, get undressed, and FaceTime me back."

My clit pulses. "I'll call you in twenty minutes."

Chapter 55
Lydia

Colby is naked and kneeling on his hotel bed in Maui, his phone propped in front of him. I'm naked and kneeling on my bed in Seattle, the fancy new dildo Colby sent me via expedited shipping in one hand and my phone in the other.

As Colby pumps his shaft, he says, "Now put the camera right up close to your pussy, baby. Yeah, like that. Right underneath it. Oh, yeah. That's good."

"Oh, Jesus, Colby. This thing feels amazing. It's unbelievable."

"The reviews said it's the Rolls Royce of dildos."

I moan. "I think it might be the Lamborghini of dildos. Oh, Jesus. This is heaven."

"Show me the view from right underneath, baby. I wanna see it buried inside you."

I move my phone so Colby can see the view he desires and he moans. "So hot. Oh, God. I'm gonna come so hard. Now put the phone right up against your clit. Rub the camera right on your clit so the lens gets kind of smudged."

I do what he wants and he pumps his shaft harder and growls.

"Now prop the phone on the bed in front of you and give me a show," Colby commands.

I do it.

"Oh, fuck, that's sexy. Fuck, I'm so turned on."

"Colby, I'm close. I'm so close. This is gonna be a huge one."

"Not yet. Hold off, baby. Wait for me."

"I can't. It's coming."

"Hold off to make it bigger. Get the other thing I sent. You're supposed to add that now—when you're on the verge. Clamp that

253

thing onto your clit and turn it on. It's gonna make you lose your shit. Best oral sex simulator on the market."

I grab Colby's second gift off the bed. A little egg-shaped vibrator with a suction opening that, according to the instructions I read before calling Colby back, is supposed to vacuum seal around my clit and send gentle sonic waves straight into my epicenter.

"Okay, it's clamped on," I report. "I'm not gonna be able to hang on much longer, babe."

"Turn it on the lowest possible setting but don't stop fucking yourself with the dildo."

"This is insane."

"Do it."

I do as I'm told. "Oh, Jesus."

"Good?"

I let out a garbled cry.

"Now turn up the clamp one notch."

"If I do that, I'm gonna pass out."

"Do it. One notch. Now."

Sweat is trickling down the canyon between my breasts. "I seriously might pass out, babe."

"*Do it.*"

I do what my beautiful pervert wants and ten seconds later, my internal muscles, the ones clamped around the dildo, constrict and warp so forcefully, the dildo shoots out of my body and spears the bed. I crumple onto the mattress, convulsing, wracked with more pleasure, all at once, than I knew possible. I rip off the clamp and writhe, my cries of release mingling with the sound of Colby coming over the phone.

Finally, when my orgasm has subsided, and so has his, apparently, I pick up my phone and behold Colby's smiling face on my screen.

"Dry eyes?" he asks.

"Yep. As usual."

"You're so ready for me," he says, his grin lighting up his gorgeous face.

"I'm *so* ready," I agree.

"Three more days."

"The longest three days of my life," I say.

"I've got my mom confirmed to watch the kids Monday night. She'll coordinate with Rosalind so she doesn't have to figure out how to pick them up and drop them off at school."

"Perfect. Thank you." I bite my lip. "God, it's gonna be an amazing night." Electricity is coursing through me. "Colby?"

"Yeah, baby?"

My heart is clanging wildly in my chest. I never thought it possible for me to feel this way again. Actually, wait... in truth, I've never felt this way before. Not *this*. This love I'm feeling for Colby is something brand-new. Something unique. It's not more or less than the love I felt—and feel—for Darren. Not better or worse. It's simply incomparable.

"There's an emotion I'm feeling for you," I say. "An emotion I want to tell you about—special words I want to say. But I want to say those words to you for the first time, in person, rather than like this."

Colby flashes me a huge smile. "Yeah, don't say the words to me over FaceTime for the first time, baby. I want to be able to touch and kiss you when you say it." He sighs. "But, oh my God, baby, I can't take my own advice. I love you, Lydia. I've loved you from the minute I laid eyes on you. I'll love you 'til the end of time." He sighs happily. "Lydia Decker, I love you and I'm one hundred percent sure I'm going to love you 'til the day I die."

Chapter 56
Colby

Josh and Kat and the wedding officiant supplied by the hotel—a Hawaiian guy in a white linen suit and flower lei—are standing before their two hundred wedding guests, exchanging promises of forever against the backdrop of an orange and purple painted sky hovering over a glimmering ocean. It's a stunning vignette. Gorgeous. But nothing compares to the expressions of pure joy on both Josh's and Kat's faces.

Man, life can shock a guy sometimes. I would have bet literally *anything* the first of us Morgan kids to say "I do" and make a kid would have been Ryan. And yet, in mere minutes, Kat will be Mrs. Faraday. And not too long from now, she'll be the mother of a little girl—Gracie Louise Faraday. And that little girl will look at my sister the same way we Morgan kids look at our mother. The way Lydia's three kids look at her.

Lydia.

Oh, shit. I'm doing it again. Obsessing about Lydia. Even while sitting here listening to Josh and Kat exchange their wedding vows.

But it can't be helped. My ache for Lydia has become all-consuming. I'm steeped in her. Drowning in her. I'm missing a limb called Lydia. No, an organ. My heart.

I force myself to tune back into the wedding ceremony.

"You're my fate, my love," Kat is saying to Josh. "My destiny. I truly believe that every minute of my life up 'til now was engineered by a greater power to bring me to this moment—to *you*—so that I could become your devoted wife."

That's exactly how I feel. Every minute of my life up 'til now was engineered to bring me to Lydia. I wasn't even supposed to work

256

the day of the fire. I'd swapped shifts with a buddy so he could attend his parents' anniversary party. But it seems a greater power had a plan for me. A plan that included me meeting and falling in love with a gorgeous woman named Lydia Decker.

Kat continues, "I'll love you forever, Joshua William Faraday. I promise to love and honor you in good times and in bad, in sickness and in health, all the days of my life and never, ever leave your side as long as I'm drawing breath into my body."

My skin pricks. I feel like Lydia and I have already pledged these very things to each other—not in words, but with our actions. In those early days after the fire, Lydia was the one who helped me get my ass onto a toilet, for fuck's sake. Talk about in sickness and in health. As I sit here now, I know in my heart I'll never want anyone other than Lydia. Even without saying the words Josh and Kat are saying in front of the entire world, I already feel like Lydia and the kids belong to me. Actually, as nice as this ceremony is, watching it is making me realize I truly don't need to do something like this to feel eternally committed to Lydia and the kids.

I tune back into the ceremony to find Josh in the midst of saying his vows.

"And, most of all, my beloved Kat, I vow to you, right here and now, in front of God and all the people we love, which includes Keane, by the way, just to be clear—"

Every Morgan in attendance, including Keane, bursts out laughing. And the minute my laughter subsides, I'm feeling consumed with a thumping need to get back home to tell Lydia I've realized how completely and unconditionally I love her... and always will.

Josh cups Kat's jawline in his palm and says, "I promise to make every day of our life together better than any fantasy, baby. *Forever.*"

Chapter 57
Colby

Walking off the plane and into the terminal, flanked by Ryan and Keane and Dax and Mom and Dad and other members of my entire extended family, I tap out a text to Lydia, telling her I've landed and would love to swing by her place on my way home from the airport, just to say hi and give the kids their presents. But her immediate reply shoots me down.

Welcome home! Dang it! Not home right now. See you tomorrow!

"Shit," I mutter. "Fuck!"

"What?" Ryan says.

I mumble something incoherent and begin banging out a frantic, desperate reply, asking Lydia when she'll be home. Telling her I'll come by, no matter what time it is. But before I've pressed send on my text, I round a corner toward the baggage claim area... *and there they are*—my family. Standing twenty yards away with huge smiles on their faces and a sign with little-kid writing on it that says "WELCOME HOME, COLBY!"

"Colby!" Izzy shouts excitedly, waving frantically and sprinting toward me.

When Izzy and I crash into each other, I pick her up and swing her around and she squeals with unadulterated glee. Quickly, I kiss her on the cheek and put her down and dole out enthusiastic hugs and kisses to the other kids. And then I do the one thing I've been dying to do all week long—something I've never done before: I take my woman into my arms and kiss the living hell out of her in front of her three kids. Not to mention my family members who've congregated to greet Lydia and the kids, too.

Oh, God, this kiss! It feels like a once-in-a-lifetime moment. A declaration of love from the highest mountaintop. *It feels like destiny.*

"Go get her, Tiger," I hear Keane say as my lips devour Lydia's, and various chuckles and titters rise up around me.

Finally, I force myself to stop kissing Lydia. I rest my forehead against hers and whisper, "I love you."

And she replies with the most awesome four words in the human language: "*I love you, too.*"

Chapter 58
Lydia

The presents Colby brought for the kids from Maui were a smash hit. Upon ripping open their hula outfits, the girls immediately insisted on dancing for Colby and me, accompanied by Theo's haphazard strums on his gleaming new ukulele. After the show, Beatrice flopped down onto the floor, eager to color in her new Maui coloring book while the rest of us looked at Colby's photos from his trip.

When bedtime for the girls rolled around, Colby read to Izzy and Bea from a book about the Hawaiian Islands while Theo and I cleaned the dishes from dinner and made lunches for tomorrow. Finally, Colby and I administered kisses and hugs and "I love you's" to all three kids, turned out the overhead lights, flipped on night lights, and then tiptoed back into the family room, both of us physically vibrating with lust for each other.

And now...

Praise be to Jesus, I'm straddling Colby's lap on the couch, kissing him furiously and grinding into the hard bulge behind his jeans.

"I've got a present for you, too," Colby whispers, his hands cupping my ass.

"Well, pop that sucker out," I say.

He laughs. "I'm not talking about my dick. I brought you an *actual* present."

"I'd rather have your dick."

He laughs again. "Patience. We're gonna do that tomorrow, remember? At my condo when there are no kiddies right down the hall."

I give him one final kiss and lean back slightly, giving him leeway to pull a little box out of a duffle bag next to the couch.

My eyes widen.

"It's nothing fancy," Colby says quickly when he sees my expression. "It's just a little token to let you know I was thinking about you while I was away."

He places the box in my hand, a shy smile on his face, and I open it to find a simple necklace inside—a black pearl pendant on a silver chain.

"It's beautiful," I say. I kiss him. "Thank you so much. I love it."

"Pearls are a huge thing in Hawaii. Apparently, they're rich in symbolism." He takes the box from me and begins extricating the necklace from it. "In Chinese culture, pearls were believed to protect a person from fire. I figured being with a firefighter, you should have that kind of protection."

"Good thinking."

He snakes the chain around my neck, sliding his fingertips deliciously over the nape of my neck. "Western cultures associate pearls with chastity and modesty," he says. "So I thought what better way to commemorate our time with Jane Austen than a pearl?" He grabs his phone and holds it up, set to the selfie function, so I can see myself wearing the necklace.

"I love it," I say, touching the pendant with my fingertip. "I'll wear it all the time. Thank you."

Colby puts his phone down and kisses the curve of my neck, making me shudder. "And, last but not least," he whispers, his warm breath tickling my skin. "Small pearls were sometimes used in Victorian times to symbolize tears." He slides his hands underneath my shirt and around my back and runs his fingertips up my back toward my bra. "I know you've shed an ocean of them in your life," he says softly. He unlatches my bra. "And I know you're scared you'll wind up shedding more with me because of what I do for a living. Who I am at my core. But I want this pearl right here to symbolize your willingness to take that chance with me. I want this pearl to symbolize we both know life is full of risk and loss and tears, but that we've both consciously decided our love is worth taking that risk."

Rather than reply verbally, I nod and kiss Colby's mouth. As he returns my kiss passionately, he pulls my unlatched bra off my breasts, letting them tumble free under my shirt. When he cups my bare breasts in his palms and pinches my nipples, I go freaking ballistic with desire. I know we've agreed to wait until tomorrow to do the final deed, but I can't wait. His final physical therapy session is mere hours away now—and, really, it's only symbolic at this point. For all intents and purposes, he's not my patient anymore. Anyone at the licensing board would be able to see he's fit and strong and of sound mind and body. Anyone would understand we're in love.

I frantically unbutton Colby's jeans as he pulls my skirt up. He grips my bare ass cheeks and slides his fingertips down my G-string and straight into my wetness, making me moan with white-hot excitement. It's the first time in two months Colby's touched the most intimate spot on my body, and, just this fast, my muscles are spasming. I cry out as his fingers slide inside me and begin strumming my G-spot. And then moan loudly when he lifts my shirt and buries his face in my breasts. His fingers inside me are doing magical things. Oh, fuck, this feels good. I pump his shaft as it peeks out of his unbuttoned jeans and he growls and takes my other nipple frantically into his hungry mouth.

My core shudders. And then squeezes forcefully. And then...

"Oh, Jesus," I choke out. I grip his dick hard as an orgasm rips through me, sending my womb slamming up and down inside me and shockwaves of pleasure scorching through every nerve ending. I don't mean to do it. Lord knows I don't. But I lose control of myself completely and let out a howl of ecstasy.

"Mom?" Theo's alarmed voice immediately calls out from his bedroom, even before my convulsions have stopped. "*Mommy?*"

In a flash, Colby throws my shuddering body off him onto the couch and leaps toward the hallway. "She's fine, Theo!" he calls out, stuffing his dick back into his jeans. "Your mom just stubbed her toe."

"I just stubbed my toe!" I choke out, writhing on the couch. "Ouch! My toe!" I begin frantically pulling myself together and scramble to standing.

"Don't come out here, Theo!" Colby shouts from the entryway. "Everything's fine!"

"Stay in your room!" I yell. "I just stubbed my toe!"

But, suddenly, there he is. Theo. Standing in the entryway to the living room, rubbing his groggy eyes. "Are you okay, Mom? Did you break it?"

Colby covertly shifts his hard dick in his jeans, looking like he's in physical pain.

"Break what?" I ask.

"Your toe."

"Oh. Yeah, I'm fine," I say, my cheeks hot. "Just stubbed it."

"But you screamed so *loud*."

Colby chuckles behind Theo. "Yeah, you really did."

"Yeah, I... um. I wacked it pretty hard. Go back to bed, buddy. I'm fine."

"Will you come tuck me in again?" Theo says.

"Sure."

Colby clears his throat. "Hey, I'm gonna head out, honey. Big day tomorrow." He rustles Theo's hair. "Have fun at my parents' house tomorrow night, Theo-Leo. Thanks for being such a good sport about doing that for us."

I kiss Colby's cheek. "FaceTime me when you get home," I say. "I'd like to continue our conversation to completion." I look down at the bulge behind Colby's jeans and wink.

"Will do," Colby says. "I'll call you the minute I get home. *For sure*."

"You don't have to leave," Theo says. "I'll just put myself back to bed. It's okay."

Colby smiles. "No, I should go. I'm wiped. It's been a long travel day and I've got a special date planned for your mom and me tomorrow that requires us to be well rested."

I smile wickedly. "Don't forget to call me the minute you get home. I'll be waiting."

Colby kisses my cheek. "Babe. Believe me. You don't have to ask me twice."

Chapter 59
Lydia

I sign Colby's release form with flourish. "Colby Morgan, you're officially done with physical therapy."

A huge smile spreads across Colby's face. "So I'm no longer your patient?"

I'm acutely aware that several other physical therapists standing nearby are blatantly eavesdropping on this conversation. I clear my throat. "Correct. As we've already talked about, you've still got some work to do on your own to get yourself into shape to pass the fire department's fitness and strength test. But getting you to heightened strength for the department's fitness test wasn't the mission of your physical therapy. My mission was to restore you back to full functionality and I've done that. But don't worry, I've mapped out a suggested workout program for you for the next six weeks to help you get into shape for the CPAT. And feel free to keep in touch if you have any questions going forward and I'll be happy to answer them."

Colby is smiling like the cat who swallowed the canary.

I glance at the other physical therapists and shift my weight. "I mean, I know you're a fitness fanatic, so you've probably got a workout program planned. But just in case you wanted a little guidance..." I hand him the workout plan I've devised for him to get him into peak conditioning for his physical fitness test for the fire department.

Colby looks down at the paper in his hand and then back up at me, shooting me an elated smile. "Well, thank you for everything you've done for me, Lydia," he says. "It's been a pleasure working with you."

"For me, too. Good luck."

Colby's smile is positively wicked. "Now, don't move a muscle, okay?"

Before I can reply, Colby sprints through the crowded clinic, past several physical therapists working with their patients—including Ramona working with a patient in a far corner—and ultimately disappears around a corner.

I stand frozen waiting for him, my cheeks blooming and my heart clanging. What the heck is he doing?

Ten seconds later, the answer to my question is answered when Colby reappears holding a massive bouquet of red roses. I'm talking about a *massive* effing bouquet of red roses!

"Oh my gosh," I whisper.

As Colby passes Ramona, he pointedly says hello to her, inducing a look of pure hatred from her that makes me laugh out loud. He makes his way past several other physical therapists and their patients before finally reaching me and presenting the bouquet to me like I've just won the Miss America pageant.

"How's this for engaging in *romantic* relations," he says.

I laugh. "Thank you. So *romantic*, Colby. Wow. And so extravagant."

To my shock, Colby leaps onto a nearby therapy table and bellows, "May I have your attention please?"

Oh my God. *No.* He wouldn't...

I look around, mortified, as everyone stops what they're doing and stares.

"I just officially completed my physical therapy!" Colby shouts gleefully, and everyone applauds and cheers. He gestures to me. "Thanks to the professionalism and expertise of my wonderful physical therapist, I'm as good as new!" He flexes his muscular arms.

More cheers and applause.

"And now that Lydia's no longer my physical therapist, guess what?" Colby's smile lights up his entire face. "*I can finally engage in romantic relations with Lydia Decker!*"

I throw my palms over my cheeks, flabbergasted, as everyone in the clinic cheers and laughs. This is so out of character for Colby, I can't even process what's happening. This man hates being the center of attention. He hates it! I've never once seen him do anything that would have suggested he'd do this.

"As some of you have probably noticed, I've had a *massive* crush on this woman since the first day I saw her. *Massive*. But when I asked her out, which I did every single day while I was still in the ICU"—everyone chuckles at that—"she made it crystal clear any kind of romance between us would have to wait until I was no longer her current patient. I guess there's some sort of policy?"

I suddenly get it. He's putting on this show to protect me from supposition and gossip that will surely follow us around after today.

"So I've waited like a good boy," Colby continues. "It's been rough, but all good things come to those who wait." At that last word, he looks pointedly across the room at Ramona, clearly giving her one last "fuck you."

Colby climbs down from the therapy table and takes my hands. "Lydia?" he says. "I've wanted to ask you something since the first moment I laid eyes on you."

My heart lurches into my throat. *Oh my God. He wouldn't.*

"Will you *please* go out on a date with me?"

I exhale with relief. "Yes!" I say, chuckling, and everyone claps.

"How about lunch right now?" Colby asks. "Are you free?"

"I just so happen to be," I say. I touch the pearl pendant around my neck. "Let's go."

Colby puts his arm out and I take it. He leads me toward the door of the clinic, pausing in front of Ramona and her patient. "I made a lunch reservation at your favorite restaurant," he says, loud enough for Ramona to hear.

"Great. Thank you."

He touches my cheekbone. "And after lunch, I thought I'd take you back to my condo and give you a tour."

"Mmm hmm." Oh, God, I'm blushing.

"And then I thought maybe we'd have sex all night long."

I blush and look at Ramona. Her jaw is hanging open. So is her patient's. "Sounds like a plan to me," I squeak out, barely able to keep from fainting from embarrassment.

"Great," Colby says. "Oh, hi, Ramona. Great to see you again." With that, he takes me by the hand, leads me out of the clinic, throws his head back, and bursts into gleeful laughter.

Chapter 60
Colby

My hands on my steering wheel and my dick rock hard, I glance at Lydia in the passenger seat of my truck and smile like a fool for the hundredth time during this short drive from the restaurant to my condo. A little champagne in my woman and, lord have mercy, my horny, dirty, born-again virgin was unleashed. Just two glasses in, Lydia took off her shoe in the restaurant and gave me a foot job under the table. Three glasses in, and she was whispering to me about the blow job she was dying to give me. *Best lunch ever.*

In retrospect, it probably wasn't the sanest idea for me to take Lydia straight to a restaurant right after we'd marched triumphantly out of the outpatient clinic, arm in arm. Based on our mutual, raging boners in that moment, the more obvious play was to drive Lydia straight to my place and begin fucking her brains out without delay, exactly the way I've been fantasizing about doing for over two months now. But, for some reason, it felt hugely important to me that Lydia and I have an actual first date to look back on and tell the kids about one day. Something classy to mark the beginning of The Story of Colby and Lydia. Plus, I think I just wanted to finally get to be out in public with my woman and be able to kiss her and nuzzle her jawline and show her off to the world as my *girlfriend.* Not my physical therapist. Not my friend. *My woman.*

Mine.

The song on the radio switches to "Unsteady" by X Ambassadors and I quickly change the station. *Enough.* The new song is "Wonderwall" by Oasis. Much better. I look over at my tipsy, beautiful Wonderwall and smile at her.

"You look gorgeous."

"I *feel* gorgeous," she replies. And then she laughs uproariously at herself, making me laugh. She adds, "And *horny.*"

"Really? I couldn't tell. The foot job you gave me under the table didn't give that away at all."

She giggles, yet again. "One more glass of champagne and I would have slipped under the table to give you something more than a foot job."

Oh my God, she's so sexy. And so full of shit. As hot as that thought is, there's no circumstance under which Lydia Decker would ever slip under a table in a restaurant to blow me and we both know it. But, still, I love hearing her talk dirty like that. "If champagne gets you thinking that way, baby, then it's an awfully good thing for me I've got two more bottles of champagne waiting for us on ice at my place."

"Oooh," she says. "You've thought of everything. But I sure hope you didn't get the same kind we had at the restaurant."

My stomach drops into my toes. That's exactly the kind of champagne I bought. And it wasn't cheap. "I thought you loved that kind from the restaurant," I say. "You once told me it's your favorite."

"Oh, it *is* my favorite," she says. "But it's way too expensive for you to be buying three bottles of it. Feed me the cheap stuff at this point and I won't even notice the difference."

I wave her concerns away. "It's all good. This is a once-in-a-lifetime occasion. No do-overs. I want to do it right."

"Once in a lifetime? Babe, we'll be having sex again after today, I promise. Many, *many* times."

"But never again after two months of making Jane Austen turn over in her grave."

"Still, honey, you're spending way too much money on me. That restaurant wasn't cheap. And neither were these flowers." She motions to the outlandish bouquet resting across her lap.

She's right. I've definitely splurged today. And not just today. Truth be told, I spent the equivalent of two car payments on presents from Maui for Lydia and the kids, not to mention those sex toys I had delivered to Lydia via expedited shipping while I was away. And it certainly doesn't help my fiscal situation that I'm on disability these days and won't be earning my full salary again until I return to work in a month or two. But when it comes to Lydia, I just can't seem to care about saving money the way I usually do. As careful as I normally am with my funds, I'd gladly spend the equivalent of *ten* car payments on Lydia if it would guarantee I'd get to see her smile at me the way she's doing right now. "Don't worry for a second about the money I've spent," I say. "I've been saving my money for today for a long time."

"You have?"

I nod.

"For how long?"

I grin. "My entire life."

Lydia visibly swoons. "Oh, *Colby.*"

Lydia's phone buzzes and she looks down at it. "Your momma says the kids are safe and sound at your parents' house. Thank you, Momma Lou! Is Ralphie already there?"

"Yup. I took him this morning. Didn't want him staring at us while we were doing it doggy-style."

She laughs. "Good thinking. That would have been creepy."

I pull up to the curb in front of my condo and gesture. "This is it. Home sweet home. It's small, but it's mine. Well, mine and the bank's. Mostly, the bank's."

Lydia looks out the window at my condo. "It's so nice, Colby. It's so *you.*"

"It's about to get a whole lot nicer. Stay put, baby. I'll come around and get your door."

"Why, thank you. Such a gentleman."

I come around the back of my truck, open the passenger door, and help Lydia down.

She slides her arms around my neck. "*I love you.*"

"I love you, too," I whisper. And then, without warning, I swoop her up and carry her in my arms like a bride, just because I can.

Chapter 61
Lydia

We've barely made it inside Colby's front door before he's kissing me passionately and ripping off my clothes. When he's got me naked, he buries his face in my breasts and sucks my nipples while frantically fumbling with the buttons of his jeans.

I help him rip off his pants and then his shirt and briefs, and the minute we're both naked, I literally leap up and hurl myself at him, taking for granted he'll catch me. And he does, of course. Without missing a beat, my strong fireman catches me in his muscular arms, hoists me up by my ass, and guides me to cling to him like a baby monkey. The minute he's positioned his tip at my wet entrance, I wrap my arms fiercely around his neck, smash my breasts against him, and I slam myself down on his steely hardness. At the sensation of him impaling me and burrowing *all the way in*, we both let out simultaneous gasps and moans of relief.

"Worth the wait," Colby chokes out.

I ride him furiously while kissing him like a lunatic, and Colby somehow manages to cross the room through my attack.

He carries me down a short hall and into his bedroom and all the while, I continue riding him. Once in his bedroom, he throws me onto his bed, making me shriek with excitement. And then, his eyes blazing, he lurches at me, opens my thighs wide, places the backs of my thighs onto his broad shoulders, slides his fingers simultaneously into my wetness and up my ass, and devours my clit with his lips and tongue until I'm gripping the bed cover and gasping for air.

When I climax, it's a big one. And from the excited sounds Colby's making, he's loving every minute of it. He sits on the edge of the bed, pulls me onto his shoulders *facing* his face, so that my thighs

270

are resting on his shoulders and my crotch is smothering his mouth, and then he stands, cradling my hips and pulling me up along with him.

I squeal. "What the hell are you doing?"

"Showing you how big and strong I am now."

I giggle. "Colby."

But my laughter is short-lived. In short order, he's got my back pinned against a wall and his face in my crotch and I'm holding onto the top of his blonde head for dear life. This is insane. But awfully exciting, I must admit.

In no time at all, I come into his mouth, probably at least partly from the sheer exhilaration of being eaten out from way up here—and when I'm done rippling into his mouth, Colby slides me off his shoulders and down, cradles my back in his strong arms to support my descent, and he lays me onto my back on his bed. Without hesitation, he slides his fingers inside me, presses his lips against my ear, and begins swiping at my G-spot with firm, confident strokes while dirty-talking into my ear.

"Holy hell, you're on fire," I grit out.

"I've had a long time to choreograph this."

My pleasure ratchets up. And up and up and up. I arch my back and whimper. I've never experienced pleasure the way I do with Colby. The kind that's so damned hot, it blurs with pain.

"Tell me how much you want my cock," he commands, still swiping at my G-spot like he owns it. I whisper to him, telling him every naughty thing he wants to know, and, within a couple minutes, the muscles deep inside my womb tighten sharply, like my body is getting ready to expel a demon. There's a deep, dull ache in my core. A crazy tingling sensation...

"Clear your mind and let go," Colby commands, his fingertips pushing me to the edge of ecstasy. "Breathe deeply."

I take a deep breath as instructed and then...

"Oh, God!" I blurt. "That feels—"

I can't finish the sentence. In a delicious torrent, my womb releases in warm rhythmic waves that leave me convulsing from head to toe.

"Get inside me," I beg. "I want you."

But Colby ignores me. He shifts his fingers inside me and begins swiping at that spot way in the back. The one I never knew existed until Colby introduced me to it.

"I can't," I whisper, still jerking with aftershocks of my last orgasm.

"You *can*," he whispers. "You're gonna listen to my voice and do whatever I tell you to do. And then you're gonna come harder than you ever have."

"Colby," I breathe. "What are you doing to me?"

"I'm taking you places you've never been before, baby. I'm taking you to The Promised Land."

As his fingers work their magic, he begins to talk to me. He tells me I'm sexy as fuck. That I taste like heaven. He says he almost came in the pool at the clinic when he first saw me in my bathing suit and that he's had wet dreams about that moment ever since. He tells me he's jerked off for months to fantasies of me. That he wakes up at night, hard as a rock, dreaming of eating me out. He tells me I smell good. Look good. Taste good. That my voice makes him hard. My hazel eyes make him come. That he's dreamed of fucking me since he was a teenager. "I used to dream of you all the time," he whispers. "I didn't know it was you until I saw you. But then I remembered you— the fantasy I've always had, ever since I got my first boner. I dreamed of you, Lydia. It's always been you. Oh, God, you're so wet for me, baby."

Jesus Christ. He's good.

"You feel how you're tightening?" he whispers. "You feel that?"

I whimper. "I feel it. What are you doing to me?" I'm so wet, I'm beginning to make a loud sloshing noise against his fingers.

"I'm showing you what your body can do," he says. "Listen to my voice. Focus on the pleasure. Clear your mind, breathe, and listen to my voice."

He continues whispering into my ear as his fingers work their magic, and when the evidence of his need drips onto my hand, that's it. My tipping point. For a split second, I feel a flash of what my brain perceives as brutal pain. It feels so damned good, it hurts. And then, a heartbeat later, I'm hovering in suspended animation, awaiting a tidal wave that's looming over my head... I spread my legs as wide as they'll go, arch my back like I'm birthing a baby, and give in to pure ecstasy.

When my savage release ends, Colby crawls on top of me like he's going to enter me, but when he sees my face, he freezes. "Tears," he says, his voice tight.

I touch my cheeks, shocked at the accusation, and when my fingertips come back unexpectedly wet, I grin. "From pleasure," I say. I touch my lover's face. "Tears of joy, sweetheart. I swear on a stack of bibles. I'm feeling nothing but pleasure and love."

Relief washes over beautiful Colby's face. Clearly, the expression on my face has convinced him of my sincerity.

I shudder with an aftershock from my orgasm. "I'm all yours, Colby. There's no guilt. No regrets. No shame. Nobody else is in this bed with us. It's just you and me."

He lays his forearms on either side of my head, pushes his wet tip against my entrance, and plunges himself inside me.

I gasp at the utter deliciousness of it... and the depth of his thrusts.

I tilt my pelvis to receive him and, soon, we're in a frenzy. Animals in heat.

He pulls out of me, flips me around, pulls me up onto all fours, plunges back inside me, and begins pounding me from behind.

We're fucking without inhibition. Growling each other's names.

Colby's balls are swinging against my backside as he thrusts in and out of me. His skin is slapping against mine. He grabs my swinging breast with his free hand and squeezes, and I come hard around his cock—so hard, I collapse onto the mattress.

Colby turns my limp body onto my back, folds my legs up and over his shoulders and slams into me again.

I grip Colby's face and pull him to me for a deep kiss, my hips tilting up and back to receive his cock, and he responds by devouring my mouth and fucking me even harder.

"I love you," I choke out, my every molecule melting and exploding with the fusion of our bodies. "I love you," I blurt again, and then again and again, over and over, euphoria swelling inside me. *I love Colby.* I'm his now. And I won't feel guilty or sorry for a minute about it. I want this. I need this. *I deserve this.*

In a flash, our mutual pleasure spikes and then quickly boils over. My interior muscles clench around Colby's hardness, sending him over the edge along with me.

Lauren Rowe

When Colby's body finishes rippling inside mine, he collapses on top of me, gasping for air.

We're silent for a long moment. Sweaty. Breathing hard. Our limbs entangled.

Finally, Colby lifts his head, levels me with his startling blue eyes, grins wickedly, and says, "Round one."

Chapter 62
Lydia

"But *exactly* what the heck is it you do to me when your fingers are way up there?" I ask. "I didn't even know I could have orgasms like that. One after the other. *Bam, bam, bam.* It's totally insane."

It's just after 3 a.m. and I'm sprawled across Colby's bed, naked and sweaty, after we just finished playing yet another round of Make Lydia Come Over and Over Again. Colby's lying next to me, on his side, also naked, his legs open casually to reveal every inch of his flaccid dick and balls. Music is playing at low volume in the room. The current song is "I Belong to You," by Lenny Kravitz. *Perfect.*

"It's called The Sure Thing," Colby says. "It makes a woman come over and over again, really hard. She's just got to be lured into the right frame of mind first and then it's off to the races. She can have as many orgasms as she can physically tolerate before passing out or crying mercy."

I wipe my sweaty brow. "Well, I guess I was in the right frame of mind."

"You sure were." He snickers.

"What's the right frame of mind?"

Colby considers that. "Really, *really* turned on. Not at all ambivalent about wanting sex. Mind and body relaxed and open and willing."

"Interesting."

"It worked so well this time because this is the first time I've had you in precisely the right frame of mind. Up until now, you've always been holding back in some way."

"Well, clearly, something was different this time because that was bananas. I mean, you had me going at your parents' and the gym way back when, but tonight has been supernatural."

Colby shrugs. "I'm good."

It's a simple statement of fact, apparently. He's not bragging. Not being cocky. He's simply being accurate.

"Show me what you're doing to me up in there."

Colby shows me the movement of his fingers—a slow come-hither motion with his index and middle fingers. "But I know the exact spot to touch," he says. "The right pressure to use. I can read your body's cues. And, most importantly, I'm talking to you the whole time in your ear to distract you. That's the magic bullet. Like I said, get you in the right frame of mind and then apply the technique the right way, it works like gangbusters every time. Hence, the reason we named it The Sure Thing."

"Who's the 'we' in that sentence?"

"My brothers and me. Well, Ryan and I were the ones who named it. But all of us use it."

I'm flabbergasted. "You've talked to your brothers about what you just did to me?"

"Well, not specifically about doing it to *you*. But, yeah. My brothers and I have always talked about sex. Specifically, the best techniques to ring the bell. That's our mutual obsession—ringing the bell. Hard and often. If you're not getting multiple O's out of a woman, you're a failure."

"All four of you know how to do that thing to women?"

"Five. Zander's an honorary brother. To start with, though, it was just Ryan and me swapping notes, just because the other guys were still thinking about Xboxes, not pussies."

"Tell me more. I'm intrigued. Who was the first to say, 'Oh, I figured out this technique, dude.'"

"Ryan. Despite being two years younger than me, he lost his virginity a full month before me, the bastard. I'm not proud of that fact, by the way, so let it never be spoken about again." He grins. "But, anyway, when I finally had sex for the first time, I raced home to tell Ryan. And he was like, 'Yeah, good boy. But did you do *this* to her? *No*? Well, what about *this*?' And I was like, 'Oh, shit! But, hey, I did do *this*! Did you?' And he was like, 'Say what now?'"

I giggle.

"So that's how it all started. We started swapping information. And the next time I got with my girl, I did the stuff Ryan told me to do and, ka-*bam*! *Way* more fun for my girl. And that made things way, way hotter for me. So then I got obsessed. And so did Ryan. And then we'd compare notes. We were never bragging. Never being disrespectful to girls. We both just wanted to get ridiculously good at ringing the bell. So fast-forward to Ryan at twenty-one or so and he had an extended fling with this wild-child who was ten years older than him. She taught him all kinds of good stuff, including about her A-spot. And the rest, as they say, is history. In one way or another, Ryan and I kept tinkering around with what she showed him for a couple years, until we finally perfected the technique we now call The Sure Thing."

"And then you taught it to the younger guys at some point?"

"Of course. Even before they started having sex, we sat them down to set them straight that sex isn't about wetting your dick. It's about ringing the bell. Embrace that and you've got the key to the kingdom."

"That older woman who taught Ryan should be hailed as a patron saint by every woman who's ever slept with a Morgan brother."

He laughs. "That woman's benefitted many happy women over the years."

"This is utterly fascinating. So the minute I go into the bathroom, are you gonna call your three brothers and Zander and tell them what a splendid job you did 'ringing my bell'?"

Colby chuckles. "It doesn't work like that. We don't brag. And now that we're older, we hardly swap notes anymore. Only if we've got a tough nut to crack or someone figures out something new everyone needs to know."

I squint at him. "You're telling me you haven't talked to any of your brothers about sex with me?"

He blushes. "Yeah, I talked to Ryan a while ago, at the beginning, when you sobbed every time you came with me. I didn't know what to do."

I grab his hand. "It's okay. I can't imagine how much that must have freaked you out. I'm sorry."

"Nothing to be sorry about. It got us where we are now."

"Which is *awesome*," I say.

"You're not feeling the slightest bit of guilt now, right?" he asks.

I stroke his fingers. "Not the tiniest bit. I feel nothing but amazing and happy."

"What about when we're not having sex? Any doubts, fears, or guilt there? Any concerns?"

I shake my head. "Not a one."

He looks unconvinced.

"What?"

"What about the first-responder thing? You're good with that?"

Oh. That. Shit.

Obviously, it's a double-edged sword for me. The very thing I'm attracted to about Colby—his heroic inclinations—makes me scared to death to be in a relationship with him for fear of losing him. But it's now clear to me nothing could possibly make me throw on the brakes with Colby at this point. We're full steam ahead. I love him and always will and there's no turning back. I squeeze his hand. "It's going to be hard for me when you return to work, I confess. I'll need to do some mental gymnastics not to throw my arms around your legs every day and not let you leave. But I promise to deal with any freak-outs head-on when we get there. I'll do whatever I have to do to keep my fears from consuming me or tearing us apart." I press my forehead against his, stroke his cheek, and whisper, "All that matters to me now is that I love you and want to be with you no matter what."

Chapter 63
Colby

I'm striding up Lydia's walkway, here to pick up Izzy for the Daddy-Daughter Dance—which, I've been assured, is commonly attended by not only actual daddies but also by uncles and stepfathers and other assorted non-daddy father figures, too. And then—*hallelujah!*—after the dance, I'll be spending the entire night at Lydia's place for the very first time. I've been jockeying to get a full-night sleepover invitation from Lydia for weeks now, and it finally came through a couple days ago as a result of me telling Lydia about the location of my firefighter fitness test tomorrow morning.

"Hey, babe," I told Lydia. "I just found out my fitness test on Saturday morning is being administered at the main firehouse near you, as opposed to the station where I used to work closer to my condo." And that's all it took. Without hesitation, Lydia told me to bring an overnight bag when I came to pick up Izzy for the dance.

And now, here I am, ascending the steps of Lydia's porch, said overnight bag in my right hand, a corsage of little pink roses in my left, and Ralph loping excitedly alongside me. And I feel like I'm walking on air.

It's been six weeks since Lydia and I first "engaged in romantic relations" that mind-blowing night together at my condo. And since then, our life has been filled with the quiet, simple joys of two people in love slowly morphing into a family of five. There have been regular dinners at Lydia's place. Bath times for Bea. Lunch-making, dish-cleaning, bedtime stories, and a backyard latch needing fixing. There have been dancing and guitar and ukulele shows. A Jasmine-themed birthday party for Beatrice followed a couple weeks later by a Harry-Potter-themed one for Izzy. Family days at the aquarium and

279

the zoo on Lydia's days off. And, of course, plenty of sexy times in Lydia's bedroom when I've rung Lydia's bell so fucking hard and often, she's had to shove a pillow over her face to keep from waking the kids.

It's been an idyllic six weeks. Magical. Perfect. Well, other than the fact that I've been chomping at the bit to finally spend the night and not have to drive back home in the wee hours with Ralph giving me the stink-eye. And now, finally, I'm going to have my cake and eat it, too.

I take a deep breath and ring Lydia's doorbell with my knuckle, electricity coursing through my veins.

Immediately, a high-pitched squeal rises up on the other side of the closed door. Four seconds after that, the door swings open, Ralph barges in, and the gap-toothed wiggler who owns my heart like none other stands before me in a pink, shimmering gown.

"Colby!" Isabella shrieks. She puts her palms on her little cheeks like the *Home Alone* kid. "You look *beautiful!*"

I chuckle. "Hey, that's my line. You look beautiful tonight, Izzy Stardust. Turn around for me, sweetie. I want to see your pretty dress."

Isabella twirls for me, her hands curved over her head like a jewelry-box ballerina, and I *ooh* and *aah* as I stride into the house.

"Whoa," Lydia says when she sees me standing in her living room. "Hunky McHunkerton!" She plants a little kiss on my lips. "I've never seen you in a suit before. You look like a trillion bucks." She slides her fingers up and down the lapel of my designer suit jacket and winks. "I've always had a thing for a sharp-dressed man."

I kiss her and decide now isn't the time to break the news that *Ryan* is the sharp-dressed man she's swooning over, not me. It's not that I'm a Neanderthal when it comes to dressing up. I own a sport coat that was tailored to fit me to a tee and always solicits compliments. But, tonight, given the importance of the occasion to Izzy, and the fact that I'll be one of only a handful of "non-daddy" escorts at the dance, I decided my sport coat simply wouldn't do.

If I'd had my usual paycheck to work with these days, rather than the slightly lesser disability checks I've been getting since the fire, I might have bit the bullet and bought myself a suit for tonight, regardless of the fact that I can count the number of times I've worn a tie on one hand. Actually, even with my tight money situation these days, I still probably would have splurged, regardless, if I thought I'd need a suit for Ryan's wedding early next year. But, last I heard, Ryan's leaning toward tuxedos for his groomsmen and me. So that was that.

And it's not like I'm going to need a suit for my own wedding any time soon. As far as I'm concerned, I'm already married to Lydia—completely committed in my heart and soul to both her and the kids—so why go through the motions of saying vows in front of our families and friends? A guy is either committed to his woman or he's not. That's a fact. I know married guys at the station who fuck around on their wives. Plenty of them. And unmarried dudes who are as loyal as the day is long. And I also know one particular woman, the love of my life, who's already been to hell and back after saying those sacred vows. A woman who promised to love her high school sweetheart "'til death do us part" and then got the shitty-ass, short-end of that stick. So I've got to figure, "Why on earth would Lydia want to go through saying those stressful words again?"

I suppose if I thought Lydia had any desire to get married, then I'd do the wedding thing for her. But Lydia hasn't even hinted at wanting to get married and I'd just as soon not put her or myself through the ritual.

Okay, yeah.

I'm not being completely honest.

If I'm digging *really* deep into the honesty bin, the truth is I'm not sure I want to put *myself* through the ordeal of a wedding. Frankly, as harsh and insecure as it sounds, I don't know if I could stand up there and look into Lydia's hazel eyes and not wonder if Lydia was thinking about the time she said the exact same vows to Darren. If maybe she was wishing things hadn't turned out the way they did with him because she'd so much rather still be married to the great love of her life, if given the choice, rather than to me. Yeah, I'm not proud of it, but at the end of the day, I'm not sure I could stand up there in a tuxedo in front of everyone I love and look into Lydia's amber eyes and hear those sacred words coming out of her mouth... and wonder if she was feeling like I'm her consolation prize.

As Izzy hugs me and Lydia gets some love from Ralph, I put my overnight bag down and glance around the quiet living room. "Where are Bea and Theo? In their rooms?"

"Bea's in her room playing dress-up and Theo's at a sleepover. Apparently, he and his two buddies are writing songs for their new band."

"Nice."

"Did Theo tell you they finally picked their band name?" Lydia asks.

"No. What is it?"

Lydia grins. "Three guesses."

"That's kind of cool."

"No." She laughs. "I'm giving you three guesses."

"Oh." I laugh. "The Smart-Alecs? The Rock Climbers? Oh, I know! Twenty-*three* Goats?"

Lydia giggles. "*The Bed Wetters.*"

My mouth hangs open. "No way."

"Yep."

"Oh my God. That's amazing. The fact that Theo can—"

I feel a tug on the bottom of my suit jacket. "Can we go now, Colby?" Izzy says insistently, her hazel eyes blazing up at me. "I don't want to be late."

I smile at my beautiful date for the evening. "It's still a bit early, honey. We'll leave in ten minutes. Oh, I almost forgot." I hand Isabella the corsage of pink buds and she gasps like I've gifted her with the Hope Diamond. "Man, you're easy to please, Izzy Stardust," I say, chuckling. I slip the delicate pink roses onto Izzy's slender wrist and she stares at it and swoons.

"*Thank you,*" she says. "Oh, *thank you.*"

I chuckle. "You're very welcome, sweetie."

"Okay, you two lovebirds," Lydia says, holding up her phone. "Stand over there in the good light for a prom photo."

Izzy and I position ourselves where Lydia has indicated, but our photo shoot is interrupted when Beatrice tears into the living room, click-clacking on plastic heels, decked out in a Disney-princess dress and smudged, pastel makeup that looks like it was applied during an earthquake. When she reaches me, Beatrice throws her arms around my knees and shouts, "I wannaguhdadda-dadda-daaaaaance-too!"

I burst out laughing and look at Lydia for a translation. "*What?*"

Lydia rolls her eyes. "She wants to go to the Daddy-Daughter Dance, too. She's been demanding to go for the past thirty minutes, ever since she found out, for the first time, that such a thing even exists."

I get down on one knee in front of my nemesis. "Hey, Newman." I touch one of her rouge-filled cheeks. "When you're Izzy's age, I'll take you to the Daddy-Daughter Dance, too, if you still want to go with me by then."

But Beatrice isn't having it. "I wanna go to da daddy-dadda-dance, too—*now!*"

I look at Lydia and she flashes me an exasperated look that says, "Lord, have mercy on my soul." I look at my watch and then at Bea again. "You know what, honey? I'm here super early. Why don't you and I have our own little Daddy-Daughter Dance right here in the living room for a few minutes before I take Izzy to her dance?"

I glance at Izzy as if to say, "Aren't I smart?" and for the first time since I've known her, Izzy Decker looks fucking *pissed* at me... which, of course, means Beatrice *loooooooves* my brilliant idea.

"But you're *mine*, Colby," Izzy says with surprising fire. "You can be Beatrice's when it's *her* turn for the Daddy-Daughter Dance. Tonight, you're *mine*."

"*Mine*," Beatrice says, grabbing my knees again, this time even harder.

Izzy literally stomps her foot with frustration. "No! He's not *yours*, Bea! He's *mine*. I've been waiting for the Daddy-Daughter Dance my whole *frickin'* life!"

I bite my lip, trying not to laugh. I've never heard Izzy "curse" before. I glance at Lydia, expecting to find her looking upset, but, to the contrary, she looks as amused as I feel. But because Lydia Decker is nothing if not a kick-ass momma, she quickly puts on her game face. "Okay, girls, enough with this '*mine*' business. And we can do without the 'frickin',' too, Isabella Rose."

"Sorry."

Lydia continues, "Colby is *everyone's*. Yours, Beatrice's, Theo's, and mine. He loves us *all* and we love him. He's belongs to *all of us*."

My heart skips a beat.

"But, *Mommy!*" Izzy protests.

"*Isabella*. It's not going to take away from your happiness to let Beatrice have happiness, too."

"Yes, it is, Mommy! It *iiiiiiis!*"

I don't mean to do it, but I chuckle. *Oh my God.*

Lydia flashes me a warning look, telling me to keep my laughter under wraps, dude, and I cover my mouth with my hand. As Lydia pulls Izzy over to the couch for a powwow, Beatrice grabs my leg and squeezes tight, claiming me for herself.

"Listen to me," Lydia says, settling herself onto the couch and touching Isabella's tear-streaked face. "*Love is infinite.* Do you know what that word means—*infinite?*"

Izzy nods and sniffles. "Like outer space."

"That's right. Never-ending. It's the opposite of everything you can see and touch. Take a cake, for instance. There are only a certain number of slices of any particular chocolate cake, right, and then it's all gone?"

Izzy nods again.

"But imagine if you had a special Infinity Cake. Every time you finished the last piece of it, another cake popped out a chute and plopped right onto your table, and it was just as moist and delicious as the one before it."

Izzy giggles. "I'd like that."

"Wouldn't that be nice? If you had an Infinity Cake, you wouldn't care if Beatrice ate a piece, would you? Or even if she ate the 'last' piece, because there'd be no such thing as a last piece. You could both have as much cake as you wanted, any time. And that's exactly how it is with love. It's like an Infinity Cake. And guess what else? Love isn't just *infinite,* it's also *indivisible.* That means it can't ever be divided or cut into slices. *Everyone always gets a whole cake.*"

Oh, for the love of fuck.

Thwap.

I feel like I just got hit upside the head with a very big "*Now* do you get it, dumbshit?" stick.

Oh, my God, I've been such a fool. An immature, idiotic, jealous, insecure little fool. Love is *infinite* and *indivisible.* Of course, it is. *Of course.* I suddenly understand how Lydia can love me *and* Darren infinitely and wholly, without one love slicing into the other. And all it took was hearing Lydia explain the way love works—that it's not a zero-sum game—to an eight-year-old.

Darren isn't my competition in a race entitled "The One Lydia

Loves the Most"! Because loving Lydia isn't a race. Or, if it is, then it's a relay race and Darren is my teammate in it, not my rival. *Yes!* It's suddenly so clear to me. Darren ran the first leg of our relay race *for our team*, and now he's handed off the baton to me.

"Do you understand, honey?" Lydia says to Izzy.

I nod, even though she's not talking to me.

Lydia adds, "Love is an Infinity Cake."

"I understand, Mommy," Izzy says sweetly. But then she looks at her little sister across the room, who's presently got her arms wrapped around my legs, and Izzy's eyes darken and turn to daggers. "But if Beatrice makes me late for the dance, I swear to God I'm going to take her Princess Jasmine purse and cut it up into a hundred pieces and then throw it into the trash."

Chapter 64
Colby

I get down on a knee and smile at Beatrice at eye level. "May I have this dance, Bea Bop a Lula?"

Beatrice giggles and nods.

I press play on my selected song—"My Girl" by The Temptations—and pull Bea to the tops of my feet. As the old-school song plays, I dance around the room with Beatrice the same way I used to watch my dad dance with Kat. And my heart soars.

When the song ends, I pick up my nemesis and hug her to me tightly, and she wraps her arms around my neck and kisses my cheek without any prompting whatsoever.

"Thank you for the dance, little miss," I say, my heart aching. "I *loved* it."

"It's a Daddy-Daughter Dance," Beatrice says matter-of-factly.

"That's right. We had our own little Daddy-Daughter Dance, just the two of us."

Bea hugs me. "*Daddy*."

My heart stops. Oh, fuck. Why didn't I see that coming? "No, sweetie. I'm not your daddy. I love you *like* a daddy. But you should call me Colby or Bee, okay?"

Beatrice looks perplexed. "*Daddy-dadda dance*." She pokes my chest. "*Daddy*."

I feel like I'm having a heart attack. "No, honey," I say evenly. "I'm *Colby*. I love you *like* a daddy. With all my heart and soul. Forever and ever. But you have a daddy in heaven."

Now Beatrice looks mischievous. She grabs my cheeks in her little palms and nuzzles her tiny nose into mine. "*Daddyyyyy*."

"Oh, boy," I say, my heart exploding in my chest. "Now I've made it forbidden fruit for you, haven't I?" I look toward the hallway,

286

my heart pounding. God help me if Lydia overhears this conversation. "Hey, why don't you call me Cheese, honey? That'd be funny, wouldn't it? Or maybe Cheese Head?" I tilt my head from side to side and make a funny face, trying to sell it. "Look at me, I'm such a silly Cheese Head."

But Beatrice ain't no fool. She runs her hand along the stubble on my jaw and coos softly, "*Daaaaaaddddyyyy.*"

Oh, shit. I suddenly feel like a felon. A very excited, gleeful, losing-my-mind felon. I shouldn't feel elated right now. I know I shouldn't. But tell that to my heart. "Dude," I say. "*Newman.* Bumble Bea. Queen Bea. Bea Bop A Lula. Don't get me into trouble with your mommy, okay? *Please.* We're Bea-Bee, remember? You and me, kid. Because I'm Col-*Bee.* And you're *Bea-trice.*"

Beatrice presses her finger into the cleft in my chin, flash-melting every molecule in my body. She whispers softly, "I love you, Daddy."

That's it. I'm toast. Gone. Done. Bury me. I love the sound of that and I can't deny it. "I love you, too, my sweet baby girl," I whisper. I close my eyes and nuzzle her little nose and breathe in the scent of the makeup on her beautiful little face. Oh, man, I'm being bad right now. But it feels so good.

"Daddy," she coos, her little palm stroking my cheek. "I love you, Daddy."

"I love you, too, Bea."

I hear Lydia and Izzy in the hallway and suddenly snap out of my trance. "Crap." I pull away from nuzzling Bea's nose, panic descending on me. "I shouldn't have encouraged you, honey. Seriously now, you've got to call me Colby or—"

"So how'd it go?" Lydia asks brightly, bounding into the room with Izzy and Ralph.

My mouth goes dry. I'm a cookie-thief caught red-handed with my hand groping the jar. "Great," I choke out.

Lydia takes Beatrice from me and kisses her rouge-smeared cheek. "Was your Daddy-Daughter Dance with Colby everything you dreamed it'd be? Did you feel like a princess with your Prince Charming?"

Beatrice nods. "I had a Daddy-Dadda Dance." She points at me. "With *Daddy.*"

My cheeks burst into flames. *Oh, shit*!

"Colby's not your daddy," Lydia says. "Remember? You've seen Daddy's picture lots and lots of times."

I choke out, "Yeah, I tried to explain—" But I'm cut off by a tug on my suit jacket.

"Ready, Colby?" Izzy asks. "We can't be late."

"*Daddy*!" Beatrice sings out, pointing at me, a smile dancing on her little rosebud mouth.

Oh my God. I feel like I'm about to choke on my tongue. I look at Lydia, a deer in headlights. "I told her," I say lamely. "I told her to call me Colby or Bee or even Cheese." Now I look at Bea. "Remember how I said you should call me Cheese Head, honey? Tell Mommy how I said that." I do that same stupid thing with my head I did before, trying to sell Beatrice on the new nickname. But she doesn't take the bait, again. Indeed, if a three-year-old can smirk, that's what Beatrice is doing right now. And yet, I continue rearranging deck chairs on the Titanic. "Or, hey," I say. "How about you call me Cheese Doodle or Cheese and Macaroni? Cheese Puff? Cheese Fries? Do you like any of those?" But my comments elicit nothing but another smirk from my three-year-old nemesis. I return my gaze to Lydia, my heart in my mouth. "I tried to tell her, Lyd. I really did."

Lydia touches my arm. "Honey, don't stress it. Bea's obviously enjoying the reaction she's getting out of you." She giggles. "And so am I. Oh my God, Colby." She puts Beatrice down and Beatrice runs off with Ralph to her room without a backward glance at the "daddy" she just nonchalantly threw under the bus.

I breathe a sigh of relief.

Lydia says, "Seriously, babe, if you stop giving her a freaked-out reaction, she'll forget about it and move on. It's classic Bea. She loves drama."

"Rookie mistake," I say sheepishly.

Lydia smiles. "No worries. Now go on and have fun, you two." She kisses me on the cheek and whispers into my ear before pulling away, "Thank you for doing this for her. It means the world to her."

"To me, too," I whisper back.

Lydia returns to full voice. "Don't keep Colby out too late tonight, peanut. He needs his sleep. He's got his big fitness test first thing in the morning so he can get back to work next week. We want to make sure Colby is well rested so he passes his test."

I wave Lydia off. "Bah. Izzy Gillespie and I can stay out all night. I did a run-through of the entire test with my buddy Dave the other day and knocked it out of the park. I'm back to my old self again and then some. I'll slay it no matter how late I stay out at the ball."

"Yeah, we're going to stay up *really* late, Mommy," Izzy says. She smiles defiantly. "The dance ends at *eight*."

Lydia and I chuckle. Oh my God, this kid slays me.

"Yeah, Mommy, don't wait up," I say. "Izzy Pop and I are gonna party like rock stars. Come on, French Fry. We can't be late." I take Izzy's little hand in mine and off we go toward the front door.

"Save some energy for when you get back home, Colby," Lydia calls after me. "I want my turn to dance with you, too."

I look over my shoulder at Lydia and smile when I see her lascivious expression. "It's a date," I say with a wink.

Out in the driveway, I get Izzy secured in the booster seat I bought this afternoon and say, "We're going to have big fun, sweet pea. I can't wait to redeem myself after the way I danced at the Climb & Conquer party on crutches. I'm going to show you some smooth moves tonight."

Izzy laughs like I've just said the silliest thing in the world. "Oh, Colby. It's not your *dancing* I care about."

"No?"

She shakes her head. "*No.*"

"What, then?"

I'm thinking Izzy is going to say it's how much she loves me. That she's thrilled to have the chance to spend some time alone with me. Or maybe even say something about how much she misses her real daddy. But she surprises me.

"I want all the girls to see how *handsome* you are and know you're with *me*."

I laugh, taken by surprise.

She continues, "When the other girls see you dancing with me, and how beautiful you are, they're all going to wish you were *their* daddy." She lets out a demonic little giggle that makes me guffaw. "But I'm going to tell them, 'Nope. Sorry. You can't have my Colby because he's all *mine*.'"

Chapter 65
Colby

Moonlight is streaming through Lydia's bedroom window.

Ryan's suit is slung neatly over a chair in the corner.

And Lydia is riding my cock like a woman possessed.

"Oh, fuck, you're gorgeous," I say, fondling her bouncing breasts as she fucks me. I'm on the bitter edge of release. And so is she. "Ride me harder, baby," I say, gripping her and guiding the snap of her hips. "Come on, baby."

She fucks me even harder, with everything she's got—and when a loud growl lurches from her throat, threatening to awaken not only the three sleeping children down the hall but the entire fucking neighborhood, Lydia freezes on top of me, covering her mouth.

Oh, God, that's the drug right there. It's my favorite game: fucking Lydia hard and watching her try her mighty best not to scream at the top of her lungs. She's never successful—I make sure of that. But watching her try, and then deliciously fail, turns me on like a motherfucker. Do I like it even better when we're able to fuck without the kids around—when Lydia can let loose and scream like a maniac? Of course. There's nothing better than watching Lydia come completely undone without a care in the world. But knowing I'm fucking Lydia so well she literally can't keep quiet, even though her brain is telling her to do it, ain't too shabby a silver medal.

I quickly guide Lydia off me and onto her back, hand her a pillow to shove over her face—something I always wind up doing at times like these—and begin banging my baby without mercy.

As I pound her hard, just the way she likes it, Lydia wraps her legs tightly around me, giving herself to me completely. Oh, God, the way this woman turns me on isn't normal. I'm insatiable when it comes to Lydia Decker.

"Lydia," I breathe, on the bitter cusp. "Are you close? I'm gonna lose it any second."

She moans her muffled reply from behind the pillow and, ten seconds later, her body confirms whatever she said in reply to me, it must have been "yes."

At the sensation of her coming around my cock, I lose it along with her. Oh, fuck, it feels good when Lydia's muscles constrict around me.

When our bodies stop jerking and our growls have quieted down, Lydia removes the pillow from her face to reveal a beaming, satisfied smile.

I collapse on top of her, completely spent and covered in a sheen of sweat. "Good lord, woman."

We lie together silently for a long time, breathing hard.

"I'm ridiculously, completely, totally, thoroughly *happy*," she says, out of nowhere.

I laugh. "Me, too. But I'd add 'absolutely' and 'deliriously' to that statement."

"Ditto."

I'm telling the truth. I've literally never been happier. I'm addicted to Lydia. She and the kids are my world. I've got my body back, better than ever. Ryan and I just signed up to do a full triathlon together in the spring, as a matter of fact, right after his wedding, so we're gonna start training pretty hard-core for that this coming week. And on top of all that, I'll *finally* be returning to work on Monday, assuming I pass my fitness test tomorrow, which is a given. When I think about myself lying in the ICU on a breathing machine not all that long ago, it blows my mind to think I'm the same guy.

"I'm so *proud* of you," Lydia whispers, stroking my back. "You've worked so hard to get your body back into peak shape. You did it faster than I thought you could, to be honest."

"I had to. I'm not completely myself unless I'm heading to that firehouse every third day."

She kisses me. "What time do you think you'll be done with the test tomorrow?"

"Around ten. But after the actual test, I'll probably stick around for a bit and shoot the shit with the guys. I'm excited to catch up and hang out."

"Oh, of course. Take your time. I'm just wondering about a

ballpark time. Whenever you get back to the house, the kids and I want to throw you a little party to celebrate you passing the test."

"You're going to throw me a *party*? Wow. I'm honored."

She chuckles. "Well, don't get *too* excited. It's going to be a rather humble little soiree. We're just going to bake you a cake, make you some cards and drawings, and put a silly paper crown on your head."

"Sounds amazing. What kind of cake?"

"Whatever you want. It's your party. Your cake."

"Carrot?"

"You got it. I've got a great recipe."

"How about I pick up lunch for our little soiree on my way home from the station?" As the word "home" leaves my mouth, my heart skips a beat. I've never referred to Lydia's house as my "home" before. And now that we're lying here together in her bed, and I'm not going back to my place for the first time ever, it feels like a particularly loaded word. I pause, thinking Lydia might correct me or otherwise comment—but she doesn't. I clear my throat. "Isn't there some barbeque place around here that's supposed to be great?"

Lydia confirms there is and tells me where it's located.

"Cool. I'll get lunch from there for our party."

"Fabulous. Do you think you'll spend the night again tomorrow night?"

"Am I invited to spend the night again tomorrow night?"

"Yes."

"Great. Then, yes, I'll be staying again tomorrow night."

She bites her lower lip. "Actually, you're invited to spend the night any night you'd like."

My heart is bursting. I kiss her deeply. And then again. And soon, I'm kissing and licking every inch of her, sucking her nipples, fingering her G-spot until she's convulsing with pleasure. Finally, when my body has recharged and my cock is once again ready to go, I crawl on top of her and sink myself deep inside her and make love to her with everything I am. When we're done, and we're lying together again, side by side, I turn on a Lenny Kravitz song I heard the other day and felt like it was about us—"I Belong to You." And then, as the song plays, I smile and say, "It sounds like I'm going to need to pack something a whole lot bigger than an overnight bag in the very near future."

Chapter 66
Colby

I'm back, baby!

The fitness test this morning was my bitch, exactly like I knew it would be.

I've now been officially added to the rotation at the main firehouse, beginning on Monday morning. And since that particular firehouse is right down the street from Lydia's place, I can't imagine I won't be spending the night over there pretty much exclusively until I get transferred to my old station. *If* I get transferred to my old station. Who knows? Maybe I'll wind up retracting that request and moving into Lydia's place full-time. In fact, I think I'll float that idea with Lydia as soon as I get home.

As I approach my truck in the parking lot, I place a call to Lydia. I already called her earlier—right after I passed my test—but I'd promised to let her know when I was leaving the station.

"Yo," she says, making me chuckle.

"Yo. I'm leaving now. I'll grab the food and head home."

"And ice cream, please."

"Of course. Goes without saying."

"You've got perfect timing. Izzy just finished decorating your carrot cake." She lowers her voice. "Just a tip? When you see the amorphous orange blobs on the top of your carrot cake, pretend to know they're carrots, mmmkay?"

I laugh. "Will do. So what do you want from the barbeque place, baby?"

"Surprise me. Oh, and it's a super popular place, so expect to be in line for quite a while. It's totally worth it, though. You'll see."

"No worries. Nothing can bring me down today, not even a long line for barbeque. I'm walking on air. I'm finally *back.*"

"I'm so happy for you."

I settle myself into the driver's seat of my truck and close the door. "Okay, baby cakes, I'll text you when I've got the food and I'm on my way—" My phone rings with another call and I check my screen. It's a number I don't recognize. "Oh, I've got another call. See you soon."

"Bye, honey. We can't wait to see you. Mwah."

I hang up with Lydia and answer the unknown call.

"Colby?" a tiny voice says.

My hair stands on end at the smallness of the voice on the other end of the line. "Yeah?"

"It's Caleb. From Theo's class? I'm sorry to bug you."

He sounds distressed. "You're not bugging me. I gave you my number so you could call me. What's up?"

"My dad is here," he whispers. "This isn't his weekend. It's my mom's. But he burst in and started screaming at my mom and when I told him to leave her alone he hit me."

My heart lurches into my throat. "He *hit* you?"

"Hard." He muffles a cry. "In the face."

"Where are you right now, Caleb?"

"I'm sitting on the curb in front of our house. He's in there screaming at my mom and I don't know what to do."

"Where do you live?"

Caleb gives me his address and I instantly recognize the street. It's only about a half mile away from where I'm driving this very minute, which makes sense considering Caleb goes to Theo's nearby school.

"Stay put, Caleb," I say. "I'm coming now."

Chapter 67
Colby

I pull up to Caleb's house to find him sitting on the curb, looking a whole lot smaller to me than he did at Theo's school three months ago.

As I get out of my truck and run to him, he stands, and it's clear to me he's got a whopper of a welt on his left cheekbone.

"Jesus," I say, appraising the angry contusion rising up on his face. "Your father did that?"

"He was screaming at my mom. I told him to leave."

I look toward the house. "He's still in there?"

Caleb nods.

"Have you called the police?"

Caleb shakes his head. "I don't want him to get into trouble. I just want him to leave. That's why I called you. He's not supposed to be here. There's a court order."

I open my mouth to tell him we need to call the cops, whether he likes it or not, because a father can't haul off and punch a kid, but before I get the words out, a loud female scream erupts inside the house.

"Shit," I mutter. "Stay here, Caleb. And call 9-1-1 right now. I know you don't want to do it, but you have no choice. Do it for your mom *now,* Caleb."

With that, I sprint at full speed toward the house, my heart racing. What am I going to find when I get in there? If this bastard is willing to punch his kid, God only knows what he's prepared to do to Caleb's mom.

I burst through the front door of the house to find a large man built like a linebacker pinning a small woman to a wall by her neck.

295

She's got her hands over his. Her face is red and her eyes wide and bulging. Clearly, she can't breathe.

"Who is he?" the man bellows as he chokes the woman, and she scratches and claws at his hands, trying to free herself.

I'm not a small man. I'm six-three and ripped. Around most men, I feel like a stud. But not in comparison to this guy. He looks like a fucking brick wall. But our relative sizes don't matter in this moment. He's literally killing her. Without a thought in my head, I lunge at the guy, put him in a headlock from behind, and pull him backward with all my might.

As we both stumble backward, I see the woman crumple to the ground, holding her neck.

I try to steady my footing, instinctively preparing myself for whatever battle lies ahead with this behemoth, but he swings his elbow back and lands a direct hit on my temple. I fall like a ton of bricks, cracking my head onto the edge of a side table as I go.

"Did you enjoy fucking my wife?" he booms.

And, just like that, I realize I'm in some deep shit here.

My head is throbbing. Blood is gushing into my left eye. "Wasn't me, man," I say. "I'm just here because you're a cocksucker who hits women and children." I leap up and lunge at him and land a solid punch to his jaw that makes my hand sting.

He stumbles back but doesn't fall, so I punch him again, dropping him to the floor like a sack of potatoes. With a primal scream, he pulls at my leg and drops me, and suddenly we're both on the ground wailing on each other. Somehow, I get myself situated on top of his chest and begin pummeling him like a madman from there while the woman screams her head off behind me.

I'm vaguely aware sirens are blaring faintly in the distance. Is that the police coming here? Or a faraway fire truck or ambulance, heading off to some car accident?

Without warning, he kicks me in the balls and throws me off him.

As I writhe on the ground, momentarily dazed and gripping my nuts... he shuffles to a nearby desk, opens a drawer... and... in slow motion... pulls out a gleaming handgun.

Lydia.

The life I was so excited to have with Lydia flashes before my eyes.

As he raises the gun, my body jerks and twitches, too shocked to move.

Lydia.

"Alexander, no!" the woman shrieks, charging at her husband and waving her arms frantically. "It wasn't him! I don't know him!"

The bastard glances at his charging wife, momentarily distracted, and I instinctively spring up and lunge at him, intending to knock the gun out of his hand. But the fucker turns my way again, just before I've made contact. As I crash into him, the gun goes off with a loud pop, shocking the living fuck out of me.

Lydia.

I go down, taking the fucker with me, every cell in my body lurching and bucking and spasming in sheer terror.

Lydia.

When I hit the ground, I don't feel it. In fact, in this moment, I can't feel my body at all. Have I been shot? Am I in shock? *Am I dead?*

Lydia.

None of my senses are working, other than my sense of taste. *Blood.* That's the only thing my body can process in this moment. The metallic taste of blood pouring into my mouth by the gallon.

Lydia.

I look down at the motherfucker underneath me and blood from my head gushes onto his face like I've turned on a bloody faucet. Is that my gray matter poetically dousing my killer as I inhale my last breath? Or am I simply bleeding from when I cracked my scalp wide open on the ledge of that table? As a paramedic, I know all too well how profusely head wounds bleed... But could it be my head is blown half off and I don't realize it?

The man who wants me dead reaches for his gun on the ground a few inches away from his outstretched hand and I scramble frantically to get there first.

"You fucked my wife!" he shouts, elbowing me in the ribs.

"No!" I scream, kneeing him in the head with all my might. "It wasn't me, motherfucker!"

There's a sound behind me. A scuffling sound. And then a male voice says, "Police! Put your hands up where we can see them!"

I leap off the fucker with my hands up and kick maniacally at the floor with my heels, frantically scooting away on my ass, skittering away from my murderer like some kind of frenzied, bloodied, hysterical crab.

"Hands up!" the cop shouts again. I glance over to the door. I see a badge. A gun. Blazing eyes.

I return my gaze to the asshole on the floor and watch, in slow motion, as he moves ever so slightly toward the gun... and then gets his head blown to motherfucking bits.

Chapter 68
Colby

I'm trembling. Twitching. Struggling to breathe. The paramedic tending to me in the back of this ambulance—Dave Rutherford—is actually a good buddy of mine. An honorary brother from way back at the fire academy. In fact, mere hours ago, I happily chatted with Dave at the main firehouse after slaying my fitness test.

I pull down the oxygen mask covering my mouth. My hand is shaking violently. "Seriously, though, can we turn off the sirens, brother?" I ask, my teeth chattering. "I think it's a bit excessive, don't you?"

Dave pushes the mask over my mouth again. "Your heart rate is skyrocketing. And that gash on your head is pretty bad. You're gonna need a shitload of stitches."

"But you swear I'm not shot, right?" I say. "You wouldn't lie to me about that to save me from freaking out?"

He smiles. "You're not shot. But you sure look like it." He shoves the mask over my mouth and nose again. "Now keep the mask on and breathe, Morgan."

I inhale a deep, calming breath, and let out a long, shuddering exhale of relief. My relief isn't for myself, though. It's for Lydia and the kids. I can't imagine how fucked up they would have been to get a phone call telling them I'd been shot and killed today on my way to pick up barbeque and ice cream for our celebration. I think it's safe to say Lydia never would have recovered. And how the hell would the kids have moved on from news like that? Would they grow up thinking every man they love is destined to get shot in the head after rushing into a stranger's house to save a woman from her abusive husband?

My body convulses violently. I'm not sure if I'm in shock. Or if it's the blood loss. Or maybe PTSD kicking in? I have no idea what's going on with me, but I'm a fucking wreck.

I pull my mask down. "I've got to call my lady. She's expecting me. She's probably worried sick."

Dave pushes the mask back on. "You're not in any shape to be calling her right now. If you call her now, you'll do more harm than good. Text her now or call her from the hospital after you've calmed down. Or give the phone to me. I'll call her, if you want."

"I'm not going to *text* her," I say. "And it has to be me who calls her."

"Then give it a minute."

Shit. I think it's safe to say Lydia's going have something close to a complete mental breakdown when she finds out what's happened, regardless of the fact the bullet from that gun happened to miss me. By mere inches, by the way. That was clear to me once I saw the placement of the bullet hole in the wall.

Oh, for the love of fuck, I don't want Lydia to have to find out about this. And I certainly don't want her to see me like this. I haven't seen myself yet, but I can't imagine I look good. I've got blood gushing out of my head. My left eye is already swollen shut, so I must have a doozy of a shiner if not some broken facial bones. Shit. If only I could hide this situation from Lydia somehow... Hey, maybe I could clean myself up and race back to Lydia's place with some barbeque and she'd never know? Yeah, I could tell her I tripped on the way out of the barbeque place or something and—

"Morgan, look at me," Dave barks.

I look at him. My teeth are still chattering.

"Hold up your hands, Colby."

I do as I'm told. They're visibly trembling.

Dave raises his hands. "Pull on my fingers."

"Dude, I've got three brothers. I'm not falling for that."

We both laugh.

"Pull as hard as you can," Dave insists.

I do it. And even I can tell my grip is fucked up.

"I think you've got a pretty bad concussion, man. Are you feeling confused?"

"No."

"What year is it?"

I have to think about it for a few seconds, but I'm able to tell him the year.

He asks me a series of simple questions and I stumble over a few of them.

"Yeah, you've got a concussion," Dave concludes. "I'll bet you fifty bucks."

"Why would I take that bet?"

"Just sayin'."

"Hey, can we turn the sirens off?" I ask. "Please? I'm getting a headache."

"No. And, by the way, if you saw yourself right now, you'd know the sirens have nothing to do with your headache."

I look at my watch and try to figure out how much time has elapsed since Lydia and I spoke about me coming home with barbeque. Maybe I can get to her house in time for her not to notice I've been gone an awfully long time? But for some reason, I can't compute the amount of time that's elapsed from the time I left for Lydia's house until now.

Dave slips the oxygen mask over my mouth and nose again. "Breathe deeply, brother. Just breathe. You're shaking like a leaf."

I pull down the mask. "I've got to call my lady."

"How about I call your mom and we let *her* call your lady?"

I shake my head. "Fuck no, don't call my mother. Momma Lou must never, ever know what happened today. Promise me, Dave."

Dave laughs.

"I'm not joking. Never, ever."

Dave lifts up the compress he's pressing against the wound in my scalp and grimaces. "Shit, man, you're gonna need a whole lotta stitches."

"Still bleeding?"

"Like a motherfucker."

"Fuck. I was hoping to get back home to my lady with some barbeque without her finding out."

Dave laughs. "What's this 'my lady' thing?"

"I don't know. She's not my wife. She's not just my girlfriend. I feel like 'my woman' makes me sound like a caveman."

"Why isn't she your wife? You were just going on and on after your fitness test about how much you love her and her three kids and she's perfect and you're in it to win it and blah, blah, blah. Why not marry her if you're done looking?"

I stare at him blankly for a long beat. And, suddenly, I know the honest answer to that question. "Because I'm scared to death she'll turn me down."

"Why would she do that?"

"Her husband was a cop who got shot and killed in the line of duty. She doesn't want to be with another first responder, but I gave her no choice."

"Oh, fuck."

"Yeah. He got shot in the head."

"Oh, Jesus. Then she's *really* gonna freak out about this." He motions to my head.

"That's what I've been trying to tell you. She's *totally* gonna freak out. Dave, her husband got shot by some fucker *who was trying to beat the crap out of his wife!*"

"Oh no. Holy shit."

"Now you see why I can't tell her about this? I've got to figure out a way to get back to her place with barbeque and ice cream."

Dave laughs.

"I'm not kidding. Help me."

"Okay, explain this to me. When you arrive at her place with barbeque and ice cream, what are you gonna tell her about the fact that your head looks like road kill?"

I can't figure out how to reply to that so I remain quiet.

Dave continues, "Or, wait. Here's an idea: hide from this woman and her three kids you love so much for the next three to six weeks so they don't discover your secret. Great idea." He gestures to what's surely a whole lot of ugly. "Trust me, man, it's going to take at least a month for you to look pretty again."

I sigh but say nothing.

"Put the mask back on, Morgan," Dave says. "You're not thinking clearly. That's what happens when you bruise your brain."

Resigned, I do as I'm told and push my oxygen mask over my mouth.

Dave leans over me to apply something to my face and I grimace sharply.

302

"Sorry. Hey, why don't I call your father for you? Let him make the calls for you."

I close my eyes and pull down the oxygen mask again. "No, I've got to call her myself."

"Who? Your 'lady'?" He snickers.

"No, my future wife."

"Ah, so you've seen the light, have you? That was sudden."

"I don't want to keep referring to her as 'my lady.' It's stupid."

"Yeah, it's pretty fucking stupid. Good call."

"I only hope she doesn't find out about this and leave me."

"*Leave* you?"

"Yeah. She might see me like this and say, 'I knew I shouldn't have gotten involved with another first responder!' And off she'd go without looking back."

Dave rolls his eyes. "She won't leave you, Colby."

"I'm not so sure. Fuck! Can you *please* turn off the sirens so I can call her? She's probably worried sick."

I've no sooner said the words than the sirens turn off.

"Thank you," I say.

"I didn't do it," Dave replies. "We're here."

The ambulance comes to a stop. Dave pushes open the back doors and pulls me out on a gurney. And while Dave and another guy wheel me toward the emergency room, I take a deep breath, pull out my phone, and place the dreaded call.

Chapter 69
Lydia

I'm a snot-nosed, shrieking, screeching maniac as I run through the parking lot toward the sliding glass doors of the ER where, I'm told, the man I love is getting examined and sutured *after almost getting shot in the head by a complete fucking lunatic*! Colby assured me he's perfectly fine. He said it over and over again, though I could barely hear him through my screams and wails.

I don't care what Colby said. I won't be okay until I've seen him with my eyes. Touched his living flesh with my fingertips. Held his hand and looked into his beautiful blue eyes and seen them open and close. Open and close.

Thank God, with Rosalind out of town to visit her grandchildren, my neighbor across the street was home and willing to watch the kids. Otherwise, I'm quite certain I would have had a legit nervous breakdown. Honestly, I don't even remember driving here. I was completely out of my head.

I burst through the ER doors and barrel to the check-in desk and babble Colby's name and describe the situation and beg to be taken to see him right away. When they tell me only family is allowed in the back, I inwardly curse myself for not being Colby's legal wife in this moment—why have I never brought up the idea of marriage with Colby? *Why*? I'm an idiot.

I furiously pull out my hospital badge and show it to the check-in woman and plead with her to make an exception. Yeah, I realize my badge is for a different hospital across town. But at least it shows I'm in the medical profession and have had a background check. Thankfully, the woman at the desk takes pity on me and covertly escorts me down a hall to see Colby.

There he is.

304

He's sitting on a gurney at the end of the hallway in a little nook, his face looking shockingly like it's been put through a meat grinder. His head is bandaged. He's visibly bruised and battered.

I choke back a sob as I run to him at full speed.

Colby.

When he sees me approaching, he reaches for me, emotion contorting his face.

"Colby!" I shriek, a sob lurching out of me. I hug him fiercely and he clutches me to him and I cry and cry and cry.

"Sssh, baby," he says, gripping me. "I'm fine. Not a single broken bone, miraculously. I'll be back as good as new in about four weeks. Just need to let the concussion heal."

I'm shaking violently. Out of my head. I'm sobbing so hard, my eyes feel like they're swelling shut. I feel dizzy. Like I literally can't breathe or hold myself upright.

"C-Colby," I choke out. "You could have d-died."

"But I didn't," he says. His voice is calm and soothing, but his body gives him away—he's trembling violently against me, every bit as much as I'm shaking against him. "I'm perfectly fine, baby. Merely a flesh wound."

But I can't be soothed. I'm convulsing with my cries and anguish and relief. On the verge of total and complete hysteria.

"I'm okay," Colby says. "Sssh. I'm right here. I'm not going anywhere, my love."

That last comment unexpectedly pisses me off. I jerk back from him, instantly enraged. "You're not going anywhere only by the grace of God!" I spit out. "He had a gun, Colby! The man fired a gun at you and *just so happened to miss!*" My teeth are chattering. My eyes are bugged out. "You came *this* close to leaving us! *This close!*" I throw my arms around him again and sob my eyes out and he embraces me again. For a long moment, we hug and kiss while I cry and cry.

Finally, my anger morphs into relief. And then gratitude that he's okay. And then love, love, love and nothing else. Finally, when I pull away from our fervent embrace, the look of pure exhaustion on Colby's face makes me realize how selfish I'm being. He's the one who's been through hell, not me. And I'm making this all about me.

"I'm sorry," I say, wiping my eyes. "Forgive me. Let's get you home. You need to rest."

"I have to wait for the nurse to come back with my discharge papers and after-care instructions," he says. "She said she'd be back in fifteen minutes."

"How long ago was that?"

He looks at his watch blankly. "I don't know."

"Oh, honey." I kiss him gently, taking great care not to touch anything that looks like it hurts. "What happened? I don't understand from what you told me on the phone why you were even there?"

"I was there because that kid had nobody else to turn to for help," he says simply.

I bring his hand to my lips and sigh. "You're *always* going to be the guy who rushes into the fire, aren't you?"

He smiles ruefully. "It's who I am, Lydia."

I nod. This isn't news to me.

In some aspects, Colby's and Darren's personalities differ sharply. It's definitely not hard for me to tell the two men apart. But with respect to this particular trait—their shared instinct to run *into* danger when everyone else is running *away*—the two loves of my life are cut from the exact same cloth.

"Please don't leave me, Lydia," Colby whispers, his eyes glistening. "I can't live without you. Please, please don't leave me."

I'm shocked. That's what Colby thinks is going through my head in this moment? *"Leave* you?" I say. *"Colby."*

He looks like he's holding his breath.

I gently brush his bruised cheek with the pad of my finger and say, "My love, yes, you scare the shit out of me. Yes, loving you is fraught with the risk and fear that I might lose you. But you're worth every ounce of worry or anguish you throw my way. *Honey, you're worth the risk.*"

Colby closes his eyes and exhales, the tension in his shoulders from a moment ago visibly releasing.

I kiss his red, swollen knuckles. "This isn't about me. You've been through hell and I've put you in a position to comfort *me*. I'm sorry. All that matters is that you're okay."

"Babe, there's no way in hell you could get a call like that and not flip out. Believe me, I tried to figure out a way for me to slip back home with barbeque and ice cream without you or the kids ever the wiser about what went down today, but I couldn't come up with a plan."

I chuckle. "Yeah, we're not all that sharp, but I think we would have figured it out." Again, I gingerly touch his battered face. "Were you scared?"

"Shitless." He smiles ruefully. "When that bastard pulled the gun, I swear to God, I thought I was done. I truly thought that was it for me."

I shudder.

"And you know what I thought about in that precise moment—when he pulled the gun and I thought I was gonna die? *Lydia*. And when he fired the gun and I thought maybe I'd been hit, I thought of you again. The life I want to live with you and the kids. How sad I was to miss all the fun."

I slide my arms around his neck and we hold each other for a very long time.

"You're my everything, Lydia," he whispers.

"You're mine," I whisper back.

Colby kisses my tear-stained cheeks and I pepper his battered face with exceedingly gentle kisses—and, all the while, we whisper words of devotion and love and relief into each other's ears.

"Have you called your family yet?" I ask.

"No."

"Not even Ryan?"

"Just you."

"Do you want me to call Ryan for you?"

"No."

"*No?*"

"I don't want anyone to know about this. They all went through hell seven months ago with me. They've had enough."

"Colby, have you been whacked upside the head or something?"

He smiles. "Cute."

"Honey, seriously. They'd want to know about this. *Of course*, you have to tell them."

He shakes his head. "No, Lydia. Kat's a month away from having her baby. Dax is furiously writing songs for the big debut album they're gonna record in LA. Ryan's on cloud nine, planning his wedding and his bar. Keane is more likely than not getting ready to go out Ball-Peen-Hammering at some bachelorette party tonight. And my parents are probably sitting at home on the couch happily watching some Civil War documentary. The thought of disrupting any of that by calling them and telling them what happened today makes me physically ill."

Okay, clearly this man isn't thinking clearly—which makes sense, of course. "Honey, I think the jig is going to be up relatively soon whether you like it or not. You told them you were starting back to work on Monday, remember? They're expecting you to drop off Ralph on Monday morning. They're going to ask you, 'How's work?'"

He makes a face that says, "Shit."

"Plus, do you really think you can avoid seeing your family for *weeks* while those bruises heal? You can barely go three days without seeing at least one of your family members."

Colby hangs his head, clearly overwhelmed.

I rub his back in silence for a moment, comforting him, until our quiet moment is interrupted by a police officer approaching and asking Colby for a statement about the incident.

Colby tells the officer his entire story, as best he can remember it with his bruised and shocked brain, and my jaw drops to the floor at what he's describing. Oh my God. My humble hero didn't tell me one-tenth the details he's explaining to this cop. When Colby called me earlier, he made the incident sound so much less dramatic than it actually was—and I *still* freaked the fuck out at his watered-down version of events. Holy crap. Hearing the real version now, I feel like I'm going to pass out. And yet, other than a few gasps and exclamations, I somehow manage to keep myself quiet and composed during Colby's interview.

The officer concludes his interview and tells Colby his account of the incident is perfectly consistent with what the wife and kid told him at the scene. And then he adds, "The wife said you saved her life, Colby. She said she'd one hundred percent be dead right now if you hadn't jumped in to help her at precisely the moment you did. You're a true hero." He glances at me and half-smiles. "*Again.*"

Colby waves at the air. "I just did what anyone would do in my shoes."

The cop shakes his head. "You'd be surprised how many people would have done absolutely nothing in your situation. Because of you, that kid has a mother tonight."

Colby shrugs and says simply, "You know how it is. We're first responders. We have no choice."

The guy fist-bumps Colby. "Much respect."

"Back at you. One of yours saved my life today. Tell that guy I said thanks, would you? Actually, no, give him my number, if you wouldn't mind. I'd like to thank him myself. I wouldn't be sitting here now if it wasn't for that guy's steady hand."

"Will do. It'll mean a lot to him to talk to you, too."

When the police officer leaves, I fawn all over my brave boyfriend, as well I should, until a discharge nurse interrupts us to give Colby after-care instructions for his sutures, concussion, and various contusions. Basically, my hero is going to be resting for about four weeks, thanks to that concussion, but in about a month or so, he'll be good as new and ready to return to work.

As we make our way toward my car in the parking structure, I grab Colby's hand. "I'm sorry this will delay you getting back to the firehouse."

Colby kisses my hand. "It's just a month. Not the end of the world, considering a kid still has his mom tonight."

We reach my car and stand next to the passenger door for a moment, embracing. "I'm sorry," he whispers into my hair.

"For what?"

"For scaring you. If I could have slipped back home with barbeque and ice cream and never mentioned what happened, I would have done it."

"Okay, enough with that. Let's get something straight right now. 'Protecting me' by keeping important things from me isn't an option. Not about this or anything else that might come up in the future. Our relationship works so damned well because we *talk*. Because we're honest. Each of us knows what's going on with the other—good, bad, or ugly. I don't want to love a fictitious version of you, Colby. I only want to love the *real* you. Forever and ever for the rest of my life."

He looks relieved. "You'll never leave me because it's just too damned stressful to love me?"

My eyes trained on his, I say, "I'm never going to leave you. If I thought *maybe* I wouldn't be able to handle the first-responder thing once you got back to work, then it's now one thousand percent clear: there's literally nothing that would make me walk away from you. I'll take the good with the bad. The stress and worry with the joy. The love with the potential for loss. I'm not going anywhere, ever."

He exhales with relief. "Thank God."

"Are you the guy who's always going to rush into the proverbial burning building, whatever that is? Yes. But, Colby." I grab his shoulders. "*That's why I love you.*"

Emotion washes over his battered face. "Let's get married."

"What?"

"I want you to be my wife. Damn. I should have bought a suit for the Daddy-Daughter Dance."

I look into his stunning blue eyes. Well, his stunning blue *eye*. His left eye is completely swollen shut. I feel electrified. Ready. Excited. But I control myself. "Now's not the time for you to be thinking about this. You're exhausted. Concussed. You don't know what you're saying."

"I know exactly what I'm saying. *I want you to be my wife.*"

I open the passenger door of my car for him. "Let's get you home. We'll talk about this again when you've had a chance to rest up."

He gets himself situated into my car and I close the door.

I walk around the car, get myself settled into the driver's side, and turn on the ignition.

"Where is 'home'?" he asks.

"Huh?"

"You said, 'Let's get you *home.*'"

"Oh. My house. I don't want you sleeping alone at your place while you've got a concussion." But I know my words are a lie the minute they leave my mouth. "Actually, I never want you to sleep another night at your place again, period. Whether you've got a concussion or not, my house is now your home."

Colby smiles. "Awesome." He melts into his car seat and exhales. "Come on, baby. Let's go home."

Chapter 70
Colby

I look down at Gracie Louise Faraday cradled in my arms and my heart melts the way it always does when I behold her singular loveliness.

"Does she look any closer to falling asleep?" Kat whispers, sounding exhausted. She's sprawled on her couch in yoga pants and a sweatshirt, her head thrown back like she's waiting for a dude with palm fronds and grapes to arrive. Meanwhile, I'm circling Kat's cavernous living room, my colicky three-month-old niece in my arms, trying to coax her to sleep so her ragged and weary mother won't have a nervous breakdown.

"I don't think she's gonna fall asleep," I say. "She's still fussing. How would I know if she's getting closer to falling asleep?"

"Her eyelids start to flutter and then she forces them open like a drowsy truck driver. Is she doing that?"

"No. She's staring at me like I've got four heads. Are you sure she needs sleep? Maybe she's hungry."

"No, she just ate a ton right before you got here. And before that, she was awake for a long time. She just fights sleep. She's just like me. She never wants to miss the party."

We both chuckle.

"It's amazing how much she looks like you, Kat," I say, staring down at Gracie's cranky little face. "For the first two months, I could see some Faraday in there, but, now, she's pure, unadulterated Katherine Ulla Morgan. Ah, there she goes. Her eyelids are fluttering."

"Thank you, Baby Jesus."

I bounce Gracie with a little more enthusiasm until, finally, her eyelids flutter closed and stay that way. "And... *scene*."

"Yay," Kat says softly. "You're my knight in shining armor, Cheese. When she gets super colicky like that, Josh usually takes over so I won't lose my mind. He's the Gracie-whisperer."

"Where is he, again?"

"Colorado with Jonas. They're looking at some more gyms to buy. He'll be home tomorrow night." She motions to a chair. "Take off a load. It's been a while since we've chatted one-on-one. I want to hear about all the things."

I sit in an armchair, cradling my sleeping niece in my arms. "How do you not sit here all day long and just watch her sleep? She's mesmerizing."

"I do, actually." Kat laughs. "Half my day is spent sitting here, staring at her. That and videotaping her every gurgle."

We both stare at Gracie for a long moment.

"Now I see why Mom loves us the way she does," Kat says. "I always assumed Mom loves all of us the way we love her, but now I see it's totally different from this side. My love for Gracie is literally *everything*."

I smile at my sister. I thought it'd be weird to see my sister as a mother. Indeed, I had my doubts she'd take to it, to be honest. But now that Gracie's here, it's plain to see motherhood is the most natural thing in the world for my big-hearted little sister.

"So enough about my sweet little baby," Kat says. "Tell me about you. What's new?"

"Nothing much," I say. "Just living the dream." I'm not being sarcastic about that, by the way. Living with Lydia and the kids has been a dream come true. Best four months of my life. I give Kat a brief rundown of the small but happy goings-on in my life. I tell her Lydia's finally gained enough seniority at work to no longer work weekends, which has been great for the kids. I tell her about Beatrice's new infatuation with dinosaurs. Theo's band. Izzy's latest dance recital.

"And how's Ralph handling his new digs?" Kat asks. "Does he love having three constant playmates or does he feel like he needs doggie therapy?"

"Ralph feels like he died and went to doggie heaven."

"And work's going well?" Kitty asks.

"Better than ever," I say.

It's the truth. I finally went back to work almost three months ago, permanently assigned to the main firehouse near Lydia's place, rather than my old stomping grounds closer to my condo—which makes perfect sense, seeing as how I live at Lydia's place now. "Oh, the sale of my condo went through last week," I say. "And I made a mint on it."

"Awesome," Kat says. "I'm thrilled at how everything has worked out for you."

"I'm thrilled, too."

Honestly, I pinch myself every day about the way things have worked out for me. I thought becoming the co-head-of-household for a family of five would make me rich metaphorically but poor literally. And I was fully willing to make that tradeoff, by the way. But the reality of the situation couldn't be further from that. These days, I'm rich in all ways a man can be. Thanks to the sale of my condo, I no longer have a monthly mortgage payment and I was able to pay off my truck with some of the proceeds of the sale. Which means the two major financial obligations of my life evaporated overnight. And then stayed that way. Because, glory be, much to my surprise, it turned out Lydia owns both her house and car outright, completely free and clear, thanks to Darren's life insurance and death benefits. So that means there's no rent or mortgage payment for me to help with at Lydia's place, even if I wanted to do it.

At the end of the day, even factoring in the kids' expenses—their clothes and toys and guitar and dance lessons and princess dresses and whatnot—there's still way more money sitting in my bank account at the end of each month these days than there ever was when I was a single firefighter going after the American Dream on my own. In short, everything about my life in every single way, physically, romantically, professionally, sexually, financially, emotionally, spiritually... *it's all awesome.* And that's what I tell my sister, in essence. That I couldn't be happier, top to bottom, in every conceivable way.

Kat beams a huge smile at me. "So does that mean you've stopped having nightmares about that *thing*?"

"Which thing?"

"The thing where the guy tried to shoot you in the head and wound up getting his own head blown off right in front of you."

"Oh, *that*."

As it turned out, Lydia was right as rain: there was no way to keep news of that incident from my family. That same day, the local news covered the story, naming me as a "hero" and mentioning I was the same guy who'd raced into that burning house to save a baby earlier this year. So, of course, some friend of my mother's saw the news story and called my mom and that was that. The cat was out of the bag. Of course, Mom was pissed I hadn't told her about the incident myself, but I blamed it on the concussion and all was forgiven.

"I haven't had a nightmare about that in a while," I say. "I only got nightmares about that for the first few weeks. Hardly even a blip." I look down at Gracie in my arms and the anxiety I'm suddenly feeling about that horrible, awful day evaporates into thin air.

"You look so natural holding her," Kat says. "Do you think you and Lydia will add to your brood?"

I stare at Gracie's long eyelashes. Her rosebud lips. Her fat little cheeks. "Yeah, I hope so. If I get my way, we'll add two. Bring my brood to five kids, just like the Morgans."

Kat's face lights up. "Aw, Colby. That'd be amazing."

"Living with Lydia and the kids, baby fever has been hitting me like a ton of bricks lately. I'm worse than Rum Cake these days."

"Impossible."

"It's true."

"That's hard to believe. Ryan's pretty baby-crazed."

I laugh. "Okay, so maybe Rum Cake and I are tied. All I know is Bea and Izzy have been calling me Daddy lately and it's flipped some primal switch inside me. I want *more*."

"Is Lydia okay with the girls calling you Daddy?"

"Yeah. Bea called me Daddy one day, out of the blue, and I was like, 'No, no,' and then Lydia goes, 'It's okay. You *are* her daddy. She's got two daddies. The one who made her and the one who's raising her.'"

"Wow. I just got a chill."

"I know, right? It gave me chills when Lydia said it. She's so amazing."

"Theo doesn't call you Daddy?"

"No, he calls me Colby. And that feels right with him. But you should hear the way he says it. It's like he's saying *Superman*."

Kat sighs. "Oh my gosh. That boy slays me."

"Me, too. He's my boy."

"Does Lydia know you want a couple babies?"

"Oh, yeah. I've been begging her to get her IUD taken out. I'm ready. We're not spring chickens."

"What did Lydia say about having babies?"

"'Put a ring on it and then we'll talk.'"

We both laugh.

"So I assume you're going to put a ring on it, then?" Kat asks.

"Fuck yes. That's why I dropped by unannounced on you, actually. I picked up the ring an hour ago and I wanted to get your expert female opinion on it."

"Well, why didn't you say so?" Kat says brightly. She sits up and puts out her hand. "Gimme."

"Hang on. Just remember I've never picked out an engagement ring before. For me, it's not about doing it 'right.' I just went with my heart. If it's not, you know, perfect cut or clarity or whatever I'm supposed to—"

"*Colby.*" Kat rolls her eyes. "Just give me the bling."

"I'm nervous."

"Why the heck didn't you take Mom ring shopping with you if you're so nervous about it? She helped both Josh and Ryan pick out the absolute perfect rings."

"I know. No shade to anyone else, I just wanted to do it myself. But now that I've done it myself, I'm scared to death I screwed the pooch."

Kat laughs. "Oh my God. Just show me the damned ring, Cheese Ball."

My stomach clenching with nerves, I shift Gracie in my arms and pull out the ring box from my pocket. "Just remember I had a much more limited budget than Josh, obviously, but also Ryan. Ryan's been killing it lately."

"Dude. Stop being a wanker and show me the ring."

I place the box in my sister's palm and she eagerly opens it.

"It's *perfect*," Kat gushes and I let out the longest exhale of my life.

"Really?"

"Really. Colby, you couldn't have picked anything better for Lydia. It's absolutely *her*."

I rake my hand through my hair. "Thank God. I know absolutely nothing about diamonds, but I saw it and it screamed *Lydia* to me so I just went with it."

"She's going to lose her mind. Honestly, I'm shocked at the size of the diamond. How big is that?"

"Just over two carats."

"*What*? Holy Hope Diamond, Batman!"

I laugh. "Dude, don't patronize me. Your ring looks like it burped my ring out after eating chili-cheese fries."

Kat giggles and glances down at the Rock of Gibraltar on her hand. "We can't compare my ring and Lydia's. Mine isn't within the realm of civilized society. Joshua William Faraday doesn't do normal."

"Yeah, I've noticed."

"Seriously, though, Mr. Firefighter, how were you able to get Lydia a rock like that? It's gorgeous."

"The sale of my condo. I'm putting most of the proceeds into a college fund for the kids, but I figured it would be justifiable to use a little off the top for two splurges: paying off my truck and getting Lydia the kind of engagement ring she deserves. She never had one with Darren. She found out she was pregnant when they were about to graduate college and they got hitched a couple weeks later down at city hall. I wanted her to get the full-on fairytale this time around."

Kat looks at me adoringly. "Oh, Colby. You're the sweetest man who ever lived, you know that?" She touches her chest. "You physically hurt my heart with your sweetness, Colby Morgan."

"I'm not all that sweet. Lydia's just worth it."

"By the way, I feel like I should tell you something, even though it's a huge secret and I'm not allowed to tell anyone yet. You don't need to put a dime aside for the kids' education. Josh is going to cover all their college expenses."

My jaw drops. "*What*?"

She nods. "That's what he said."

"Josh said he's going to cover Theo's and Izzy's and Bea's college educations?"

"Well, no. Not specifically like that. But when we found out about Baby Rum Cake baking in the oven last week, Josh said our baby gift to them will be paying for their kid's college education. Every dime. Tuition. Living expenses. The whole nine yards."

"*What?*"

"And then he picked up his phone right then and there and called his lawyer or whoever and repeated the same thing to him. And that was that. The thing is already funded, apparently. But that's Josh for you. He says something and then he does it. He said by the time Baby Rum Cake is ready for college, his or her trust fund will have well over three hundred thousand bucks in it."

"What the...? Oh my God, Kat. But what does that have to do with my three kids?"

"When Josh was on the phone with his lawyer or whoever, I heard him say he wants to do the exact same thing for 'all his nieces and nephews, no matter how many kids the Morgan family eventually spits out.' Those were his exact words. But don't tell anyone yet. Josh wants it to be a surprise. But, yep, he's already got some trust fund he's started and he's just going to keep adding money and names to it with each new kid that's born, however many that is."

My stomach clenches. "Each new kid 'born' doesn't mean Lydia's kids, Kumquat. Think about it. Josh planning a trust fund for Baby Rum Cake doesn't mean he's planning the same thing for Lydia's kids, too. They're totally different scenarios."

"Why? We all know you think of those kids as your own. For crying out loud, they call Mom 'Gramma Lou.'"

"I know, but let's just be real: Josh probably thinks step kids are different than blood relations. Lots of people think that way."

"Not Josh. And you know how I know? Because he told the lawyer to add Coco to the list, too. Just because he thought she was so cute in Maui and he wants to make sure she has all the opportunities in the world. That's what he said. So if he's doing that for Julie's stepdaughter, why wouldn't he do that for Lydia's kids when you marry Lydia?"

"Holy fucking shit."

"By the way, Josh came up with this whole idea all by himself. I haven't pressured or cajoled or even politely asked him to do it. He said every single kid in our family will never need to worry about paying for their education or living expenses while they're in school, no matter where they go or how many degrees they want. He'll just keep adding money to the trust fund, no matter how much is required."

317

I rub my face, completely flabbergasted. "That's... oh my God."

"That's Josh."

I feel disoriented for a minute, but finally say, "Honestly, I don't know if I could accept a gift that big for the kids. That'd be close to a million bucks earmarked for them. That's a lot of money."

Kat shrugs. "To normal people, yes. But not to Josh. If it makes you feel any better about it, that's funny money to my hubsters. I mean, it's a hugely generous gift, I know. But a million bucks to Josh isn't the same as it is to us. You know that diamond necklace he bought me?"

I nod, even though I don't remember a diamond necklace.

"A million bucks."

"Jesus."

"You know those earrings Uncle William gave me from his deceased wife's collection? The ones I wore at the wedding?"

I nod, even though, to be honest, I didn't notice Kat's earrings at her wedding.

"Three-quarters of a million bucks. Oh, and did I ever tell you I've got a million bucks just sitting in the bank with my name on it, thanks to Josh? It's just sitting there, lah-de-dah, but he's so generous all the time, I don't have any use for it. I literally have no need for a million bucks. Honestly, at some point soon, I'm just going to divide it up and give it to all of you."

"Okay, enough," I say. "I'm freaking out. This is unbelievable."

Kat laughs. "I know. It's insane, isn't it? I never talk about Josh's wealth, but he recently told me his personal assets will cross the billion-dollar mark in about a year."

"*Billion*? Buh? With a *B*?"

"*Billion*. In a year's time, I'm going to be a *billionaire's* wife. And Josh is only turning *thirty-one* next week! Ha! It's totally insane."

"I had no idea," I mutter, still in shock. "I thought Josh was rich, but I didn't... *Jesus*."

"You know the craziest part? He didn't make me sign a pre-nup! Ha! He just said, 'My money is yours, babe. Do whatever you want. Please don't fuck me over.'"

"*What the fuck*? What man in his right mind would say that—especially to *you*."

"*Hey.*"

We both guffaw.

"Kat, I'm so mind-fucked right now."

"Don't be. Just be happy. And let Josh be happy. He doesn't have any family besides Jonas and his uncle. Literally. There are no other Faradays besides those three. Well, and now Sarah and Gracie and me. But that's it. We're a tribe of six at present. And Jonas and their uncle both have the same amount of money as Josh, if not more. So, really, who the hell would Josh spend his hundreds and hundreds of millions on, if not his new family he adores? He already gives truckloads to charity. Like, more money than you can possibly imagine. So let the man spend his oodles of money the way he wants to do it. He's already talking about taking the entire extended Morgan family on another big trip. Probably in a year or so when Gracie can walk. Next time to Bali."

"Bali? Oh my God. Kat, stop."

Kat cocks her head. "Or, wait, maybe it was Bora Bora? I dunno. Whatever. Somewhere good that starts with a B. Bermuda? Belize? I can't remember."

I shake my head and sigh. "Well, shit, now I feel like a total cheapskate."

"What? Why?"

"All I got Josh for his birthday next week was a coffee mug."

We both burst out laughing.

"Mom's getting Josh some crazy-expensive bottle of rare tequila. Chip in on that."

"Thanks for the heads up."

"So, any idea how you're going to propose, Cheese Head?"

"Yeah, I've got a couple ideas. I'm still mulling it over, though. Do you have any brilliant ideas for me? Something heartfelt but simple."

Kat twists her mouth, considering. "Well, for Josh's birthday next week, he's arranged a romantic dinner for two-and-a-half here at the house. A chef, waiter, flowers, musicians. Basically, he's turning our dining room into a five-star restaurant."

"Wow. Sounds amazing."

"Yeah. *Amaaaazing.* But fuck that shit."

I laugh.

"Josh *thinks* he wants a quiet birthday dinner at home with his two girls, but I know him better than he knows himself. After being cooped up for three solid months in Babyville, he's dying for an adrenaline rush, even if he doesn't realize it. So I've cooked up a little surprise for my beautiful adrenaline junkie. Which means, of course, unbeknownst to my darling husband, that quiet dinner he's already arranged and paid for will go to waste unless I can pawn it off on someone who might appreciate it. So what do you think? Why don't I send the five-star restaurant to your place? Seems like the perfect ambience for a marriage proposal to me."

"Thanks. Yeah, I'll take that off your hands, for sure. But I don't think I'll propose to Lydia that way. My gut tells me my proposal should be a family affair."

"Aw, that's sweet. Okay, well, either way, the dinner is yours." She pulls out her phone and taps out a text. "Okay. I just texted The Mighty T-Rod about it. She'll coordinate."

"Thanks."

"Just don't ask Mom to be your babysitter that night. She's coming here to watch Little G for me when I kidnap Josh."

As if on cue, Gracie stirs in my arms and I look down to find her big blue eyes staring serenely up at me.

"Hello, Little G," I coo softly. "Got yourself a little power nap, did ya?" My niece smiles at me and my heart melts. "Man, she looks exactly like you did when Mom and Dad brought you home from the hospital, Kitty Kat. Have I ever told you about that day?"

"Many times. But tell me again."

"I held you in my arms the way I'm holding this little angel right now and I fell deeply and totally in love with you. And right then and there, I swore to myself I'd always protect my little kumquat, no matter what." I look up from Gracie's face and the expression of pure love on Kat's face brings a lump to my throat.

"I love you, Colby."

"I love you, too, Kumquat."

"And I'm so happy for you. Lydia's your perfect match. The minute I laid eyes on her in the bathroom at the hospital, I knew she was perfect for you."

I throw my head back and hoot with scornful laughter. "You're so full of shit! Oh my God."

Kat giggles. "Okay, yes, maybe that's a bit of an exaggeration."

"You think?"

"But in all seriousness, I saw Lydia and thought she was exactly your *type*. Is that better?"

"Still bullshit."

"*No*. Now, granted, you were lying in the ICU down the hall on a breathing machine and Lydia mentioned she had three kids so I wasn't in the mindset to play matchmaker for the two of you at that particular moment. I think I assumed she was married at the time, actually. But, regardless, I *did* think, 'Wow, this woman is *exactly* Colby's type.'"

"Bullshit. Revisionist history."

"No. It's one hundred percent true. You think I don't know your type? Colby, we all know your type. For like three straight years in high school, you'd stop whatever you were doing and stare over my shoulder any time I watched a Beyoncé video."

I laugh. "No comment."

Gracie begins fussing in my arms. "Someone's hungry," I say, handing my niece back to Kat. "Thanks for the vote of confidence on Lydia's ring. I appreciate it." I get up. "I'll see you Sunday at Mom and Dad's for Dax's going-away party."

"I'll see you then."

I kiss my sister on top of her head, kiss Gracie on her fat little cheek, and race gleefully out the door, the ring box burning a hole in my pocket.

Chapter 71
Lydia

"This is seriously the best champagne I've ever tasted in my life," I say. "And these scallops are amazing."

"Amazing," Colby says, but he seems preoccupied.

I glance at the musicians in the corner of my small dining room—a violinist, violist, and cellist—and giggle. "I think three musicians probably made a whole lot more sense when this dinner was planned for Josh and Kat's house. Here, it kind of feels like those poor ladies have been stuffed into a clown car, don't you think?" I laugh again... but Colby doesn't laugh with me. His features are tight. His brow is furrowed. Clearly, he's got something on his mind. I put down my fork. "Okay, love. Talk to me. It's obvious you've got something you need to get off your chest."

"Yeah, um, hang on." He gets up and whispers to the three musicians in the corner and they nod, put down their instruments, and quietly leave the room.

And, just like that, I understand what's going on. *Colby is finally going to propose!* Just last week, when he asked me to start trying for a baby, I said, "Not until you put a ring on it." *And now he's going to put a ring on it!*

Colby returns to the table, but instead of kneeling like I think he's going to do, he resumes his chair.

I exhale, vaguely disappointed.

Colby takes a deep breath. "Lydia, I love you with all my heart. And I love the kids. I truly consider them my own."

Okay, we're back in business, folks! "I know you do," I say, trying to keep my voice from rising three octaves. "And we all love you."

322

Colby takes another deep breath. "I don't know if what I'm about to say is going to offend you or be insensitive. And if it is, just know my intentions are good."

Um. Huh? "Sweetheart, your intentions in everything you do are good," I say. "I'd never doubt that. Just say it, whatever it is."

"You're sure you want to marry me, right?"

I furrow my brow. Was that Colby's idea of a marriage proposal? Because if so, it sucked balls.

"Oh... *no*," Colby says. He laughs, apparently reading my facial expression. "That wasn't my *proposal*. I just meant..." He exhales. "Crap. Let me start over." He takes a quick sip of his wine. "I mean *when* I ask you to marry me, which I'm going to do in the near future and not like *that*, I'm thinking I'd like to involve the kids in the moment because our marriage won't be two people coming together, it'll be five. Would that disappoint you if I included them?"

I melt. "I think that'd be lovely."

He exhales. "Okay, good. That's the first thing I wanted to ask you. And the second thing is this." He swallows hard. "Can I please legally adopt your three kids?"

My heart stops.

Colby puts up a palm. "Don't answer me right away. Just, please, give it some thought. I know Darren is their father and always will be. I would never want to take that away from him or the kids. But I want to be their legal parent in case anything ever happened to me or to us. To make sure they'd get my death benefits if something happened. To make sure my parents would have a say in their care if something happened to both of us." He shrugs. "And, honestly, I just want to be their legal parent for no other reason than I want to be their parent. But if that's an offensive or insensitive thing to ask, then I understand."

As I listen to Colby speak, Darren's mother's face keeps flashing across my mind. I can physically *hear* her sobbing in my ear and saying I've betrayed her son and that if anything were to happen to me, she and Darren's father would be the ones to care for my children, not Colby or the Morgans. If I say yes to Colby about this, it's a hundred percent certainty Darren's mother will never, ever forgive me as long as she lives.

I tune back into Colby. He's still trying to convince me to let him please be the legally responsible, living father of my children. "So just think about it," he says in conclusion. "No rush on your decision."

I grab his hand. "*Yes*."

Colby's face lights up. "Yes?"

I nod. "Yes."

"You don't need to think about it?"

"Nope."

He squeezes my hand. "I'll always honor Darren. You know that, right? He's their daddy. I just want to be their Colby. Or, if they're up for it, their *other* daddy. The one holding down the fort on earth while their other one is waiting to see them in heaven."

Tears spring to my eyes. "And that's why saying yes to this is such a no-brainer." I wipe my eyes. "We'll have to talk to the kids about it first. Explain it to them. Gauge their reactions. And I'd recommend you talk to Theo separately. He's the only one who remembers Darren well. He'd probably like being given the choice."

"Sounds good." Colby kisses me and then kisses me again, and soon, predictably, our kissing turns passionate. He whispers, "I've lost my appetite for food. I'm hungry for Lydia. Let's tell all these people to get out. The kids will be back at eleven and there are at least ten ways I want to fuck you before then."

"Check please!" I shout to no one, raising my arm, and we both laugh.

With a quick kiss to my lips and a playful little honk of my boob, Colby gets up, throws his napkin down, and heads off to clear the house.

Chapter 72
Colby

Theo rings the bell at the top of the highest rock wall and I cheer wildly. I'm about two feet below him and to his left, secured by a rope running parallel to his. I could have smoked him to the top, of course. But I've hung back to watch him as he climbed, making sure I could help him out if he needed it. But, I'll be damned, Theo barely needed a single word of instruction.

"You slayed it, buddy!" I say, my excitement equaling his. I ascend the last few feet, reach the top of the wall, and ring the bell on my side. "You're getting so good at this, Theo-Leo. Better than me, that's for sure."

"I'm not better than you. I asked for help a bunch of times. And you're on the harder side of the wall."

"Yeah, but I'm six foot three. Look at my arms and legs versus yours. Pound for pound, inch for inch, you're way better at this than me, dude. Swear to God."

Theo positively beams at me.

"Hey, don't belay down yet," I say. "Sit back on your harness for just a sec. I want to ask you something while we're sitting on top of the world together."

Theo looks at me expectantly.

I quickly signal to the Climb & Conquer staffers managing our ropes below that we're staying put for a second and they shoot me a thumbs-up. I return to Theo. "You know I love your mom with all my heart, right?"

He nods.

"Just between you and me, I'm going to ask her to marry me later today at the party, and I'm hoping as the man of the household for three years before I came along you'll give me your blessing."

"My *blessing*? You mean like my *permission*?"

"Well, no. I don't need your *permission*. I'm going to ask her later today, no matter what."

"Then what are you asking me to do?"

"Give me your *blessing*."

Theo looks at me like I'm a moron.

"Okay, never mind. Belay down, you punk. This isn't going as planned, at all."

Theo laughs, calls down to the staffer below, and begins belaying down. Shaking my head, I follow suit.

When we get to firm ground and begin taking off our harnesses, Theo says, "So what happens if I say no? If I don't give you my *blessing*?" He snorts.

"Then I'd give you a knuckle sandwich, you smart-alec."

Theo laughs.

"Are you planning to say no?" I ask.

"No. I'm not planning to say anything. It's not up to me. Asking an eleven-year-old kid for permission to marry his mom is just weird."

"I'm not asking for *permission*." I sigh. "It was a gesture, you little smart-ass. A gesture. It's like, you know, a ritual. Excuse me, but I just thought it would be a cool thing to do. Like, you know. A *moment*. I stand corrected."

Theo's laughing his head off and soon I'm joining him and the moment is just patently ridiculous.

"Well, just so you know," Theo says. "Not that I need to give you *permission* or anything, but I've been dying for you to ask my mom to marry you forever."

"You have?"

"*Dying*."

"Oh. Well, good. Because I'm going to ask her and nothing and no one could have stopped me, not even you, you little punk."

"Good. Because I want you to ask my mom to marry you, so you're playing right into my hand."

"Good."

Theo laughs. "Good."

"You know, this could have been a poignant moment if you'd just played along," I say. "You're totally screwing with my Hallmark moment."

Theo chuckles. "Hey, you're the one who asked an eleven-year-old permission to marry his mother. Why do you think they don't let eleven-year-olds get married? Because we're not mature enough to make decisions like that."

I lose my shit laughing. "Oh my God. You slay me." I wrap my smart-ass boy in a bear hug. "You've been hanging around my brothers way too much, you know that?" I kiss the top of Theo's head. "They're teaching you to talk like a Morgan. *So* not good."

We pull apart and Theo's smile is wide and beautiful.

"So, you're gonna ask her today?" he asks.

"Yeah, at the party for Dax this afternoon."

I'm talking about Dax's going-away party. In a few days, my baby brother will move to LA with his two bandmates in 22 Goats, Fish and Colin. There, the threesome will move into an apartment building owned by Reed Rivers, finish writing songs for their debut album, and eventually begin to record said songs with one of the top producers in the music industry. To say it's a dream come true for Dax and his friends would be the understatement of the century. And so, of course, my family, being who they are, is using the occasion as an excuse to get together to party with the ones we love the most. Plus, with little Gracie's arrival three months ago and Ryan's baby news coming just last week, it seemed like a good time for all of us to get together all around.

"So you're gonna ask Mom in front of our whole family?" Theo asks.

My heart lurches. It didn't escape my notice Theo said *our* whole family... not *your* whole family. "That's the plan," I say. "Why? Are you going to tell me that's a lame idea, too?"

"No, I think it's a great idea. The sooner the better. Are you gonna give her a big ol' diamond ring? She's never had one, you know. I think she wants one."

"Well, of course, I got your momma a big ol' diamond ring. I got your momma the biggest and prettiest diamond ring you ever did see, son. She's going to need a crane to cart her hand around whenever she wears it."

Theo nods his approval. "Kewl. And, bee tee dubs, when I say that, I'm spelling it k-e-w-l. Because that's next level cool."

"Oh my God! No! Keane's brainwashed you!"

We both laugh.

"So, um, Theo..." A flock of butterflies releases into my stomach. "There's actually one more thing I wanted to talk to you about today." I take a deep breath. I suddenly feel overcome with nerves. "Do me a favor and let me get everything I want to say out before you reply, okay? Just hear me out."

He nods.

Oh, God, I feel like my stomach is stuffed into my throat. "Even though I've never met your dad, I've come to feel like I know him through your mom and you kids. And the way I feel about him, he's like my brother." I take a deep breath. Holy shit, I've never been this nervous to say something in my entire life. "I'd never, ever want to take your dad's place. You know that, right? He's your dad and always will be and that's that." My chest is tight. My breathing is shallow. "But that said, I want you to know I love you and your sisters like you're mine. As far as I'm concerned I couldn't love you any more if you were my own blood. You're my family, the same as Ryan or Keane or any other Morgan."

Theo's face turns red.

I swallow hard. "So, um, after I marry your mom, I was thinking I'd very much like to legally adopt you and your sisters. I don't need a piece of paper from the government to feel like you three are mine. I already do. But the legal paperwork would tell the world you're mine, no matter the situation. It would make things easier with school registrations and stuff. And it would give me peace of mind to know that if something were to happen to your mom—not that it's going to, but you've got to think about these things when you're an adult—nobody could ever take you away from me. This way, you'd be a *bona fide* Morgan in the eyes of the government and the world. Of course, you wouldn't have to call me dad. You could keep calling me Colby. And you'd still be a Decker. But I just think that—"

"*Colby*," Theo says sharply, forcefully enough to instantly shut me the hell up. "I know I agreed to wait for you to finish talking before I say anything, but can I just say yes now?"

I press my lips tightly together. If I speak, I'll surely lose it. So I simply nod and open my arms to my boy. And I might be imagining it... I probably am... but when Theo crushes himself into my belly, I'm almost positive I hear him whisper, in the faintest little voice, "*Dad.*"

328

Chapter 73
Colby

I survey my parents' living room. It's filled with a whole bunch of people I love the most. My entire immediate family and Zander, of course. Fish and Colin—the two dudes who've been in 22 Goats with Dax since high school. There are also about ten members of my extended family here who made the three-hour drive from Portland, including my cousin Julie with her husband, Travis, and stepdaughter, Coco. And, last but not least, Josh's twin brother, Jonas, and his wife, Sarah—who's also my sister's best friend since college—are also here. In other words, it feels like a pretty big crowd to get up in front of for a guy who *hates* talking in front of a crowd.

I touch the ring box in my pocket. Holy fuck, my heart is thumping a mile a minute. I absolutely hate talking in front of large groups of people and avoid it at all costs. Except today. Because when I thought about how to ask Lydia to be my wife, there was no scenario I could envision that felt more right to me than doing it here, like this.

Speaking of which, it seems to me it's about time to get this show on the road. We've eaten dinner. Dessert is laid out. People are feeling loose from the booze that's already flowed but not yet drunk from the booze that's yet to come. And, most importantly, there's been plenty of time for everyone to fawn all over Dax and his bandmates, as they should, and to gush over Gracie Louise and the sonogram image of Baby Rum Cake. At this point, I won't be stealing anyone's thunder.

I gaze across the room at Lydia. She looks absolutely radiant as she chats with Kat and Kat's best friend, Sarah.

I look at Theo, hoping to catch his eye. A couple times today,

329

he's flashed bug-eyes at me when our gazes have met, like, *Do it now, dumbass!* But each of those times, I've subtly shaken my head like, *Not the right time yet, dude.* I'm kind of hoping he'll catch my eye now and give me that same look to give me a much-needed shove. But, nope. Theo's too enraptured by the conversation he's having with Dax and Jonas Faraday to pay me any mind. I'm guessing they're talking about music.

I let my eyes wander to Izzy. She's playing some sort of playground-style, hand-slapping game with Coco. I smile to myself. I knew those two would hit it off. Hey, I just realized they're about to become cousins. *Awesome.*

My eyes wander to Queen Beatrice sitting on Zander's lap on the couch. Not surprisingly, Bea's cheek is pressed against Zander's broad chest as he talks and laughs with Josh and Ryan. Uh oh. Bea looks like she's on the cusp of nodding off. Well, shit. If I want my nemesis to be awake for this proposal, I guess I'd better get a move on.

I quietly slip into my mom's nearby office, grab the poster board I'd stowed there yesterday, and return to the living room. "Hey, can I have everyone's attention, please?"

Everyone stops what they're doing and stares at me, surprised. I don't think they've ever witnessed me uttering those particular words in my entire life.

I clear my throat. "Can everyone gather around, please? I have a little story I want to tell you." I catch Theo's eye to find him bursting with excitement. I wink at him. "Lydia, sweetheart? Can you come over here and stand next to me while I tell everyone a little story?"

As Lydia works her way to me, the energy in the room noticeably elevates. Clearly, my family knows what's up. Colby Morgan has asked for everyone's attention and for Lydia to stand next to him? There's only one thing that could mean.

"Hey, baby," I say when Lydia reaches me. I kiss her on the cheek. "Everyone, I want to take this opportunity to tell you a little something about Lydia Decker. The woman I love more than life itself."

Everyone exchanges excited glances with each other.

"I met this incredible woman right after experiencing the worst, most horrific catastrophe of my life. To be honest with you, when I met Lydia, I felt a darkness inside me the likes of which I'd never felt before. I felt *hopeless.* And then she walked into the room and she was hope for the hopeless. Her very presence was a torch of light that chased away the darkness."

Everyone in the room swoons.

I face Lydia. She's teary-eyed. "Lydia, as you know—but not everyone here does—during our first encounter in the ICU, I was quite the charmer: broken bones, busted spleen, burns down my side, high as a kite on painkillers, singed lungs, and breathing on a ventilator. Unfortunately, as a result of all that, I can't remember much of what transpired between us during our first encounter. I wish I could—it's not every day a guy meets his future wife."

Mom squeals.

I glance at my siblings and they're all chuckling at Mom.

I return to Lydia. "But even though the details of our first encounter are blurry at best, I do remember a few things about it. I remember the way you made me *feel* when you held my hand and talked to me. That the sound of your voice was a balm for my broken body and a salve for my aching soul."

Lydia's face contorts with emotion.

"And I also remember, quite distinctly, that the minute I saw you, I knew in my heart and soul and bones that I *loved* you."

Lydia blinks and the tears welled in her eyes squirt down her cheeks.

"Now, to understand what a mind-blowing statement that is, you need to realize I'm not a guy who's ever believed in love at first sight." I look at my parents. "Sorry, Mom and Dad. I know you've always said it happened to you, but I just couldn't wrap my head around it." I return to Lydia. "So I didn't trust my feelings completely. I figured they had to be the result of my vulnerable emotional and physical state. And, of course, the fact that you were so frickin' gorgeous, you took my breath away." Movement out the corner of my eye catches my attention and my gaze flickers momentarily to Izzy. She's standing a few feet away, wiggling in place with excitement. I wink at her and she squeals loudly.

Everyone laughs.

I look at the crowd. "Now, some of you might be skeptical about love at first sight, the same way I used to be. You're thinking people fall in love and then look back and *claim* to have fallen head over heels right out of the gate, just to make their love story sound more poignant and magical. Well, to all you doubters, here's what I say: *Ha! Love at first sight is real and I've got objective proof!*" I turn the poster board around to reveal a blow-up of my handwritten note on the white board. "These are the words I wrote to Lydia within minutes of meeting her."

Lydia puts her palms on her cheeks—a gesture mirrored by several other females in the room, including sweet little Izzy.

"How did you...?" Lydia whispers. "I didn't know you knew about that!"

"I saw it on your phone at the Climb & Conquer party," I say, and Lydia palms her forehead.

"Way back then?" she whispers.

"Sorry I didn't mention it. I thought you'd be annoyed I looked at your phone."

She laughs. "It's okay."

I look at the crowd. "I was sneaky and saw this photo on Lydia's phone a while back and that's when I knew she'd fallen in love at first sight with me, too. Or else why would she have snapped a photo of this and saved it?"

Lydia nods effusively and giggles through her tears.

I take Lydia's hands in mine. "Lydia, my love. I've now shown the world proof positive I loved you at first sight."

"I loved you, too. From the minute I saw you."

My heart leaps. "And my love for you only grew from there. I fell in love with you at second sight, Lydia. And then third, fourth, twentieth, and one-hundredth. And I know without a doubt I'll keep loving you for the rest of my life to infinity. You and your three beautiful kids. I want to love and protect all of you for the rest of my life." Slowly, I kneel and everyone titters and gasps and ooohs and aaahs. With a shaking hand, I pull out the ring box. "Lydia Decker, will you *please* make me the happiest man alive and marry me?" I open the ring box and Lydia gives me the exact reaction I'm hoping for: she completely loses her mind.

"Yes," Lydia says, putting her shaky hand over her mouth, her eyes watering. She nods effusively. "*Yes, yes, yes!*"

As everyone claps and cheers, I slide the ring onto my future wife's finger and stand to kiss her, but just as my lips make contact with Lydia's, Izzy barrels into my legs and hugs me with all her might, practically knocking me over. Of course, not one to be shown up, Beatrice leaps off Zander and joins her sister in hugging me, which prompts Theo to stride over and join us, too. It's by far the best moment of my life. And there's not a dry eye in the place, including mine.

Wiping my eyes, I say, "I'm just getting started here, folks. There are three other people I need to get yeses from, too."

Everyone shares huge smiles and swoons.

I look at the three kids staring up at me. "Theo, let's start with you, bud. *You're my boy.* As a symbol of my love for you and my promise to take care of you and your sisters and love you, always, I hope you'll accept this gift." Ryan appears from the hallway holding a gleaming electric guitar with a bow on it and Theo whoops with joy.

When the guitar is slipped into Theo's hands, he sees it's covered in signatures and he whoops again.

"Those are the signatures of the guys from 22 Goats," I say. "Plus, thanks to Josh and his connections, those are the signatures of all four members of Red Card Riot and a whole bunch of other bands signed to River Records, too."

"Thank you!" Theo says, furiously looking at every square inch of the autographed guitar. "Oh my God!"

"Thanks again, Josh," I say.

"You bet. Enjoy it, Theo."

"Oh my God!" Theo shouts, perusing the various signatures on his gift.

"So is that a yes?" I say. "Did I effectively buy your affection?"

"Yes!" Theo says, laughing. He gives me a hug. "Thank you."

After my embrace with Theo, I turn to my little wiggler next. "Isabella," I say and the sight of her smile makes my heart melt. "From day one, you've been buyin' what I'm sellin', sister."

"It was love at first sight," she says, and everyone chuckles.

"For me, too," I say. "One look at you, and I was a goner, Izzy Stardust. So to show you how much I love you and to symbolize my vow to take care of you and our family, I got you this." Ryan hands me a small box and I hand it to Izzy. With an anticipatory squeak of excitement, she takes off the top of the box to find a dainty gold-chain necklace with a tiny diamond-star pendant dangling from it.

"Is this a... *diamond*?" Izzy chokes out.

"Yep. And you know why it's a star? Because you're my Izzy Stardust." I secure the necklace onto Izzy's slender neck and she wiggles and prances like her pants are on fire, making everyone guffaw. "Thank you for always showering me with your infinite and indivisible love, Isabella. One smile from you and I always feel like I'm wearing a jetpack on my back."

Izzy does a little dance of joy and everyone laughs.

I peel my eyes off Izzy, though it's hard to do, and move along to my former nemesis. "Beatrice," I say. "*Newman*."

Everyone laughs.

I look at Bea sideways and she mimics my gesture, making me laugh. "Man, you've made me work for it, haven't you?"

Everyone chuckles again.

"But it's okay. It's made winning you over all that much sweeter." As I've been talking Beatrice's eyes have wandered to the pendant around Izzy's neck and I'm getting the distinct feeling she's about to demand rather loudly that it be hers. "Let's cut to the chase, shall we?" I say quickly. "I got you a present, Queen Bea."

Boom. Miss Bea's hazel eyes are back on me.

I put out my hand. Ryan places a medium-sized, purple-wrapped box in it, and I hand the box to Bea. When she opens the lid and sees the sparkling tiara inside, her jaw goes slack with awe. The thing isn't made of diamonds, of course. They're cubic zirconia. But to this three-year-old's eye, this tiara might as well be the crown jewels.

"Queen Bea," I say, placing the sparkling tiara on top of her head. "I promise you'll always be my Bea and I'll be yours."

"Bea-Bee!"

"That's right. You and me, kid."

I bend down and hug Beatrice at eye level and she grabs my cheeks in her little palms, pulls me by the scruff toward her, and lays a little kiss on my lips. "I love you, Daddy."

"Thank you, my baby," I say, nuzzling her nose. "I love you, too."

My mom makes a sound that can only be described as losing her shit and everyone laughs and wipes their tears.

I stand, take Lydia's hand on one side and Izzy's on the other, and say, "And that's a wrap, folks! I give you... my family!"

Everyone cheers and converges on us. There are hugs all around. Dad grabs the bottles of champagne and sparkling apple cider that have been on ice in the kitchen and Ryan quickly opens them and passes around plastic cups. Once everyone's got their assorted bubbles, Ryan says a quick toast, and we all drink.

"Can I say a toast?" Theo asks. But it's clear nobody has heard him but Keane and me.

Keane sticks his fingers into his mouth and whistles like he's calling a faraway dog and everyone abruptly stops talking.

"Yo. The brahito burrito has something he'd like to say," Keane explains.

Theo raises his cup. "I just want to say I'm really happy to be a Morgan."

Oh my God. The kid just hit a grand slam homerun with this crowd.

"Talk about playing to your audience," Ryan says, and everyone laughs and cheers.

"*I* have a toast!" Izzy yells above the din. "I'm really happy to be a Morgan, too!"

More cheers and whoops.

Of course, Beatrice mimics her brother and sister and everyone turns into a puddle at her cuteness.

I look at Lydia and what I see on her face reflects back to me exactly what I'm feeling. Joy and Love. That's all I'm feeling in this moment. Joy and Love. And absolutely nothing else.

Chapter 74
Lydia

Colby closes the door behind us. We're both giggling. Or maybe that's just me, giggling enough for both of us, thanks to the *many* glasses of champagne I've had at this fabulous going-away party that unexpectedly turned into my engagement party.

I put my hand over my mouth to muffle my giggles. "How have we never done this before?" I whisper, looking around Colby's childhood bedroom, which nowadays apparently serves as Mr. Morgan's quasi-office. But even though the room is no longer in the exact form it was in back in the day, it's definitely got enough memorabilia of Colby's high school days to set the stage. The bed in here is a full-size, rather than the king Colby insists on these days. His high school football and cross-country trophies line a top shelf, along with several adorable class photos and yearbooks. All in all, it's not hard for me to imagine we're both sixteen-year-old versions of ourselves sneaking in here to have a little fun while Colby's parents sleep soundly down the hall.

"You never had sex with anyone in this room?" I ask.

"I never did. I fooled around a couple times in here, but I never did get the pootie."

"I'm shocked."

"There was always someone in this house at all times, growing up. Impossible to sneak someone in without getting interrupted. Trust me, I wacked off in this room a ton. It's always been my biggest fantasy—fucking someone in this bed. You have no idea."

I laugh. "Well, it's your lucky day, sweetheart. Lock the door."

Colby checks the doorknob. "Fuck, there's no lock. There used to be a lock!"

"Crap."

"Help me push that dresser in front of the door, baby. Where there's a boner, there's a way."

I giggle. "Oh, man, that's funny."

Colby shoots me a snarky look. "Hey, Giggler. *Help me push the dresser.*"

"Sorry." I try to help Colby move the dresser, as requested, but I can't stop giggling long enough to be of any use.

"Shh, baby," he whispers. "You're gonna get us caught. We don't have much time before they miss us."

But I can't stop laughing.

"Okay, move out of my way. For cryin' out loud, if you're not part of the solution, you're part of the problem."

I move out of the way and Colby the Firefighter has the dresser moved in front of the door in ten seconds flat.

"Not sure why you thought you needed me," I mutter.

"Ssh. Clothes off. *Now.*"

We both begin ripping our clothes off like they're on fire, and when we're both naked, and I behold his beautiful, naked body before me, I immediately stop giggling. Holy hot damn. He's absolutely stunning to look at these days, especially like this—when he's hard as a rock.

He pulls me toward the bed and I happily let him lead me. Hell yes, I do. Because he's the sexiest man alive and he loves me and my kids and he's noble and true and kind and funny and I love his family and his dog and he's promised to take care of me and love me forever and ever and ever. And did I mention he gave me a big-ass diamond?

Colby sits on the bed and leads me to straddle him and I slide myself down onto his hard-on. I'm wet, wet, wet, and so is his tip, which means the sensation of him burrowing inside me feels like a knife cutting through warm butter.

I throw my arms around his neck and my press my forehead against his and say, "Fuck me, Teenage Colby. Fuck me exactly the way you've always fantasized you'd fuck a girl in this room."

"Not 'a girl,'" he whispers. "You. I fantasized about fucking *you* in this room."

"*Me?*"

"*You.* Except you were Beyoncé." He grips my ass as I begin moving my pelvis ferociously on top of him.

"You have a type," I grit out as my pleasure ramps up.

"Yeah. *You.* You're my type. Oh, fuck, this feels good."

"Yeah, me and Beyoncé. Because we're basically the same thing."

"Not you *and* Beyoncé. Just *you.* Beyoncé was just a placeholder for you."

I grab Colby's face and kiss him and ride him ruthlessly and soon we're both in a frenzy of excitement.

"Oh, God," he says. "This is so hot for me, Lydia. You have no idea how many times I wacked off in this room and wished I could be doing this very thing on this bed."

I quicken the pace of my movement, sliding my clit against his shaft with each furious snap of my pelvis—and, soon, we're both growling with pleasure. I press my forehead against Colby's, fucking him relentlessly, run my fingertips over the sexy burn scars trailing down the left side of his torso, and, all of a sudden, I'm jolted with a current of electricity that takes my breath away.

Colby grabs my face passionately and I grab his and we kiss *desperately,* like the fusion of our lips is giving us both eternal life.

I'm on the verge of losing myself completely and I know it. "Mayday," I squeak out. "*Mayday.*"

It's our code.

My last line of defense before the shrieking starts.

Without hesitation, Colby hands me a pillow and I shove my face into it, just as a rippling, clenching, magical rainbow of a unicorn of an orgasm rips through me and makes me scream at the top of my lungs.

As I come, Colby does the same, groaning into my ear with his release.

For a moment, we lie tangled up in each other, catching our breath. Finally, I lift my head off his shoulder and look at my ring. "I'm engaged, sucka."

Colby laughs. "You're funny when you're drunk."

"I'm horny when I'm drunk. And in love. And happy." I nuzzle my nose into his. "Oh, and I'm Beyoncé, too. Because, apparently, all black girls are Beyoncé to white boys."

"Dude, all black girls aren't Beyoncé to me. *You objectively look like Beyoncé.* People must tell you that all the time."

I bite my lip. He's right. They do.

"Admit it," Colby says.

I giggle. "Okay, yes. I get that all the time."

"I knew it!" He kisses my shoulder. "You're much prettier than her, by the way. Beyoncé wishes she looked like you."

"Yep. No doubt about it. Who runs the world? *Lydia Decker.*"

Colby nuzzles his nose into mine. "I love you."

"I love you, too."

We kiss tenderly for a long moment, until Colby pulls away and grins.

"Guess what?" he says. "Theo said yes. He wants to be my son."

I touch the cleft in Colby's chin. "Izzy said the same thing. She actually cut me off mid-sentence to say yes."

Colby wraps his arms around me and holds me tight for a very long moment. "Now that I put a ring on it, will you *please* get your IUD taken out?"

"Psst. Come here and I'll tell you a little secret, hot stuff." I press my lips against Colby's ear, a huge smile on my lips. "*I already did.*"

Epilogue
Colby

Mia throws back her little head and bawls at the top of her lungs.

"Aw, honey," I say. "It's okay. I've got a whole jar of worms. We'll just put another one on the hook and you'll be good to go."

"It's okay, Mamma Mia," six-year-old Beatrice echoes. She kneels on the sand of the lakeshore to address her little sister at eye level. "Daddy will just put another worm on the hook for you. That's how fishing works. You don't get *one* worm to last you all day. Daddy always brings lots and lots of worms, just in case we lose one." Beatrice gets up and grabs the nearby worm jar off the ground. "See, Mamma Mia? Daddy has a whole jar. He has *infinite* worms."

Just that fast, Mia becomes mesmerized by the jar in her big sister's hand and her tears dry up.

"Thanks, Bea," I say. "You're the Mia-whisperer."

Beatrice looks at me like, "Stick with me, kid..." and I chuckle.

"I don't think we're gonna need more worms," Ryan says as he casts his line out into the lake. "Surely, after Mia's Wilhelm Scream just now, every fish in the lake just hightailed it to the other shore."

"No worries," I say. "Fishing isn't about catching fish, anyway."

"Oh, it's not?" Ryan says, a smirk overtaking his lips. "What's it about, if you don't mind me asking?"

"It's about hanging out with the ones you love the most. Making memories."

Ryan chuckles. "Wow, Master Yoda. You're so Zen these days. I seem to recall you getting awfully annoyed with Keaney for being too loud during a fishing trip to Green Lake back in the day. Remember that?"

"Wasn't me." I reel my line in and begin casting out again when

I catch Mia's movement out of the corner of my eye. "Mia, honey, don't eat that! Bea, will you take that from your sister, please? Mia, sweetie, that's for the fish to eat, not the people. That's fake cheese, not real cheese."

"I'm hungry," Mia says simply, her hazel eyes looking forlorn.

"I know. But Mommy and Auntie will be coming back with sandwiches and juice boxes any minute now. Just hang tight and leave the fish food for the fishies, okay?"

"I told you she's too young to come fishing," Ryan says dryly.

I roll my eyes. *Smart ass.* As we both know, it was Ryan who insisted my tempestuous two-year-old could survive one day of her life without taking her usual morning nap. I'd planned to stay at the vacation rental with Mia while Ryan took the older kids down to the lakeshore, since Lydia and my sister-in-law were off at a nearby market to pick up supplies. But, no, Ryan insisted Mia and I absolutely had to join in the fishing.

"Come here, Mamma Mia," Theo says calmly to Mia, taking her hand. He stands behind her and helps her cast out her line. And then he helps her hold her rod, sacrificing his own chance to fish for the sake of the greater good.

"Thanks, Theo," I say, shooting my boy a grateful look.

"Daddy! Noooooo!" It's Ryan's almost-three-year-old son, Zachary. He's standing on the far side of Ryan on the lakeshore, energetically palming his forehead like Homer Simpson.

"What's up, buddy?" Ryan asks.

Zachary holds up his empty hook. "My worm! He's *gone!*"

"Oh no! Where'd he go?" Ryan asks.

"I dunno." Zach makes a presto-change-o motion with his free hand and whispers, "He just... *left.*"

My brother and I both chuckle.

"He just... *left,*" Ryan says, mimicking Zach's exact inflection and hand gesture and we both laugh our asses off.

"Daddy!" Beatrice calls from her spot next to Mia, drawing our attention over there. Beatrice has her line pulled out of the water and her mouth is forming a flabbergasted O. "*My worm left, too!*"

Ryan yells, "It's the Worm-ocalypse! God help us all!"

Theo laughs. "Or maybe it's an *uprising*—a Worm-olution."

I sigh. "Well, either way, it sounds like we need a whole lot more worms." I look around the shore for the worm jar. "Anyone seen the jar? Bea had it a minute ago."

"I put it right there." Bea points to an empty spot on the ground.

"Well, they're not there now."

"*No worms?*" Mia says breathlessly. She sounds like she's responding to someone telling her, "You'll never eat ice cream again!"

"No worms," I confirm evenly. I'm not proud of it, but, on occasion, I kind of like pushing Mia's buttons.

And push them, I have, apparently. At my confirmation of The Great Worm Shortage, Mia throws down her rod, drops to the sand like she's been hit by a tranquilizer gun, and wails.

Ryan and I exchange a dry look that says, "Fuck my life."

"See?" Ryan says. "I told you making her skip her usual nap was a bad idea."

I scratch my nose with my middle finger. "Paybacks are a bleep, mofo. When Claire gets here, she's going to teach you all about the innate differences between boys and girls. You'll see."

"Gender stereotyping," Ryan says. "I don't believe in it."

"Yeah, let me know how not believing in it works out for you two years from now when you've got an emotional little girl on your hands sobbing her eyes out about whatever is her equivalent of a shortage of worms."

"It's okay, Mamma Mia," Theo says. He's bending over, talking to Mia on the ground. "Dad? Mia says can she pretty please have another worm. She says she *begs* you."

I laugh. "Yeah, but we have to find them first." I look around the immediate vicinity for the worm jar again but to no avail. "Dang it. I can't find that jar."

Well, that does it. Mia's now utterly inconsolable.

Ryan laughs. "Whose bright idea was it to rent a lake house for a long weekend in the first place? Whoever he is, he's a moron."

Again, I roll my eyes. The moron of which Ryan speaks is Ryan, of course. About a month ago, Ryan and I, along with our beautiful wives, Josh and Kat, Zander, Keane, and Keane's fiancée, were hanging out backstage before a 22 Goats concert in Seattle—the band's world tour had finally come through the boys' hometown. And that's when Drunk Ryan somehow got the brilliant idea the Morgan siblings absolutely, positively *had* to rent a lake house for a long weekend *as soon as humanly possible*. "The missus is gonna be popping out Baby Claire in two months," Ryan said, "and after that, the Rum Cakes will be out of commission for a solid three months. We'll call it a last-hurrah lull before Hurricane Claire."

And so, since Captain Morgan is a guy who always goes after everything he wants in life, big or small, we're now here for that long weekend. Although, unfortunately, only the Rum Cakes and the Cheese Heads could make it. Dax couldn't join us, obviously, since he's still being his rock-star self on tour. That goes for Zander, too, since he's working on the security staff for the 22 Goats tour nowadays, thanks to a chance encounter with Reed Rivers one fateful day a few years ago when Zander and Keane visited Dax in LA. Keane isn't here, either, thanks to some exciting job he just landed. And, of course, Kat and Josh aren't here, thanks to Baby Jack's arrival two weeks ago.

"No woooorms!" Mia screams from her spot on the ground.

I put down my rod, intending to go to her, but Theo puts up his hand.

"I've got her, Dad," Theo says. "Just help Bea and Izzy. Their lines are crossed." Without another word, he scoops his baby sister up and begins making silly faces and she immediately calms down.

My heart flutters. I swear to God, that boy is my hero.

"Anyone want a sandwich?" a voice calls out. It's Lydia, thank God. Our family's patron saint. She and a rather pregnant-looking Mrs. Rum Cake are walking down the narrow pathway from our vacation rental, holding large plastic bags.

"In the nick of time," I say. "I think Mamma Mia maybe needed her morning nap, after all."

"Ya think?" Lydia says. She mock-glares at Ryan and he laughs.

I take the bags of food from the ladies and Lydia heads straight to Mia and Theo.

"Are you tired, missy boo?" She takes our baby girl from Theo and, instantly, Mia crumples into her mother's arms, absolutely exhausted.

"Aw, what's going on, little Mamma?" Lydia asks. "Give me the lowdown."

Without taking a breath, Mia tells her mommy about the tragic worm situation and how daddy was mean because she wanted to eat the funny cheese but he said she couldn't eat the funny cheese because it's for fish, not people, and now she's sad. Lydia nods and expresses sympathy, all while trying her mighty best not to laugh in her adorable daughter's sweet face.

"I got a bite!" Izzy shrieks. "A bite! A bite! A *bite!*"

I race to Izzy and try to help her reel in the fish, but quickly realize her hook isn't being assaulted by a fish—it's caught up in some lake grass.

In a flurry, several kids express various fishing-line and hook-related catastrophes and fiascos, and for the next ten minutes or so, I find myself doing nothing but troubleshooting while Lydia gets Mia fed. Finally, all problems have been solved, except, of course, for the mystery of the disappearing worms. Everyone seems happy again, so I tiptoe away from the kids and pull my wife aside.

"Did they have pregnancy tests at that little market?" I whisper, nuzzling my nose into Lydia's.

"They sure did."

"And did you buy one?"

"I sure did. And then I peed on a little stick the minute I got back to the house."

I hold my breath.

"*And I was right,*" she says, beaming. "I am, indeed, officially 'with Morgan' again."

I whoop with glee. "Lucky number five!" I laugh and kiss my wife enthusiastically. "I've always wanted five."

Lydia laughs. "Yes, I know. You've mentioned your dream of having five kids once or twice or a hundred times, my love."

"Wouldn't it be fun if it's another girl? Four girls and a boy— the exact opposite of my family."

Lydia giggles. "That'd be great. But we've got to root for a boy for Theo's sake. You know how much he wants a baby brother."

"Bah. He'll take what he gets. He's already got Zach. Zachy is more like a baby brother than a cousin. And now he's got Jack, too. He'll be fine."

My wife slides her arms around my neck. "Hey. Let's not tell everyone about the new cheese ball in my oven for a couple days. I always love having a little secret with just you. It turns me on. Makes me want to do crazy things to you."

"With a pillow shoved over your mouth?"

She giggles. "It can't be helped."

I lean into Lydia's full lips and kiss her. As my tongue and lips lead hers in slow and sensual movement, a deep sense of gratitude and serenity fills every nook and cranny of my soul.

Love.

That's what I feel.

Love.

It's what I always feel these days.

It fills me so completely, it seeps out my pores and drips down my flesh.

Love.

It's coursing through my blood.

Love.

It fills my lungs. My thoughts. My belly. It's fused to the very tissue of my heart.

Love, love, love.

I pull away from Lydia and smile at her. God, I wish I knew how to explain this love I feel for her. This sense of rightness. But my paltry words just aren't enough. After much contemplation on the topic, a lot of it done while staring at Lydia's face while she sleeps—or at Izzy's, Mia's, Bea's, or Theo's—I've concluded there are no words in the English language to fully encapsulate the perfect communion of love, joy, serenity, and certainty that exists inside me these days. The clarity that comes from a man knowing, without a doubt, he's living the life he's meant to live. And so, as usual, I fall back on saying the words that aren't nearly enough but are all I have: "I love you, Lydia."

"I love you, too," my beautiful wife replies. She's my life. My savior. My patron saint. "More than all the words invented could possibly describe."

We share a smile.

"This is fun, isn't it?" I say.

"It's awesome," Lydia replies. "Although I sure wish Mia had had her morning nap."

"No, not the mini-vacation. *This.*" I motion to her and me. "*Us.*" I motion to the kids. "*Them.*" I put my hand on her flat belly— acknowledging the new Morgan we're soon going to love with all our hearts. "*Him or her.*"

345

A huge smile spreads across Lydia's face. "Yes. This is most definitely fun."

"Daddy!" Beatrice yells. "Mia's melting down again. We need to find those worms! *Stat!*"

We burst out laughing. Beatrice just learned to yell "Stat!" the other day when she dressed up as a doctor for Career Day at school and someone taught her to say it.

"Okay, okay," I say, pulling myself together from laughing. "I'll find that jar, if it's the last thing I do." I look and look and finally find the jar underneath Izzy's jacket... far, far away from where Bea said she left it... *and it's empty*. And, just like that, I know exactly what happened to those wiggly creatures. The Great Wiggler herself became The Great Emancipator. I look at Izzy's sweet face and her guilty expression confirms my suspicion.

"Looks like the worms made a break for it," I say, my eyes trained on Izzy's.

"*What?*" Zach says incredulously. He begins looking down at the ground beneath him like he thinks he's about to get mobbed by a gang of worms.

I continue staring at Izzy, not saying a word. Her face is getting redder and redder. I raise an eyebrow, inviting her to confess her sins.

"I did it!" Izzy finally blurts, throwing her hands over her face. "It was me! I freed the worms! I felt sorry for them!"

Lydia and I share a chuckle.

"What about the fish?" Theo asks. "You don't feel sorry for them but you feel sorry for a bunch of frickin' worms?"

"That's different," Izzy says. "We *eat* fish. It's called the food chain." She rolls her eyes like she thinks her brother is a supreme dumbass.

"Izzy, worms are part of the food chain, too," Theo says. "Humans eat fish. Fish eat worms. See? *Food chain.*"

Izzy puffs out her little chest and boldly explains to her big brother that feeding worms to fish without making the fish work for their meal isn't part of the frickin' food chain. It's the same thing as calling a human who eats a Big Mac a hunter. Theo disagrees and, soon, the conversation escalates, which leads to Beatrice jumping into the fray to defend her big sister—not that anyone asked Beatrice's opinion, of course, but she's always got one handy. Soon, Theo is

346

telling Beatrice to please kindly butt out, which prompts Beatrice to shout that Theo's a big ol' meanie and she can talk if she wants! Which means Mia begins crying because she hates it when Beatrice is unhappy and, damn, the poor kid just needs a fucking nap...

"You're honestly excited to add one more to this insanity?" Lydia asks, sliding her hand in mine.

"I couldn't be more excited. You?"

"Same."

I squeeze Lydia's hand... and sigh contentedly... and let the love I feel in every fiber of my being, every cell of my body, every beat of my heart, waft over me and consume me.

Love.

Playlist for Hero

"Lean on Me"—Bill Withers
"Bailando"—Enrique Iglesias
"Fix You"—Coldplay
"Unsteady"—X Ambassadors
"My Girl"—The Temptations
"Wonderwall"—Oasis
"I Belong to You"—Lenny Kravitz

Acknowledgements

This book took a village to write. Thank you to everyone I consulted for your valuable expertise and insights. Thank you to the firefighters of Rancho Santa Fe Fire Station 2 in San Diego, California. You handsome and heroic gentlemen went above and beyond to help me with my research for this book. Thank you for the tour of the firehouse, the ride-along in the fire truck, allowing me to attend a spectacularly exciting training day during which a bunch of cadets went into a burning building and lived to tell the tale, and especially thank you for talking about the emotional toll of your very heroic and important job. Thank you to Dr. Scott Bisheff for helping me injure poor Colby realistically and depict his recovery properly. Thank you to Melissa Meissner, the extraordinary physical therapist who helped me bring Colby back to life, slowly but surely, in as accurate and professional and healing a manner as possible. Special thanks, as always, to Sophie Broughton. But this time especially thank you for the idea that spawned my beautiful Beatrice. Thank you to Selina Washington for your insights on Lydia's background. I greatly appreciate you and your lovely heart. Thank you to Wander Aguiar for the beautiful, customized cover photograph of Colby Morgan and to cover model Jason Dickinson for being my Colby. Fun fact: Jason is an *actual* firefighter in Seattle, Washington! *Swoon.* And, yes, those are his real tattoos. Thank you to Rachel, my dear friend, for so honestly sharing your journey as a young widow with a child. Much love to you, my sweet friend. Keep chasing that joy. Thank you to my readers, the Love Monkeys, as always. I love you so much and am deeply indebted that you love my stories the way I do. Thank you to Cuz and Baby Cuz for inspiring me in my artistic journey, always. And, last but not least, thank you, Dad, for listening to me tell you the story of *Hero* over my birthday lunch and for welling up with tears as I talked. *Now that's why I love you the most.*

Author Biography

USA Today and internationally bestselling author Lauren Rowe lives in San Diego, California, where, in addition to writing books, she performs with her dance/party band at events all over Southern California, writes songs, takes embarrassing snapshots of her ever-patient Boston terrier, Buster, spends time with her family, and narrates audiobooks. Much to Lauren's thrill, her books have been translated all over the world in multiple languages and hit multiple domestic and international bestseller lists. To find out about Lauren's upcoming releases and giveaways, sign up for Lauren's emails at www.LaurenRoweBooks.com. Lauren loves to hear from readers! Send Lauren an email from her website, say hi on Twitter, Instagram, or Facebook.

Additional Books by Lauren Rowe

All books by Lauren Rowe are available in ebook, paperback, and audiobook formats.

The Morgan Brothers Books:

Enjoy the Morgan Brothers standalone books in any order:

1. *Hero.* This is the epic love story of heroic firefighter, **Colby Morgan,** Kat Morgan's oldest brother. After the worst catastrophe of Colby Morgan's life, will physical therapist Lydia save him... or will he save her? This story takes place alongside Josh and Kat's love story from books 5 to 7 of *The Club Series,* beginning with *The Infatuation,* and also runs parallel in time to Ryan Morgan's love story in *Captain.*

2. *Captain.* A steamy, funny, heartfelt, heart-palpitating insta-love-to-enemies-to-lovers romance. This is the love story of tattooed sex god, **Ryan Morgan**, and the woman he'd move heaven and earth to claim. Note this story takes place alongside *Hero* and The Josh and Kat books from *The Club Series* (Books 5-7). For fans of *The Club Series,* this book brings back not only Josh Faraday and Kat Morgan and the entire Morgan family, but we also get to see Jonas Faraday and Sarah Cruz, Henn and Hannah, and Josh's friend, the music mogul, Reed Rivers, too.

3. *Ball Peen Hammer.* A steamy, hilarious enemies-to-friends-to-lovers romantic comedy. This is the story of cocky as hell male stripper, **Keane Morgan**, and the sassy, smart young woman who brings him to his knees on a road trip. The story begins after *Hero* and *Captain* in time but is intended to be read as a true standalone in *any* order.

4. *Rock Star.* Do you love rock star romances? Then you'll want to read the love story of the youngest Morgan brother, **Dax Morgan,** and the woman who rocked his world, coming in 2018 (TBA). Dax's story is set in time after *Ball Peen Hammer.* Please sign up for Lauren's newsletter at www.laurenrowebooks.com to make sure you don't miss news about this release and all other upcoming releases and giveaways.

5. If you've started Lauren's books with The Morgan Brothers Books and you're now intrigued about the Morgan brothers' feisty and fabulous sister, **Kat Morgan** (aka The Party Girl) and the sexy almost-billionaire who falls head over heels for her, then it's time to enter the addicting world of the internationally bestselling series, *The Club Series.* Seven books about two brothers (**Jonas Faraday** and **Josh Faraday**) and the witty, sassy women who bring them to their knees (**Sarah Cruz** and **Kat Morgan**), *The Club Series* has been translated all over the world and hit multiple bestseller lists. Find out why readers call it one of their favorite series of all time, addicting, and unforgettable! The series begins with the story of Jonas and Sarah in the first four books and ends with the trilogy of Josh and Kat.

The Club Series (The Faraday Brothers Books)

If you've started Lauren's books with The Morgan Brothers books, then it's now time to enter the world of The Faradays. *The Club Series* books are to be read in order*, as follows:

-*The Club* #1 (Jonas and Sarah)

-*The Reclamation* #2 (Jonas and Sarah)

-*The Redemption* #3 (Jonas and Sarah)

-*The Culmination* #4 (Jonas and Sarah with Josh and Kat)*

*Note Lauren intended *The Club Series* to be read in order, 1-7. However, some readers have preferred skipping over book four and heading straight to Josh and Kat's story in *The Infatuation* (Book #5) and then looping back around after Book 7 to read Book 4. This is perfectly fine because *The Culmination* is set three years after the end of the series. It's up to individual preference if you prefer chronological storytelling, go for it. If you wish to read the books as Lauren intended, then read in order 1-4.

-*The Infatuation* #5 (Josh and Kat, Part I)

-*The Revelation* #6 (Josh and Kat, Part II)

-*The Consummation* #7 (Josh and Kat, Part III)

In *The Consummation* (The Club #7), we meet Kat Morgan's family, including her four brothers, Colby, Ryan, Keane, and Dax. If you wish to read more about the Morgans, check out The Morgan Brothers Books, a series of complete standalones. These books are set in the same universe as *The Club Series* with numerous crossover scenes and characters. You do *not* need to read *The Club Series* first to enjoy *The Morgan Brothers Books*. **All Morgan Brothers books are standalones to be read in *any* order.**

Does Lauren have standalone books outside the Faraday-Morgan universe? Yes! They are:

1. *Countdown to Killing Kurtis* — a sexy psychological thriller with twists and turns, dark humor, and an unconventional love story (not a traditional romance). When a seemingly naive Marilyn-Monroe-wanna-be from Texas discovers her porno-king husband has thwarted her lifelong Hollywood dreams, she hatches a surefire plan to kill him in exactly one year, in order to fulfill what she swears is her sacred destiny.

2. *Misadventures on the Night Shift* — a sexy, funny, scorching bad-boy-rock-star romance with a hint of angst. When Rocker

Lucas Ford checks into the hotel where Abby Medord works the night shift, sparks fly... This is a quick read and Lauren's steamiest book by far, but filled with Lauren's trademark heart, wit, and depth of emotion and character development. Part of Waterhouse Press's Misadventures series featuring standalone works by a roster of kick-ass authors. For more information, visit misadventures.com.

3. *Misadventures of a College Girl*-a sexy, funny romance with tons of heart, wit, steam, and truly unforgettable characters. When college freshman Zooey Cartwright meets bad boy football player Tyler Caldwell at a party, she decides she wants to lose her V card to him and then never see him again. But things don't go according to plan... Part of Waterhouse Press's Misadventures series featuring standalone works by a roster of kick-ass authors. For more information, visit misadventures.com.

4. Look for Lauren's third *Misadventures* title, coming in November 2018.

Be sure to sign up for Lauren's newsletter at www.laurenrowebooks.com to make sure you don't miss any news about releases and giveaways. And if you're an audiobook lover, all of Lauren's books are available in that format, too, narrated or co-narrated by Lauren Rowe, so check them out! Thank you for reading!

Made in the USA
Lexington, KY
08 May 2018